"A splendid debut novel! Nicole M. [...] experience with horses, her love for W[...] for storytelling into a rich novel, complete with a lovely romance. Focusing on war's innocent victims and humanity's duty to protect them, *Until Our Time Comes* is both sweeping and deeply personal. Fresh, original, and not to be missed!"

Sarah Sundin, bestselling and Christy Award–winning author of *Embers in the London Sky* and *The Sound of Light*

"In this breathtaking tale of danger, courage, rescue, and love, Nicole M. Miller shines a light on an incredible true story of World War II Poland and the magnificent Arabian horses caught up in the turmoil of war. Sweeping and deeply inspiring, this reading experience is not to be missed. Highly recommended for fans of Sarah Sundin and Kate Breslin."

Amanda Barratt, Christy Award–winning author of *The Warsaw Sisters* and *Within These Walls of Sorrow*

"This beautifully written story captivated me from the first page, with its heroic characters in a seemingly impossible situation and a resilient orphan boy who proceeded to steal a bit of my heart. Nicole M. Miller filled the remaining pages with a fascinating cast, heart-pounding suspense, and heartwarming romance. I loved reading her fictional account of this unlikely, remarkable partnership to rescue Poland's Arabian horses during World War II. *Until Our Time Comes* is an extraordinary debut!"

Melanie Dobson, award-winning author of *The Curator's Daughter* and *Memories of Glass*

"Nicole M. Miller weaves a page-turning tale with a hero and heroine drawn together in the midst of Hitler's takeover of Poland. Full of peril, intrigue, and romance, *Until Our Time Comes* takes readers on an unforgettable journey along with the characters through the years of World War II. Fascinating, little-known history fills every page of this heartfelt and hope-filled novel."

Amy Lynn Green, author of *The Foxhole Victory Tour*

UNTIL
OUR TIME
COMES

UNTIL OUR TIME COMES

a novel of WORLD WAR II POLAND

NICOLE M. MILLER

Revell

a division of Baker Publishing Group
Grand Rapids, Michigan

© 2024 by Nicole M. Miller

Published by Revell
a division of Baker Publishing Group
Grand Rapids, Michigan
RevellBooks.com

Printed in the United States of America

All rights reserved. No part of this publication may be reproduced, stored in a retrieval system, or transmitted in any form or by any means—for example, electronic, photocopy, recording—without the prior written permission of the publisher. The only exception is brief quotations in printed reviews.

Library of Congress Cataloging-in-Publication Data
Names: Miller, Nicole M., 1986– author.
Title: Until our time comes : a novel of World War II Poland / Nicole M. Miller.
Description: Grand Rapids, Michigan : Revell, a division of Baker Publishing Group, 2024.
Identifiers: LCCN 2023043650 | ISBN 9780800744700 (paperback) | ISBN 9780800745905 (casebound) | ISBN 9781493445578 (ebook)
Subjects: LCSH: World War, 1939–1945—Poland—Fiction. | Horses—Breeding—Fiction. | Arabian horse—Fiction. | Poland—History—Occupation, 1939–1945—Fiction. | LCGFT: Christian fiction. | Historical fiction.
Classification: LCC PS3613.I5464 U58 2024 | DDC 813/.6—dc23/eng/20231016
LC record available at https://lccn.loc.gov/2023043650

This book is a work of fiction. Names, characters, places, and incidents are the product of the author's imagination or are used fictitiously. Any resemblance to actual events, locales, or persons, living or dead, is coincidental.

Cover design by Laura Klynstra
Cover image by Ildiko Neer / Trevillion Images

Published in association with Books & Such Literary Management, BooksAndSuch.com.

Baker Publishing Group publications use paper produced from sustainable forestry practices and postconsumer waste whenever possible.

24 25 26 27 28 29 30   7 6 5 4 3 2 1

For John, Anthony, and Aiden—
who bring love, laughter, and inspiration to my life every day.

GREAT
BRITAIN

Manchester

Oxford
London

NETHERLANDS
The Hague •   ✪
Amsterdam

BELGIUM
✪
Brussels

✪ Paris   Luxembourg

Strasbourg

FRANCE

Basel

✪ Bern   Zurich
SWITZERLAND

Nice
Marseille

Genoa

Milan

ITALY

Florence

SWEDEN

DENMARK
Copenhagen

Hamburg

Hanover   Berlin
✪

Poznań

Cologne   GERMANY

Dresden   Breslau

✪ Prague

Kötzting   Hostau
Furth im Wald   Brno

Asch   CZ

Stuttgart

Munich   Vienna

AUSTRIA

HU

Venice   Zagreb

YUGOSL

Riga ✪ **LATVIA**

Moscow ✪

LITHUANIA
Kovno
✪

• Smolensk

• Konigsberg
Danzig ▪

**EAST
PRUSSIA**

• Vilnius

• Minsk

• Grodno

Vistula River   *Bug River*

RUSSIA

✪ • Wygoda
Warsaw   Janów Podlaski
• Lodz

POLAND   • Kovel

Kharkiv •

Kiev •

• Kraków   • Lviv

ECHOSLOVAKIA

✪ Budapest

• Odessa

NGARY

ROMANIA

AVIA

EUROPE
1939

Prologue

The movement was swift. The fingers light. The absence of his pilfered pocket watch barely noticeable—and yet it was as if a blaring siren sounded through his skull.

Bret Conway whirled and spotted a small, short frame slipping through the crowded marketplace. Despite the summer heat, the afternoon shoppers fresh from Sunday picnics and church mass filled the town square. Vendors called out wares as the smell of spices and hot cobblestones filled the air.

Bret followed the little thief's path, a glimpse of the boy's tattered fedora popping in between the sundresses and tan shirt jackets.

Polish conversation drifted around him. After his three years in Warsaw and now six months in this quiet town, it was almost as natural to his ears as the conversations on the streets of London.

He kept at a distance, watching the boy, no more than six or seven years old, as he stopped at Babka and Ludwik's fruit stand. The slender child stood beside a woman in pale riding breeches with a grass stain on her right thigh. Was the boy going to steal something from this unsuspecting victim too?

Her back was turned to Bret, though the angle of her head and her elegant stance sparked something in the back of his mind. She had the recognizable, practiced posture of an equestrian— something he recalled from his own time on horseback and among Olympians.

Ludwik and the woman leaned over the harness of a cart horse, lost in their discussion. The leather straps were crisp and new, and it appeared the woman was helping fit the cart to the small, chestnut-colored mare. Babka was sorting through the fruit and helping old man Pieter with his purchase. The thief stood in their midst casually, his relaxed posture almost seeming bored.

Bret needed that watch back—it was too priceless an heirloom to lose so embarrassingly to a little pickpocket. And yet the scene intrigued him.

"Amerykanka? Can we go now?" the boy said in heavily accented English. He reached up and tugged her sleeve impatiently.

The woman turned, her features fully in Bret's view now as she smiled brilliantly while speaking with Ludwik. She stroked the horse's neck confidently, kindly. "Yes, soon," she assured the boy before resuming her conversation with Ludwik.

Something tightened in his chest. He knew of this Amerykanka. Everyone in Wygoda knew of this woman. She was a rarity. An outsider beyond what even he, a Brit, could boast.

The American horse trainer. Adia Kensington.

She tightened up the final harness strap and patted the horse's rump as if about to say her farewell, and Bret's feet compelled him forward.

The boy peeked over his shoulder in Bret's direction, and his eyes widened. Ducking behind the American, he put his hands over his eyes as if it would make him invisible. "No, Amerykanka, I am sorry. I did not mean to do it!"

"Do what?" Adia asked, looking down at the child.

Bret stepped up beside her and cleared his throat.

"Przepraszam," she said. Then she seemed to recognize that he wasn't a local. "Oh, excuse me," she said in English, her American accent more unfamiliar than the slurry of Polish.

He'd spotted her a dozen times in town but had never stood so close. At this distance, the curve of her lips and her long, dark lashes caused his heart to speed up. Her dark hair shimmered in the brilliant midday sun. Momentarily, he forgot what had even brought him over.

"My apologies for the intrusion." Bret cleared his throat. "I believe the boy"—he nodded to the little thief—"has something of mine."

She frowned and narrowed her gaze at the boy. "Myszko," she said firmly, "we talked about this."

"I am sorry, Adeeea," the boy she'd called mouse whimpered.

She crossed her arms, standing as a confident barrier between accuser and accused. Her long hair was pulled into a cascading chocolate ponytail that curled in soft waves at the ends. Her shoulders were narrow, her hands cut and blistered but radiating strength. The dirt under her nails and the natural creases in her work shirt set her apart from the high-society women Bret's mother had thrust upon him. None of those girls had the natural beauty or presence this woman had.

Ludwik, within earshot, harrumphed and pointed a finger at the child. "And I'm still missing my set of playing cards, little one."

The boy, wide-eyed with unkempt brown hair poking out from his hat, ducked his head and whimpered again. He pulled Bret's brass watch and a deck of cards from his pockets.

Adia took the watch and held it out to Bret. He took it from her flattened palm, his fingertips sizzling at the touch of her skin.

"I'm so sorry." She smiled. "He's compulsive about . . . collecting things even though he knows it's wrong. Please forgive him."

"Perhaps the lad should not be so easily forgiven," he said.

She captured his gaze with her deep brown irises, and a fire seemed to spark inside her. "He's only a boy."

Babka, the heartbeat of Wygoda and the chef of the best pierogi in all of Poland, wandered over and smiled at Bret. She had deep wrinkles and wiry gray hair but always exuded energy and warmth. "Ah, so good to see you, Mr. Conway. What is all this commotion?" She looked to Adia. "You surely have met before, yes?"

Adia's gaze remained skeptical.

Who was this street urchin to the American horse trainer? How had the lad commanded such loyalty of her?

"The boy took something of mine," Bret explained to the matron of the town square.

Babka waved a hand. "Harmless, harmless. All little boys go through rebellious times."

"It's a dangerous world," Bret countered. "He could pick the wrong pocket and face far more severe consequences."

Adia crossed her arms, angled her head. "Would you have the boy flogged, Mr. Conway?" Her voice deepened as if she were digging a trench and burrowing in for a fight. "Sent to prison? His hand cut off?"

"I'd settle for far less." He grinned.

She drew back as if sensing a trap.

"And what is that?" She crossed her arms.

"Dinner. With me."

Her lips fell into an *O* as Babka clapped her hands and squealed excitedly. "That's a wonderful idea! I'll prepare my best table for you both. Ludwik, haven't I said for months now these two should meet?"

Ludwik grunted distractedly, still messing with the horse's harness.

"And how would that help Ewan's bad habit?" Adia protested.

"What does that matter?" Babka elbowed her sharply and smiled with crooked teeth. "You need a night off. As I always tell Filip, you work too much in those stables of his."

Adia shook her head and rolled her eyes. Clearly, she'd had this discussion with Babka before, and it was a tired one.

"I should have started with a proper introduction." Bret put a hand to his chest apologetically. "My name is Bret Conway. I'm a correspondent for the *Daily Express* in London." The lie slid easily off his tongue. He'd perfected it in his three years in Poland and two in Spain.

Her eyebrows, slender and arched, lifted ever so slightly. Skeptical or surprised? She was tough to read. And reading people was his true occupation.

Babka looped her arm through Bret's, beaming. "Oh, he's just being modest," she crooned. "This fine man here also helped Ludwik and I when we were renovating the kitchen a few weeks back—finding us all the supplies we needed and wielding a hammer or two. He's a jack-of-all-trades."

Bret chuckled at the compliment. Truth was, Charlie had gotten them into that to earn a few extra meals from Babka, since good cooking was sparse in their line of work.

Adia glanced down at the boy. "I'm still unsure of how my accompanying you to dinner will teach little Ewan the dangers of stealing, Mr. Conway."

"Well, we could discuss that very thing over Babka's unforgettable pierogi." He smiled and tucked his pocket watch away.

She chuckled softly, a musical sound like that of a sea siren. He needed to hear more of it.

Babka beamed and poked Adia's arm. "I can vouch for the man. It's just one dinner, after all."

"I do have a weakness for your pierogi," Adia said to her. And then to Bret, "But I also have a history of relying on the wrong men."

"Just a dinner." Bret put a palm to his chest. "Nothing more, nothing less. I give you my word."

Adia bit her lower lip, and her eyes slid to meet Babka's expectant gaze. The older woman nodded firmly.

Hope soared within Bret.

Adia turned slowly, holding Ewan's shoulders as if he were a shield. "Fine. Tomorrow at seven o'clock," she tossed over her shoulder. "I'll meet you at the restaurant." She waved farewell to Babka and Ludwik and slipped away.

Hope crashed into dismay. Tomorrow?

He and Charlie were to meet one of their contacts outside Warsaw tomorrow night. How on earth would he manage this?

Charlie emerged from the crowd, crunching an apple loudly. Bret's redheaded friend, partner, and brother-in-law watched Adia's disappearing form. He nodded a greeting to Babka and Ludwik and then leaned in to whisper to Bret. The smirk on his face indicated he'd overheard it all.

Babka and Ludwik both turned to a group of shoppers to help fill their orders, out of earshot of Charlie and Bret.

"My, my," Charlie droned in his thick Irish brogue. "Dare I believe my eyes and ears? The avowed bachelor, going on a date?"

Bret ignored the barb. His fingers curled around his grandfather's watch in his pocket. The engravings were worn, and a familiar dent on the edge served as a reminder of the time and war it had endured. Colonel Harold Conway had always claimed it was lucky. It had deflected a bullet in the trenches of France back in 1914, saving his life.

Bret had never believed in such superstitions—until now. Had his grandfather's luck endured in a different form?

"This is a mistake." Bret shook his head. "What am I thinking?"

Charlie lifted a bushy eyebrow, his green eyes sparkling in jest. "From the looks of her, I know exactly what you were thinking. She the lass who works at Janów?"

"I'll send a message to the farm to cancel with her. We meet our new contact tomorrow and there's no time for distractions."

Charlie fed his half-eaten apple to Ludwik's cart horse, then took Bret's shoulders, staring him down. "I can handle the contact alone. Trust me, mate. You can't pass up this particular distraction. You won't get another chance with her."

No, he wouldn't. Nor would they get another chance at a rendezvous with this contact claiming to have access to high-level German intelligence. A source like this had been three years in the making.

Charlie elbowed him in the ribs. "Come on, let's go."

Bret followed his partner in the opposite direction that Adia and Ewan had disappeared.

They went through the motions of checking in with their various sources and embedded spies for the rest of the afternoon. Bret's mind constantly darted back to Adia and the lie he'd so easily shared about his occupation. His cover as a reporter was easy to repeat, but she'd seemed almost skeptical about it. Sparring with her over dinner would be far too fascinating—he could already predict as much. His mind worked through a hundred different scenarios on how the dinner might go. It soothed his mind to war-game every possible outcome.

At dusk, Charlie drove them back to their small safe house south of Wygoda. The sun was deep into the horizon, and yet the dim lighting did little to hide Charlie's toothy grin. Apparently, Charlie had been thinking about his upcoming date as much as Bret had. Since they'd known each other nearly all of their respective twenty-seven years on this earth, it didn't take much to communicate between them.

"Shut it," Bret fired over.

"I'm just tickled I can wire yer sister and give her a little bit of hope. She's been praying for years you'd find someone who might tame yer wild ways."

Elizabeth—Charlie's wife—certainly would be happy to hear even the possibility of a romantic interest. She hoped for anything to anchor Bret and Charlie back to England. It was Bret, after all, who'd convinced his friend to join British Intelligence instead of becoming a boring old lawyer or doctor.

"It's just dinner."

"So you say," Charlie said, glancing in the rearview mirror and hesitating. His brow furrowed slightly.

Bret knew that look. All humor fled between them. He reached for his pistol and turned in the seat. "We have a tail?"

"Coming fast." Charlie pressed the accelerator, and the car lurched forward.

The headlights behind them grew larger, brighter.

"In front!" Charlie shouted. Bret turned to see a car barreling toward them. They were pinned. And neither threat slowed or veered off path.

This wasn't an accident or wayward driver. They'd been targeted somehow. Their cover blown.

"Brace yourself," Bret called.

Everything flashed through his mind in the span of a heartbeat.

The information and potential leads he'd be unable to pass along.

The obvious leak in their network he'd be unable to rectify.

The trouble he'd be in with Elizabeth for putting her husband in danger.

The realization that he'd miss his dinner with the elusive and mysterious horse trainer. And he'd have no way to let her know.

And then glass shattered, metal screamed, and pain pulled Bret from the sea of his regrets. Darkness overtook all.

PART ONE

THE REFUGEES

1

SEPTEMBER 1, 1939
WYGODA, POLAND

Adia reached over the fruit cart to accept the canvas bag of her weekly produce from Ludwik and smiled. "Thank you and send my love to Babka."

She fed one of the apples from the bag to their old cart nag, Lyra, one of the first horses Adia had trained when she first came to Janów. The horse crunched on it happily and lazily flicked her tail.

"I will," Ludwik said. "Better get on home. Something seems amiss in the air today."

He'd said that every time she picked up groceries for the past few months. Truth was, Adia had felt the same unease throughout Wygoda. Perhaps all of Poland felt the distant storm rising.

She looked down to see Ewan's hand mid-reach into a woman's coat pocket. She cleared her throat, and Ewan flinched and retracted his hand, smiling up at her as if he hadn't been trying to steal.

"What am I to do with you?" Adia sighed.

A distant rumble drew her attention, and a hush fell over the town square. Something roiled deep within, and she put one hand on Ewan's shoulder. The noise, like a swarm of bees building up steam and drawing close, intensified.

Whatever it was—it was headed their way.

The sea of bodies around them swayed unsteadily. Adia had seen the same movements, anxiety, and building tension in livestock herds before a stampede.

From over the ridge of towering trees, two dark gray, single-engine planes with black swastikas dipped over the town square, lighting the fuse of panic and terror.

Shoppers clutched their goods and elbowed through the crowds. It was every man and woman for themselves, seeking refuge. Carts were knocked over, women screamed, dogs barked and fled.

Adia braced herself as she pulled Ewan toward their truck. They needed to get to Janów as soon as possible—the town could be the planes' target. From the corner of her eye, she saw Ewan, who'd seen enough terror in his life, reach for a passerby's pocket, and she pulled his hand away.

"Now certainly isn't the time," she called to him among the din of the stampede.

Ewan flushed and tucked closer to her as he avoided elbows and stomping feet.

Time had run out, for all of them. She'd expected the German invasion after they'd seized Austria but had hoped for more time to put precautions in place. She wouldn't allow a repeat of what happened to the Arabian horses of Poland in the Great War, when German and Russian forces had annihilated nearly every horse—priceless champions of distinguished lineage—at Janów Podlaski. Hungry soldiers didn't care about the finely bred horses or see them as art or culture or thousands of years of history in the flesh. They saw only horses to pull their carts, meat to feed their soldiers.

The herd at Janów would need to evacuate to safer regions.

Adia gripped Ewan's hand tighter as they wove through the tangle of bodies and trampled debris. But the unmistakable equine whinny of fear caught her ear, and she looked back upon Ludwik and Lyra.

The rickety wagon was tilted on its side, two wheels broken. The chestnut mare reared in her harness and kicked out in desperation. The leather lines were tangled and tight as the animal pulled harder against the pressure. Her eyes bulged in terror and her body rippled with tension.

Ludwik's hands flailed helplessly as he tried to reach out to untangle the lines.

The elderly man was in over his head. It was only a few months back that the couple had even begun to use the horse and cart instead of the wheelbarrow that Ludwik pulled by himself.

"Come on, Myszko," Adia said, changing their course.

Wood shattered as Lyra kicked panels on the cart, and one of the poles at her side splintered. If she sidestepped, she could be impaled.

They drew near, and she let go of Ewan's hand and told him to stay back. She dropped her groceries to the ground, raced to Ludwik, and pulled him away just as a hoof sailed past his head.

She pushed him back to where Ewan stood and focused on the horse. The mare fought the pressure, each pull on her bit adding to her panic. Adia held her hands up, taking deliberate steps while she moved close, anticipating Lyra's moves as she jumped from side to side.

"Easy, girl." She reached for a rein that flew about and caught it. She held firm but gave a little when the mare shied away.

The mare's hooves settled, though her body remained tense, muscles rigid. Her brown ears flicked back and forth amid the surging crowd, but her eyes watched Adia for direction.

Adia leaned over carefully to unbuckle the cart from the harness. She maintained a steady pressure on the reins and ran her hand slowly over the horse's sweaty, matted fur. She darted a glance at Ludwik to see him holding Ewan's shoulders protectively, both watching with furrowed brows.

As she unclasped the last strap and the cart dropped free, the mare hopped forward, but Adia was prepared. She let the mare walk, gently pulling her nose toward herself so she could circle the horse and keep her close. This brought the horse's focus back to Adia and away from the chaos beyond.

"That's a good girl," Adia said. "We're all right now, see?"

Despite her steady tone, the mare was like a rubber band pulled to the breaking point. She could snap at any minute, giving in to her most primal instinct of flight. Adia needed to maneuver the horse out of the crowd or she'd bolt and hurt someone.

Adia looked through the bustle of people for Ewan, her heart thumping at seeing the spot empty where she'd left him. "Ewan?" she called out. She gripped the horse but lost her focus on her.

Another pair of planes dipped overhead. The loud pop of gunfire erupted nearby, and people cried out in horror. Plumes of gunpowder filled the square, the acrid smell overpowering that of human sweat and smashed produce.

Adia braced for the mare's reaction a heartbeat too late.

Lyra pulled the reins free, the leather searing Adia's palms. She lunged forward, knocked Adia over, and kicked her back hooves out as she turned to flee. A hoof slammed Adia in the shoulder, which sent her stumbling back into the overturned fruit stand.

Pain coursed through her body as the bright daylight and the roar of the crowd faded away.

Bret pushed through the crowd toward the brave—or was it foolhardy?—woman trying to calm the panicked horse. The panic was so thick in the air, he could taste it. He neared Adia and the horse right as planes appeared again and well-meaning but ill-informed civilians fired rifles into the sky.

Those were pellet guns compared to a plane.

The horse reared, kicked, and sent Adia sprawling into a pile of crates. The animal took off into the crowd, but Bret rushed to the woman. She smelled of fresh hay and lavender soap.

The little thief, Ewan, scurried over, and they reached her at the same time.

Her tan breeches and blue jacket were dirty. A small cut bled at the edge of her hairline where she'd hit a crate. Her ivory forehead was smooth until she stirred from unconsciousness and grimaced.

"Move slowly," Bret commanded softly.

She blinked and struggled to rise to her feet. He grasped her elbow and eased her upward. She pressed a palm to her head as she leaned against him.

"Easy there," he said.

She groaned, and her gaze settled on his face as she regained focus. A hint of recognition clicked, and she stumbled back. "You?"

He owed her a thousand apologies and an explanation for missing their dinner over a month ago. Her face had filled his thoughts often. He should have orchestrated a reunion far better than this one.

"I can explain—" he started.

"Adia!" Babka rushed up and grabbed her arm. "Thank you for helping Ludwik." The woman was short and robust, and her age wasn't visible in her movements or the strength of her voice. "We should have sold that horse years ago. She'll have to take her chances in the countryside."

"She'll return to her paddock, I'm sure." Adia winced a smile. "Is Ludwik okay?"

Babka waved a hand, her apron still fresh with flour and sauce stains. "He's fine. Are you okay?" Babka's gaze swung around and froze on Bret. Her eyelids narrowed and her neck flushed red. "Bret Conway. The nerve to show your face—"

"Babka!" Adia scolded, flushing as well. "We have bigger concerns right now."

"What?" Babka scoffed. "The Germans? They're utter fools. They will not defeat Poland."

Bret bit his lip to keep from arguing. He was in enough hot water with Babka as it was for standing Adia up. No one escaped her justice.

"I need to get back to the farm." Adia turned and located the little pickpocket, gripping his shoulder and wobbling unsteadily. She closed her eyes, the blush in her cheeks faded to white, and her head listed to the side.

Bret stepped forward and caught her as she fell. The jolt of his body against hers seemed to snap her back to awareness.

Babka reached out to her. "Adia!"

Blood dripped into Adia's eye. Bret pulled out his handkerchief and pressed it to the cut on the side of her forehead. She gritted her teeth but didn't pull away.

"She cannot drive home like this." Babka shook a crooked finger in his face. "Bret, I'll trust you to see her back to the farm safely."

"I will," he said, meaning it with all his being. He owed Adia as much.

More gunfire erupted on the other side of the square, followed by screams of terror. Babka bade them farewell and turned to find her husband.

"Where's your vehicle?" Bret asked Adia.

She pointed to the eastern road. "Near the boardinghouse."

Bret motioned to Ewan to follow, and they pressed through the sea of people. The boy lugged the heavy bag of groceries along. With each step, Adia seemed to regain more of her strength and had fled Bret's grasp by the time they reached the truck.

He helped Adia into the passenger seat, his fears over her injury assuaged slightly as her shoulders straightened into her proud, upright posture. She shook off his hand. "I'm fine."

"Keys, please."

She patted her pockets and groaned. "Ewan? Did you take the keys again?"

The boy flushed and pulled out handfuls of items from his pants pockets. Thread spools, a few coins, a photo of a young girl, a set of keys, and a box of playing cards—Ludwik's playing cards, he guessed.

Bret took the keys and shook his head. "You'll return all of those when this settles down."

"This might not calm down anytime soon with the Germans so

close," Adia mumbled as she leaned her head back against the seat and rubbed her shoulder with a grimace.

Bret fired up the truck, and once they were on the road bound for Janów Podlaski, he looked over. "The Germans aren't close. They've only breached the port of Danzig."

She frowned. "But the planes?"

"Single prop planes—reconnaissance." He gazed at the empty sky through the towering trees. "If the Luftwaffe were here, we'd know it."

"How can you be so sure?"

"My sources in Danzig. War is still here, just not on the doorstep."

She raised an eyebrow. It was the same questioning look she'd given him when he'd told her his name and profession. "Your 'sources'?"

"Any reporter worth his salt has ways of getting information."

"If you say so." She looked out the window as the town buildings and panicked crowd faded and gave way to lush forests. "As you said, it's only a matter of time. We need to get the horses out, now."

"The horses?"

She tensed. "You have your job, Mr. Conway. I have mine."

"Miss Kensington," he said, striving to keep his voice from sounding patronizing. He admired her heart and dedication, sure, but she must not understand the full picture. "With all due respect, you need to leave Poland. Immediately. I know these horses are prized and you have worked with them for some time, but you need to leave them behind."

As he kept his gaze on the road, he sensed her sharp stare settling on his face. A wall rose within her expression, as tangible as the steering wheel beneath his hands.

He'd underestimated her. His warning only cemented her resolve and his role as her opponent. The way she'd dove into the crowd and broken free Ludwik's cart horse, the constant smudges and stains she had on her clothes—they all pointed to how meaningful these horses were to her. They weren't just her job. They were her duty.

It was the same way he viewed his calling—and why he'd given up hope of a normal life to pursue it.

But he'd already paid a dear price, and in the moment, he wasn't sure it was doing any good. War had begun anyway. Charlie's sacrifice, Bret's years in the shadows—none of it had made a difference.

Adia's voice was deep and resolute, her eyes fixed on the road ahead as the pristine white buildings of Janów Podlaski peeked through the trees. "I have a plan to keep the horses out of Nazi hands. Leaving the horses is the last thing I intend to do."

2

Adia straightened in her seat as Bret Conway turned the vehicle onto the long driveway, a lane of white rock among lush green pastures, white fencing, and brilliant emerald trees.

The white clock tower at the center of the main barn gleamed in the sunlight, the regal sight sending a jolt of admiration down Adia's spine. The square tower, reminiscent of a medieval castle, stood in proud testament to the hundreds of years it had faced invaders and near destruction.

Horses of all colors decorated the countryside. Mares grazed contently while foals nursed or frolicked at their sides, oblivious to the distant planes. Within the stables and fields, there were more than two hundred and fifty horses.

Arabian horses. Lean, built for endurance, speed, and elegance. Arched necks and tails, wide eyes, attentive ears, and sloped faces. Honed for what they were best at: racing, long-distance trekking, companionship. Even battle.

The truck neared the circular driveway, and her chest tightened.

Janów Podlaski was her home. It had been for three years now and had been her dream for a lifetime prior.

In a flash, it could all be gone.

Would history be doomed to repeat? No. She'd prepared for this very thing.

"A plan?" Bret said. She wasn't sure if he'd asked her a time or two before. She'd tuned out his voice.

Panic and restlessness seized her, and she opened the passenger door and jumped out before Bret pulled to a stop. Ewan ran off to wander the halls that were his playground.

Escaping Bret Conway's presence did little to reduce her unease. It had taken nearly all of the past month to overcome her anger at allowing herself to indulge such foolishness. Agreeing to dinner, only to be stood up by the cocky and overbearing reporter. The sad, patronizing looks from Babka and the other diners—they still burned deep.

Of all the people to find her unconscious, bested by a horse, no less.

She rubbed her forehead. That ornery old mare. Who would have expected Lyra to get the better of Janów's best trainer?

"Wait," Bret called out behind her.

She walked with hurried strides over the gravel, wishing to be rid of this man. He was as mesmerizing as she remembered, his deep gaze seeing through to her core. The pit of her stomach filled with lead at the recollection of sitting at Babka's for so long. Babka had apologized, claiming there must be a good reason for Bret to stand her up. But Adia had seen it before—had allowed such flights of fancy. Would she ever learn? There was no one to depend on but herself.

"Adia—Miss Kensington." His voice and footsteps drew nearer.

The fall and bump on her head had thrown her off balance. In a literal sense. Now Bret seemed intent on doing the same to her. His clipped British and the deep timbre of his voice were alluring.

He caught her arm and gently pulled her to a stop. "If I may?"

They paused outside a row of stalls with a dozen pregnant mares casually looking on. The scent of straw, hay, and horse comforted her.

The familiarity of the setting did little to ease the effect of Bret's piercing green eyes. As she studied him further, a fresh scar along his jawline stood out, the pink edges of the wound indicating it had healed only recently. A matching scar peeked out from the hairline on his forehead. She didn't recall seeing that back in July when he'd asked her to dinner.

"Won't you allow me to apologize?" The frown at the edges of his lips and the crinkle between his eyes lent credence to his genuine regret.

But she'd spent weeks burying the memory and pain of being jilted at the restaurant. What good would come from dredging it all up?

"We have bigger worries now, Mr. Conway." She straightened her shoulders, pushing away the ache and stiffness. "Thank you for seeing us home. I'm certain Filip, the director, will provide you with a vehicle to get back to town—"

"What is going on here?" a heavily accented voice cut in, loud boot steps echoing down the paved aisle.

Bret and Adia turned at the same time. Adia stepped toward her employer and mentor. "Director—"

Filip held up a hand. The man, though in his sixties, was tall and lean and carried himself as confidently as a young international show champion—which he was several times over. His skin was darkened and freckled from years of working in the sun.

His gaze narrowed on the British man beside her. "Conway? What are you doing here?"

"Director Maier." Bret stepped forward and held out a hand in greeting.

The older man's face burst into a rare, enthusiastic smile, and he gave an even rarer jovial laugh. He pulled Bret into a hug and slapped his back. "It's been too long, my friend."

Adia glanced between them, and her heart sank. Janów and the nearby towns were a tight and small community, so how was it these two men knew each other when she'd known nothing of this Bret Conway?

She cleared her throat. "You're acquainted?"

Filip turned to her with a tilted grin and sparkling gray eyes.

"Mr. Conway here has done several stories on the farm over the years. He's a big proponent of our work and quite an accomplished horseman himself."

That last little bit caught her attention, but she smothered her interest. No more distractions.

Filip crossed his arms. "As happy as I am to see you, why are you here?"

Bret glanced at Adia. "Just helping your trainer and her assistant get home from the market."

Filip angled his head at her. "What happened to your forehead?"

Adia shook the question off, ashamed enough by the incident. She didn't need Filip to learn that Lyra had bested her. "Filip, the Germans are close. We need to move the horses out of here."

Filip's smile faded, the light in him extinguished. He looked at Bret. "Is this true?"

Bret put his hands in his pockets. His jaw flexed. "We've seen an increased number of reconnaissance planes. The armed forces have settled in Danzig, but they'll most likely advance south over the next few days."

A flutter filled her chest as everything he said only validated her plan. But as he continued, her hope flew away.

"Your horses aren't any safer on the roads." His voice was deep and foreboding. "You'd best tell any nonessential staff to leave while they have a chance. Then hunker here with the horses and a select few men." He sent Adia a pointed glance.

She straightened her spine and shook off his words, stepping close to Filip. "You know what happened to the horses in the Great War. We can't just sit here and let that happen once more."

"You needn't remind me." Filip tensed and anger flashed across his features. "I bear the scars—same as Janów, same as the meager herd I have cobbled together over the past twenty years from the ashes of that war."

Bret shifted. "I was not aware you were here during that time, Director."

Filip glared at them both. "I, like the entire stock of Janów, barely survived. You don't need to tell me the stakes. Even so"—he looked at Adia—"I'm not sure how we could manage two hundred and fifty horses on the road, even with a full staff, which I doubt we'll have after news of this invasion spreads."

"We can offer more money, use family members to help corral the horses." Adia held out her palms in desperation. "The foals will stick with their mothers. We can herd the stallions in a smaller group a fair distance behind. I've already reached out to Antek Dabrowski. He lives near the Soviet border, southeast, near the marshes. His farm can accommodate all our horses."

Bret shook his head. "A herd of horses is too big a target from the air—you might never reach the Bug River. There are rumors of hundreds, even thousands of German planes. Fighters and bombers. This won't be like anything seen in the Great War."

It would be far worse.

Shivers raced down her spine at the implication. "The horses will die or be seized if the Germans come. We must give them a chance at survival."

"You must find passage back to the States, Miss Kensington," Bret said, his shoulders tense as he stared at her. "Before it's too late."

Filip pressed his lips together as if in agreement but reluctant to say as much.

"My work is not done here." She turned to Filip, wishing she could block out Bret entirely. "Antek has a dozen barns and three hundred acres of pastures. The Germans won't risk war with Russia by marching that far east. Then we could smuggle a few at a time south into Romania and ship as many as we can to my farm in America."

Filip growled. "These are Polish horses, not Romanian, not American. Their place is here."

Adia matched his irritated tone with her own snarl. "If the Germans seize them, we have no say in the matter. Right now, we still have a choice."

"Getting humans through the border will be hard enough," Bret said softly. "Civilian evacuations have already blocked roadways, not to mention the amount of Polish military movements."

Impossible. Foolish. Doomed to fail.

She'd heard the words all before. No one had ever understood her.

She could not let go of her horses—these priceless horses. They were the last piece she had of a mother she'd never known. Ewelina Bartosz-Kensington had died to save the Polish Arabian horses.

Adia could do no less.

There was no reasoning with this woman.

Bret watched a flame ignite deep inside Adia's expression and fan into an inferno as he voiced his concerns. Her resistance only grew as Filip agreed with Bret.

It would take more than strong words to move her to safe borders.

"We must rely on diplomacy," Filip said.

"Diplomacy didn't get us out of the last conflict," she hissed.

A young, high-pitched voice cut in. "Amerykanka!"

The three adults turned to young Ewan, who scampered down the row of stalls. Horses snorted and nodded in excitement as he ran past.

The boy tugged on Adia's hand. "Zuza. Her baby comes."

Adia glanced between Filip and Bret, her hesitation evidence that this discussion was far from over. "Excuse me." She followed Ewan down the aisle, her shoulders back and her stride as confident as if she owned the farm.

"Quite a strong-willed subordinate you have there, Filip." Bret turned to the director. "You won't give in to her plans to go east, will you?"

"I don't know." The man crossed his arms. "But to hear the Germans have invaded . . . is most upsetting."

He looked tired, defeated. Bret could only fathom the terror Filip had faced twenty years earlier when his life's work had almost been wiped away. The Great War had taken so much from the world and especially Poland. What more might this new conflict strip from Europe? From its people, its history?

Bret turned and studied a dark brown mare whose head hung over the half door of her large stall. Her belly was swollen with foal, and she flicked her tail against the occasional fly. The stall was twice as big as a regular one and padded with extra straw in preparation for a new resident.

A pang struck his stomach at the thought of what might happen to this soon-to-be mother and her coming progeny. He wished against all hope that there was a way to protect them, to get them to safety. Adia and her lofty plans were no match for the coming conflict. He'd heard the reports, seen the rumors of the true power Hitler had amassed in the form of metal, men, and firepower. Nowhere would be truly safe.

"Bret, you recall that favor you owe me?" Filip watched the same mare with a deep *V* etched in his brow.

Filip had been a loyal source of information on the Polish government and international relations through his role as the farm's shepherd and a pillar in the field of horse breeding, which crossed diplomatic boundaries throughout Europe. On top of that, he'd been instrumental in helping Bret out of a pickle several years back involving a weapon-smuggling operation. He and Charlie were just two green agents whose mistakes nearly ended their careers—and their lives.

Bret nodded. "Of course. I still have the scars from that particular incident."

Filip chuckled. "It could have been worse if I hadn't showed up."

A debt he'd be glad to repay. "What do you need?"

"I need you to watch out for Adia—if possible, get her out of Poland in one piece."

Bret hesitated. Weapons, information—most anything would have been easier. His orders could change at a moment's notice.

How could he possibly commit to looking after such a stubborn woman who seemed to have no sense for her own well-being?

No, Bret refused to make promises he couldn't keep, especially where Adia Kensington was concerned.

"I made a promise to look after her," Filip continued. "Her parents were dear friends of mine. Her mother, bless her soul, is the very reason we have what little breeding stock was left after the Great War. I promised her mother and father to keep her safe if she ever made it to Poland, and to see that she not be treated differently because of her mother's patronage."

"Wait, her mother was Polish?"

Filip nodded. "I think you know to whom I'm referring."

A muscle tensed in Bret's neck as his curiosity was tickled. No wonder Adia looked as though she belonged in the halls of Janów. She carried herself like royalty, like the daughter of a countess.

"Please, my friend," Filip continued. "I hate to ask this of you, but I fear I'll have a lot on my hands in the coming months. And I don't expect that she'll return to America until she has what she wants."

"Then give her a horse and let her be gone."

"It's not in my power to give her what belongs to the Polish people, and she has yet to earn enough for the particular stallion she covets."

"The Polish state has more to worry about now than losing profit on a horse."

"My hands are tied in the matter," Filip growled. "You said it yourself—she wouldn't be able to get out with a horse even if I could arrange it. Our best hope is that the Germans leave this place alone. What concern will they have for horses anyway? Now there are tanks and planes. This is an entirely different world."

Bret shook his head. Though he'd seen reports of their mechanical might, the German army still relied on horseflesh to pull the artillery and supplies as much as any other army. Horses might not lead the charge in the German invasion, but there was still a place in this war for them, especially for the Polish, French, and Russian armies.

No, Janów and its fine horses would not go unnoticed.

Adia and her convictions would be right in the path of war.

"Bret?" Filip pressed. "Can I count on you?"

3

Adia stepped from Zuza's stall and leaned against the doorway. She wiped her hands on a rag and closed her eyes against a throbbing headache.

The smell of sweat, blood, and new life clung to her nostrils as soft nickers from mother and newborn echoed off the tall walls of the broodmare stable. Within moments of delivery, the dark brown baby had wobbled to its feet and began nursing. Zuza, the sheen of her white-gray coat sparkling even in the dim light, turned her head to lick the foal's wet and matted fur.

Adia smiled as Ewan chattered to the new little colt. "I think you will like it here. There are sugar cubes and many horses who will be your friends."

Adia grimaced, leaning forward to put her hands on her knees and fight a wave of nausea. Was it the concussion . . . or the dread that the paradise Ewan described would not exist once war fell upon them? It could be a matter of weeks.

Or days.

She left the thief and the new colt behind, listening for any sign of Filip and Bret. She wove through the tall aisles filled with decorative iron bars along the stalls and pristine floors. Janów, in all its ancient splendor, was more of a castle than a barn overrun with mice or dust.

Here, they cultivated the pride of Poland. Racehorses of world renown, cavalry horses of the highest caliber.

Her feet led her, without instruction, to the place where she found the most solace. A gentle nicker greeted her, and the burst of joy that filled her chest pushed away the remnants of her fear.

"Hello, my prince," she said. She unlatched the stall door and slipped inside.

The three-year-old stallion, Lubor, the most renowned and promising horse of the entire farm, perhaps the entire country, pressed his dark muzzle into her hands and sniffed in expectation of his favorite treat.

She laughed softly and pulled two sugar cubes from her pocket. He gathered them with his lips and chewed them.

He stood tall for an Arabian—fifteen hands, or five feet tall, at the top of his shoulders—though the traditional means of equine measurement didn't account for the high arch of his neck and regal way he carried his head. He had a deep brown body with black accents along his legs and a midnight-black mane and tail. She'd always adored this bay coloring. It was the color her mother's horse, Zalina, had been.

Lubor had been born only a few days after her arrival in Janów, and she knew right away he was special. The Polish Department of Agriculture, who oversaw the stud farm, had agreed and taken note of him. His sire and dam had been equally noteworthy. They anticipated Lubor would surpass his ancestors in prestige.

Lubor pushed his muzzle back into her hands, demanding more goodies, but she ignored his persistence and brushed her fingers through his long, silky mane.

"What will we do, Lubor?" she asked softly.

Though the grounds had always hummed with life—grooms running to and fro, trainers exercising the horses, mares and stallions nickering, bickering, and crunching on grain—a quiet unease now settled in.

All of Poland waited with bated breath.

Lubor tensed and looked to the right at the sound of footsteps.

Bret approached in the clean trousers and pressed collared shirt he had worn earlier, but his sleeves were rolled up to his elbows, hands in his pockets and shoulders relaxed. He seemed comfortable here in the surroundings where she'd spent years working to fit in.

He nodded in greeting to her, but his gaze locked onto Lubor. It was the way most everyone responded in the prince's presence. The horse was mesmerizing, magnetic, and Lubor seemed to know it.

Bret approached slowly, pulling his hands out and offering them flat for the horse to smell. Lubor poked his head through the rail and snorted in appraisal.

Adia studied their interaction. Horses had their particular preferences, same as any person. Some preferred certain hays or grains, while others got along better with certain grooms or no one at all. Lubor, from the very start, had held a fondness for Adia and Ewan and misbehaved more often for Filip and other men. "Horses are an excellent judge of character," Filip said often. "They see more than we ever can."

So, when Lubor licked Bret's hand and then began to sniff his face and hair, Adia felt a tick of annoyance.

"His reputation hardly does him justice," Bret said as he stroked Lubor's neck and looked through the stall window to admire the horse's form.

"Why are you still here?" she asked softly.

He kept his focus on Lubor, rubbing the flat area between the horse's eyes that boasted a white diamond mark among the dark brown fur. "Filip asked if I might stay on for a few weeks. Maybe longer."

She lifted her head sharply, her heart thudding. "What?"

Lubor pulled away from Bret's touch and looked over to her, sensing her unease.

"It seems he needs extra help since many of the staff are evacuating with their families." Bret put his hands in his pockets and shrugged. "I'm awaiting a new assignment from my editor, so I have a little time to spare."

"And you're an *accomplished* horseman."

He smirked. "Some might say that."

"Care to elaborate?" For Filip to be impressed, he must be remarkable.

"Nothing much." He hesitated and glanced away, which triggered a warning bell in her mind. What was he hiding? "I rode in my youth and in university. Polo, jumping, and such."

His casual tone irked her. He must have come from an affluent family to participate so easily in the sport of kings. While her mother had left the bay Arabian mare to her daughter upon her death, Adia had scrimped and saved. Though she could ride better than the boys, she couldn't afford to enter the shows or transport her horse the long distances to compete. She hadn't owned a saddle until she was in her teens. After her mother's horse died tragically, she'd taken in every broken and hopeless horse that others had cast aside. She then trained the horse, sold it for a significant profit, and after doing this a dozen times, earned her way into the show ring among the best. And finally, she'd saved enough to make her way to Janów Podlaski.

"And you intend to pester me until I return to America, is that it?" She straightened, still a bit unsteady on her feet.

He offered another charming smile and shook his head. "I imagine that would be a waste of time. You seem to have your mind made up."

She raised her chin a half inch. "I do."

He pulled out his hands and clapped them together. "Then let's not bother with such things. How might I be of service?"

Her mind raced. How could she keep Bret busy and out of sight? Something rattled her about his presence and the conflicting feelings he stirred in her.

"Aside from convincing Filip to evacuate the horses?"

"Also a waste of time."

"That, we agree on."

Filip, when his mind was set, could not be swayed. More than once, she'd suggested different pasture arrangements based on the herd hierarchies, and it was only after several horses were injured in rivalry disagreements that he'd gone with Adia's suggestion and claimed it all to be his idea. Still, he had done incalculable work as the leader of the largest stables in Poland. He was no fool.

She gave Lubor a final pat and slipped out of his stall, closing the door behind her and facing Bret with new resolve. "I'm sure we can manage just fine around here, Mr. Conway. Certainly, you have more important work to do."

She turned away, but he caught her elbow and gently turned her to face him. Her mouth went dry.

"Adia, I know I've done you wrong and made a twit of myself. But in the meantime, can we find peace between us?" He looked at Lubor, who watched them with his ears perked forward and his eyes intent. "Despite what you may think, I care for these horses as well, and I'll do whatever I can to help you and the director."

She couldn't rationally turn away the help—they were short-handed. Adia stared at the stallion next to them. What if one extra set of hands could better protect Lubor, Ewan, and all the treasures of Janów?

Part of her wished to rebel against a truce with this man. A compromise could open the door for friendship, for flirtation . . . for something more? She'd so easily fallen for his first request of dinner. Look how that had turned out.

She would not allow this line of thinking. She couldn't let him know how he irked her—and intrigued her. She'd keep the wall firmly in place around her heart.

She nodded and then pointed to a stack of pitchforks and wheelbarrows at the end of the aisle. "Very well. The stalls in this barn need cleaning. Grab a pitchfork."

He smiled. "Mucking manure it is."

He fell into step beside her, and she felt him studying her discreetly, perhaps still concerned after her fall.

42

As they walked toward the wheelbarrows, Ewan raced past them, brushing by Bret as he chased one of the barn cats. In an instant, Adia reached over, scooped up his arm, and slid the brass object effortlessly out of his hand. The young boy turned, blushed, and took off after the cat as if he'd done nothing amiss.

Adia lifted Bret's pocket watch by the chain. It glinted in the sunlight streaming in from the high windows as it swung from her grasp.

"If you plan to stay here at Janów, Mr. Conway, you'd better keep hold of your pocket watch."

SEPTEMBER 8, 1939

The sleek gray stallion with shining white fur and deep black eyes pushed Bret with his nose, breaking him from his stupor.

They stood outside the white-fenced outdoor arena where Adia rode a five-year-old solid black stallion bound for the racetrack next spring. As arresting as the horse was in conformation and attitude, it was the rider who captured every ounce of Bret's attention. Mesmerized him.

She rode with strong hands, confident and focused eyes, a straight back, and a sturdy seat. Her moves were effortless, her cues subtle as she commanded the spirited animal to walk, trot, and canter in sequence.

Over the past few days of working together, they'd fallen into a quiet rhythm where she gave him polite orders and he asked little of her. She was on guard around him, and he understood why. She'd already raised the drawbridge. Any advance he attempted would be met with a full-on retreat.

He'd agreed to Filip's request with the darkening fear that he couldn't guarantee Adia's safety with the oncoming threat. But neither could he turn down his friend or leave this woman when he might be able to help.

The stallion at his side, Palermo, nudged Bret again, and he chuckled. "All right, chap." He patted the horse's neck, which was sweaty from their ride. It was hard enough to focus on his mount while riding in the same ring as Adia, but here from the ground, his attention wandered even more.

Focus, Conway.

He'd agreed to watch after the American, not stare her down.

It had been years since he'd ridden, and getting back in the saddle dug up memories—and muscles—he'd long forgotten. He knew Filip admired his riding accomplishments, particularly his competing in the 1936 Olympics in Berlin. But he'd reminded Filip to keep the title of bronze medalist quiet or he'd risk his cover as a reporter. It was just easier and cleaner this way.

Only military men were granted places in the equestrian Olympic events, and most with that background didn't become a lowly reporter. The games were a showing of military might, an exhibition of the prowess of the horseman. And that year, under Hitler, Germany had taken the gold in every equestrian event.

A distant rumbling swelled, and Adia looked up from her horse to search the skies. Bret followed suit and tightened his hold on Palermo.

A set of planes swooped overhead, the third in as many days.

Adia's horse bolted forward, but she expertly pulled back the reins and directed Balik into a controlled circle. The horse snorted and his ears twitched at the unfamiliar sound.

Once the horse stilled, she looked over to Bret and met his gaze. She cued Balik to walk to the arena fence where Bret stood with Palermo, then stopped several paces away to keep the stallions from drawing too close. As she dismounted, stray dark brown hair from her long braid floated around her face.

"It seems ridiculous to just continue as if it were a normal day," she said.

Rumors of the Germans' location had been filtering through Wygoda for days. Bret knew her deep desire to prepare the herd for transport. Something in the way her eyes sparkled, the strength of her convictions, and the easy way she confronted him reminded him of Charlie. It had been a partnership he'd taken for granted until the moment it was gone.

And as the planes reminded him, danger was so close. What if Adia suffered the same fate as Charlie?

He shook his head and swallowed back bile at the thought.

Balik nipped at Adia's arm, and she distractedly pushed his nose away, looking off into the distance, west.

"Adia! Bret!"

They both turned at Filip's voice.

"The Germans have moved on Warsaw," Filip said, his voice deep and raw. "They are advancing far more swiftly than anticipated. Warsaw is less than two hundred kilometers west of here. Should it fall . . ."

Adia and Bret exchanged a silent glance. A thousand emotions flickered through her deep brown eyes in seconds.

Filip shook his head. "I can't believe it has come to this." He looked between the two of them.

Adia's straight posture slackened, her lips turning downward and her confidence deflating. There was no sense of glory or gloating in her demeanor. Bret could see she knew what this meant.

They all did.

"We'll go east as you suggested, Adia. I'll send word to Antek." Filip turned and looked over the emerald fields and white barns that he'd shepherded for several decades, his gaze turning to the setting sun on the horizon. "We will leave as soon as everything can be arranged."

4

SEPTEMBER 14, 1939

The Germans continued to lay siege to Warsaw. Radios had fallen silent across the country, but the inevitable hung on the wind in rumors and the stream of refugees fleeing east.

Once the city fell, the invaders would be only hours from Janów.

Lubor snorted as Adia slipped a leather halter over the long, sloping bridge of his nose. His shining black nostrils flared, and his deep black eyes sent her looks demanding an explanation for this noise and disturbance in their routine.

The usual tranquility of nickering horses, rustling leaves, and frolicking foals felt like a distant memory compared with the slamming of stalls, the stomping of boots, and shouts from grooms.

Planes now swooped overhead several times an hour. The sand in the hourglass was running out.

Adia pressed her forehead to Lubor's jet-black nose, and his hot breath grazed her skin. She traced her fingers over the ridges of his nose, as familiar as her own. She'd been with him every step of his life, from birth to near accidents as a frolicking foal, to the anxious days when he was first weaned from his mother. She had planned to be at his side next spring when it was time for him to learn the saddle and bit and make his debut on the racetrack, where all Arabian stallions were tested to prove their worth.

But would those days ever come?

"This isn't the exit from Poland I'd hoped for you," she whispered against Lubor's nose.

She'd envisioned a triumphant send-off once she scrounged enough to purchase him with Filip's blessing. A royal farewell with a host of broodmares to start a breeding empire back in the States.

She pressed her lips together. She couldn't give up on this future. Somehow, she'd find a way.

Soft footsteps padded up the aisle, and she looked up to see Ewan running toward her, then past her, with a sack of jangling items.

"Myszko, what's in that bag?"

He came to a stop, his mouse-brown hair flopping over his forehead. "Meester Bret said I need to give back these things I took."

She sighed. She'd asked Ewan to do that a dozen times. How did Bret get him to actually do it? Among the swell of her nervousness with the evacuation, her anger rose at Filip for leaving the child in her charge. Perhaps if someone better suited to child-rearing had tended him, Ewan would have overcome this compulsion to steal.

"Better move quickly!" She lifted her eyebrows to emphasize her point. "We leave soon."

Ewan's eyes widened and he dug around in his bag. He pulled out a pair of small, silver spurs and handed them to her before he dashed away, arms clenched around his loot.

She ran her thumb along the short spike on the back of the U-shaped metal. So that was where these had gone. Again. She should have known.

What would become of Ewan in the wake of Germany's invasion? What did he have aside from the looming buildings that were Janów? No family, no shelter.

What would she do? All she could think of was the horses, not her own safety. She figured Ewan would stay at one of the new farms and continue to pilfer trinkets and help with the horses.

Bret's voice floated down from the hallway that intersected with the stallion barn, repeating the instructions the two of them had decided after Filip put them in charge of the evacuation. "Distribute the food among the staff in case we get separated. We need a few days' worth before we reach Antek's farm. Let's hide the tack or take it with us to keep it from any soldiers who pass through."

Bret and Filip turned the corner, their shoulders hunched, focused on their discussion.

Her heart tripped over itself. Though she hated to admit it, the British journalist had proven invaluable with the preparations, his commanding presence and confidence assuaging her own fears.

She and Bret had worked together to group horses and assign staff based on experience. They would travel in groups of yearling mares, yearling colts, mares with new foals, and stallions.

The change in Bret—his lack of questioning and challenging compared with their earlier encounter—stumped her. What had truly prompted him to stay in Janów the past two weeks?

He and Filip paused ahead, out of her earshot as their voices lowered, both seemingly unaware of her and Lubor's presence. Bret's sleeves were rolled up, dust coating his pants and a short-brimmed hat covering his dark hair. He'd worked as tirelessly as she had in the days since Filip had ordered the evacuation. Her only visit back to her small cabin beyond the stables had been long enough to pack a small bag of her essentials: passport, cash, a few letters from Aunt Bea, a change of clothes.

Lubor pawed the ground, drawing her mind back to the present. He commanded attention in every way. She ran her hand down his neck. His muscles tensed under her touch, but as she scratched lightly, his nerves settled and his shuffling hooves stilled.

She yearned to see Lubor prove himself at the races. Instead, he was running for his life.

"Tomasz says we'll be ready by sunrise." Bret's voice beside her startled her. He stood at Lubor's nose, stroking the silky muzzle gently. Filip was no longer in sight.

She cleared her throat and moved around Lubor's rump so they stood on opposite sides, a barrier between her unsteady knees and Bret's all-seeing, green gaze.

"Thank you." Despite this being her plan, her charge, she wondered if that was enough time. There were still wagons to pack, grain rations to inventory, horses to document and account for.

Bret watched her for a beat longer and then fished a sugar cube from his pocket for Lubor. The stallion instantly swiped it with his lips and nudged Bret for more.

"You should get what rest you can tonight." He turned to leave.

"Mr. Conway?" Stirrings deep inside compelled her forward.

He half turned and chuckled. "I think for simplicity's sake, you should just call me Bret."

"Well . . . I wanted to thank you. I-I'm not sure I could have done this alone—." Pride choked her. Lubor swished his tail as if sensing her discomfort. "Just . . . thank you."

Amusement flickered in his eyes. He tipped his hat and smiled enough that a faint dimple appeared on one side. Then he turned and strode away, leaving her alone again in a mix of emotions.

A stillness settled over her and the stallions in their stalls. She glanced around at the aged wood, painted with care and attention and spectator to hundreds of years of history.

Would she see these barns again? This had been the only place that had ever felt like home. And now she'd venture east into the uncertainty with all of Janów's wards.

Żegnam i dziękuję. Farewell and thank you.

A tear welled at the corner of her eye, and she batted it away, striding down the hall toward her next task.

The feat ahead of them commanded all her focus. Not pesky regret or distracting Brits. She'd need to keep her head—and heart—on what mattered most.

Lubor. And the two hundred and fifty other horses fleeing for their lives.

SEPTEMBER 15, 1939

The sun crested the horizon as the uniformed staff of Janów and herds of horses took shape in the paddocks of the white stables. Dozens of grooms saddled the broke-to-ride mounts and distributed them to the thirty townspeople who had been called upon to help wrangle the Arabians.

It required every ounce of Bret's willpower to keep him from taking Adia by the shoulders and shaking her. Frustration swelled at his inability to simply whisk her and Ewan away into France and dump them on a boat to America. This was no place for either of them.

That was the only way to truly keep his promise to protect Adia during these uncertain times. But in truth, they'd missed the narrow window to evacuate Poland.

Now, she led the coordination of Janów's exodus with masterful attention to detail. She was a vault of information about every single horse and staff member and worked harder than anyone else on the grounds.

"Crystal is temperamental with men, so we should assign Zara, Henryk's wife, as a handler. Moonlight needs to be among more dominant mares or she feels unsettled, so put her alongside Zuza."

Adia knew which stallions were foaled within days of each other and put them in the same group with the most competent handlers, including herself and Ewan. Apparently, Lubor, the son of the famed Odwaga, and Ewan got on well. Tomasz, the most experienced and longest-employed trainer, and his twin sons, who were both trainers, would round off the stallion handlers, along with Leonard and Jok.

Bret checked the saddle girth and bridle straps on Samir, his chestnut-colored gelding with a wide blaze and four tall white stockings on his legs. Samir was calm enough to lead the group of excitable stallions and boasted a stockier build that resigned him to the farm fields instead of the show ring. An outsider among a sea of horses that knew their purpose, not unlike Bret when he'd lived in England.

"Two peas in a pod, you and I," he said to Samir, giving him a sugar cube. He had learned the value of buttering up his horses with sweets back in his Olympian days. If a horse decided he didn't like you, not much would change his mind. A little sugar could go a long way.

Bret planned to stick close to Adia with the stallions but wanted to be able to ride ahead or behind to check on the other groups as well.

Down the gravel road that led to the clock tower barn in the center of the stud farm, Adia helped Ewan into the saddle on an old dapple-gray gelding named Captain. She turned to her mount, a golden-colored gelding named Dancer with a brilliant white mane and tail. The half-Arabian was a fast and well-trained companion used to race against the stallions on the track. The horse watched Adia's movements closely, obviously enamored with his rider. Bret didn't blame him.

Filip blew a whistle from the front of the driveway as the biggest batch, the mares with swollen bellies and the mares with young foals on their heels, started off on the road to the east toward Włodawa. They'd be the slowest-moving group, so they'd be the first to get started. The one-year-old fillies would follow, then the colts and stallions, with a wide berth in between to keep the males and females apart. Where there weren't fences to keep the sexes apart, distance would have to suffice.

Horses danced and shuffled nervously as the herd moved forward, ebbing and flowing like a wayward swarm of bees. Handlers walked horses on the outer edges of the group, but most of the animals were halter free and clinging to their companions in the uncertain new surroundings.

Slowly, the long stream of horses disappeared over the horizon, and the rear of the procession followed. The groups needed thirty minutes in between departures or they would risk mares and stallions clashing.

Minutes turned into hours as the stallion group handlers sat anxiously on their geldings.

Adia and Ewan trotted to Bret's position to the side of the circular driveway, which provided the clearest view of the herd. The stallions were gathered in a paddock, each one haltered and held by trainers or grooms. These were far too valuable and unpredictable to leave loose.

"Watch out!" Tomasz shouted, causing Bret and Adia to both twist in their saddles and look back at the commotion.

His son Lukas held tight to the rope of a rearing Wojownik, Lubor's half brother, who looked almost identical but didn't boast his brother's ideal temperament. The stallion lashed out and jerked his lead rope free of Lukas's grip. He kicked against the fence and broke the top board. With a quick hop, Wojownik soared free of containment and thundered down the road toward the departing mares, black mane whipping in the wind.

"Loose horse!" Tomasz cried out.

Bret kicked Samir's sides at the same moment that Adia and Dancer bolted forward. The pairs raced down the lane after Wojownik. Adia leaned forward, flat against Dancer's neck, as the horse's long strides covered the ground. Samir fell back the slightest bit, unable to keep up, but Bret squeezed his sides encouragingly to keep on pace.

Wind whipped Bret's face and his eyes watered as they closed in on Wojownik. The pure speed sent him back to fast-paced foxhunts of his youth. How had he forgotten the immense joy of this?

Pebbles flew from under the three sets of hooves, drawing his focus back. Strands fell free of Adia's braid and streamed behind her. She reined Dancer closer to Wojownik and leaned forward to reach for the flapping lead rope. Bret kept Samir along the other side to keep Wojownik from changing direction.

Wojownik nipped at Adia's outstretched arm, but she kept out of range. Her movements were deft and her control of Dancer exceptional. She waited for the perfect moment when the lead flicked upward and snatched it from the air. With a firm hold she pulled back on Wojownik's and Dancer's noses equally. Bret pulled his own reins back to ease Samir down to a walk.

All three horses snorted and panted. They were a few hundred meters from Janów, where they'd left Ewan and the rest of the stallions, but luckily the herd of mares was safely out of sight.

When Bret looked back at Adia, his pulse quickened even further. Her hair fell in waves over her shoulders, her cheeks rosy and her eyes shining. He felt the same joy that radiated from her smile. The race, the excitement and adrenaline—they were intoxicating.

So was the glow of her.

"Well," she huffed, her grin deepening, "I do hope the rest of our journey is a bit less exciting."

"Though it'd be nice if it were that speedy."

She laughed, a melodious tone that sent a ripple of shivers down his arms. Her attention shifted back to Dancer as she patted his sweaty neck under his thick white mane and whispered praise.

He tore his gaze away. She captivated him. But she'd be out of his life for good in a short while. As it should be.

Men in his line of work weren't allowed the luxury of long-term relationships. He knew that better than anyone.

For now, they'd need to focus on hiding the horses throughout the farms of Eastern Poland and smuggling them through occupied territory. Until that happened, he needed to keep Adia and her magical smile at arm's length.

5

Dead in their tracks. The entire column of horses was stopped after only six hours of painfully slow travel.

Adia's chest tightened as she circled Dancer for the twelfth time, her nerves getting the better of her. At this rate, they'd never make it to Antek's farm, let alone a single kilometer farther.

The heart-pumping race to catch the wayward stallion had not hinted at what was to come. Once the group of horses emerged from the small roads that led to the stud farm, their meager progress screeched to a halt.

The roads overflowed with civilians on foot, in vehicles, in carts pulled by mules or draft horses, and on the occasional motorbike. Horns honked, men shouted, children cried.

Adia looked over and met Bret's unreadable gaze, his handsome features still full of resolve. Their gazes held, just for a moment.

"Well, at least there's one good thing to come from this predicament," he said.

"What's that?" she grumbled.

"At least you can confidently say that you were right to push for an earlier evacuation." He smiled, somehow able to make light of all this.

But the affirmation didn't soothe her unease.

They'd hardly traversed half a kilometer since leaving the farm and still had seven and a half more to go to cross the Bug River and reach the town of Kovel, where Antek's farm sat on the outskirts. They had enough food and supplies for those few days, but would that be enough if it took them twice or three times as long as they'd planned?

Every handler and rider struggled to hold on to the excited stallions amid the chaos and odors of gasoline, sweat, and hot gravel. The heat bore down on them, the luxurious shelter of the trees that encased Janów a distant memory.

Adia watched Ewan and his horse closely, both their eyes wide and sweat beading down the child's face. "It will be all right, Ewan," she said softly. He blinked, nodded slowly, but didn't look her way.

A loud crash sounded just in front of Bret and Samir, who led two stallions and rode ahead of Adia. Samir reared and pawed the air, but Bret leaned forward and managed to keep his balance, steadying the horse and holding fast to the lead ropes of the stallions in his charge.

Two men had crashed their rickety cars on the road and now emerged to shout at each other. One man threw a punch, and his wife screamed from within their vehicle. Most of the crowd simply averted their eyes and trudged forward.

Bret dismounted, handed the horses off to Adia, and broke up the brawl. He ordered the men to return to their vehicles. The timbre and power of his voice seemed to shake the ground, and both men turned with flushed faces and reluctantly did as commanded.

The line of fleeing families and horses inched forward another few feet before coming to a stop again.

Would it have been better for them to remain at Janów? No. Everyone else was fleeing because they knew their best hope lay in escaping the coming danger.

The moments turned to hours. Adia's clothes stuck to her damp skin. Her forehead burned under the sun. She'd forgotten a hat in her haste to leave.

Ewan was also melting beneath the cloudless sky. He clung to the saddle, brown eyes wide, long hair askew, and arms tucked into himself as if he could hide. But not even a mouse could escape the sun pressing down upon the roadway and the swarms of mosquitoes and other bugs.

Near midday, several hours after they'd departed Janów, the traffic on the roadway parted like the Red Sea as a row of mounted Polish cavalrymen wove through.

The leader tipped his hat to Bret and Adia. "Greetings! You are the group from Janów Podlaski, are you not?"

"Yes, Captain Sven," she said. "We met last fall."

"Ah, Miss Kensington, yes. I bring a message from Director Maier," he said. "The roads are far worse ahead. You'll not make much progress in this manner. With the heat, the staff are falling ill as well. And these blasted mosquitoes. He advises camping in the forests during the day and traveling by night."

She looked over at Bret, feeling a mix of relief and despair at the obstacles within that plan itself.

Bret leaned forward. "Any other news—or threats—we should be aware of?"

"We don't know where they're at." The Germans. The captain flinched ever so slightly. And these solders were off to face the oncoming Germans, no doubt.

Adia looked at the young faces. Some had never even shaved their first beard and yet they were Poland's most highly trained soldiers. Several hundred men on horses with rifles, against the might of Germany with tanks and planes.

She closed her eyes, a cavity opening in her chest and a feeling of horror spreading to every limb. Her stomach roiled as soldiers rode past, toward the west. Toward war and danger and death.

"Let's get off this roadway." Bret motioned to a grove of trees a hundred yards away.

The broiling earth had left even these spirited animals muted. Their heads hung low, and their hooves dragged on the gravel. As the group moved slowly from the road, the horses perked up ever so slightly at the patches of grass among the shade of the trees.

The lush green fields and barricade of trees had protected Janów from much of the summer's heat. But there was no shelter on the road. Not from the sun or any mechanical predator in the sky.

The shade of the canopy of leaves provided instant relief, along with the added effect of dampening the noise from the road packed full of evacuees.

The men and Adia quickly set to tying off the horses to trees and keeping them spaced out to prevent fighting. The horses lowered their heads to graze.

After they tied off Dancer and Captain, Adia walked up to Bret with Ewan on her heels.

"Now what, Amerykanka?" Ewan asked.

"I was going to ask the same thing," Lukas said, approaching with his hands shoved in his pockets. His long blond hair dipped over his forehead and his smooth skin was far too clean and dry after such an arduous voyage. The nineteen-year-old was the heart-stopper of his family, and he knew it. Every week, a new young girl from town would fawn over him and drop by the farm for a tour.

"What's with the picnic, brave leader?" Lukas's eyes sparkled as he looked at Adia.

His flirtations landed on Adia more often than not, no matter how much she insisted she was far too old for him—seven years his senior.

Rafał and Tomasz joined them, both a little worse for wear. Though Rafał had shared the same womb as his two-minute-older brother, his muddy brown hair was close-cropped, and his features lacked the sharp definition Lukas's had.

"We'll camp here until dark," she explained, unsure they'd heard the message relayed by the cavalrymen. "Filip's orders."

"Fine by me." Lukas smiled. "It was about as much fun out there as stacking hay in summer of '36."

Adia recalled the first summer she'd worked in Poland and the unusually oppressive heat. Those were hot days mucking stalls and muggy nights learning Polish, with the help of Lukas and Rafał's mother, Elena. Elena had fallen ill the following winter and never recovered. Adia still missed her.

Rafał shook his head and scoffed at his brother. Lukas was brilliant with the horses, same as his brother and father, but he was always itching for adventure beyond the emerald pastures and dirt racetrack.

"The horses aren't used to this much walking, especially on a roadway." Tomasz winced. "Olark's hooves are already showing sores."

Adia silently ran through the treatments for stone sores: soaking the hooves in salts, draining the sores, wrapping the hooves. And rest. But they still had so far to go. And no soaking salts.

Bret shifted his weight and gazed eastward. The sun still shone high in the sky. It was barely past noon. "I'm going to scout ahead and check on the route through the forest."

"I'll go with you." Adia straightened.

"You should stay and treat the horses." He glanced between Lukas and Rafał. "Either of you care to come?"

Rafał stepped forward and nodded wordlessly, turning to his horse.

She stepped closer to Bret and narrowed her eyes. "Why couldn't I go?"

"We should try to be inconspicuous." He smiled. "A beautiful woman astride a Janów-bred horse isn't very subtle."

Indignation surged in Adia, but Bret chuckled. "I mean no offense."

She crossed her arms.

Rafał trotted up, and Bret mounted Samir. "We'll be back before dark."

The two trotted through the trees toward the roadway and vanished from sight.

The insolence of that man. And yet her neck flushed at his words "a beautiful woman." She shook her head and walked toward Tomasz, Lukas, and Ewan as they bent over the gray stallion's hoof several paces away.

Lukas winked at her. "So, we both got left behind? I thought you'd have a better chance, since he fancies you."

She glared and pushed him off balance, the way she might have done if he were her brother. He felt as close as one, as did Rafał. After all, Tomasz and Elena had taken her in without question and guided her through her first few months at Janów.

Lukas chuckled, righted himself, and wiggled his eyebrows. "Did I strike a nerve, Amerykanka?"

"Enough." Tomasz stepped up and growled at his son. "Adia, look at this sore. Tell me what you think."

Ewan looked between all of them, blinking with a confused expression. "What does 'fancies' mean?"

The sun sank ahead as Bret and Rafał returned to where the stallions and handlers waited. The two of them had made good time along the congested roadway, able to canter along the road's grassy banks. Hordes of refugees now thinned as some broke off to camp or find shelter at a nearby town for the night. They'd be able to move much faster by moonlight.

"How exactly did you meet Adia, anyway?" Rafał asked once they slowed their mounts to a walk.

Bret looked over and tipped a smile. "Why so curious, if I may ask?"

Rafał shrugged. "She's like my sister. My mother took her under her wing before she died."

Bret softened toward the young man, hearing the genuine concern laced in his words. "I'm only looking after her as a favor to Filip. Once I know she's safe, I have my own work to get back to."

"Why would Filip ask you?" Rafał tilted his head and spoke softly, a total opposite of the boisterous Lukas.

The lie came swiftly. "He knew how busy you'd all be caring for the horses. And my friendship with him goes back quite a while, that's all."

He couldn't talk about the years of training and combat experience that Filip surely was counting on. Or the fact that if needed, Bret could call upon his network of spies and trade a few more favors to keep Adia safe. Those were all the pieces he kept hidden.

The camp of staff and horses poked through the tree line as the sky blazed orange, and Rafał nodded, seeming to accept Bret's explanation.

The younger man had proven a good rider and insightful conversationalist in the past few hours. Bret wondered what else brewed beneath his quiet demeanor. Above all, Bret was glad to know Lukas and Rafał would also look out for Adia amid the chaos that was to come.

When they reached the horses, Adia, Ewan, Lukas, Tomasz, and the other riders sat in a circle, nibbling cheese and bread from their packs. They stood at the men's approach.

"How is Olark?" Bret asked Adia, dismounting and smothering the groan that rose in his throat from his back's stiffness. Even the training work of the past two weeks hadn't prepared him for this much riding.

"He'll be all right." She reached out to scratch Samir's neck. "How is the road ahead?"

"We'll be all right." He forced a smile. "As long as we don't have any surprises along the way. For now, I'd love a bite to eat. I'm famished."

She took Samir's reins and lifted her eyebrows expectantly. "So is your horse."

"Yes, of course." He nodded and led the horse over to the others as she followed. "Isn't this the way of the cowboy from those dime novels you Yanks like? The cowboys always take care of their horses first?"

"It's the way of all proper horsemen, Conway. I'd expect nothing less from you. Since you're so *accomplished*."

He smiled at her barb, a common one since he'd never filled in the details about why Filip admired his horsemanship so much. He had ignored her inquiries and especially the memories of the Olympics— the beginnings of his career in espionage, rumors of a rigged competition with a German colonel who had stolen the gold medal, and of course, the laughs and memories he'd shared with Charlie along the way.

Bret loosened the girth but didn't remove the saddle completely. They'd be back on their trek in a few hours. He unlatched the bridle's throat strap and slid it off over Samir's ears, waiting for the horse to open his mouth and release the metal bar.

But the horse sat there, ears swishing and jaw clenched as if defiant, preventing the bit from coming free.

Adia crossed her arms, smirking. "Need help there, Cowboy?"

Bret jiggled the bridle, confused by the horse's indifference and insistence in keeping the bit in his mouth. He'd never seen a horse act this way. Most were eager to free themselves from the metal bar.

After several more minutes, Bret's own stomach now grumbling, he sighed and turned to Adia. "It seems I require your assistance, Miss Kensington."

"Certainly." She stepped closer, the trace of lavender soap wafting over him. She stuck her finger into Samir's mouth right at the bit, where a gap in his wide, flat teeth gave way to soft gums. Instantly the horse opened his mouth, and the bridle came free. Samir licked his lips and then lowered his head to graze.

"Ah. So that's the trick."

Adia studied him. "Are you going to tell me more about what's ahead? What shape is the roadway in?"

"I'm hungry. Perhaps you'll join me for dinner, and we can talk more then."

She pressed her lips together. "I've heard that before. And somehow, I'm not sure I believe anything you say, Mr. Conway. I'll ask Rafał instead."

She spun to leave, but Bret caught her arm. "Adia," he said, drawing her back. "I tried to explain—I can explain."

Why did his throat suddenly close? All he had to say was that he'd been in a car accident. A reasonable, understandable delay, surely.

Her penetrating gaze burned into him.

It was all still so fresh. And the loss of Charlie . . . it was so much more than an accident. He hadn't fully come to terms with all that he'd lost.

Her voice cut into his thoughts. "You'd better grab a little rest and some food. I'll check on Lubor again." She slipped away and disappeared into the darkness that spread like an inky fog through the heavy, humid night.

He stomped back to the staff, where Tomasz and Ewan played cards. Ewan surely had pocketed at least half the deck and a good portion of the bounty of trinkets used for gambling that had been set along the forest floor.

Though he was famished, Bret's stomach churned in frustration and confusion. How could he make her understand? Or was it better that she held her anger as a shield between them both?

An hour later, Lukas emerged from the trees, the same direction Adia had disappeared in toward Lubor and the other prized stock.

"How much longer—another day or so before we reach the river?" Lukas asked as he sat next to Bret and reached for a canteen of water. "Think we'll beat the Germans across?"

"Pretty sure Adia will scare them away if they get too close," Bret quipped, ripping off a chunk of cheese.

Lukas huffed a laugh. "She has that way with some people."

Bret lowered the block of cheese, angered by the way thoughts of her consumed his mind.

Tomasz muttered under his breath, tossing his hand of cards down in frustration. Ewan giggled and scooped up his winnings as the elder man rose and announced he'd no longer play poker with the little mouse.

"We should probably start packing up to get back on the road," Bret said, wishing Adia was at least in sight. Every moment these past few weeks had felt tense, uncertain.

An instinct deep inside him seemed to shout that the worst was yet to come.

6

Adia closed her eyes, silently berating herself for even hinting at the failed dinner date.

They were fleeing German invaders. Lives were at stake. Dwelling in her regret was frivolous.

She walked around the encampment, unsure of how long she'd wandered before weaving back through the trees to the cluster of stallions. Several horses lifted their heads, while most continued to graze on the thick grass.

Lubor's distinctive white diamond mark on his forehead peeked through his silky black mane, shining above the rest. His curiosity overruled his hunger, and he lifted his head to watch her approach. He nickered at her, and she fished out a sugar cube, though her pocketful would not last much longer.

She bent over each of his legs, each hoof, and ran her hand over his neck, shoulder, and hindquarters. And after realizing she hadn't really paid attention, she started again.

Lubor. These stallions. This was her mission. She couldn't afford to get lost in other distractions.

She buried her face in Lubor's thick mane of silky hair. He nudged her softly with his nose and then startled. His quick jump and snort of fear set her heart racing.

Footsteps snapped twigs as two shadowy figures approached. She ducked behind Lubor, but even in the dim light, she could see their focus narrowed in on her.

"Hello," they called out. "We spotted the horses and were curious."

Two men shuffled into view. They wore civilian clothing with short-brimmed hats pulled low over their faces, coat collars turned upward despite the heat of the evening. One had an unlit cigar between his lips. The other peered without reserve through crooked, thin-rimmed glasses.

She recognized them instantly from town. Roman and Stefan, two thugs who routinely rustled bribes and extorted businesses. Though they'd never been arrested for it, they had been reported to rob travelers who came through Wygoda.

She looked toward the camp where the rest of the staff were finishing their meals and gathering up their supplies. Were they within earshot if she cried out? With the thick mass of trees, they certainly couldn't see her.

The stallions lifted their heads at the strangers' approach and shifted uneasily.

"What do you want?" she asked harshly.

"Your accent is funny." Stefan, the taller of the two, tilted his head like a dog. "Are you English?"

She bristled, sweat beading anew on her brow, and said again, "What do you want?"

The stout man with the cigar, Roman, answered with a half smile, "My, my, these aren't the famed horses of Janów Podlaski, are they?"

She stepped in front of Lubor as they drew closer. "They're very spirited. Don't come any closer."

"Or what?" Roman taunted.

They paused a few feet in front of her. Stefan scanned her body with not even a feigned interest in the horses. Lubor stomped his foot and bobbed his head in agitation, picking up on her unease.

"He'll bite," she said. Lubor had bitten a few grooms he wasn't fond of, but there wasn't any guarantee she could count on it as a defense.

Stefan laughed. "We're not that concerned with the horses."

How could she slip away? Could she leave the horses behind? What if they took Lubor? She thought back to the brawling fights along the roadway earlier in the day. These were violent, uncertain times. And no doubt Stefan and Roman knew the value of these stallions.

Her mind whirled. If she hesitated, she'd never get the chance to flee.

She bolted, but Roman grabbed her. Lubor struck out with his front hoof and hit him in the arm. The man cried out, his arm clenched tight against his chest. That kick was more than strong enough to fracture the bone. Stefan slipped around his counterpart and grabbed her arm, keeping well out of Lubor's reach. The young stallion whinnied and snorted angrily, pulling against his tied lead rope.

Adia screamed and kicked wildly, landing the heel of her riding boot on Stefan's shin. When his clamp-like grip loosened for a heartbeat, she wrenched her arm free and elbowed him in the sternum. He coughed and swore.

She sprinted free, scrambling toward the camp. Now all the stallions were whinnying and crying out. She screamed again.

Hear them. Hear me.

Roman lunged toward her, grabbed her waist with his good arm, and yanked her back, throwing her to the ground. She landed hard on her side, branches and stones digging into her hip, arm, and face.

He pulled her up by a handful of her braid at the base of her head. She gritted her teeth against the pain. He lowered his face next to hers, his rancid breath hot on her face. "Funny little trick there with your horse."

She thrashed and tried to scream, but he clamped a hand over her mouth. The taste of dirt, cigar, and sweat filled her mouth and she gagged against the force of it all.

The burly man dragged her clear of the rows of horses and deeper into the thick brush of the forest, farther from Bret, Lukas, and Ewan. Farther from salvation. Stefan followed and glanced behind to ensure they weren't seen.

Panic overwhelmed every sense and she clawed, scratched, and bit at her attacker. Roman swore as her fingernail scratched his eye, and he clenched his hand on her throat.

She gasped and gulped for air that would not come, and her head swam and ached from the lack of oxygen. Nausea roiled in her stomach and blackness brushed at the edge of her vision. She could hardly stay on her feet.

A loud snap rang out, and the squeal of horses and thundering of hooves echoed on the ground.

They all turned to see Lubor stomping up to them, teeth bared, his broken lead rope hanging from his halter. Roman pushed Adia away to avoid Lubor's hooves, and she fell to the ground. She rolled to the side, barely escaping being struck as the horse thrashed.

Several other stallions screamed and snapped their ropes, biting at each other. Adia coughed, sputtered, and tried to stand, but the world spun around her. Lubor circled her and charged Stefan, who ducked behind a tree.

The attacker reached under his coat and pulled out a revolver. He pulled back on the hammer and leveled it at the diamond on the stallion's forehead.

"No!" Adia screeched. She clawed and stumbled up to her feet to push Lubor away.

A chorus of footsteps drew close. Bret broke through the brush and grabbed Stefan's arms, knocking the gun free of his grip. He punched the man across the jaw, sending his spectacles flying and his unconscious body to the ground in a heap.

Adia whirled to see Lukas with Roman in a choke hold, a wrestling move that he and his brother had perfected over years of constant bickering.

Bret picked up Stefan's pistol and quickly checked the man for another weapon before striding over to Roman and doing the same.

He helped Lukas haul Roman to his feet and handed the gun to the twin.

"Shoot either of them in the leg if they move." His gaze bore into the younger man, and Lukas nodded confidently, any trace of the jokester and daredevil replaced by the weight of his task.

Bret knelt at her side, a wildness and intensity in his gaze that both calmed and terrified her. His lips moved, but she couldn't comprehend what he was saying. The din of her racing blood and surging fear drowned out everything else.

She'd always felt so safe in Poland, the bricks of Janów's barns her sanctuary and shield. Now those walls were gone.

"Adia?"

She blinked as his voice emerged from the haze of her thoughts. His voice was soft, firm.

"I'm . . . I'm okay," she mumbled. Was she? Her head pounded and her hands trembled. Her gaze darted to Lubor, who stood nearby, sniffing the ground and eyeing Lukas, who loomed over Roman and Stefan. Lukas's attention darted between his prisoners and Adia, his eyes dark with concern.

Bret reached for her, his fingers brushing her shoulder, and she jerked away without thinking. He pulled back his hand, his expression dark with anger and sadness.

She swallowed, her jaw clenching against the pain in her throat from Roman's grip, as if he still pressed down on her. She wished she could wash away the feel of it all.

"I'm fine, really."

"All right," Bret said softly, keeping his distance.

Her breath came in short gasps as emotion swelled in her chest and tears scratched at the corners of her eyes, frantic to escape. But she would not—she could not—cry in front of him, in front of them.

Roman glared at her, and Stefan began to wake.

Fear and shame flooded through her, driving her to her feet. She brushed off the leaves and grass and wished she could brush away the men's stares and Bret's hovering presence.

She needed to flee from them all.

Tomasz and Rafał and several other grooms emerged through the trees and looked around, taking in the two men held at gunpoint and the scattered stallions with loose lead ropes.

Knowing Ewan wouldn't be far behind Tomasz and Rafał, she strode away from the circle of spectators through the trees toward their makeshift camp. As she did, tears broke free of her hold and her lungs pulled in large gulps of air.

And still she was drowning.

Bret looked to Tomasz, who nodded at Bret's silent request.

"I'll stick close to her." Tomasz nodded toward Rafał and pointed to the two men at Lukas's feet. "You help them deal with this mess."

Rafał nodded, approaching his brother, and asked what had happened.

Bret ran his hand over his face, his blood and skin on fire, aching to beat each of the thugs to oblivion. And what could they do with them now? Bret knew of their reputation to break the law in Wygoda, but he'd never expected them to attack a woman.

Times had changed. Desperation, chaos, ruled all.

The sun had nearly set, and the herd needed to push forward. Or should they delay and allow Adia some time and space to recover from the shock of it all?

She had fled the small clearing so fast, with hardly a look back at Lubor to ensure his security. That was not the Adia he knew. The stallion still roamed free, now sniffing the grass with infrequent glances back at the intruders.

The man with the bleeding arm, Roman, grunted and glared up at the twins, and Bret could smell the sinister thoughts flashing through his head about overpowering them and escaping.

Bret walked over and held out his hand to take the pistol from Lukas. He had a Luger tucked in his own waist but knew it wasn't as common for horse trainers, or supposed journalists, to wield so casually.

"You round up the stallions," he said to Rafał and Lukas and the other Janów grooms behind them who looked on silently. "Jok, Leonard," he called to two of the largest men who seemed capable of handling themselves in a fight. "Will you escort these men back into town and see they find the inside of a jail cell?"

Jok and Leonard nodded without hesitation. Janów and its staff were a tight community, and Roman and Stefan had messed with the wrong horse trainer.

While Rafał, Lukas, and the rest gathered up the stallions and brought them back into order for their march, Bret helped secure Stefan's and Roman's bindings, not caring one bit how Roman's bloodied arm might ache against the strain. He deserved every bit of it and more.

Stefan spat on the ground, glaring at Bret. "The world is falling to ashes. We won't be locked up for long."

"Maybe not." Bret smiled. "From what I've heard, the Germans have no patience for criminals. I'm sure their sentence will be far more severe than anything you'd find in Wygoda. But if you come near the woman or our horses again, a broken arm is the least of your concerns."

Bret handed the pistol to Jok, who turned and kicked Stefan in the back of his leg, making him stumble forward. "Walk, you cowards," Jok said.

Bret watched until they'd disappeared through the forest back to Wygoda, a sense of unease still filling him. Stefan might have been correct. The local and national governments could collapse at any moment. The only other option was vigilante justice.

All he could do was keep Adia as far from harm as possible. So far, he wasn't doing a great job. If the horses hadn't broken loose, if Lukas hadn't come to camp and mentioned not seeing Adia . . .

He swallowed back the sickness that rose in the back of his throat.

"Should we camp another day?" Rafał asked. Both brothers awaited instruction from Bret.

He shook his head, giving them a small smile of appreciation.

"You know how Adia would react to such a suggestion. We'd better get the herd back on course."

They nodded and dispersed, weaving through the trees back to camp and retrieving their saddle horses.

Now darkness had seeped between each tree and stained the sky above. A dull gray light from the full moon spread across the ground and provided just enough light to guide their steps.

His heart flipped when Adia came into view. She checked Captain's saddle and then reached down to help Ewan mount, as calm as if nothing were amiss.

But when she angled back in his direction, he caught the faint outline of tear tracks on her dirty cheeks.

His chest constricted painfully. How had he failed so utterly to keep her from harm? Why had he let her out of his sight?

She set Ewan in the saddle and handed him the reins. Ewan's gaze followed her as she turned away, his insightful young expression soaking in the silent signals Adia radiated.

Her hands trembled at her sides and her braid was still askew, though it looked like she had tried to smooth away the dirt and bits of forest caught in her hair.

He needed to know if she was okay, even though he knew she'd deflect any concern or care on his part.

She untied Dancer from the thin tree trunk and turned as if sensing his approach. She avoided his gaze and shifted from one foot to the other.

"We're all packed and ready to go here," she said, scrutinizing the barren area where they'd rested for the afternoon. "Are the horses—Lubor and the others—" Her question halted, and her voice wavered, her unease spilling over.

"They're fine. Rafał and Lukas are tending to them."

She clamped her jaw as if hesitating to ask the question he knew she wanted the answer to.

"Those men are gone now, Adia. We've sent them to Wygoda. They won't be able to hurt you again."

She turned away. "They didn't hurt me."

Bret nodded, glad to hear the telltale stubbornness in her words.

She checked her saddle again, and in the dim light, Bret caught sight of the bruising around her neck. He held back his words, focusing all his energy on the swift anger and protectiveness that bolted through him.

She stepped into the stirrup and swung her other leg over the saddle. "We'd better go. We're wasting moonlight."

Her words rang with finality. The conversation was over.

He glanced over to Tomasz, the man's gaze darting between the two of them from under his bushy gray eyebrows.

Far in the distance, rumbling from bombs or artillery stirred the ground, reminding them of the army closing in behind them.

With the threat of Polish ruffians and the river crossing ahead, no corner of Poland was safe for Adia or these horses.

His mission shifted in his mind. He wouldn't just look after her until they'd reached the border like he'd promised Filip. He would do everything in his power to take Adia out of Poland.

Better yet, out of Europe.

7

SEPTEMBER 16, 1939

Adia did everything she could to hide her trembling hands from Bret and the rest of the group.

The faint, wretched odor of Roman's cigar breath still lingered. She couldn't get the visions from her mind, couldn't push away the terror that swirled in her stomach or the feel of Roman's hands on her body. They were gone, but still she flinched at each broken branch.

The night slowly passed, and as dawn peeked through the trees, the forest gave way to wider fields that offered little protection from the sun and heat to come.

The roads were less crowded after sunset, as most evacuating civilians pulled their vehicles to the side of the road to sleep. The smell of oil, gasoline, and dust still choked the air, even though the temperature had dropped slightly.

"There's a farmhouse ahead we spoke with when we scouted," Bret called out. "The owner agreed we can rest there for the day."

Adia turned. "And then how far to the river?"

"Another few kilometers. At this pace, we'll reach Antek's farm in one more night."

Only one more night. Thank God.

The pop and clatter of gunfire grew far behind them, the slight whiff of smoke caught on the breeze. Could they truly escape what was coming?

Her mind was lost to the noises beyond, the smoke and ash in the air that hinted at horrors beyond imagination.

Less than an hour later, as the sun inched higher, a small farmhouse rose on the horizon and Bret led the column of sixteen horses and seven riders down the long driveway.

Rafał motioned to the barn for the horses. "There are enough empty stalls for the stallions for the day."

Relief pricked at the knot of tension in Adia's chest, though she glanced around, still expecting to glimpse Stefan or Roman.

An old woman emerged from the house and lifted a hand in greeting to Bret. She smiled and beamed at him, and he gave his charming grin in return.

"Ah, there you are! Been waiting for your arrival all night. I'm so honored to host Janów Podlaski horses." She clasped her wrinkled, tanned hands to her chest.

Bret made a round of introductions as Rafał and Lukas led the stallions and riding horses into the large stables. Adia slowly dismounted and let Lukas lead Dancer away, then felt utterly exposed, unable to hide the twitch that plagued her hands and the hitch that caught her breath.

Lukas looked at her with a gentle furrow in his brow, avoiding the teasing and flirting that usually accompanied every interaction between them. The absence left Adia even more on edge.

The woman, Karina, fussed over Ewan and smiled brightly at Adia, not seeming to notice her angst. "Come inside. I don't have much, but I have some bread, cheese, and eggs."

At that invitation, Ewan, the twins, Tomasz, and the rest of the staff stampeded into the small farmhouse.

Bret waited behind, a few strides away from Adia, unimposing with his hands in his pockets and his shoulders drooped in exhaustion.

An explosion echoed to the west, more than a hundred kilometers away where Warsaw lay under siege. They both turned in the direction at the same time, then exchanged glances. She saw the dozens of worries and possibilities flash through Bret's mind. But the heat of the day was falling upon them, and only the horses mattered now.

"I'm not hungry," she said, her voice coming out in a rasp. "I probably should tend to Olark's sore hoof."

"I'll help you, if you want it."

She nodded, had expected as much. Deep down, she was glad for his company.

They turned toward the large barn, its white paint chipped along the boards and many pieces in disrepair. But inside, two rows of ten stalls stood proudly, now full of stallions happily eating hay. It appeared to be an old milking barn, though the cows seemed to have vanished. If she had to guess, she'd assume the cows had been seized for the armies.

She and Bret fell into silent synchronization, something they'd developed during the past two weeks at Janów. While she feared him pressing her into conversation at first, her worries eased as the quiet settled between them. He seemed to understand her need for time, silence.

She picked up Olark's hoof and winced, seeing a small sore, red and tender, on the bottom of it. It would need lancing, draining, cleaning, and wrapping. And several days of rest.

She set down the hoof and glanced toward Bret, who stroked Lubor's face at the stall adjacent to Olark's. "Do you think Karina will let Olark stay for a few days? We'll need to keep him stalled and come back for him later."

"That bad?"

"Yes. These horses aren't used to this much walking on rocks."

If they pushed Olark, his sore could turn into an infection. A bad hoof made for a lame horse, which usually led to putting the animal down. Horses' legs were too frail, supporting too much weight comparatively, for them to survive with severe hoof or leg injuries. As sturdy as they were, as fast as they could run, the animals were often startlingly frail.

Her stomach whirled at the thought, and all her other emotions crashed down upon her.

"I'm sure it's fine for him to stay here a while," Bret said quietly.

Until the Germans passed through. Would they make it this far east? Or would they just stop if—when—Warsaw fell? What would happen to Olark if they seized this farm?

The morning had already grown hot, and her neck flushed in frustration. She put aside all distracting fears and set to work tending Olark's hoof. Bret was quick to hand her supplies before she even asked for them.

An hour later, Olark ate his hay in silence, the wound drained and wrapped.

Adia checked her wrist for her watch, dreading that they still had an entire day ahead before they could progress toward Antek's farm, but her timepiece was missing. Her stomach flipped. Had she lost it in the struggle with Roman? All the memories and terror pulled at her once more.

Bret stepped closer and caught her elbow gently. "Adia. There's something I've been meaning to tell you."

Her body stiffened, terror filling her at what he might say, or do, next.

He held up her watch with the worn leather band. "I snagged this from Ewan last night."

The tension and breath that were caught in her lungs fled her body. She couldn't contain a burst of laughter, the same way Ewan couldn't seem to control his compulsion to steal.

She took the watch and tilted her head in thanks. "Well, I certainly owe you one—"

A shrill whistle, at first no louder than the buzzing of a bee, grew louder and louder, cutting off her words. Bret took her arm and covered her body with his as the whistle turned into a scream and an explosion rocked the earth below their feet.

Bret knew the percussive blast of a firearm quite well. He'd been shot at and fired his sidearm more times than he cared to count. He'd experienced mortar blasts and set off a few hidden explosives in his training years. He remembered the depth of the blast and how it seemed to turn your bones to pudding.

All of those were nothing compared to the ordnance that fell outside the barn, the rumble of the impact like an earthquake that sent bullets of rocks, wood, and heat shooting in every direction.

He held Adia tightly, pressing his palms over her ears. She struggled against him for a heartbeat as if caught in a different nightmare. His ears rang with a high-pitched scream, and it was impossible to tell if it was the artillery, the horses, Adia, or just the result of the impact.

The growling of plane engines filled the skies outside, and the stallions kicked at their stalls, eyes wide and nostrils flared.

Bret pulled Adia to her feet and looked for better shelter—a root cellar or mound of earth. The run-down barn provided little cover.

The second blast arrived too soon, closer, blowing out the end door and knocking them both over with the force. They landed against the ground, tucked between some bales of hay, as a third, fourth, and fifth bomb struck the vicinity like the banging of drums in a destructive symphony.

The explosions faded as the planes passed over and carried their mission of death to the next unsuspecting souls.

Bret paused in the relative silence, his head buzzing and his ears throbbing. Adia lifted her head and looked at him.

Her lips moved, but her words were muffled. From the way she looked him over and furrowed her eyebrows, she must be asking if he was all right.

He nodded and stumbled to his feet, helping her rise as well.

The barn, aside from the large door broken from its hinges and the splintered wooden siding, was still intact, though the stallions continued pacing their stalls in a frenzy. None of them appeared injured.

Adia raced away from his side. He didn't need to hear her to know she was worried about Ewan.

The house. Was the house even standing?

They ran down the aisle of the barn and emerged into daylight seeped with smoke and ash. The echoes of screaming and crying floated on the air in a haunting melody. The road. The bomber had struck those fleeing on the road.

Vehicles were charred, overturned, and people wailed in agony. Others emerged from the forest line—those who had abandoned their vehicles along the road.

Was this what the war had come to in just a matter of weeks? Targeting civilians rather than military encampments?

"Ewan? Tomasz?" Adia shouted, bolting toward the small farmhouse.

The windows were shattered, roof tiles blown askew, but the house somehow stood as stalwart as the barn. Lukas and Ewan emerged from the front door and, upon spotting Bret and Adia, raced toward them. Adia knelt and swung Ewan into her arms, relief painted over her face as she clung to the child.

Lukas knelt, seemed to ask if she was all right, then approached Bret. Neither he nor Ewan seemed injured, and the rest of the staff and Karina poked their heads out the door, eyeing the skies suspiciously.

"You all right, chap?" Bret asked Lukas, his ears still feeling as if they were underwater. His voice sounded strange.

"We're all in tip-top shape." Lukas looked to the barn. "We were scared for you and the horses."

"We got lucky." *This time.*

Adia turned and stood to face Bret and Lukas while Ewan

clutched her leg. "They'll be back, won't they?" Dust smudged her face, but her eyes shone with fierce determination and an inkling of doubt.

Bret nodded, his thoughts seeming to echo hers.

How long would their luck hold?

8

Planes rumbled in the distance, but as sunset drew near, the Janów trainers and grooms tended to the injured along the nearby streets and then patched up the damaged barn doors and the house's windows.

Adia slipped through the flurry of activity, retrieved the small first aid kit from her saddlebags, and sought out her unsuspecting patient. Somehow, the clear mission at hand helped still the trembling that had taken hold earlier.

Weariness weighed down each limb, but with the distant whir of engines and the punctuation of explosions, she wasn't sure sleep was an option. Except for the scrappy little pickpocket, of course. He had curled up on the sitting room couch and slept soundly.

Bret stood on the small porch with Karina and Lukas, speaking quietly. He caught her gaze as she approached, and her stomach tightened with nervous energy.

"Miss Kensington, you should be resting," Karina admonished, her short gray hair falling in waves along her forehead, framing her wide cheeks and expressive eyes.

Adia nodded to Bret's arm. "I thought I'd help you tend to that cut first."

Bret's brow furrowed in confusion, and he looked down at his arms, his hands tucked casually in his pockets. A stream of red soaked his left bicep, a four-inch gash, but as she'd suspected, he'd not yet noticed.

"Oh, yes." Karina waved a hand. "There's a water basin in the kitchen. Please help yourself."

Lukas crossed his arms and lifted his chin. "Don't fret, Conway. Adia's patched me up a time or two and I have barely a scar to my name, despite all the kicks and bites I've earned. From horses, of course."

Adia smothered a groan at Lukas's arrogance and joking nature. She led the way to the small kitchen draped in floral curtains, Bret following behind.

The oppressive heat dipped slightly as they stepped inside, moving carefully around piles of window glass still needing to be swept away. In the adjacent room, Ewan snored loudly.

Bret took a seat on a stool near the sink and craned his neck to look at the tear in his shirt. "It's nothing. Not even worth a stitch or two."

"We'll see. Take your shirt off."

He lifted an eyebrow and smirked.

She smothered her own smile. "Unless you want me to just tear the sleeve off at the seam."

He did as commanded, and she busied herself laying out the needle and catgut, salve, and gauze. She set the teakettle on the burner and lit the flame.

When she turned back, he had one arm pulled from his shirt, a plain undershirt beneath the collared one loose against his torso. Relief flooded her that he wore an undershirt, but she shook herself out of her confounded emotions. This wasn't the time or place.

Or the right man.

Roman's face also flashed before her eyes, causing her to wince. Would she ever be rid of him?

A swipe with a wet cloth on Bret's arm revealed a deep cut crusted with dirt and dried blood.

"Nothing, huh?" she muttered to herself.

He chuckled but kept quiet as she worked.

Moments of silence floated between them, both half listening to the skies, Adia distracted by the thrumming of her heart against her rib cage. She'd taken a kick or two to the chest in her time working with horses, and she marveled at how closely that pain mirrored the feeling now.

"Thank you," she said softly, the words forced out and only intensifying the ache in her chest. Her hands trembled slightly as she held the needle over the edge of his wound. "For saving me . . . before . . . and then in the barn."

The slight trace of humor in his smile disappeared, a wash of concern filling his gaze. She'd seen the look before, knew what was next. Pity.

She started stitching to quell any conversation down that path. Bret winced, but he didn't pull away from the pain.

After long moments of silence, she felt compelled to fill it.

"You're wondering why I'm even here," she said. "Everybody does."

"And why are you here?" he asked, his voice gruff and his face tipped close to hers as she hunched over his wound.

Flashes of a bay Arabian mare drifted through her mind, and vague memories of a woman who had the same dark hair, dark eyes, and small frame as Adia.

"My mother and father died when I was six."

Ewan snoring in the next room only intensified the pressure that brought her blood to boiling. Ewan's age. She'd only been Ewan's age and as frail as he seemed at times. Also an orphan.

"I hardly knew them. They left me with my aunt in the States. Mother gifted me a Janów-bred mare, Zalina, who I had nearly ten years with until a mountain lion attacked her." She swallowed a lump in her throat. "We were forced to put her down. She was all I'd ever known of my mother. My only connection to her."

More memories raced through her mind. Lazy summer afternoons sitting on Zalina's back while she grazed through fields of green. Riding her through the trails at full speed, only to have the mare dip under a low branch and knock her off. Hiding in Zalina's stall whenever Aunt Bea called her to finish her chores. Skipping school to ride through the forests of her quiet Oregon hometown.

And then the smell of antiseptic, of blood, of gunpowder. Adia's only friend and confidant in the world, lost.

"I'm so sorry, Adia."

Bret's voice pulled her to the present, and she hurried to finish the last stitch and tie off the line. She pressed the salve and bandage over it, then turned away to clean the needle and repack her kit. She spoke without facing him.

"Zalina was Lubor's aunt. And he looks just like she did. Same star on his forehead, even."

Bret touched her elbow, and she spun to face him. His shirt was back on and buttoned up.

"We're not giving up, Adia. We'll reach Antek's farm. I promise."

The red-crusted cut in his shirtsleeve haunted her. At what cost?

Bret smiled at the little thief burrowing closer to Adia and using her arm as his pillow as they both napped on the couch. Though it had taken an hour of urging and Karina's firm insistence, Adia finally relented and lay down on the couch, initially alone but joined by Ewan when he spotted her nearby.

What a pair they made.

Shaking his head, Bret strode out of the sitting room into the kitchen. The rest of the house was silent, still. Exhaustion pulled at each man, woman, child, and horse, along with the breathless trepidation of waiting for the next strike.

He fell into a chair and propped his elbows on the dining table, ignoring the dull throb of pain along his arm where Adia had stitched his wound. His thoughts whirled around all she'd shared, and the way her soft fingers had grazed his skin. He'd hardly felt the sting of the needle when her nearness overshadowed all else.

To learn of her mother's horse and all it meant to her, how could he insist she return to America empty-handed, leaving the Polish Arabians at the mercy of invaders? She'd never agree to it. And how long before his orders pulled him away?

Would he fail to protect her as he had failed his partner?

Why hadn't he been more insistent from the moment the Germans invaded that Adia be shipped back home?

Filip had put his trust in the wrong man. Bret had failed to anticipate any of this—her dedication to the horses, the speed of the German attack, or the depravity of men.

He'd been told to observe and report German and Russian positions through his network of contacts, knowing Poland was a hotbed for political maneuvering. Both the Germans and the Russians had vied for the land time and again. Bret had known traveling with the Janów horses was better cover than his life as a correspondent.

He desperately wanted to give MI6 the edge to stop a war before it began. He believed that was more important than any of his longings or desires. Lives were at stake.

What if Adia was killed because of his need to find all the answers?

What if his quest for peace, an end to this violence, truly led to the end of himself? Losing Charlie had brought every decision he'd made into question. Was the sacrifice of one worth the cost if it prevented hundreds—or thousands—more deaths?

He sank back into the chair, his mind far too restless to find sleep.

"Lord, help us," he whispered, compelled by something deep within to utter words that hadn't surfaced in many years. Hadn't he gotten on just fine without God the past decade? How could a powerful, just God stand by when Charlie had been betrayed, when Elizabeth blamed Bret for her husband's death?

He straightened in his seat and bit back waves of emotion. He didn't have time to wallow. He couldn't change the past, nor could he simply wish Adia out of harm's way. They'd carry on with the plan and he'd do everything in his power to keep her safe.

As the evening shadows shifted beyond the empty window frame, Bret managed only a few hours of sleep. His dreams were filled with horses, lions, and memories of his own childhood equestrian adventures with the animals that he'd once called friends.

Distant gunfire and explosions woke him just after sunset, the rest of the house stirring too. Jok and Leonard had returned from Wygoda, where they'd ensured the two criminals were locked behind bars. At least they were back to full strength in the number of handlers.

Adia and Karina watched Ewan eat platefuls of cooked potatoes and carrots, shaking their heads in wonder at how much food the child could consume.

Tomasz and Rafał followed Bret into the kitchen. The ground trembled, the glass cups clinking in the cupboards.

"Shall we get underway?" Tomasz asked. He looked at Adia, who glanced to Bret and nodded in confirmation.

The elder man and his son bade farewell to their hostess and slipped from the house, calling orders to the rest of the staff, then pulled horses from the barn.

Bret hid a smile of appreciation at the reverence the men held for Adia. Without Filip around, she was the clear authority, though it seemed to make her a little uneasy. She was used to working tirelessly in the background—he'd learned as much in two weeks at Janów.

Minutes later, the ragtag band of horses and staff set out at a slow pace through the trees and back onto the road, which was sliced here and there with deep gashes in the rocks and dirt.

Bret kept Samir close to Adia, with Ewan astride Captain on her other side. Dancer and his gold fur glowed in the light of the stars. They passed discarded and destroyed cars, carts, and livestock.

The air around them reeked of smoke and death.

Adia pulled close to Ewan and muttered something to him. He swiftly stood upright on ever-steady Captain's back and jumped onto her saddle. She held him close and covered his eyes as they passed a ditch strewn with burned and battered bodies. Beyond that, a pair of dead cart horses rested on their sides, still attached to the mangled and burned wagon.

Bret's stomach tightened. He wished he could shield her from all this too. Despite her tough exterior, he'd seen through to her tender soul.

It would be a long night.

"Think the other groups made it to the Bug?" she whispered to Bret, still holding Ewan close. Dançer snorted uneasily.

"Filip knows these roads and woods well. I'm sure they're well ahead of us."

"The marshes will be extra sticky this year with the heat."

He hummed his agreement. "Filip probably used the southern bridge—it's the widest for crossing."

"It will all be fine once we reach Antek's farm. They have pasture space, hay, and grain and enough shelter for winter." Her voice trailed off as if she was trying to convince herself. Kovel sat one hundred and sixty kilometers from the Russian border. Germany certainly wouldn't bomb the Russian border—it'd be far too risky to wake the Russian bear.

"It's a good plan," he assured her. It was. But she had little control over the German Luftwaffe and how far they'd go. War destroyed even the best-laid plans.

She stared straight ahead, her expression unreadable in the gray dusk.

Silence enveloped them, the rowdy stallions now subdued, their hoofbeats soft even on the rocky road. This peace was temporary, tense.

Behind them, black smoke billowed into the sky from the direction of Warsaw and the rest of Poland that was already lost.

9

September 17, 1939

The river neared like a dark green snake along the horizon, and a single wooden bridge—the only one for dozens of kilometers in either direction—stood as their sole lifeline from the bombardments behind them.

This was their only measure of hope.

Adia's hands tightened on the reins, her body going against her deepest training on how to keep her horse calm and focused. If she felt uneasy, so too would her mount. But only a few more hours remained until they reached Kovel. The goal was in sight, as sure as the sun rose and marked the end of yet another night of walking through brush and briars.

She glanced over at Bret, wondering what he'd do after tomorrow. Would he go back to Janów, or Warsaw? A war correspondent, she imagined, would run straight back into the fire.

Her stomach churned uneasily at the thought. But what other option was there? She knew this was a short-lived partnership, and she'd been counting the days until he'd be gone and her life could return to normal.

But then, there was no going back.

87

Nothing would ever be the way it was before, not even when they were finally tucked away near the Soviet border in Kovel and near the Pripet Marshes, where heavy trucks and artillery dare not tread.

Adia and Dancer, leading Lubor, were the first to reach the rotted boards of the bridge. It would easily pass two vehicles in either direction, but the edges were splintered and sun-bleached. The air over the river smelled stale and rancid in the growing heat of the day.

With all ears attuned to the sound of planes, Adia and her horses stepped onto the wood. After a few strides, she glanced behind her to Ewan and Bret. "Keep to the center, no more than two horses wide," she yelled. "It's steady enough."

"Sun's rising fast," Bret called back, angling his gaze up to the sky.

Her heart pounded, and she nodded her acknowledgment of the unsaid. Daylight meant planes. Planes targeted bridges. The fact that this one still stood was a miracle. At least once they crossed, they could hide among the trees.

"Three wide, then," she relented.

She urged Dancer ahead, pulling the hesitant Lubor forward by his lead rope. He snorted at the sight of the rushing water beyond. The horses' hooves clomped onto the wooden boards, the texture and reverberation different from the soft forest floors and gravel roadways they'd endured for a handful of days.

Water rustled beneath them, the Bug waters fast flowing but low and dark green from the dry, hot summer. The river was probably ten or twelve feet deep—far too deep to walk across. Each thump of a hoof punctuated the tense atmosphere around them, grating on Adia's raw nerves.

This had been her plan. This was her burden. They had to find a moment's peace on the other side.

She blinked, focusing back on the moment instead of the endless worries that swirled in her mind.

Minutes passed until the sound of soft dirt replaced that of the wooden bridge. She whirled Lubor and Dancer around to the side of the bridge to watch as Ewan and Captain followed, then Bret and Samir with Wojownik.

Her gaze met Bret's, a familiar jolt of energy shooting down her spine as he and his horses stepped off the bridge. He offered a wry smile. "Never a dull moment."

"Won't you be sad and bored once you return to reporting from the front lines?" she quipped.

"Indeed, nothing shall ever compare," he said, lifting an eyebrow teasingly.

She flushed and scolded herself. It was far too easy to laugh in his presence. She ought to discourage the banter, but it came so effortlessly between them.

She cleared her throat and schooled her expression as Tomasz with his horses and then Rafał crossed the bridge. "Let's aim for the tree line and veer to the north." She twisted in the saddle, watching the rest of the herd cross the bridge and fall back into line. "Only a few more kilometers to go."

"About time," Lukas said, winking at Adia as he passed. "My backside's never felt so flat—"

"Hush," Tomasz called to his son from the back of the line of horses. "And stay vigilant."

Adia kicked Dancer into a trot to move to the front of the column once more, Lubor keeping pace. She noted again how exhausted Ewan was astride his gray Arabian, and yet it was only at Kovel and Antek's that they'd find true respite. Then they could sleep for days after securing the horses, once the nearness of the Russian border offered a sliver of protection.

Around the nearing tree line, she squinted in the morning hue of orange and red to see a rickety barbed wire fence. She turned. "We'll need to stick to the road—"

The nearing rumble of planes cut her off. The horses instantly tensed. Each had been inside the barn when it was shelled. Their instincts were primed to panic.

And primed to run.

"Hold on!" she said, gripping Lubor's lead as the horses all danced and bunched together nervously.

The planes were far away and the sound didn't grow near, but the horses' energy only spiraled until the herd bumped into one another.

Two young colts—Amir, led by Rafał, and Makin, led by Jok— broke free. They tore away from the group toward the forest ahead.

Adia's heart leaped to her throat. The light was still dim, and the horses couldn't see the loose, broken fence ahead.

At the same time the planes' rumble faded into the horizon far north of them, the shrill scream of the two colts echoed from the forest. Amir and Makin had run straight into the rusted barbed wire, instantly trapped.

She didn't need to see them to know how their fearful thrashing would further deepen the cuts on their fine, delicate legs. They were doomed.

She dismounted and led her horses to Bret, who had gotten off Samir. His lips were set, jaw flexed.

She reached out with the reins. "Hold these—I might be able to get them free."

Bret held his own horse's reins with one hand and then grabbed her shoulder with his other, shaking her slightly. "Adia—no." His tone was deep and somber. "You should take Ewan to the tree line. I'll see to the colts."

She looked over, hearing their screams and imagining exactly what would need to be done. She'd seen horses tangled in wire before—the wounds wouldn't be able to heal, especially given how far they'd have to walk to Antek's farm. Tears seared her eyelids and pain clawed her chest apart.

He squeezed her arm, prompting her to hold his gaze. His deep green eyes, now visible in the light of dawn, were sorrowful but resolved. He would ensure they didn't suffer. And pushing back would only delay what needed to be done.

She nodded as a lone tear escaped. Instead of handing off her own mounts, she reached for Samir and Wojownik. Bret ran toward the wayward colts. Lukas followed to assist.

She gasped for air and then pulled all four horses forward, gripping the lines so tightly her knuckles were white. No others could be lost.

"Ewan, hurry. We must move ahead." She knew Bret wouldn't wait for her to stop the horses' pain.

"I want to go with Meester Bret," Ewan said, pointing in the direction he and Lukas had gone.

"No," she screamed. "Follow me. Now!"

Ewan's eyes widened and his lower lip quivered. Adia had never, ever screamed at him. But now wasn't the time to apologize. Instead, she ran ahead, trotting the horses in her grip, Captain following dutifully without even needing Ewan's urging.

Her sides ached from her sprint to flee as far from the fence and forest line as possible. She didn't want Ewan to hear what came next. The barbed wire fence ended a few hundred meters ahead, so Adia led the horses to the protection of tree cover. She tied them off securely and then turned to Ewan, ripping the boy from the horse to shield him behind a tree before she tied off Captain.

Tomasz and the rest of the handlers filtered in behind her. A sharp crack echoed around them, and she covered Ewan's ears with her hands.

The boy was startled but froze and tensed as she held him close.

Two shots rang out in the direction of the bridge, followed by another two shots, and then silence settled over the trees as if in reverence.

Adia closed her eyes, her heart still racing and her hands still tight over Ewan's ears. But there was no amount of protection she could offer to shield him from what this war could truly heap upon him.

God, let Kovel be our sanctuary. Let Ewan and the horses find shelter from this chaos and pain.

But God felt so, so far away as all of Poland bled. Could He even hear the crying of her heart over the agony of a million people?

Bret's shoulders hunched forward as he walked alongside Lukas to catch up with the herd, the smell of gunpowder and blood still seared into his nostrils.

They couldn't save the colts. It had taken only a moment to determine they wouldn't be able to extricate the colts from the loose barbed wire, and Lukas confirmed what they had to do.

Had Adia and Ewan been far enough from seeing it happen?

Bad luck, bad timing. Only a short distance from their destination and two lives were snuffed out by a broken fence. If they'd crossed the bridge in daylight . . . If the horses had jumped the fence instead of getting tangled and cut in the loose wires . . .

But there was no time to mourn or question. They had to move forward.

Lukas cursed and let out a long breath. "Thought we'd catch a break today."

Bret grunted his agreement.

"Was she okay?" Lukas asked quietly, his tone exploratory. "Adia?"

Bret glanced over and saw Lukas avoiding his gaze, trying to appear uninterested. The younger man truly cared for Adia—and beyond the sibling affection she clearly had for him. Perhaps more than infatuation. He was only seven years younger than her. Perhaps he could be good for her one day, if she stayed in Poland, if this war dragged on.

Bret's stomach hardened, and his fists involuntarily clenched at the thought. "She'll be okay when we reach the farm," he said, sounding more confident than he felt.

"What are your plans after we reach Kovel?" Lukas stared at the thick grass beneath their boots as they trudged onward. "I mean, you only promised Filip to deliver her and the horses to Kovel, right?"

He swallowed a lump of befuddled emotions rising in his throat. "I promised to keep her safe."

Lukas huffed a short laugh at the absurdity of that promise. "For how long?"

"Good question." What would he do? He had to connect with a local contact and establish an intelligence network within Eastern Poland to funnel the latest troop movements. Could he do that from this remote town along the Russian border? Or would he need to be near Wygoda again?

Could he ask Lukas to step into his shoes? The boy was impulsive and immature, but perhaps the combined efforts of Tomasz, Rafał, and Lukas would be enough to keep Adia from getting into trouble.

They saw the herd in the trees ahead, once the fence had ended and disappeared, and Lukas held up a hand to stop him. "Can I just ask—" He hesitated, his eyes shifting nervously. "What are your intentions toward Adia?"

Bret smiled, putting a hand on Lukas's shoulder. "Rest assured, my friend, I have no intentions."

Lukas nodded, his body relaxing slightly. "I mean, I just see the way she looks at you . . ."

His breath caught in his chest. "What?"

"She doesn't look at me that way."

"Meester Bret!" Ewan ran up to him, throwing his arms around Bret's leg. "Where did you go?"

Lukas walked ahead, their conversation over.

But Bret struggled to process his words. Adia looked at him how?

She stepped out from the trees and approached Lukas. They spoke for a few seconds, then she took his shoulders, leaned forward, and kissed his cheek. Lukas's cheeks turned pink.

A moment of jealousy flared within Bret.

"Meester Bret?" Ewan asked, staring at him critically.

Bret patted the boy's head. "Sorry, Ewan, but I didn't go far," he said, looking down at the kid. His face was smudged with dust. "We'd better get back on the road."

Adia approached and crossed her arms. "Get back to Captain, Ewan, and mount up." Her tone was terse, and the boy jumped to do as she said.

Once they were alone, she met Bret's gaze and tilted her head. "I'm sorry you had to do that," she said softly.

"Are you okay?" He stepped closer, itching to take her in his arms and hold her.

She shook her head. Her brown eyes swam with regret. "This was all my fault," she said, shaking her head.

"You're not the one dropping bombs on civilians, Adia."

"If we'd stayed at Janów—"

"We're here now," he said, cutting her off and holding her gaze. "Don't get lost in 'what if' or you'll drive yourself mad."

She closed her eyes and nodded.

Despite his advice to her, his own mind wandered. What if he stayed at the farm in Kovel? What if he learned more about these looks she gave him? What if he did set his mind to getting to know Adia Kensington better?

The what-ifs had always been his weakness, his distraction, the guilt that kept him from healing and truly learning from the past and his mistakes. But he wanted to sit with them if it meant a moment longer with her.

She stepped away. "We'd better get back."

As she walked off, he felt the absence of her as acutely as the blast from the bomb in the barn the day before.

But what it all meant, he wasn't certain.

He moved in a haze as they mounted, reorganized their column, walked steadily along the forest, and followed the road to the east. He felt Lukas's gaze on his back as they walked. Ewan also stuck close to him, uneasy since the bridge crossing and the strange behavior from all the adults.

"Where are Amir and Makin?" Ewan asked Adia quietly.

"We lost them," Adia muttered. "Eyes ahead, Ewan."

As the morning hours passed, the heat of the day pressed upon them. A road sign for Kovel, one kilometer ahead, passed and faded.

And then the smell of scorched earth, smoke, and ash filled the air. Bret trotted ahead to fall in step with Adia as they reached the edge of the town. A sense of dread wrapped around him.

Kovel, a sparse town of a dozen buildings and a distant church, was on fire without a soul in sight.

10

Adia whirled Dancer around to motion Lukas over. "Hold Lubor and Wojownik for us. Bret, we'll ride to Antek's—" Her voice caught. *If there's anything left.* "Tomasz, keep everyone here and hidden."

No one questioned her, but no one spoke either. The sense of disappointment so thick around the herd was like being mired in a mud pit.

She and Bret handed off the stallions to Lukas. The young groom gave her a somber look. "Be careful," he said firmly.

She kicked Dancer's sides, and Bret on Samir followed closely. She wouldn't promise Lukas anything.

They galloped through the town, and no matter how hard she tried to focus on the roadway, the realities of their surroundings sank in like lead.

Houses smoldered like black shells, and the air still smelled of fuel and burned wood and rubber. Flames had melted vehicles' tires to the ground and charred metal sheets. Fresh bullet holes pockmarked the brick houses and wooden fences.

Where were the civilians? Had they been able to flee in time? Where were Filip and the more than two hundred horses with him?

She turned Dancer up a small country road, which she'd visited only twice before in her entire time in Poland but had been seared into her memory as their only hope. Then she pulled the horse's reins back to skid to a stop as a lone hunched figure walked into view along the road.

Bret stopped Samir next to her, his Luger in his hand and ready, his face unreadable, his eyes focused on the potential threat ahead.

After a few moments, Adia recognized the limping figure. "That's Antek." She jumped off Dancer and ran toward the man. "Antek!" she called out.

Antek was a beast of a man, more than six feet tall, with curly, shoulder-length hair and a long beard peppered with gray. His face was dirty and smudged and his eyes red along the edges. He looked up and blinked in surprise.

"Adia? What are you doing here?" He coughed roughly and doubled over. He dropped the bag he had slung over his shoulder and leaned on his knees to catch his breath.

"Where is Filip and the rest of the herd?" Her voice shook. She glanced up and could see the smoke hovering over what she knew was Antek's farm.

Bret caught up and handed Antek his canteen of water. The man accepted it and drank. Water dripped down his beard and over his soiled clothes.

Adia's gaze locked on the splotches of blood on his shirt. "Are you injured?" She reached for his shoulder, shaking him gently to gain his attention and focus.

Antek waved a hand and straightened. "I'm fine."

Bret watched him from a step away, hand on his hip as if ready to pull his Luger again. "What happened?"

Antek shook his head. "They came through so, so fast. We didn't have any warning."

Bret and Adia fell silent and exchanged a glance.

"They burned everything, took anything of value. Filip never made it here, thankfully. He sent a rider to tell me they'd turned back yesterday. If they'd been here . . ."

Adia stepped closer, glancing at the burning farmhouse in the distance amid the sea of charred fields and fences. Her thoughts turned to his family. She'd only met them twice, but their faces were clear in her mind. "Where's your wife and boys?" Her heart rammed against her rib cage, and her gaze fell back to the dark red on his shirt.

Antek cursed and his features twisted in agony. "Dead. They're all dead." He elbowed Bret aside so he could continue walking down the road as if fleeing from the wreck behind. He growled over his shoulder, "Go back to Janów. There's nothing for you here."

Sorrow swirled in her stomach, and her mind went hazy. Dead? His entire family?

She followed him, dragging Dancer behind her. "Where are you going?"

"Anywhere but here."

"Come back to Janów with us," she said. "We'll fight the Germans together."

Antek sneered. "It wasn't the Germans."

The air fled Adia's lungs, and panic electrified every single limb.

"It was the Russians," Antek said, his gaze stony. "The Soviets are here, and they're far worse than the Nazis."

The Soviet Union? Invading Poland?

"Come again?" Bret asked, unsure he'd heard the man correctly.

"The soldiers said they came to save us from the Germans." Antek spat blood. "Protect the descendants of the Soviets here in the east."

"But why the destruction?" Adia asked.

"Some of the townspeople resisted . . ."

Adia's gaze drifted off to the east for a moment, then she looked at Bret with a new expression of resolve. "We have to get everyone back to Janów," she said. "I'm going back to the herd and will ready them to cross back over the river."

He nodded to Antek to indicate he had more to ask of him. "I'll be right behind you."

She mounted Dancer and kicked hard, the horse's hooves flying over the road.

Bret turned to Antek. "Are you going to be all right?"

Antek studied him. "You're the British bloke, right? Conway?"

Bret nodded, sensing what his next words would be.

"I'll be your new contact with the company," he said, his voice low and well out of Adia's retreating earshot. "They reached out before this mess, and I've been ordered to Wygoda to help the resistance."

The man's family had just been murdered, and he'd already received new orders from British Intelligence. But then, didn't Bret also want revenge for those he'd lost?

"Come with us. We can find another horse for you."

"No." Antek shook his head. "I have a rendezvous in Pinsk, the opposite direction of Janów."

"How will I reach you in Wygoda?"

"You're not hard to find in Janów. I'll contact you," he said, resuming his slow trudge away from the ashes of his life's work and his murdered family left behind. "And keep away from the Russians, if you can."

Bret mounted and followed Adia's path, finding the herd where they'd left them outside the skeletons of Kovel. Beyond the horizon, several explosions rang out and the ground trembled beneath their hooves. Those were close, really close. How near had they come to walking right into the troops as they trampled the people of Poland?

Knowing those were Russian bombs, Russian troops, changed everything. Whatever pact Russia had had with Poland was now voided. No border was safe. No city inside Poland would offer sanctuary.

All they could do was regroup with Filip and the rest of Janów's horses and come up with another plan. There had to be another option.

As for his mandate—it didn't change. He had to protect Adia and deliver her back to whatever shelter the white buildings of Janów could provide. It would take two or three days to make it back the seven kilometers, if they pushed the weary horses and staff to the very limit. When they set out eastward, they'd all been well rested and healthy. Now they were ragged and exhausted.

Adia stood in the lead position, holding Lubor. She looked over her shoulder at him, her jaw set and her eyes ablaze with purpose. "Ready?"

He nodded, Samir prancing beside Dancer in a nervous state.

No one spoke. All held their charges with a silent unease as the new threat dawned.

They'd all gone nearly twenty-four hours without rest or sleep, and the colts that had bolted earlier still lay along the roadway. But the group couldn't stop, couldn't slow down.

Not now that a new, more dangerous threat lay beyond.

They kept at a fast trot until they reached the river, and then the tension nearly broke everything—and everyone.

The bridge over the expanse of the Bug River was gone.

11

We have to swim the horses across," Adia repeated, staring down each of the men surrounding her.

Tomasz shook his head. "'That's suicide." He motioned to the raging river. "Most of these horses are scared of a puddle."

She pointed toward Kovel and the horizon that still echoed with explosions and gunfire. Upon seeing the bridge destroyed the night before, they'd been forced to camp in the trees and wait until daylight to venture farther. "We don't have a choice, and we don't have time. The next bridge is a day north and probably also destroyed."

"I've never swam with a horse," Rafał said, arms crossed and brow furrowed.

"Trust the horse," she said. "And hold on tight."

Tomasz turned to Bret, which he'd never done in challenging Adia's leadership in the past few days. "Bret. Please be the voice of reason here."

Bret stood on the ground and leaned against his saddle as Samir grazed the sparse grass along the bank. His expression had been guarded and his gaze thoughtful as he'd listened to their arguments for the past half hour. He hadn't weighed in with his opinion, and

Adia's stomach clenched in nervousness that he would side against her.

And yet, she valued his opinion. He'd proven knowledgeable and dependable, no matter her personal reservations about his flaws.

"I'd like to know what you think, Bret," she said.

Silence settled over the group, and even the horses seemed to pause their grazing to await Bret's verdict.

He looked toward the river and drew in a long breath. Adia braced herself for him to turn down her ideas once more. Hadn't he also been against her plan to leave Janów? And he'd been right.

Now two stud colts had paid for her folly. How many more would? How many people might suffer because of her decision? What if Ewan were hurt? Or worse?

Kovel and Antek's farm had been the only option—it had been the obvious choice to Adia when Germany had first invaded. And when Germany was the only threat. Now they could end up sandwiched between two armies that would have only one purpose for the horses and the staff. Prisoners.

"Adia's right," Bret finally said. "We don't have a choice."

Adia blinked, unsure she'd heard him clearly though she was only a few meters away from him.

Rafał cursed.

Tomasz growled at his son and then crossed his arms. "Fine. How do we do this?"

Bret nodded to Adia, directing the question back to her. This was her call.

Her chest swelled, and she was surprised by the warmth and gratitude she felt for him. But she'd have to mull more on that another day.

"I'll take the younger horses that might be more flighty in the water," she said, turning to Lukas. "You take Lubor, and Bret, you take Wojownik. He's high-strung, but he and Samir have bonded. We'll go one pair at a time, and if the current takes you downstream, meet back up here where the bridge was."

Bret and Lukas nodded, and the rest silently turned to ready their horses.

Everyone spread out, and Bret stepped up to her. "What about Ewan?" He nodded to where Ewan sat on Captain, his eyes wide and his grip tight on the saddle.

"Can he ride with you?" She drew in a deep breath. "Captain will cross without hesitation, but Ewan could get swept away."

Bret nodded. "Be careful," he said, low so no one else could hear. "The water's strong and there's probably debris from the bridge littered all over the river floor."

She appreciated that he told her quietly, not in front of the rest. "Let's go a few meters down to cross."

"I'll see you on the other side." He flashed that charming smile he always seemed to drop when she needed it the most. It soothed yet needled her in the most irritating way.

"I guess I didn't even ask if you've ever swam with a horse," she said, unable to smother a small smile of her own.

He chuckled. "Oh yes. It was one of my favorite summer activities. The local girls were always impressed."

"I might have guessed as much, you Casanova you." She smirked. "And as such an accomplished horseman."

He shrugged, but his eyes seemed to twinkle as if he was fond of her calling him by nicknames. "I had my priorities skewed in my youth, but I'm not disappointed with where I've ended up."

"Oh, really?" Her eyebrows lifted. "In another life, you could be on a beach in Morocco."

He shook his head. "I quite detest Morocco. And beaches."

She pressed her lips together to keep from agreeing with him further. She felt the same after spending a few weeks in Morocco showing horses with Filip. Beautiful culture and cities. Far too much heat and sand.

"And there's truly not one of those local girls waiting back at home for you to return and sweep her off her feet?" Adia asked as she checked the girth on Dancer one more time.

"I'm sure that's what they're hoping . . ." He winked. "The same way that I'm sure you have suitors back home who pretended not to like you in their youth but now yearn for your return."

She huffed a laugh. "No one is lining up to court the local horse trainer spinster."

He went still and leaned close. "I would."

Electricity shot through her body, setting off every manner of warning through her brain and heart.

Then he winked and muttered a weak "Only kidding, Amerykanka." But something felt forced in his disclaimer.

She mounted her horse and shook off the words. They didn't mean anything.

"Will you talk to Ewan?" She avoided his gaze. "I'm afraid he's cross with me right now."

Bret nodded once. "Of course. Don't worry about him. Just get your little spinster self and those horses across."

"I will." She moved away hesitantly, wanting both to say something more and to hide from him completely. "Be careful too."

He turned to find Ewan.

She directed her horse toward the river and gathered every ounce of gumption and resolve left within her. She collected the leads of two younger stallions and nodded to Lukas before handing off Lubor.

"Anchors aweigh," Lukas said with a smirk. "Isn't that what your American navy says?"

"Aye, aye, Captain," she quipped, tempted so strongly to glance back at Bret just once more.

Instead, she drew in a long breath and kicked Dancer forward into the waters. The horses behind her hesitated, but she held firm and clucked to them encouragingly. Soon they were up to their knees.

The cold water wrapped around them and then closed around their jowls as the center of the river dropped beneath their hooves.

"This is a bad idea," Tomasz hissed to Bret as Adia and her three horses walked into the rushing waters. Bret's stomach tightened in fear as he watched Dancer go up to his neck in the water.

He wasn't fond of the situation either. But Adia knew what she was doing. She and Dancer moved slowly through the center of the river, and the current moved them slightly to the south. In the murky water, Dancer's bright white mane and flaxen coat completely disappeared.

When they reached the other shore safely, Bret let out a rush of air and a quiet prayer of thanks. "Start crossing," he said to Tomasz, silencing the fear and growing unease. "Hold tight and kick the horse forward the whole way."

Tomasz nodded and waved toward his sons.

Bret towed Wojownik over to Captain and Ewan. "Ride with me, Ewan. We'll get across together, okay?"

Ewan shivered and refused to look at him. "No. I wait here."

"Ewan, come on," Bret said firmly. "We have to go."

Lukas, Rafał, and Tomasz all rode into the river in a line with their horses in grips. Now he just had to get himself and the boy across.

"Come on, Ewan. We have to go."

"I cannot swim," Ewan whimpered.

Bret reached out a hand. "Samir will swim for us. You just hold on to me, lad."

Ewan looked over, trembling, and then slowly reached out. Bret bunched Captain's reins with Wojownik's lead in his grip. The young stallion nipped at Captain, but the old, patient gelding just snorted and ignored the ribbing.

Bret tucked Ewan in the saddle ahead of him and wrapped his arm around the boy's small body. And then they moved into the water to join the rest of the horses.

Ewan squirmed nervously as the water rose to his toes and then up his calves. It was cold and foreboding.

"Hang on, Ewan," Bret called, holding on to the boy with every ounce of strength he had. Adrenaline coursed through him. Adia trusted him with the boy, and he couldn't let her down.

The cold water cut like a sharp knife in contrast to the warm summer air above, and Samir jerked his head up in nervousness. The footing below was unsteady, the horse struggling to place each step in what seemed like thick mud.

Captain and Wojownik pulled on the reins in Bret's grasp, as if wanting to turn back away from the river that seemed like certain death. Bret's arm twisted and his shoulder strained to hold them, the reins of Samir, and Ewan.

The other side of the river was only a dozen meters farther.

Then the ground fell out beneath them. Samir slipped and fell to the side.

Water rushed over Bret's head and muffled Ewan's cry of terror. Bret fought to stay in the saddle and keep a sense of direction and grasped for Samir's neck and mane as an anchor. He let go of Wojownik and Captain, hoping they found their way to the other side of the river.

Samir's legs flailed in the water and churned waves around them. Ewan floated away for a moment, but Bret yanked him back as the horse broke back through the surface. Samir's legs paddled frantically as Bret hauled Ewan upright. The boy sputtered and coughed, spitting out river water.

After a few more terrifying moments of Samir swimming and kicking to more shallow ground, the horse's hooves hit the earth and he wobbled to find his footing. Behind them, Captain and Wojownik swam toward the rest of their herd. Rafał and Tomasz scooped up their lead ropes as they rose out of the water.

From the western bank, Adia, astride Dancer, splashed into the river. She reached for Samir's reins to pull them free of the river's grasp.

Once they were all on shore, dripping wet and gasping for air, Adia dismounted and reached for Ewan. The boy dove into her arms and held her tightly. She looked up at Bret, scanning him as if to check for injury.

She let out a breath and hugged Ewan as he whimpered against her neck. "Thank you," she said. "Thank you for saving him."

His gaze held hers—he could see how deeply she cared for the boy. And there was something else in the way she looked at him. Or was it just because of what Lukas had said earlier? Or his foolish joke about lining up to court her that had gone too far?

So be it. Bret had spoken the truth. Of course he'd line up to vie for her time and attention—but that was in another life, another time. In this version of their worlds, the stars might never align. At least she should be aware that she had a lot to offer a good man. If it were Lukas, so be it.

Whatever fixated his mind on her in that moment after the treacherous river crossing, he wasn't quite sure. Perhaps the constant brush with death put things into perspective.

Or the lack of sleep had pushed him into delirium.

"Let's try to reach Karina's tonight," Bret called out to Tomasz and Adia.

They both nodded, and the rest of the crew finished wringing out their clothing. Horses snorted, shook off the loose water, and huffed nervously.

A rumbling echoed in the distance and the drone grew louder. Everyone turned at the same moment.

"Plane!" Lukas cried out. He kicked his mount forward, jerking Lubor's lead. "Take cover!"

Several other horses screamed and panicked at the same moment. Wojownik and Lubor both jerked free of their handlers' grasps.

Lubor bolted to the north along the banks of the river.

"No!" Adia screamed. She swooped up Ewan and lifted him back onto the saddle with Bret. "See him safely to Janów. I'll get the horses."

"Adia, wait," Bret called out as the staff all attempted in a frenzy to wrangle the dozen horses that remained.

But in a flash, she jumped on her horse and took off.

His blood raced and his heart pounded wildly. She couldn't go off alone.

He kicked Samir forward and stopped beside Tomasz. "Take Ewan and get everyone to Janów as quickly as you can. I can't leave her alone out there."

"Meester Bret! I can come too!" Ewan screeched at the top of his lungs. "Don't leave me!"

Tomasz took Ewan, dodging his flailing arms. The elder man pointed a finger at Bret. "You find our Amerykanka, and you bring her home."

Bret gathered the reins as Samir stomped his feet anxiously. "I will. I promise."

With the slightest urging forward, Samir bolted in the direction of Adia and Dancer.

Bret wouldn't lose her. He couldn't break one more promise. Not when it could mean her life.

12

Tears streaked from Adia's eyes at the breakneck speed at which she and Dancer flew along the forest paths as she tracked Lubor and Wojownik.

After hours, she drew Dancer to a stop and paused along the bank of the Bug. Her chest tightened, her heart sinking.

Cold. The trail had gone cold.

Lubor, where are you?

She twisted in the saddle, the width of the Bug before her. Her river-sodden clothes were now completely dry. She whistled a high-pitched trill, a familiar call that had always brought him running to her. She waited. Nothing. Was he out of earshot? Captured? Injured or dead?

What about the others that she'd left behind?

The sandy banks were soft, and she reined Dancer out of the marshes. Mud covered his legs and body from their pursuit. Adia's shoulders drooped forward in defeat.

Had she lost it all? There was no place for the horses in Kovel, no option but their white-bricked cage at Janów. And now the prince of Janów himself was missing.

A crack cut through the hot afternoon. A gunshot. The sudden break in the silence startled Dancer, who stepped into a deep pocket of mud and slipped. Horse and rider lurched forward, and Adia sailed over his shoulder into the swampy ground. He fell onto her leg, and though the soft ground cushioned her, the air escaped her lungs in a rush.

Dancer snorted and jerked back upright, spooked by the smell of gunpowder on the breeze.

She rolled over and reached for the reins that dangled on the ground. Mud covered her limbs and dragged her down. *Slow down, Adia, or you'll scare him more.* But her thoughts surfaced too late. The horse balked at her outstretched hand as if she were a viper.

The gelding tore free of the bog, head swinging from side to side in confusion. He trotted in a circle and looked like he'd come to a stop, but when another gunshot erupted, the nervous horse bolted.

The realization didn't sink in right away. Not until Dancer had disappeared from her line of sight.

"No. Please," she croaked. She fell back against the mud, her body crushed under the weight of despair. Her ears buzzed in the numbness that crept over her.

Move, Adia. Find Lubor and the others. You can't give up now.

More gunfire sounded, and she located the source, down the riverbank. Close.

Were the Germans at the Bug already? Or was it the Russians here on the western side?

Her heart lurched. If only Bret was here. He'd have a plan. He'd never have led Dancer into a marsh like she so foolishly had.

She hoped he was watching over Ewan, Tomasz, Lukas, Rafał, and the rest of the herd.

When a series of shouting voices drew nearer, she rose to her elbows but kept low. The banks offered tall, dry grass that sprouted from the dark mud. If she could shift a few hundred yards to the south, she could hide in a small grove of trees along the winding Bug.

She inched along on her stomach, her hands and boots sinking into the mud. If she'd been spotted, she assumed she would have already been shot. They—whoever they were—must not know of her. Yet.

From the small grove and dim shadows, she saw a group of five armed Germans leading a band of Polish soldiers. Cavalry soldiers, by the look of their soiled uniforms. Her heart broke at the vacancy in their eyes, the defeat in their slouched shoulders.

And then she recognized some of the faces.

Captain Sven and a handful of his soldiers who had passed them on the road. The men who'd relayed Filip's message.

The Germans spoke loudly among each other and poked at their victims with the barrels of their rifles.

Footsteps sloshed in the mud behind her, and she froze. Her body trembled. Where could she go? What could she use as a weapon? She had nothing.

To her right, a vast river offered no protection. To her left, an open field and road were filled with Germans and their prisoners.

The steps drew nearer. Her blood went cold. The engine of a vehicle rumbled in the distance. Her luck had run out.

She rose to her feet to bolt to the river—she might be able to outrun or outswim whoever was behind her. She wouldn't give up without a fight.

But as fast as lightning, a hand clapped over her mouth and an arm looped around her waist, wrenching her off her feet.

———

Bret pulled Adia to the ground behind the thick brush just as a truck of Nazi soldiers drove into view from the north. If he hadn't taken her down, they would have had a clear line of sight to her.

Adia elbowed him in the chest with a powerful jab. Pain shot through his rib cage as he held her down while keeping a hand firmly over her mouth so she wouldn't give them away.

Her eyes, wide and wild, scanned his face, and she blinked as if unsure he was real. Her body slackened in relief, and he took away his hand slowly from her mouth. She leaned her head against his shoulder.

"It's okay," he whispered. He tightened his hold on her. She was alive. But she was far from safe. They were trapped, with Germans all around them. He wasn't sure where Samir was now—he'd dismounted a dozen meters from the river's edge and raced toward Adia, and there hadn't been time to tie him up. Bret had seen the soldiers and knew the risk of them spotting her. He guessed Samir had returned to the group of stallions.

But she was here. In his arms. The faintest waft of her floral soap drifted atop the mud and grime of the embankment.

He released her to peer through the brush at the German patrol on the road. Adia did the same and inched closer to him, still trembling. Five Germans, a dozen Polish soldiers.

The captors paced along the road, and the officer gave a sharp nod and shouted a command.

They lined up the prisoners at the edge of the ditch.

A wave of nausea rolled through his stomach and thousands of needles pricked his skin. He took Adia's shoulders, ripping her gaze from the road. "Don't look, Adia. Don't listen."

A chorus of gunfire preceded the screams of death that echoed along the banks of the Bug.

Adia's eyes darted back to the troops as if involuntarily, then she shut her eyes. Her fingers dug into his arms as the blasts continued.

Then all of Poland fell silent. Twelve dead Polish soldiers. Five triumphant invaders, destroying all.

Bret concentrated on his breath, in and out in a measured flow. He had to keep it together or he and Adia would be next.

Adia shook violently, tears streaming from her closed eyes. Her forehead wrinkled in sorrow, her breath hissing through clenched teeth. He pulled her closer as he watched the road.

The soldiers strode back to their vehicles and, one by one, disappeared.

Several moments of silence passed before he released Adia. She was covered in thick mud, her braid matted against her back. The smudges on her chin and forehead did little to dampen her gentle beauty. Her cheeks were pale, her eyes unfocused. After she glanced around, she stood on wobbly knees.

"Easy, Adia."

She stumbled away from him, her eyes darting back to the road.

"Don't look." He took her hand. "There's nothing we could have done."

She sank to the ground and hugged her knees to her chest. He glanced around, nervous another patrol would venture down the road at any moment. This bank wasn't well shielded if a vehicle came closer.

But he wasn't sure she was ready to move. He'd lost his bearings in his chase after Adia along the river to the north. They could be two hours or two days of hard riding from Karina's farm, with no telling how many other patrols between here and there.

And now they had no horses, no supplies.

"You were right." She pressed her hands to her face. "We never should have left Janów."

He knelt beside her and pulled his small canteen from his pocket. "No one could have anticipated the Nazis moving so fast, or the Russians invading."

"You did." Her words were filled with quiet acceptance. She took the offered canteen and sipped.

"No, I never expected this." He pulled her to her feet. "Right now, we need to keep moving."

She brushed away a tear that escaped and searched his face. "Is Ewan okay?"

"He's with Tomasz and the rest of the herd, on their way back to Janów."

"Lubor and Wojownik came this way." She swallowed and glanced toward the road. "I can't leave them behind. If we lose our two best stallions? Then this was all for nothing."

His promise to Filip warred in his mind with the orders Antek had passed to him. Look after Adia, the daughter of Filip's dearest friends. Observe and report on enemy activities. Keep her safe. Provide information that might save Allied lives.

He also pictured the way Adia's hands ran over Lubor's neck and face and how animals and children alike, especially orphans, flocked to the American horse trainer. She seemed oblivious to the magic she possessed, the protector and advocate for the helpless.

Perhaps she needed the horses for something deeper.

If she could push through with such drive and devotion, perhaps he, too, could step out in blind faith. He could report back to his commander and gather intel while they searched for the stallions. Perhaps that was the only way to keep her truly safe.

He nodded, plans and strategies forming in his mind to get them through the countryside and track down the colts. "We'll find them. Together."

13

Adia woke with a start, light streaming through rotted wooden boards overhead, the smell of molding hay assaulting her nose.

This wasn't her clean, quiet cottage at Janów.

She rolled over and stiffly sat up, the events of the past forty-eight hours rushing back. The river crossing, the destroyed town of Kovel, the bombardments shredding all hope, the priceless stallions slipping from her grasp. The massacre echoing over the Bug River.

Bret saving her.

She glanced around the empty hayloft. Where was he?

She brushed hay from her clothes, braided her tangled hair, and crept slowly down the creaking ladder. This hadn't been her first time sleeping in a barn. She'd often escaped Aunt Bea's overbearing ways by running away, but with Bret at her side, this felt different.

They'd planned to venture carefully through the area and see if the horses had stumbled into a barn or hayfield. Though the animals could be anywhere, most horses had a fair sense of direction—most managed to find their way back. There was a small shot, at least, of finding the colts.

Silence surrounded the abandoned farm. The house had been a pile of rubble when they came upon it, but the barn was intact. Wygoda sat due west, and out here she felt so utterly alone, exposed.

"Bret?"

"Good morning," came his soft voice and chipper accent from behind her.

She whirled, warmth filling her gut at his confident half smile and sparkling green eyes.

"Sleep well?" he asked, his hands behind his back, a playfulness in his tone. It was something that had surprised her especially in the past day—his humor in spite of everything.

In fact, that thread of humor, as strong as iron, may have kept her from the depths of utter despair.

"What are you hiding?" She pressed her lips together, her mind racing at the possibilities.

He lifted an eyebrow at her vague question. She knew he was hiding a lot about who he was, what his true purpose for being in Poland was.

"Behind your back," she clarified.

He held up two brown eggs. "Freshly boiled."

She gasped as her stomach growled. "I thought we couldn't chance a fire."

"The fog covered the smoke. I went a few hundred meters away and kept it small."

She cupped the warm egg in her palm. "Don't you ever sleep?"

"Not lately." He sat on a bale of hay and looked out through the open doors, half the wood splintered from the blast that had destroyed the house.

Adia stepped over the broken leg of a chair—shrapnel from the house—and brushed off other wood debris from a bale next to Bret's. She sat down and focused on her breakfast, a comfortable silence settling between them as they peeled the perfect brown eggshells.

She missed Ewan. The absence of his normal chatter left a void in her soul.

"Do you think Tomasz and the boys are close to Janów yet?" Her voice trembled.

Bret didn't meet her gaze, brushing the bits of shell from his hands and swallowing the last of his egg. "If the Russians are truly allied with the Germans, the bombings will probably cease. That should make the return voyage a bit smoother."

She fell silent. Small mercies.

"Lukas will watch over Ewan," he said, as if reading her thoughts and true intent behind the question.

After she finished eating, he stood, his posture tense as if he needed to broach something, and motioned for her to draw closer. She did so.

He pulled out a silver handgun. The small breakfast churned in her stomach.

"Have you ever fired a gun before?" His voice was somber, heavy.

She drew in a nervous breath. "Just shooting cans with the neighbor boy and his .22 rifle."

"Good, you know the mechanics. This will pack a bigger punch, so hold it firmly, wrists straight. Never aim at anything you don't want to shoot. Don't put your finger on the trigger until you're ready to fire."

He stepped closer and showed her more of the components, unloading and reloading the revolver. Then he handed it over and let her test the weight of it, positioning her hands over the grip.

The metal was cold, heavy in her hands.

"We don't have enough ammunition to practice, only a handful of spare rounds." He pulled out a half dozen bullets from his pocket and gave them to her.

She closed her fingers around the ammunition, letting his words sink in.

"We need to talk about some contingencies in case we run into any patrols."

She blinked, looking up into his blank expression, the professionalism and confidence in his voice filling her with both a sense of safety and a deeper suspicion. "How do you know so much about all of this?" she whispered.

The soft buzz of flies echoed through the air as the morning sun warmed the ground around them.

"I was embedded with a unit when the Spanish war started." He glanced away, eyes troubled and saddened. "Saw more than I'd ever hoped to see."

She nodded, heart lifting at the hope that he was being honest with her for once. Perhaps this was why she'd always picked up such inconsistencies in his behavior and professed field of work. "A regular old Hemingway, huh?"

"I met Hemingway. And he's a cad." He growled. "I resent the comparison, even if he is a half-decent writer."

She perked up at the tender spot and couldn't resist teasing. "Is he as handsome as they say?"

Bret inclined his head, unable to hide the flash of humor in his gaze. "Will you please focus on the matter at hand?"

She lifted her chin and arched an eyebrow, meeting his challenge. "Only if you promise to tell me more about Hemingway one day."

"I didn't realize you carried such a flame for writers."

Her heart skipped a beat. "Well, novelists, perhaps."

"And if I had written a novel or two under a nom de plume?"

Her mind whirled as she realized he'd inched even closer. She cleared her throat. "Um, have you?"

His eyes searched her face, and her smile widened ever so slightly. Then he chuckled and stepped away, reaching down to pass her a small bundle. "No, I haven't." He pointed at the brown cloth sack. "I scrounged up a few blankets and cooking supplies from the farmhouse. Let's go northwest for a few hours to see if the horses went toward Białystok."

He picked up his bag and peeked out the barn door before stepping into the sun.

The heat of him still radiated next to her, along with the intensity of his stare. She shook her head and pushed it from her mind, jogging to catch up to him and keeping an eye on the sky.

For every one of his strides, she took one and a half, and she longed for two horses to even the field.

He spoke low, crafting a tale of them as a married couple trying to get to her family in Kraków in case they came across an unfriendly patrol.

"Why are we spending so much time on this?" she huffed, frustrated when he ordered her to repeat it all back to him for the third time.

He stepped in front of her and stopped, and she collided with his chest. "If we're separated or I'm killed, this could save your life."

Her ears began ringing. If he were killed. The thought hadn't even grazed her mind.

Now the potential blinded her to anything else.

How had she gone from disliking this man so strongly to now feeling such terror at the thought of his absence?

He took her arms and squeezed gently. "Adia. Repeat the directions again. Please."

In a daze, she did as he asked. Word for word.

———

Adia wasn't enjoying their conversation any more than Bret, as evidenced by her pale face and haunted eyes.

He suspected she might miss him if he were gone, and at least the thought comforted him. The past thirty-six hours had shown her to be hardy and resilient even in the face of more primitive accommodations than what they'd faced during the herd's evacuation.

He prayed contingency plans wouldn't ever be necessary. He would not fail her.

After half a day of walking, they reached a small farmhouse that appeared untouched by bombs or soldiers. If it was still occupied, the residents might have seen the horses.

"Why don't you wait here." He motioned for her to stay in the shade of the forest.

"You think whoever lives there would trust a man off by himself rather than a lost married couple?" She shook her head and took his elbow, looping her arm through his. Her touch sent electricity coursing through him.

In the past two days, he'd come to realize the depth of his fondness for her. He should have taken her in his arms and kissed her back in the barn when the moment felt right. Forget the consequences. What if today was all they had?

But she led him onward to the farmhouse, and he brushed a hand over his sidearm out of habit.

Adia knocked on the wooden front door. "Możesz nam pomóc?" she called, pleading for help.

The sound of loud boot steps shook the house from inside. Bret pulled her back, his hand gripping his Luger. The door flung open, and a shotgun was leveled at them both.

"Get off my farm!" a man shouted.

Adia held up her hands and put a hand over Bret's arm swiftly to keep him from drawing his weapon. "Sir, please," she replied. "We are looking for two horses that have been lost. Fine horses from Janów Podlaski. We are desperate to keep them from German or Russian soldiers. Have you seen them?"

The old farmer's hold on the gun wavered. "How do I know you mean what you say?"

"We want nothing from you, sir." Her Polish was precise and nearly free of her American accent. "Just information and a direction to keep searching."

The farmer cursed, lowered the gun, and slammed the door.

In the silence, Adia lowered her hands and looked at Bret. He reached for her arm and kept one eye on the door as they moved away slowly.

At the sound of hinges creaking, he turned. Behind them, a small woman peeked one eye through the narrow opening. "Northeast," came the aged woman's gravelly voice. "Two horses trotted through yesterday, heading northeast."

Then the door closed, and Bret and Adia looked at each other. Relief sparked in her bright gaze. Was this Lubor and Wojownik? Or two others from the Janów herd? Something in his gut told him it was those two stallions.

Northeast. Farther from Janów. Closer to the Russians.

He set an ambitious pace to reach the next town by nightfall. Adia stuck close to his heels, though it didn't escape his notice how much more effort she had to put in. Yet she didn't complain. Not once. Again he thought of the fair women with lace gloves back in London whom his mother had insisted he court—their parasols, heeled shoes, satin gowns. Not one would have lasted a day in occupied territory, let alone kept pace with Bret across the countryside.

Adia walked close enough that they brushed elbows occasionally, which was a relief after losing her too many times in the past few days.

The moon shone as their only light after they covered another five kilometers to town. They needed a place to hide for the night. They could question townspeople tomorrow and scan pastures by daylight.

They snuck past several Russian road patrols in the shadows. As they reached the brick exterior of an old warehouse, Adia tripped and fell into him with a muffled "oof."

He held her with one hand and glanced around to ensure no one had heard. He peered around the corner of the building. Two Russian soldiers strolled in the opposite direction, talking between themselves and seemingly unaware of their presence.

Adia winced and leaned against the brick wall.

"You all right?" he whispered.

Her forehead wrinkled in pain, but she nodded in contradiction. "Peachy."

Bret drew in a deep breath. He shouldn't have pushed her so

hard. Being in shape to ride horses day after day didn't mean she was primed for a cross-country venture.

"Let's see if we can find an entrance here." He peeked around the corner again and darted back at the sight of the soldiers. They'd swung around and closed in on them, mere meters away.

He took Adia by the arm and led her swiftly along the building and around the other corner, which revealed an arched, recessed doorway. They ducked inside and pressed their backs against the wall. He held a finger to her lips, and she nodded, eyes wide and chest rising and falling rapidly.

The Russian voices were still lighthearted and jovial, and after a few moments they faded into the distance. Bret slumped and pressed his head back against the cold stone.

Adia sank down, folding her legs against her chest and pressing her forehead to her knees. "Lubor, when we find you . . ." Her voice faded.

He sat down beside her, the thudding in his chest so loud he feared the soldiers would hear it and return. "No more sugar cubes for him," he agreed.

She laughed softly and lifted her head, turning to him. The moonlight shone upon her smooth skin, and the deep pools of her eyes drew him closer.

"I'm sorry I got you into this mess," she whispered.

"I'll reserve my ire for Lubor and Wojownik."

"You're just being nice."

"I'm not very nice when I'm tired, hungry, and surrounded by Russian patrols."

"Here I was hoping this was the first time you've been hungry, tired, and surrounded by Russian patrols." Her voice was airy.

"Well, it's been a while." He kept his tone light, but the words were true. This hadn't been the first time. He hoped she didn't read too much into it. She was too perceptive for her own good. All he could do was pepper the truth with as many omissions as possible.

"Are we camping here?" she asked, fear and hope mixing in her voice.

"Not the best option, but it's too dark to risk much else. Tomorrow we'll keep to our grid search in the same direction."

"Mmm," she mumbled. "I'll take first watch, then."

He wasn't sure he'd be able to fall asleep regardless. She was so close, and her presence consumed every thought. But after a few quiet moments, stillness and darkness wrapped around him and pulled him into a dreamless sleep.

14

SEPTEMBER 25, 1939

Six days of sun-scorched trekking and uneasy, sleepless nights left them without any horses or further leads.

"I think we should go back to Janów." The words hurt Adia to say. She rubbed her aching neck as Bret paused from packing their meager supplies: blankets, a dented canteen, and a small sack of dried goods that did little to ease the nausea in her stomach.

"Are you sure?" he asked.

She nodded and turned away when a tear clawed at the corner of her eye.

Failure. What an utter failure she was.

She'd lost Lubor and Wojownik, the finest horses in all of Poland. If she hadn't come up with the plan to evacuate in the first place, they might still be safe at Janów.

Bret set the cloth bag down and took her hand in his. He tilted her chin toward him, and the tender gesture threatened to unleash the tears buried deep inside her.

"Adia."

She ripped away, wishing she could take solace in his warm embrace but knowing it would only make matters more complicated.

"We're not doing any good out here, and we're bound to run out of luck soon."

They'd dodged a dozen patrols, and though the skies were void of bombers, the constant stream of fighters and reconnaissance planes left them both on edge.

"Who knows," she said with a forced smile. "Perhaps those unruly colts found their way back to Janów already."

She missed Ewan. And Tomasz, Lukas, Rafał, and Filip.

"All right." Bret gathered the rest of their items and slung the bag over his shoulder. He turned the direction opposite of the previous day.

Her fingers tingled as if sensing the loss and defeat of her decision. She wished so desperately for Lubor and Wojownik to be close and safe. Yet they could be long dead, never to grace the history books of Polish breeding. It was time she faced reality.

They wove through the dense forest that had become so familiar in the days since they'd fled Janów with the false hope of sanctuary beyond.

They had a careful rhythm, and Bret seemed to smell enemy patrols. As they came into a clearing, Bret hesitated just as a German command rang out. "Halt!"

The sharp click of a rifle chambering a round sent chills down her spine.

Their luck had run out.

Bret stiffened beside her, and she glanced down to see his fingers twitching as if he wanted to reach for his gun but restrained himself. He carefully lifted his hands and turned slowly. She did the same to find two soldiers with rifles leveled at them.

"Papiere," one of the men demanded, putting his hand out for their identification.

They didn't have documentation showing Polish citizenship— only British and American passports. They would be detained as suspected spies.

Bret cast her a side glance, and the message was clear. This was what he'd told her again and again. Option one was to negotiate or bribe. But these soldiers were on edge, ready to strike. Bret clearly wanted her to follow their plan for option two, which would only work when there were two or three soldiers at play.

She would distract—he would fight.

She drew in a deep breath and braced herself. Gasping and swaying dramatically, she collapsed to the ground and pretended to pass out.

Her sudden motion distracted the soldiers, and Bret seized the moment. He punched one soldier solidly in the jaw, and the man fell to the ground beside Adia. She scurried back as Bret pulled the rifle from the second man's hands and struck him with the stock across his temple. As the soldier collapsed, Bret reached down and took her hand, pulling her to her feet.

He took her around the waist and propelled her forward. "Run," he said roughly.

They darted through the trees and came upon a small clearing with a dozen run-down buildings. They'd passed through it only twelve hours earlier and it had been empty.

She skidded to a stop, Bret colliding into her. Terror froze every limb.

A dozen gray-suited Nazis stood in a row, all of them armed and sneering as if they'd caught a pair of mice in a trap.

Within seconds their hands were upon Bret and Adia, wrenching them apart, pulling the rifle from Bret's grasp.

"Adia!" Bret roared, struggling against his captors. "Run!"

Her mind clicked to this scenario that they'd discussed. The one she'd never agreed with.

As two men dragged her back, laughing among themselves and brushing the side of her face with the handles of their pistols, she kept her gaze locked onto Bret's.

He clenched his jaw and jerked his chin in the direction of Janów. She knew the way. She knew the directions by heart.

She read his expression so clearly: *I'll create a distraction so you can escape.*

Her heart raced and her head spun. The men around her studied her and snickered. Her mind flashed back to the two men who had accosted her that first night out on the road and how close they'd come to getting away with whatever they'd intended for her. Bret had saved her then. But now? He was so close yet so far away.

Bret again tried to get his arms free, knocking one soldier down and earning a punch to the nose from another one. Blood poured down his face, but he blinked through the impact and again motioned his orders, his plea.

Go, Adia.

She winced as one of her captors patted her down roughly. The men pulled her pistol from her belt and tittered at the weapon like mocking schoolchildren. The fire in Bret's face raged.

She slowly, deliberately held his gaze and shook her head. She would not abandon Bret, the one who had risked everything to save her time and time again. She could not simply leave him behind to die alone.

Somehow, her view of him and their working partnership had shifted.

They were in this together.

To the end.

Rage consumed Bret, blurring his gaze and making it hard to think. Or breathe.

He had to get to her. He had to break free.

But they were outnumbered. Outgunned. Out of luck. Out of time.

His nose throbbed, not fully broken but bleeding steadily. The soldier he'd knocked down, a man half his weight and a head shorter, brushed himself off and pulled his Luger, shouting angrily at Bret and jabbing his side threateningly.

But he couldn't process the words—not when Adia held his gaze and shook her head, drawing her position in the sand.

Foolish woman. Why wouldn't she try to escape?

After her message had been conveyed, she seemed to snap from her stupor and looked to one of the men who appraised her. She lifted her knee swiftly between his legs, sending him crumpling to the ground and writhing in agony. The other man laughed heartily and dodged her kick easily.

The small soldier grabbed Bret's hair and jerked his head around, forcing him to look the angry man in the face. Spit flew from his lips as he shouted and cursed Bret.

Then a volley of gunfire echoed through the forest, and all the soldiers jumped, looking around in confusion.

Bret elbowed the man holding his arms behind his back and then slammed a shoulder into the short fellow. Free of their hold, he raced toward Adia, all the soldiers ducking and spinning to identify where the assault was coming from.

Bret only cared about getting to Adia, no matter who was behind the gunshots.

He dove into the man who held her, knocked him to the ground, and wrestled his pistol from his hand, then fired a bullet into his shoulder. The man screamed and rolled in pain.

Bret stood and took Adia's hand, pulling her to the shelter between the abandoned brick buildings.

The soldiers had ducked behind their vehicles and fired on the buildings, where a hidden enemy fired back. Bret prayed the enemy of the Germans would be their friends as he and Adia slid into an open doorway.

"Hold!" a voice commanded in Polish.

Bret and Adia held their hands up. As Bret's eyes adjusted to the dimmer light, he recognized several Polish residents from Wygoda.

"Don't shoot! They are friends!" a voice said firmly. A tall blond man appeared, ducking from the open windows where gunfire peppered the walls.

"Lukas!" Adia rushed from Bret's side and hugged him.

Lukas smiled and then pulled her from the line of fire, and they ducked down against the solid wall. He nodded at Bret. "We'd just about given you up for dead."

"We almost were." Bret raised his eyebrows. "How did you find us?"

"Well, we were looking for Germans, mostly." Lukas blushed and looked down at Adia. "Though I'm glad we could help."

A bullet ricocheted off the stone wall, close to Adia's shoulder. She jumped, and Lukas lifted his rifle to his shoulder.

"Let's catch up later." He winked at Adia. He tucked under a windowsill and aimed his rifle, squeezing the trigger to return fire.

Bret knelt beside Adia, checking the magazine of the Luger he'd taken from the soldier to see there was a full load, minus the bullet left in the shoulder of her attacker. After he slotted the magazine back into place and pulled the slide back to chamber a round, he looked her over.

Blood seeped into her sleeve along her arm where the bullet had struck close.

She followed his gaze and looked down. "Just shrapnel. I'm fine."

The shattering of rock walls from gunfire intensified. Bret pulled her away from the wall, crawled over to a table, and tipped it over to provide an additional barrier from shrapnel.

"Machine gun!" one of the rebels cried out. Several screams of pain sounded as the crumbling brick wall gave way to the more powerful weapon and the bigger bullets.

"Stay here!" Bret yelled over the din of the battle. He pulled a small derringer from his ankle, checked the ammunition, and handed it to her. How he wished he had something more. Perhaps he could get to Lukas and see if he had anything else. The other weapons had been seized by the Germans outside.

"Grenade!" someone cried.

The warning registered in his head just long enough for him to duck behind the table and pull Adia close to cover her body with his. He covered her ears with his palms.

The blast ripped through the building and sent rocks clattering over every surface and jabbing Bret's back and neck.

His ears echoed with a high-pitched ringing and dust stung his eyes. Adia coughed and wiggled underneath him, calling his name, though it sounded as if she were a mile away.

He slowly moved each limb and turned his neck gingerly. Nothing felt broken or injured, though the ringing drove him to distraction.

Finally, silence fell over the building and surrounding area.

"It's over. They overtook the Germans." Adia shook his shoulders until he met her gaze. Her face was covered in soot and dust and her hair was frayed in all directions, but the wildness made her all the more attractive.

Get it together, Conway.

He forced the noise to the back of his mind, and his training emerged. He surveyed the building facade, able to see the expanse of soldiers and the damage the civilian fighters had managed to do. Bodies of Germans were strewn across the grass and behind the vehicles.

The gunfire had ceased, though the shouts from the partisans continued as they checked in on each other.

Adia rose to her feet, looking around at the fallout. Bret stood and glanced to where Lukas had been firing back at the barrage.

His heart plummeted. A pile of rubble sat where the horse trainer had been.

Adia recognized it at the same moment and jumped toward the pile. Bret hurried after her. He caught her and pulled her back as Lukas's body came into view, his legs and torso covered in rocks, his face and chest at rest—a bullet hole clean through his forehead.

15

Adia screamed. The sight of her friend against the cold, unforgiving ground pulled her heart from her chest and pummeled it with the power of a thousand bombs.

This couldn't be.

She collapsed to her knees at his side, her mind numb and oblivious to any lingering threat beyond this cursed building.

Not Lukas.

He was an arm's length away, motionless, his skin lightly tanned, his eyes closed peacefully.

"Adia. He's gone." Bret took her hand, his touch breaking her trance.

Her gaze shot to his. His sorrow and pain mirrored hers, etched with the same disbelief.

"What is he even doing here?" Her breath came fast, uneven, and her head swam. "Why isn't he at Janów?"

"I don't know." He pulled her closer, but she pushed away. She couldn't accept that any of this was real.

"No," she said, shaking her head and suddenly desperate for fresh air. She stumbled out of the brick coffin and into the blinding daylight. Bret followed close behind.

German soldiers were fallen across the grass, some rolling in pain and gasping for help. The rebels strode up to each one, mocking and prodding them with the muzzles of their guns.

Adia turned away, her stomach churning. No one was innocent in this war.

Bret chided them, instructing them to treat the wounded and take them as prisoners.

"What are you two doing here?" Antek stormed over to them, his features furrowed in anger and concern.

Adia blinked. "What are you doing here?"

Bret went quiet, as if not surprised by Antek's presence. But Adia's mind and emotions were too wild to make sense of anything.

Antek glared at Bret, ignoring Adia's question. "Get out of here. It's too dangerous. There are more enemies close by."

Bret took her arm. "We'll leave. How are the roads to Janów?"

Antek snorted. "Stick to the forests."

Panic seized Adia. "Wait." She bolted back into the building, emotion choking her as she knelt beside Lukas.

She reached a trembling hand to his neck and unclasped a locket she'd rescued a dozen times from Ewan's stash. She pulled it free and stood, staring at the small brass oval etched with ornate flowers. Inside she knew it held a photo of Lukas and Rafał's mother. The woman who'd welcomed her in, helped her learn Polish, and tried again and again to get her to marry one of her sons.

She clutched the necklace to her chest, and tears streamed freely down her cheeks.

Careful, slow footsteps sounded behind her and then paused.

"I'm sorry, Adia. We must go." Bret's voice was filled with regret. "Antek promised they'd bring his body to Janów."

For Tomasz. For Rafał.

At least he could be buried beside his mother.

She sniffed and lifted her head, kneeling to tuck the locket into her boot lining. She pressed it against her calf, wishing she could do more. That she could have done more.

Her breath exhaled in shaky waves. Had it only been a few hours earlier that life was simpler, that Lukas was alive and his jokester self? Now it was all gone. Her focus had been entirely on Lubor and the missing stallions. Now another presence was forever missing from the world.

"Adia."

She stood, swiped at her face, and turned to walk past Bret into the daylight, where the stench of death hovered like a vile fog.

Memories assaulted her of Lukas and Rafał bantering in the hallways of Janów, of Tomasz's constant admonitions and their mother's gentle smile that always followed. When Adia had first come to Janów, it was their family that had drawn her in, taught her Polish with patience and constant laughter.

A lifetime of hardly knowing family, and she'd now lost so many of them. Elena to illness. Lukas to the Germans.

Who else might be stripped away from her world with so little warning?

As they resumed their path toward Janów, she paused next to Antek, who spoke quietly with a partisan who was wrapping his injured hand.

She glared at the older man. "Why didn't you send him back to Janów?"

Bret took her by the shoulders. "Now's not the time."

She shook him off, still focused on Antek. "He was too young to be out here. His home is at Janów."

"We tried to get him to go home," Antek said, his gruffness tinged with a rare tenderness. "We're all fighting for our homes. Mine was flattened by bombs. And there are boys even younger dying every day—most without the chance to defend themselves or their families. Now get out of here or you'll follow Lukas to the grave."

Ewan's face flashed before her eyes. This was his home too. He was entirely helpless and a victim as much as Lukas, Rafał, and Tomasz. She had to protect him now.

Bret gently pulled her down the path toward the road as they moved west toward Janów, positioned deep enough into the forest brush to avoid detection from any patrols.

When they were far enough away from the bodies and dwindling Polish resistance fighters, her mind broke from the endless swirling thoughts and she twisted free of Bret's hold. Nausea roiled in her stomach, her skin crawling and her head pounding.

How could she go back to Janów Podlaski?

Lubor and Wojownik were missing.

Lukas, one of their best trainers and a lifelong employee of the farm, was dead. Tomasz's son. Rafał's twin.

This was her fault. It had been her plan from the beginning to move the horses to the east. If they'd stayed within the white walls as Filip and Bret had urged, Lukas would never have joined Antek's band of fighters. Ewan would be by her side. Lubor would be in his palace, where he belonged.

She turned to face the direction of Janów. Her hope for a future that she'd dreamed of all her life.

She walked at a steady pace to keep from Bret's reach. She couldn't bear his pity. Not when she'd created such a mess of everything.

She'd put those around her in danger, and the world's best Arabian stock was now scattered in enemy territory.

Tears blurred her vision again, and she snagged her foot on a tree root, stumbling and nearly falling to the ground. Bret caught her and held her close.

This time, she didn't pull away. She buried her face in his chest, breathing in the smell of smoke and earth and strength. Her mind, body, and soul were numb. He tightened his embrace.

Despite every thought pushing back against the warmth and comfort she felt from his hold, she clung to him like a desert nomad to a watery oasis. Her knees wobbled and yet adrenaline still surged through her veins.

Flashes of Lukas's body and vacant face played over and over in her mind.

She dug her fingers into Bret's shirt, willing the images, the reality, the pain to disappear. But the ache folded in on itself, deepening and burrowing into the void of her heart.

———

Bret pressed his lips lightly to the top of Adia's head as she fought against the demons raging inside her. He knew those demons all too well.

The guilt of survival.

The disbelief of the loss.

The sliver of hope that it was all just a bad dream.

He had no idea how to defeat those particular demons.

He glanced over his shoulder to ensure they were well out of sight and that no movement rustled in the bushes. Clear, for now.

He had let them fall into that patrol. If they hadn't been there, if Lukas hadn't been distracted by Adia, perhaps . . .

No.

The endless what-if loop was just another game of those demons. A game in which no one survived with their sanity.

He could feel the anger and regret pouring from her as she clutched him. Rushing the process wouldn't help. But he worried about remaining stationary for too long.

He drew in a small breath to speak, and it somehow broke her trance. She jerked back, wiped her nose and cheeks with the backs of her hands. Clearing her throat, she straightened.

"I'm sorry. I shouldn't have—" She paused and drew in a deep breath. Her cheeks flushed. "We should get moving."

Her absence left him cold and yearning to take her back. But he needed to get back to reality.

He'd been reckless. The growing depth of his emotion for her left him distracted. And when she'd been in the hands of those German soldiers . . .

He shook his head. Forget his own distraction and mistakes. She'd disobeyed his command to run. What was the real reason? He dared not ask.

He dared not hope.

You'd do her more harm than good, Conway.

Keep her safe. Help her as much as he could. Anything more, anything deeper, was a liability. Hadn't the past few hours proven that?

He thought of the dozens of bodies in the abandoned town behind them. German or Polish, any death was a tragedy.

Wasn't this why he had been drawn to espionage?

He had been naive to think he'd be responsible for fewer deaths than any man on the front lines. The General, his father, had expected him to move up the ranks like the three generations had before him. But what if counterintelligence could save thousands—millions—of lives? What if the right question, the right document, held the key to peace or a path toward peace?

What a fool he'd been. And now? He was stuck in a corner of Europe on the verge of Nazi domination after a fruitless summer attempting to find any scrap of information.

His hands were empty, and now stained crimson.

He studied Adia's lithe figure as she walked ahead in the direction of Janów, which was only a half day's walk away. Back straight, shoulders square. Ever the trained and disciplined equestrienne, though she clenched and unclenched her hands at her sides, betraying her true feelings.

After they reached Janów, he'd need to meet again with his contacts, learn his new orders. Would he be required to leave Poland? Perhaps it was the best thing for them both, having hundreds of kilometers between himself and the American horse trainer.

Yet he was terrified at the thought, and at the swift reminder that he had no choice in the matter.

As they strode silently through the forest, the distance between his heart and mind widened.

They didn't speak until the rise of the white clock tower appeared in the hillside, a speck between green trees.

"Thank God," Adia breathed. She paused and closed her eyes,

the wind lifting the long wisps of hair that had escaped her braid days ago.

But was Janów any safer than anywhere they'd wandered in the past days? Bret smothered his doubts, Adia's soft words bringing to mind memories of his grandmother's devoted and loving stories of how they'd endured the Great War. *"We cannot fathom the depths of His love, nor the complexity of the path He's laid for us. And so we must persevere."*

Perhaps they had no other choice but to call upon God when the devil was on their heels.

PART TWO

THE ASHES

16

Oh, my beloved Janów.

    At the long driveway and the sight of the clock tower, Adia's exhaustion fled, the pain in her legs and back disappeared, and her heart raced. Her strides gained speed as she spotted a handful of horses in the front pasture. Liza, Eagle, Serena, Zuza and her foal, and Crystal. Where were the rest?

Filip was due to have returned with the main group of horses. Was Tomasz here? Ewan? Dare she hope—Lubor?

Her heart lurched as she thought of encountering Tomasz, the necklace in her possession and what it implied, but she pushed the thought aside. The white gravel flew beneath her boots, and she skidded to a stop at the base of the clock tower and looked down the long row of stalls.

Oh, God, no. Her body went rigid, cold.

The stalls were empty.

She gasped for air and ran to the foaling barn. The smell of fresh straw and the rustle of hay instantly set her stomach at ease. Still, there were only half a dozen stalls filled out of the twenty-four.

She wove through to the back pastures. Her gaze flicked across the scattered herd. Ten, twenty. Forty or so.

Her throat went dry.

She spun around. Another two fields and about the same in each,

141

when there were typically twice that. A little more than one hundred horses on the grounds? Out of two hundred and fifty? Their heads hung low, and their tails swished idly.

The stallions.

She pivoted, blazed past Bret, and turned into the stallion barn. She ran to Lubor's stall and clung to the railing with white knuckles. Tears stung her eyes, burning like fire.

Empty.

And Wojownik's. And those of the other stallions they'd lost along the way.

A few nickers echoed and she moved a few stalls down, but none sounded like the familiar voice of her prince.

"Odwaga," she whispered, brushing the soft muzzle of a speckled gray stallion. Lubor's sire. One of Janów's legends. At least he was here, safe. So Tomasz had made it back, surely.

"Adia?" a familiar deep voice rasped.

She turned. "Filip! Where is Ewan? Tomasz? The stallions?" She ran to her mentor, and they embraced, the weariness of the road still surrounding her.

"You are back," Filip said with a sigh. "And Bret?"

"I'm here." Bret strode down the hallway and nodded to the director in greeting. His shoulders were hunched, and the lines had deepened in his brow. He had covered his own exhaustion so well until this moment. He looked over at Odwaga. "So, Tomasz and the rest, they've returned?"

Filip hesitated. "Where have you been?"

Bret met Adia's glance. Where hadn't they been?

It all felt like too much to explain. She put her hands in her pockets, itching to reach for the locket secured away in her boot.

"Where's Tomasz?" she asked, her voice cracking. Why hadn't Filip directly answered her question?

Filip drew in a long breath. "I don't know. He and his sons, they went looking for you both. And for Ewan."

Her pulse came to a stop and her ears buzzed. She looked around.

The silence that had settled over the aisles wasn't just because of the vacant stalls.

Ewan.

Bret stepped closer, his arm brushing hers lightly, as if he sensed her rising panic. "Ewan wasn't with Tomasz?" he asked.

Filip lowered his head somberly. "On the trek back, we all lost so many horses in our group. Tomasz said his group did as well. He said Ewan ran off after you both."

The air around them went heavy. Her stomach churned. If she'd had any food in the past day, she would have lost it.

"Where was Ewan last seen?" she asked, already mentally preparing what she'd need to gather to join the search.

Bret picked up the pack he'd just set on the ground, and Filip held up his hands. "He took off after you both after crossing the Bug," Filip said.

After they'd left Ewan behind.

Adia met Bret's gaze. "I'm coming with you."

He nodded. There was no question or room for argument.

"Now, wait just a moment. Eat a meal first and get a good night's sleep." Filip shot Bret a glare. "You know better than this, Conway. And you promised me—"

"Circumstances have changed." Bret's gaze turned steely.

She frowned. There was something coded in their exchange, something she wasn't privy to. What did Filip mean? Why was Bret so sensitive about whatever he'd implied? What had Bret promised? Even in the past week of facing death and all manner of stress, Bret hadn't ever looked so cross.

Bret jerked his chin to her. "Come on. Let's get a few supplies on our way out."

She followed without a word, the steps beside him now feeling familiar, yet the pull of Janów grabbed her heart and squeezed.

As much as she wanted to stay, it simply wasn't home without Ewan.

"Bret, Adia, please." Filip stomped after them. "Please, wait."

As they rounded the corner to the entrance to the barn, they all froze midstep.

Adia's sweat went cold on her brow, and her body trembled at the sight of six monstrous tanks rumbling down the white gravel driveway of the stables, along with nearly a hundred soldiers.

It was too late.

———

Bret caught Adia's arm and pulled her back from the entrance at the sight of distinctive green military uniforms and the flag that adorned the sides of the tanks. This changed every priority within the span of a heartbeat.

Now he had to hide her, somehow.

He pushed her through an open doorway into one of the tack rooms brimming with saddles, bridles, and halters. He closed the door behind her and glanced around the tack room, then swept up an old cap and coat hanging on the wall.

"Listen to me, Adia," he said as he put the hat on her head and shoved her long braid inside it. "You must stay hidden. Be invisible. There may still be a chance we can get back out to look for Ewan, but we'll have to tread lightly."

She stared up at him, eyes wide in terror and disbelief. "They— they're here. They're really here." Her voice had a soft lilt to it, as if she were in a daydream and questioning all reality.

He took her face in his hands, cupping her jaw and shaking it slightly to bring back clarity and focus to those beautiful brown eyes. "Adia, you hear me?"

She nodded and pressed her hands over his, her touch electric. "How are they here already?"

"Stay calm, Adia." But in truth, his own heart raced, his mind whirled.

He'd expected to see the shiny boots and crisp uniforms on the doorstep any day. But this? These uniforms weren't the ones he'd expected. These were green, not gray.

144

The Soviets—not the Germans—had seized Janów Podlaski.

He tore himself away from her side, appraising her slender form in the impromptu disguise. Even with her hair hidden, she moved too gracefully, her face was too fair, her eyes too dark and innocent, her jaw too slender.

He cursed himself for not thinking of this. The Germans might treat an American fairly, but the Russians? He knew from his study of history that the Russians were unpredictable.

"We'll still go looking for Ewan?" she asked, voice unsteady.

Bret walked over to a small window and looked through the hazy glass, unable to answer her. Dozens of soldiers milled about in the courtyard and in the barns. Several already had horses in hand, eyeing them with interest.

He swallowed the lump in his throat. This wouldn't be easy on Filip or Adia. Hopefully a few horses were all the Russians would take with them.

The handle rattled on the door. Bret bolted to Adia's side and whispered in her ear, "Keep your eyes down, shoulders hunched forward. We'll get through this."

"I trust you." Her voice was thick with emotion.

Warmth filled him and a tick of confidence returned as two soldiers burst through the doors.

"Hands up!" they shouted in Russian, pointing at them with Mosin-Nagant rifles.

Bret held up his hands and Adia followed suit. The soldiers stepped toward them and pushed them to their knees. One man kept his rifle on Bret and Adia while the other rushed through and gathered up armfuls of equipment as if in a frenzy.

Adia sat silently, keeping her gaze down to the floor, while Bret watched her out of the corner of his eye and sized up the enemy forces. They didn't give their captives any attention, focused on the spoils instead. They picked up bits and bridles, turned them over in their hands, tossed them aside.

Good. Let their greed distract them.

"Wager you a week's pay we're home in a month," one soldier said. Bret's Russian was a bit rusty, but he was able to catch most of the words.

The other soldier scoffed. His face was youthful—no trace that a razor had ever grazed his chin. "I'd prefer we bet a week's rations, what little it is."

"Let's move to the next town. There's nothing here but horses."

"At least we'll have meat tonight," the younger man said and stomped out, slinging his rifle over his shoulder.

The man who'd towered over Bret and Adia lowered his gun and stepped toward the door before hesitating. Bret's pulse tripped.

The soldier's eyes locked onto the huddled groom in disguise.

Though every instinct in Bret cried out to take out the threat, he would only bring an entire army down upon himself if he acted rashly.

Adia shifted ever so slightly but kept her head down.

Under the scrutiny, each second passed as if it was hours. The footsteps of the other soldier had faded.

Bret could take one easily, but it could expose Adia further. It could bring about harm to the whole staff at Janów.

The soldier stepped forward, reaching as if to remove Adia's cap.

Bret cleared his throat. "Can I help you?" he asked in Polish, not wanting him to know he understood them.

The soldier's gaze turned to ice. He instantly swung his rifle and swiped the side of the wooden stock across Bret's temple. Pain shot through his face and down to his toes, and he fell backward. Nausea swirled in his stomach, and he gritted his teeth to beat back the dizziness and darkness.

"Don't speak to me, Polish filth!" The sharp Russian voice pierced his throbbing skull.

Bret staggered and Adia's hands gripped his arms. The soldier spat on him and leaned over Adia again.

Stay awake, Conway.

Despite channeling every inch of his willpower to fight off the rising unconsciousness, everything around him slipped from his grasp.

The last image he saw before blacking out was the soldier lifting Adia's hat, her only manner of protection. Not again. He'd failed her just as he'd failed Charlie.

17

Adia fought the urge to cower. The soldier's hand lingered closer to the brim of the hat that covered her face.

Her mouth dried. Her heart hammered against her rib cage. Her throat tightened. She'd be worse than dead if he found out she was a woman.

"Vlad!" a loud voice echoed from outside the tack room.

Vlad's hand disappeared and his boots clattered from the room, taking with them the energy, fear, and anxiety swirling about her mind.

Bret caught himself as if fighting to maintain consciousness. Blood streamed from the cut along his temple, which now swelled as a testament to the severity of the blow.

"Stay with me, Bret," she whispered, lowering him to the floor to avoid his falling entirely. Her heart thudded and her breath caught. She was still consumed by the fear she had tasted so clearly on her tongue. The Russians could return at any minute.

Outside the room, clattering, shouting, and scraping sounds resonated, each sending a new jolt of fear through her. What was happening? The moments dragged on, but she couldn't leave Bret behind.

Slowly, the ruckus in the barns faded to a distant rumble. Where had the enemy gone?

She pulled her handkerchief from her pocket and pressed it to the cut on his brow. "Bret," she whispered. *Please wake up.*

He grunted and his eyes fluttered open. The knots in her stomach loosened so quickly, it left her woozy and nauseous. He pushed himself to a seated position, glancing around the tack room.

"I think they're in the southern barns now," she said.

His forehead and eye were already deep red and purple. She winced and cupped the side of his face. His gaze snapped to hers.

"I'm so sorry," she rasped, her voice as shaky as her hands. She continued to hold him as he blinked and seemed to struggle to focus. "Why did you do that? They could have killed you for standing up to them like that."

"Are you all right?" He looked her over. "What happened?"

"I'm fine. The soldier was called away right after he hit you."

"He didn't see your face?" Bret's voice was urgent. The tone did strange things to her heart.

"No."

"You're sure?"

A laugh escaped. "Yes. I'm sure."

But her laugh only covered the taut nerves under the surface. So close. Too close. If Bret hadn't spoken up and distracted that soldier . . . She could still feel the fresh-faced Russian drawing closer and the pressing doom of being discovered.

"Goodness, they were so young," she breathed. Not even eighteen.

"And strong." Bret pressed several fingers to his cut and winced. "They said they'll be moving on soon. We won't have to hide you for too long."

"You speak Russian?"

He chuckled, then grimaced. "Enough of it."

She shook her head and absently rubbed his cheek with her thumb in a slow, tender motion. Then she caught herself—and the danger in their closeness—and started to pull away her hand.

He caught her wrist gently. "Hmm," he said in protest. "It was just starting to feel better."

149

Her face and neck grew hot. He certainly didn't mean to say such things or imply she stay so close. He was simply rattled. That was all. Discombobulated, was all.

The smile faded from Bret's lips, and he grew serious as if contesting her theory. His gaze was clearer, his faculties seemingly in place. And there was a tension stretching between them of something unsaid. As if they weren't crumpled on the tack room floor, surrounded by discarded bits, bridles, and halters.

Say something, Adia. Or back away.

She didn't like the glint in his eye or the weight behind it.

She wrenched her hand free and rose to her feet, letting him regain his footing and stand slowly from where they'd fallen to the floor.

She cleared her throat. "We need to find Ewan. As soon as you've recovered."

Bret nodded and rubbed his neck. "The Russians are most likely patrolling every town and road, more than what we saw before."

She swallowed. "But we'll still go?"

Even with the growing danger, she ached to find Ewan. She feared he was all alone out there.

"Yes, of course," he said with a trace of a smile, followed by a wince of pain.

She took his hand and led him back to the rows of small, one-room cabins that housed the Janów staff. The grounds were quiet and seemingly soldier free. His domicile was at the far end, as far from hers as possible. When he'd first come to the farm, it was the only available room, but now all but a handful of cabins in between were abandoned.

He opened the door slowly and studied the small room before stepping in, unbalanced. She followed, bolted the door, and closed the curtains. Then she strode to the sink and dampened a cloth with cool water.

"Sit down," she commanded softly.

"I'm fine," he growled, but obeyed.

The room layout mirrored her own—bed in one corner, desk and chair in another, a small kitchen area, a walled-off privy and bath. He sank to the small desk chair and leaned on the tiny, empty table. The room hardly looked lived-in at all though he'd stayed there for two weeks before evacuating the horses.

She flipped on the small light switch, and a bulb flickered overhead. The dim lighting revealed the cut along Bret's hairline. It didn't need stitches, but the bruising was quite significant.

Avoiding his studious gaze, she bent forward to dab the cloth along his forehead. He remained motionless, and she dared not even breathe.

The chaos of the past few days pressed in on her, so heavily it could snap her bones. Lubor. Lukas. Ewan.

"The soldiers will move on soon," Bret said softly, as if reading her concerns.

"And if they don't?"

Bret took her hand, and she reluctantly met those deep emeralds. "We'll take it one day at a time."

The intensity of his gaze locked her in place.

"Adia." He rubbed his thumb along her wrist, sending chills down her spine. "When the German patrol captured us, why didn't you run?"

Her heart skipped a dozen beats. With everything that had just occurred, this was what he asked?

"I don't want to talk about that." She pulled back slightly, but he held firm.

"If Antek and his men hadn't shown up . . ." His husky voice faded, the implication clear. Those men who'd held her captive could have easily done anything. The other soldiers probably would have killed Bret the same way they'd slaughtered the Polish prisoners along the banks of the Bug.

They'd been lucky. Lucky and at the same time so unlucky that Lukas had been a part of the group.

Was her life worth more than Lukas's? Than the lives of any

of the other rebels who had died? Than those of the Germans, even? They had wives, mothers, sisters at home who'd mourn their deaths too.

Her stomach churned, empty and yet filled with a sinking regret.

"Why, Adia?" Bret pressed.

She closed her eyes. "Why does it matter? Lukas died. Ewan is missing."

"Will you tell me anyway?"

His voice was so earnest, pleading.

She opened her eyes, tears slipping from the corners. "I couldn't just leave you. You never would have left me behind." Her heart wrenched and her stomach tightened at her words, and she ripped free of his hold. Now she needed to escape or she feared she'd spill even more. "You should rest." She wiped her face, put the rag back in the sink, and fled to the door.

He groaned as he rose to his feet, followed her, and caught the door before she could close it. "Stay in your cabin until I come for you." He leaned on the doorframe as if he couldn't stay upright without it. "We'll leave in a few days once things quiet down."

"What are you going to do?" she whispered.

He shrugged. "I'll work as normal and listen to what I can. But it's too dangerous for you—even with the coat and cap."

Her heart dipped in disappointment. How would she ever remain in her cabin for more than an hour with nothing to do?

"Adia, I'm serious." He held her gaze. "Don't venture outside. It's likely they'll leave Polish citizens alone, but you will raise too much attention."

She looked toward the barns, itching already to check on the remaining horses.

"Promise me." His mouth tipped down into a deep frown, and exhaustion saturated his features.

"Get some rest." She closed the door behind her and strode quickly toward her own cabin.

As she opened the door to her musty room that was covered in a week of light dust, she drew in the familiar sight of her small desk in one corner, next to the lumpy cot she'd grown to love.

She stood before the small square window near her bed and crossed her arms. Soldiers shuffled around in the distance, watching the horses. To what end? Why were they here? How long? Helplessness tightened her muscles, caused her joints to ache.

She bit her lip to keep from cursing the men. These horses belonged to Poland.

Anger flared. Her neck hot, she stripped off the coat and hat. Her braid fell over her shoulder, and she eyed it thoughtfully.

She caught her reflection in the small, round mirror over her desk. This woman's face was thinner, paler, than the one she'd seen there about a week prior. There were scratches and tearstains and dark circles under her eyes. She was a ghost of her past self.

She couldn't sit here and do nothing. Nor could she move around freely as an American horse trainer. Especially as a female American horse trainer. She moved to her desk, opened the solitary, shallow drawer, and lifted a heavy set of shears that rested next to unused pencils and paper.

If Bret could walk among the Russians as a groom, surely she could too—as a young boy whose beard hadn't yet grazed his chin.

Grabbing hold of her hair, she held the scissors to the base of the thick braid. Her hands trembled as she remembered her mother with the same dark hair, the same long braid. Ewelina Kensington would have done anything to save the Arabian horses. She'd given her life for them. What was a little hair?

Adia closed her eyes and squeezed the handles together.

OCTOBER 5, 1939

Bret moved silently and unnoticed through the perimeter of Janów as he mentally cataloged the dozens of Russian soldiers milling about. He clenched his jaw as he recognized the broad shoulders and scarred face of the lieutenant who'd knocked him out in the tack room nearly two weeks earlier.

At least Adia hadn't been discovered in all this time. The deep blue and purple coloring at his temple was a small price to pay.

They'd settled into an uneasy routine while under the Soviet dominion, meeting quietly by darkness with Filip but not yet venturing beyond the walls of Janów for fear of greater risk or violence from their invaders.

His mind constantly drifted back to his conversation with Adia in his room after the Soviets had first arrived and her vague reply to his prodding. *"Why, Adia?"* He couldn't seem to pry the memory from his mind. It replayed each night in his dreams, bringing with it the conflicting desire and fear of the deeper reason she hadn't admitted to.

"I couldn't just leave you," she'd said.

God help him, could he leave her if—when—his orders demanded it? Antek hadn't yet contacted him with further instruction, and he did all he could to help Adia and Filip care for the meager herd left from the evacuation.

It was early in the day, and a dozen tasks lay before him to keep the horses fed and comforted when a flash of movement caught his eye. A hunched figure darting into the broodmare barn. He followed, a nagging uncertainty tugging in his mind. He knew that figure.

As he rounded the corner slowly, ensuring it was free of Russians, he peeked into the extra-wide stall freshly piled with straw, used for delivering foals. A slender figure wearing a familiar tan coat and cap leaned over a thick-bellied mare lying on her side in labor. Filip stood in the corner, arms crossed, face contorted in concern.

Bret growled at the figure in the tan coat. "I told you not to leave your cabin unescorted."

Adia whirled, the large cap covering her hair falling over her forehead. She'd smudged dirt over her face, though her eyes shone with a fire that set his body ablaze.

When the mare groaned, she turned back, rubbing her hand

gently over the bulging belly as the animal pawed her legs against the ground and shifted her head in discomfort.

Filip cleared his throat. "Czysty's foal is breech, and Adia is the best at turning babies."

Bret checked the aisles again, grateful for the midday hour when the soldiers would be eating.

She turned in time to catch his survey of the surroundings and said, "Any rumors of the soldiers moving on?"

"No news," Bret mumbled. "From what I've overheard, they're all confused, restless."

"We'll have to wait even longer to search for Ewan, won't we?" she asked softly. She turned back to the mare and massaged the animal's stomach.

"Yes. Soldiers are everywhere."

Adia didn't respond.

"Tomasz and Rafał are still out there. Don't worry—Ewan is resilient and they will find him."

"Can you bring more cloths and warm water?" Adia asked Filip. "I need to turn him soon and pull him out."

He nodded and strode down the aisle.

The mare squealed and pawed at the bedding.

"Keep watch for me?" Adia asked Bret, removing her coat and rolling up her sleeves. Her smooth, slender arms and dainty hands would give her away to anyone who looked closely enough.

His gaze traveled up and caught at the frayed, freshly cut ends of her dark hair that now went only to her ears. He hadn't quite gotten used to the sight, even in the past two weeks of seeing it. But her entire disguise—short hair, dirty face, and bulky clothing—seemed to work. The soldiers paid her little mind.

The air between them was tense—as it always seemed to be now. There was still far too much left unsaid. And he knew the weight of Ewan and Lubor missing rested heavily on her conscience.

Filip returned, and the two of them set to work as the mare's contractions grew closer and more intense. So far, the soldiers hadn't bothered or shown any interest in the animals, but the noise could still draw an unwanted crowd.

Bret kept an eye on the aisles as he watched Adia focus completely on the task at hand. Her face emptied of the worry and fear that had etched deep lines in her forehead for weeks, filled with the calming confidence of a woman who'd dedicated her life to these animals.

Adia carefully washed, then reached into the mare to loop a rope around the foal's hooves to pull it out. It was their only recourse when nature would not allow for a smooth delivery.

After a short struggle and a great deal of pulling from Filip and Adia, the wet foal rested on the bed of straw. Within moments, it rose on shaky legs.

Adia wiped the sweat from her brow, and Filip helped clean up the mess of cloths and buckets. They watched the young one move cautiously toward its mother to nurse as Czysty rose to her feet and snorted. The mare squealed and bared her teeth at the uncertain foal.

Filip and Adia exchanged a glance.

"She's a first-time mother," Filip said hesitantly. "Perhaps she'll need some time."

Czysty bit at the foal again and slashed out a front hoof. Adia stepped in and pulled the foal clear of her range, but the mare's teeth caught Adia's arm, ripping her sleeve and drawing blood from her forearm.

Bret took hold of Czysty's halter and pulled the mare to the opposite side of the stall. Filip moved to check on Adia, but she waved him off.

"It's not that bad," she said through gritted teeth. "Can you take her into the next stall?" she asked Bret. Then, to Filip, "Would you fetch some goat's milk for this little one? He needs to eat."

After the director disappeared, Bret led the broodmare from the stall and froze as three Russian soldiers approached. He glanced into the stall to confirm Adia had her head down and covered by her cap as she checked over the foal, wiping away the slime of the afterbirth.

"What are you doing?" a soldier demanded of Bret. "Give us that horse."

He reached out for Czysty, but the mare lunged forward and bit his hand. Bret didn't try to stop her.

The Russian cursed and pulled his handgun. "We'll eat this one," he said.

Bret jumped in front of the gun and held up both hands. He attempted a Polish-accented, broken Russian plea. "She's exhausted. She has just given birth."

The soldier wavered, the two behind him snickering and then batting his arm playfully.

Pride mixed with embarrassment painted the young soldier's face. His hand tightened almost imperceptibly over the pistol's handle.

Instead of fear, Bret felt relief—relief that he'd be able to block another blow to Adia. For him to take the bullet instead of the mare felt right. He hadn't stopped the vehicle that stole Charlie or saved his sister the ache of losing her husband, but he was now in the right place at the right moment.

A long stretch of held breath passed before the man holstered his weapon. The soldiers all stomped away without another word.

The unease still clung to the air.

Adia jumped from the stall, her face dark and contorted in disbelief. "Are you itching to get shot?" she hissed. "What were you thinking?"

He let out a long breath. His feet were cemented to the floor, and Adia quickly took the mare into a nearby stall and then turned back to him.

Her mouth fell open into an *O* as she scanned him again. Her concern delighted him and surprised him. The Adia Kensington he'd known weeks ago, at the start of the German invasion, would never have thought to fret over him rather than the horse. Something had changed in her.

"Stop jumping in front of Russian guns!" she whispered. "We don't need any more death around here."

He blinked away the daze and smiled softly, lifting her bloodied arm. "I'll stop when you quit jumping in front of unruly horses."

"That is hardly as dire." She rolled her eyes and tried to pull free, but he gently pulled her closer to examine the U-shaped bite mark. It was deeper than he'd thought. A stream of blood ran down to her hand.

He pulled out a fresh handkerchief. "We need to clean this."

She looked at the wobbling foal that watched them with ears forward and nose in the air, sniffing curiously. "He's more important right now. There are so few stallions left. Who knows how many horses will even survive this conflict?"

"You are equally irreplaceable, Adia."

She grew still, her eyes darting to his lips for the briefest of seconds.

Hope, possibility, desire lifted his soul. Excitement surged in him, as exhilarating as the parachute training he'd done in '34. Forget the consequences—he had to jump. He leaned closer, putting a hand to the back of her neck, her skin warm and soft.

"Thank you for saving Czysty," she breathed. "But you—" Her voice caught. "You are irreplaceable too."

The space closed between them as their breath mingled for a heartbeat. Their lips nearly touched.

A booming voice cried out in Russian down the hallway. "Halt!"

Followed by a thunderous gunshot.

18

Adia jumped apart from Bret as the voice and gunshot cracked through the silence of the barn.

Her heart, already racing far too fast from Bret's proximity—from what they had almost done—tumbled in her chest as she turned to the sound.

Russian shouting echoed from the direction Filip had gone. The director's voice cried out, and Adia took off running toward him, Bret close behind.

They turned the corner. Three soldiers bent over the fallen director, punching him and ripping away the supplies he had clutched in his arms.

Bret grabbed her shoulders and drew back. The soldiers hadn't noticed them. "Wait," he said. "No more jumping in front of guns."

She clenched her fists and pulled against him only for a moment before settling. She turned away from the sight as the soldiers left Filip alone, passing the items among each other and discussing them as if they'd just gone to the store, not beaten a man to the ground.

Bret had probably known, as she did, that the soldiers were nothing but bullies. If she or Bret had challenged them again, the violence would have gone a step further than what Filip had suffered.

As the Russians' footsteps and chatter faded, they rushed to Filip's side. He rose to an elbow, wincing in pain. Blood poured from his other arm from the graze of a bullet.

Adia ripped his shirt open to look at the wound. "Not too deep."

"I'm fine, I'm fine," he grunted, coughing a smattering of blood into his hand.

Bret hoisted him to his feet, glancing down the aisle where the soldiers could still be heard in the distance. "That needs stitching."

"I've had worse scars," Filip wheezed. Dirt filled the gashes and cuts on his hands and face. "Just let me lie down awhile. I'm not sure I translated correctly, but I overheard that they are leaving today."

Leaving. Finally.

She glanced at Bret, and the lines of his face softened ever so slightly.

Janów would be free of this terror at its gates—still under occupation from afar but left on its own to rebuild.

Bret took a few steps forward with Filip's arm slung over his shoulder, and Adia dipped under his other side. "I'll patch you up," she said.

Filip held up a shaky hand. "Adia, you must see to the foal. He'll need milk, and they took what I brought."

Bret's gaze connected with hers, and a fire still seemed to burn within him. She knew without a doubt that he didn't want her out of his sight.

She nodded at Filip's request. "I'll feed the foal and then meet you both in Filip's cabin."

He hesitated, but Filip groaned and pressed his free hand to his bleeding lip, which drew Bret's attention back to the more urgent matter.

"Be careful." Bret squinted and angled his head. "No stepping in front—"

"Of guns." She nodded. "Or unruly horses. I know."

She dashed through the stables silently and unearthed a buried cache of milk bottles from a tack room chest. If only her little Myszko were here. Her heart ached at the fear that he could be subject to a soldier's violent wrath.

She warmed a bottle over a small stove in the stable's kitchen and poured the goat's milk into a large bottle with a long rubber nipple. She'd always insisted the farm keep a ready supply from the neighbor's goats in case a foal lost its mother. This time, it paid off. She raced back to the foaling stall and found the little black colt lying on the ground, legs tucked beneath himself and head hung low. He nickered softly at her approach.

She ran her hand along the still-damp fur. "Easy there, small one. I'm so sorry your mother left you. She just doesn't know any better."

She offered the bottle to the teacup-size muzzle. His lips and gums clamped down, and he gulped heartily. Silence closed in around them, aside from Czysty in the stall next to her. The foal drained the bottle greedily, a good sign for the new life.

Adia's shoulders fell forward, and her head rested against the broad, fluffy forehead of the little orphan. The new life in the midst of so much death.

"Dorek," she said against his fur. "I'll call you Dorek." *Gift from God.* She'd heard the name once before and now it felt fitting. "The future of Janów may rest on your shoulders, Dorek."

If no other stallion returned, this new life would be even more precious. On top of it all, Dorek and Lubor shared the same father.

Should Lubor not find his way home . . .

The sound of suckling filled the silence as she leaned her head back against the stall wall, closing her eyes. When Dorek finished, he rested his head on her lap, and she was in no hurry to move.

Could life ever return to normal? Would these aisles bustle with mares, foals, and the up-and-coming stars of Janów who would breed hundreds upon thousands of show horses, racehorses, and cavalry and hunting mounts?

She thought back to her mother's horse, the fiery but patient Arabian mare who had toted Adia from one side of Oregon to the other. Her loyalty, intelligence, temper, and humor. She'd tried one moment to knock Adia off with a low-hanging branch and the next to lie next to her in the field for a nap under the noon sun.

A loud clatter in the distance startled Adia from her reverie. She slipped from the stall and walked through the barns, ducking behind a stack of hay at seeing the group of Russians near the entrance to the barn. The men cheered and shouted, ripping decorations from the walls, putting anything loose into a box and loading it into trucks in the driveway. Vehicles roared to life, filling with young soldiers who seemed eager to leave. A moment later, a smell tickled her nostrils and set her heart racing.

She reached for a small halter hanging outside the stall as waves of orange rolled toward her, Dorek, and Czysty, swallowing every blade of hay and straw and every wooden board in its path.

Fire.

"I'm fine," Filip told Bret from his cot. He waved a bruised hand. "Go check on her so you can wipe that scowl off your face."

It annoyed Bret that his thoughts were so obvious. He leaned back in the chair beside Filip and rolled up the last bit of gauze after wrapping the director's arm. Bret had been lauded for his ability to mislead and shield his true emotions. Why couldn't he do that when it came to Adia?

"We need to get her out of Poland," Bret said with a long sigh.

"How do you suggest we manage that?" Filip grumbled as he leaned back onto his wooden bed.

"Antek has connections within his partisan group who could find her some papers, smuggle her through Belgium."

"She'll never agree to it. Not without Ewan or Lubor."

The thought pained him as much as it relieved him. He wanted Adia out of this war zone. Safe. Of course, with her curiosity, he wasn't sure anywhere would be truly safe.

"She must see things differently now. With Lukas—"

A soft shudder vibrated the ground, cutting him off. He walked to the door and held his ear to the wood, listening.

Moments ticked by in silence, punctuated by the soft ticking of the grandfather clock. The hair on Bret's arms raised, and he slowly reached for his holster tucked in the back of his belt.

He carefully opened the door, startled to see a roiling black cloud of smoke over the stables. He turned to Filip and commanded, "Stay here!"

The barns. Smoke bellowed from every window, door, and stall opening. The foaling stalls, the barn closest to the cabins—that was where Adia had been.

He circled around the building, looking for any gap in the smoke.

From the west side below the clock tower barn entrance, a steady stream of Russian soldiers departed with the meager herd of one hundred Janów horses in tow. Spoils of war.

His stomach lurched in horror. But he couldn't save those horses now.

Where was Adia?

He stepped closer to the foaling barn, lifted his shirt collar to his mouth, and dove into the sea of black smoke.

19

Adia burst through the world of heat and smoke with the mare and foal in tow, grazing past a tall, stalwart figure.

Bret.

She sensed his bewilderment, his frantic searching through the sea of smoke.

Pushing Czysty and Dorek free of the barn walls, she released them into the clean atmosphere beyond and turned back, reaching through the blinding cloud for Bret. She opened her mouth to call for him, but her voice turned to a whisper. He'd been right there behind her. Now she reached and felt nothing but the heat of the nearing flames.

Then she heard his voice to the right, reached for him, and yanked his arm as they tumbled from the inferno into the daylight beyond.

She held to his hand as tightly as her buzzing adrenaline and rush of fear allowed. He was covered in dark soot, and flames had singed his pant legs at the ankles. He turned, looking her over. They spoke over each other, both in rough, rasping voices as if the fire had blazed through their throats.

"Are you all right?" he asked.

"Are you burned?"

"No," he panted. He brushed her hair and cupped her face as if to reassure himself that she was standing before him.

Czysty and Dorek watched the barns with eyes wide, tails arched, and necks erect.

She swallowed back a tidal wave of emotion. "Is Filip okay?"

Bret nodded. "The cabins are safe from the fire."

Her head whipped around, and she looked to the clock tower floating above the plume of smoke. "The other horses!"

She ran to pick up a water bucket from a paddock fence and tossed the contents on the flames at the stallion barn. She rushed back to the larger trough in the same paddock to refill it and hefted the water onto the doorway. The stretch of a dozen meters felt too far. It wasn't enough. By now the horses could have inhaled too much smoke.

Bret picked up another bucket and followed suit. Together, they tamped down a few hot areas, enough for her to look in and peer into one of the stalls. Her heart lifted with hope.

Empty.

Then her heart shattered at the realization.

Why were the stalls empty?

She moved to the next one.

"Adia, wait."

She reached the main doorway, the interior untouched by the flames. She looked down the driveway.

The distant row of horses and Russian soldiers along the road sent chills down her spine, even with the embers glowing at her back. From afar, she could see Lubor's father, Odwaga, the mares Liza, Eagle, Serena, and Zuza, and the darling month-old foal at Zuza's side. And dozens of others—those who'd endured the bombings of their evacuation and river crossings, only to spend mere days back at Janów.

"No, no, no . . ."

A thousand thoughts flashed through her mind in a single moment. The horses were alive, safe, but in Russian hands. The Russians wouldn't be interested in them as breeding stock. These horses would be forever lost to her, to Poland.

She lunged toward the driveway. "No!"

Bret's arm looped around her waist and lifted her, hauling her backward.

She kicked, cried out. Tears stung her eyes. She had to stop them. She had to retrieve the horses—those precious few horses they had left.

She coughed and sputtered, though ultimately, she slackened against his hold.

"It's too late." Bret's voice echoed around her. "We need to stop the fire, save what we can of the barns."

"For what?" What was left except a few staff and an undernourished foal and his evil mother?

Shouts in Polish echoed around her as the grooms and Filip hobbled over with buckets and hoses. The hiss of water suffocating the fire lifted from all corners of the barn before the small crew moved to the next building. But her gaze was fixed on the street and the last of Poland's best breeding stock as they grew smaller on the horizon.

Bret tightened his hold on her, his lips to her ear. "Don't give up." His voice cracked. From smoke or emotion, she wasn't sure. "Stay with me."

Adia's ears buzzed, and her wiser, more rational thoughts cut through the haze. *Move your legs. Don't let all of Janów go up in flames.*

The hundred-year history of Janów was as familiar as her childhood. It had fallen to ruin again and again and had been rebuilt from the ashes. This could not—would not—be the end.

She fumbled to find her footing and straightened her legs, Bret's strong grip giving her extra strength. She turned and looked into his eyes, which mirrored the kaleidoscope of emotions in her.

"Let's get to work."

———

OCTOBER 6, 1939

After working through the night, Bret stood next to Adia in silence at the new day's sunrise, surveying the damage as the final wisps of smoke lifted into the air. He struggled for each breath amid the physical and emotional exhaustion.

The foaling barn and yearling barn had suffered the most, but the quick work of buckets in the hands of the meager staff and half-beaten director saved the iconic clock tower barn, the tack and equipment rooms, the arena, and the stallion stables. After such a long, hot summer, the trees and grass and buildings had ignited as if drenched in petrol.

As further injury, the Russians hadn't left behind anything other than straw, halters, and ropes. They had pilfered every item that could fetch a ruble or two. They'd even ripped the windows from the frames.

The best and worst news of all was that not a single horse had been lost to the fire. But that was because the foal and ill-tempered mare were the only horses left behind.

Bret had watched Adia wrestle with the reality of it for the past twelve hours, and it gutted him.

"The fires are out." He turned to Adia, studying the weary wobble of her knees and the smoke smudged across her face. Her clothes were stained black, and the handkerchief he'd wrapped around the bite on her arm was crusted with blood and ash. "We can't do much more right now."

She pointed to the charred beam at their feet. "Let's move this last one aside to clear the pathway."

Stubborn woman. She was admirable, magnetic. He inhaled deeply, and they lifted the beam together and carried it outside to a pile of discarded pieces of Janów.

With one final shove, his energy evaporated, his mind hazy.

Hold it together. Just a little longer. But his body disconnected from his mind.

A swift movement next to him drew his eye, and he reacted. He caught Adia as she collapsed, his own knees buckling.

He cupped her head, holding her close to his chest and taking the brunt of the impact to the lower half of his body. Pain shot through his entire being as he clenched his teeth to keep from blacking out. She landed on top of him.

He paused and pulled in a shaky breath, taking silent stock of his toes and fingers to ensure they still worked. "Adia?" he whispered, his voice raspy.

She groaned and lifted a hand to her forehead. "What?"

Her warmth against him filled his mind and pushed away the pain shooting through his nerves and his legs, which they'd landed on.

"Can you move?" he asked.

"The earth is spinning." Another groan.

Gathering every inch of strength left inside him, he eased to his elbows, preventing her from falling onto the burned and soiled ground. Though slender, she was heavier than he expected—perhaps from the muscle required to ride and wrestle one-thousand-pound animals every day.

Or he was weaker than he realized.

He clung to her as he wavered to his feet. A hand clamped his elbow and helped him regain his footing. He glanced over to Filip, whose black-and-blue, swollen face darted to Adia.

"Her cabin wasn't touched by the fire," he said. "Do you want me to bring her anything?"

"A doctor?" It would set him at ease to have her examined.

"No doctor," she grumbled, her eyes closed and her forehead wrinkled. She lifted a hand but then faded back into sleeping stillness.

"Still defiant." Filip shook his head. "I'll bring whatever food I can find and fresh water for when she wakes."

Bret nodded and carried her to her cabin, then laid her down gently on the cot. His mind cried out for him to go and fall into his own bed. His body desperately needed time to recover. But that bite of hers needed tending, and his chest ached at the thought of leaving her just yet.

He brought over a basin of water and a cloth like she had done after the Russian soldier struck him, and wiped her forehead to reveal the soft, ivory skin below the layer of soot.

She stirred and mumbled at the cool touch.

He untied the handkerchief and looked at the jagged mark from the mare. It had somehow stayed clean under the layer of protection. He dabbed at it and she winced, pulling her arm back.

Her eyes fluttered open, wide with concern. "Oh, we can't forget to find another goat to milk for Dorek, since Czysty won't let him nurse." She sat up, but he held up his hands for her to lie back down.

"Easy there. Dorek?"

She reluctantly settled back against her pillow and drew in a breath. "The little black colt. He's all we have left."

Bret leaned forward and tucked back a stray lock of her dark brown hair that had fallen across her forehead. "I'll remind Filip."

"Thank you."

He paused. "Adia." He waited to go on until she met his gaze. "If I make it my only goal to find Ewan and Lubor and ensure they return to Janów where they belong, would you consider leaving Poland now?"

She held his stare, her stillness betraying the acceptance that slowly seemed to dawn. "How would I get out of Poland?"

"I've asked around. A contact of Antek's can get you to France and then to America."

In a low, unsteady voice, she asked, "Do you want me to leave?"

His chest tightened, a familiar panic surfacing that appeared anytime he thought of her disappearing from his life. If he told her as much, if he spoke the truth, it'd be selfish. It'd be dangerous. It'd only ask for further pain and heartache.

"I think you'll be safer beyond the borders of Poland." That was no lie, at least.

She tilted her head. "You didn't answer the question."

Was she teasing him or just not thinking quite clearly?

"I can't protect you here," he said.

"It's not your job to protect me, Bret."

But it was—he'd agreed to as much to help Filip. And he yearned to do so, even if he hadn't pledged to Filip. He squeezed her hand. "Would you at least consider it? Please."

She frowned and nodded.

Relief filled him and broke him in half. He leaned forward, kissed her forehead, and then fled her domicile.

She was the strongest person he'd ever met—seeing her work against all the odds to help smother a raging fire after witnessing the whole of her life's work taken from Janów's grounds. And here he was, hardly able to say what needed to be said and truly convince her to leave.

A moment longer in her cabin and he would have lost all resolve.

A moment longer and he would have begged her to stay.

20

OCTOBER 8, 1939

Adia kicked a loose board as she wandered around the charred perimeter of the broodmare barn, Dorek following close at her heels, playfully nudging her elbow.

She'd moved Dorek into a small paddock beside her cabin. He needed constant feeding and reassurance after his traumatic first day of life. And now he'd escaped the rickety pen she'd set up for him so he could follow her nonstop.

Two long days had passed since the fires burned and soldiers fled with the lifeblood of the stables. Adia had fallen into a restless sleep for an entire day before dragging herself from her bed to bathe and put on a fresh set of clothes. Filip stopped by often with food, fresh water, and milk for Dorek.

Today, when she'd ventured out for the first time, she walked by Bret's cabin and knocked but found it vacant. Bret was free to come and go—surely he had responsibilities of his own.

Still, she wondered how he fared, where he was. If he was healing well. If he had considered any plans to look for Ewan. If he thought back to their near-kiss as often as she did—that moment of innocence, peace, and hope before her whole world had fallen to ruin.

She knelt and ran her hand over a brass door hinge that had escaped the carnage. She closed her eyes, picturing how the rows of stalls with brass fittings had looked only days earlier. The vision stung.

Her mind then flashed to a similar style with simpler flourishes back home in Oregon. Twelve stalls as far from Janów's splendor as they were distance in kilometers.

She swallowed. Former splendor. Compliments of the brutal Russian invaders.

Now the stables played host to the mice and barn cats. A few of the felines still had singed whiskers and tails.

Janów was as barren as her little Kensington Acres.

What would her mother say, to know everything she'd fought for had once again been utterly wiped away? Adia hoped her mother would at least be proud that she'd tried. Was this what Ewelina had faced, too, in the Great War?

Ewelina, the daughter of a Polish aristocrat, had run toward adventure, danger. She'd been the same age Adia was now, twenty-six, when she came to Janów. And in war, she lost her family of Polish loyalists and fell in love with a British spy. Adia's mother and father had saved a handful of Arabian horses that rebuilt the bloodline in Poland.

From where she stood, Adia had no hope of living up to such esteem.

She brushed the wrapped wound on her arm from Czysty's bite a few days ago, still tender. All of Poland bled. Its people, its history, its treasures.

Dorek nudged her face with his feather-soft muzzle. She cupped his jowl and scratched his neck. Odwaga, Dorek's and Lubor's sire, had been taken by the Soviets, but at least through Dorek, a piece of the bloodline could live on.

"What should I do, Dorek?"

The colt nibbled on her shirttails, offering no useful opinion on the matter.

Bret pulled out his pocket watch, flipped it open without bothering to look at the time, snapped it closed.

He wasn't happy to be gone from Janów this long. Antek's contact was late.

Never a good sign.

They were to meet here in the shadow of a now ghost town, every building window dark and hollow like a long-decayed skull. In the husk of a stone mill, the grinding wheel sat motionless and purposeless outside, and the interior looked as if all its workers had simply walked away and never returned. Lunch boxes still lay open on a table at the end of the big room, food rotten and decaying.

He'd observed this scene again and again on the road throughout the wreckage of Eastern Poland, and still it unnerved him.

The evening light streamed through the cracks in the mill's wood and the open doorways. Bret sat in the back-corner shadows where he had a view of every entrance and pathway. But hardly a leaf fluttered in the hour he'd waited.

Too quiet.

"Yer more punctual than I anticipated," a voice said from outside the main doorway. A lean figure stepped into the building, his hands in his pockets and a hat tipped over his forehead.

"And you're far less punctual." Bret tucked his watch away and let his hand rest on the handgun at his hip. "How do I know you're the one I'm supposed to meet?"

"Ye don't." The figure stopped and leaned against a beam. He had a cigarette between his lips and his Scottish accent cut through each word. "Hard to know anything for certain these days."

"Except that death is coming for us all, sooner or later." Bret recited the phrase Antek had instructed him to use. The code words used among the trusted band of rebels Antek had cultivated these past few weeks.

The man lifted a hand to his cigarette and extinguished it between two fingers. He removed his hat, revealing a mop of red curls, a kid no more than eighteen or nineteen smiling from underneath the unruly locks. "Call me Scottie. How can I be of service?"

"I need to get someone out of Poland. Out of Europe."

He whistled. "Ye and about a million others. I was hoping ye'd ask for something easy like heavy artillery. Or a crate of medicine."

"What will it take?"

"What've ye got?"

"Money."

"We have all the money we need."

"Then name your price. I don't have all day."

"Information." He stuck another cigarette between his lips. "I 'ear you're mighty handy when it comes to diggin' up a secret or two."

"That so?" Bret's jaw tightened and he glanced through the open windows again, seeing no movement.

"Ye agree to lend us a hand when we need it, we'll get yer girl out."

Bret opened his mouth, then slammed his lips shut. There was no use in asking how Scottie knew that his "someone" was a girl. Surely Antek had told him. It was what Bret would have assumed were the situation reversed. And it was common practice to work in assumptions to pry a bit more information from your mark. Scottie knew what he was doing—but then, he would, or Antek wouldn't have recommended him.

"Fine." Bret nodded. "For as long as my orders keep me in Poland."

"Brilliant." Scottie popped his hat back onto his head, wrestling it against his thick hair. "Meet at the southwest well at Janów in a week's time. Sunday, at sunrise, and my man will see that she gets back to her safe little home in America."

Bret bristled at the fact that Scottie knew Adia's destination as well. But again, he had probably done his research before ever meeting with Bret. "Your man? I agreed to work with you."

"My time is in high demand. Ye can trust me man."

He bit his tongue to keep from complaining further. "Are we done here?" He stood and slipped out an open doorway without waiting for confirmation.

Anger, unease, and sorrow all ripped at his heart, but he tamped them down like the smoldering flames of Janów.

This was best for her. Best for him.

Bret returned to the stables astride a mud-colored old farm horse abandoned by one of Janów's neighbors. The roads were quiet and the other towns lifeless as all of Poland sat on edge in the wake of the Russians' departure.

He circled the farm's perimeter before putting the plain, mixed-breed saddle horse into one of the open paddocks. The horse grazed lazily, as if oblivious to the fate he'd escaped by evading Russian capture.

Bret roamed the halls until he stumbled upon Adia in the clock barn, bent over a broken saucer containing a puddle of milk as a bedraggled kitten lapped up the lavish meal.

Dorek nibbled on a discarded halter hanging from the stalls nearby. She stroked the animal's fur gently, her forehead furrowed and her eyes pouring out every bit of love and tenderness within her.

The sight rocked his gut. For someone so seemingly cold to him at times, she sure attracted all manner of orphans and needy things.

He couldn't fathom a life, a time without her there. Had it really only been five weeks since they'd reunited in the town square after the first Nazi plane sighting?

The thought of Adia leaving before Ewan returned caused his heart to seize. Of course, it was hard to know if Ewan ever would find his way home.

Adia turned, her face smudged with some of the soot and dust that lingered in the air. Her arm was still bandaged, her clothes singed and stained.

The sight still utterly took his breath away.

He cleared his throat and stepped forward. "Have you thought about leaving?"

She stood, picking up the kitten with milk droplets on its whiskers and petting it gently. "I've thought about it."

A small part of him was relieved at her mild concession, but he couldn't let it show. "I've found someone who can get you out in a week."

"A week," she said, voice trembling. She looked down at the kitten.

Confound it all, he should have pressed Scottie. It should have been tomorrow. It should have been yesterday.

"Is a week long enough for us to go out and look for Ewan, just one more time?" She lifted her gaze to his, her pleading eyes matching those of the little feline begging Adia for more milk.

His heart thudded, and he was delighted at the thought of being out on the road again. With her.

But was it too dangerous?

A lot could happen in one week.

His body ached from exhaustion, his chest tight as he breathed through the torrent of emotion. As stiffly as she moved, he anticipated she felt the same soreness and tiredness.

"You sure you're up for that?" he asked.

She nodded slowly, lacking real enthusiasm, but her eyes were on fire. "I need to find him."

Perhaps it was too great a risk. Bret could search on his own in hopes of finding the boy—and if he could be found in time, perhaps Adia could take him with her to America.

"Don't even think of trying to go off on your own and leave me behind, Conway," she said sharply, a faint smile tugging at the corners of her lips.

He let out a long breath of frustration. "We'll leave tomorrow at first light."

21

Venturing through the countryside and emptied towns of Poland, Adia felt more at home than at the hollow shell that was Janów Podlaski.

She was avoiding the realities of all that had been lost, but out here, she could hope that they'd return and find it all back to whole.

Something had shifted in the winds now that the Russians had fully retreated to the border of Poland and Russia. German patrols were sparse—most occupied Warsaw or Kraków and left the smaller towns in their decimation. Poland was fallen, but at least some parts were left to rest and rebuild.

For the moment.

Bret had secured fake Polish papers for both of them—and she didn't ask how. As before, they'd fallen back to the story of being a married couple with family in Kraków.

At the end of their first day moving east, they entered a small, abandoned town to find a flash of a chestnut-red horse bolting away from them. A broken halter and lead rope dangled from its nose.

Adia spotted the Janów brand instantly—a perfect white crown. "That's Apple!" She kicked her mount into a sprint and wove to the right. "Cut her off."

177

Bret mirrored her actions, pushing his horse to the left, and they caught up to the mare easily. Bret caught her lead and they all slowed to a walk, the silence of the town settling back over them as they drew to a halt.

Adia dismounted and quickly looked over Apple for any injury to her body, neck, or legs. She looked underfed and a bit feral but unharmed.

Bret tied some extra rope he'd brought to her halter and patted the horse's neck. "Apple, eh?"

Adia's shoulders drooped. "Ewan named her."

Bret held her gaze with steely resolve. "We'll find him, Adia."

At the edge of the small town, a few empty fields offered a secure location for their horses. She turned away to unlatch the blanket from behind her saddle. "Let's stay here for the night and use that paddock over there for the horses."

"I'll make a sweep of the town to be sure there aren't any patrols and find us somewhere to take shelter."

They fell into a familiar routine, moving silently and comfortably around each other. Once Adia had seen to the horses, digging up a bag of grain from some rubble and ensuring the paddock fencing was solid, Bret returned and led them to a small rowhouse that overlooked the pasture. The house was empty and disheveled, the doors fallen off their hinges and any valuables stripped by the passing intruders.

"I'll take first watch," Bret said, motioning to a small room for them to share.

She'd grown used to the close proximity in the evacuation and while searching the eastern countryside before for Lubor and Wojownik. She didn't mind being so close to Bret, but now she had a deadline pressing down upon her shoulders.

She paused. "Perhaps we should split up, cover more ground in the next six days. We haven't seen a patrol all day, so—"

"No," Bret said softly, kindly. "Chivalry won't allow me to do that, I'm afraid."

"Chivalry." She laughed and shook her head. "What time do we have for chivalry in days such as these?"

His expression went somber and weighted. "If not now, then we might as well give up all hope."

A shiver shot down her spine, but the stubbornness deep in her gut wouldn't let go. "I'd be fine on my own." Ewan was out there all alone, and if Bret was pushing her to leave Poland, there was so little time.

"We're not gonna press our luck." His tone left no room for negotiation. He pointed to a small bed in the corner of the room. "Get a few hours of sleep."

She sighed. "You're insufferable."

"The feeling is mutual, madam." He looked away, seeming to smother a smile as he put his saddlebags on the ground and then lowered himself to lean against the wall near the doorway.

Heat flared on her cheeks, and she sat down on the bed across the room. "Have you always been like this?"

"Charming and courteous?" Now he wasn't hiding his smirk.

Suddenly the despair and anger of the past week, of the Russians pillaging Janów, faded away. In the same way Bret's easygoing nature had kept her grounded on their journey back from Antek's, his jokes were like a balm to her soul.

"I'm guessing you're the firstborn and have always gotten your way." She sat upright on the bed and crossed her legs, holding them to her chest. The last time they'd scoured the countryside, they hadn't conversed much. They'd been surrounded by patrols and danger. Now something had shifted between them. Was it the clock ticking until her departure?

"You'd be right." He shrugged. "Though my father was quite upset that I didn't follow in his footsteps."

"Let me guess—banking?"

"Military." Bret looked away. "I come from a line of generals moving chess pieces on a board in an office in London."

Disdain dripped from his words, surprising her. "So, you became one of those pieces instead?"

179

He looked over sharply, startled. "What?"

"A spy," she said.

"You're off your trolley."

She held up a hand. "I've known for some time." It was her turn to smirk. "Your family might have been generals, but mine were spies."

Bret's expression didn't change as much as she might have expected at such a revelation. She stood, inching closer to combat the dimming light so she could see his reaction. And the longer she read his face, the more obvious it became.

"You knew," she breathed.

"They were famous in this region." He motioned to the spot on the floor beside him. "Terence Kensington and Ewelina Bartosz."

"Sounds as if you knew them better than I did." She sat down next to him, closer than she meant to, their knees nearly brushing. "They shipped me about as far away as I could possibly get."

"War was brewing." He leaned toward her, elbows on his knees. "They knew better than anyone the danger they faced."

And they'd both paid the price for it. That war had claimed millions, her parents among them.

"Are your parents still alive?" She was eager to divert the conversation.

He studied her silently for a moment, eyes narrowing as if he saw straight through her deflection. Then he nodded. "At the family manor outside London, with my younger sister, Elizabeth."

She angled her head. "How much younger is she?"

"Only a year." Bret smiled fondly. "So we'd always been quite close."

She picked up the subtle language. "*Had* been close? You're not now?"

His mood shifted. "We had a bit of a falling-out recently." It didn't sound as if he wanted to share further.

"How did you end up assigned in Poland?"

His dark gaze shimmered and a grin lilted to one side. "Luck, I guess."

Adia bit down on the inside of her bottom lip to keep from playing into the obvious flirtation. She was transported back to the same bashful woman she'd been in Wygoda's market when Bret had asked her to dinner. Butterflies fluttered inside her, but everything that had held her back before was only further intensified.

"When did you figure it out?" Bret continued to study her intently.

"You being a spy?" She chuckled. "When you started talking about Hemingway."

"That was entirely truthful." He held up a finger of protest. "I did serve with him in Spain, and he is an utter cad when it comes to women."

Despite the jesting tone, now her mood shifted. She shook her head. "But how am I ever to know what to believe?"

That was the crux of it all. Ewelina and Terence Kensington had died during the war, abandoning her for what? Some government secrets?

Bret looked down at his hands and leaned back slightly. There was no avoiding the reality of his job and the lies he'd spun. "I only sought to protect you, Adia."

"That's not your job."

He laughed softly. "Well . . ."

"What do you mean?" Adia's face flushed. "No more lies, Conway."

————

The air went still around them in the deserted house, and Bret felt the anger radiating from Adia. It was time to come clean. She would be gone soon, and he might never have the chance.

The shock at her so easily knowing his role in espionage had yet to fully settle. But as she'd pointed out, she had more history than most in the world of intelligence gathering.

He sighed. "Filip asked me to look after you, in honor of a promise he'd made to your father."

Anger, confusion, indignation all flashed through her eyes in an instant. She stood and turned toward the cot. "That at least makes more sense," she said, her voice trembling. From what? Why would this upset her so?

He rose to his feet and reached for her elbow. "I never meant to miss our date, Adia. My network was compromised. My partner was killed."

She seemed to weigh his words and the new information.

"I was in a hospital bed that night and for two weeks after. Nothing less would have kept me away."

Broken ribs, fractured vertebra, head trauma. It was a long recovery and a lengthy, careful search within his contacts to find where the leak had occurred—how they'd been discovered and targeted, leading to Charlie's death. Only months later did he turn up with nothing other than a rumor that the German officer they'd intended to meet had also disappeared without a trace.

"When I brought you to Janów back in September, Filip asked me then to stay and look after you." He hesitated. "But that was before I realized just how much I cared for you, Adia."

She flinched and then wrenched her arm free of his touch. "I don't believe anything you say."

He shook his head. "You're looking for excuses, you mean."

She gasped and turned, enraged, allowing him the moment to seize her hands and hold her close, their gazes locked.

"Aside from who my true employer was, I have never lied to you," he said, his throat constricted with emotion. "And I'd give anything to go back and eat pierogi with you at Babka's that night."

She closed her eyes. "To what end?"

"I think you know."

Her eyes opened wide at the boldness in his words. He released her hands, sliding his fingers up her cheeks and cupping her jaw to angle her face upward.

Her breath caught, lips trembling and eyes filled with tears as the moonlight cast shadows across the room. Something about the pain in her expression halted him. He wanted to hold her, kiss her, and beg her forgiveness—but this wasn't the time. She'd be gone in less than a week.

She'd return to her life in the States and find love and happiness elsewhere. It would be selfish of him to anchor her here with emotion or guilt about what could have been between them.

She appeared to be thinking the same thing. She broke free of his hold and strode to the other side of the room. The moonlight dimmed and the room filled with darkness.

"We only have a handful of days left," she said, brushing a tear from her cheek but avoiding his gaze. "We'd better focus on what matters. Finding Ewan and Lubor. That's it—no more of this foolishness between us. Wake me in a few hours when it's time for my watch."

Bret sat back by the doorway, the distance between them now a gaping wound. "Yes, Miss Kensington."

"Don't call me that."

"Don't be so terse." Bret crossed his arms and looked away, the air between them now thick and suffocating. "You're right. We need to focus on what matters."

Though he said the words, his heart and soul couldn't have disagreed more.

22

After five days of tension and near-fruitless searching, the familiar road brought Janów into view. Adia felt more than just the pain of returning empty-handed. She felt as if she'd let down everyone around her—Bret, Filip, Ewan.

They'd even gone back to Karina's to see if the injured stallion, Olark, was still there, but the house and barn had been leveled, the area barren. It was another cut to their deeply battered souls. Though they'd found two other Janów mares, the victories felt small.

The gap between her and Bret felt like a raw wound. They'd barely uttered a word since their midnight conversation less than a week ago. He'd been polite, quipped a few well-timed jokes, but maintained the distance they'd agreed to in not so many words.

She hated it.

But what was the point in hoping for anything different? They were worlds apart. And she'd be back in America within a month's time.

The added sorrow of failing to find Ewan and Lubor crushed her bit by bit.

Bret led two mares and Adia led one behind her terrible mount as the crunch of gravel under their hooves surrounded them. The peak of the clock tower rose in the distance.

"What time are we meeting the contact tomorrow?" Her voice was unsteady as if rusty from the days of silence.

"Dawn. I'll fetch you a few hours before."

Hardly an evening to say goodbye to the place on earth she loved most. The people, the historic buildings, and picturesque green pastures. The horses. Dorek. Czysty. She kept her head straight and her eyes glued to the white bricks that had once offered such comfort.

Don't think about it. Don't dwell on how you'll miss it all, how you'll leave every bit of your shattered and trampled heart here.

The decision was made. Now she simply needed to be free, to be as far away as possible. Back to her solitary life and mission to grow the Arabian breed that had driven her for so long. It was the most logical, the most safe. Now Bret could be free of this burden and go back to whatever served British Intelligence.

As they traversed the bend in the road and the driveway of Janów loomed a short distance away, she pulled back and started. The tired mare she rode even perked up and snorted anxiously.

A stream of gray-uniformed soldiers with red patches and black swastikas led a line of dozens of Arabians. She recognized them instantly: Kasia, Lilac, Blaze, Pixie, and so many more. The initial flare of fear in her chest twisted into curiosity and confusion.

Shiny black vehicles filled the circular driveway beneath the clock tower, and handfuls of men worked with hammers and boards to repair the charred foaling barn.

Bret pulled his charges to a stop next to her and stared, his slackened jaw evidence of his own surprise. "Let's circle around, approach from the south," he said. "Then find Filip to learn what's going on."

She couldn't pull her eyes from the stream of horses, scanning for a particular gleam of brown coat and the distinct arched neck of the prince of Janów. But she didn't see Lubor in the visible line of horses. Her heart thudded in hope. What did all of this mean?

Bret and Adia circled the fields and trotted through the rows of cabins. They left the horses in a paddock and crept carefully through the foaling barn. Most of the soldiers were clustered near the entrance where the majority of the structural destruction had been wrought by the Russians. The other barn had been fully patched, fresh white paint sparkling on the boards.

Adia darted to the stallion barn and raced to the first stall, not caring if she ran into a soldier. Her mind was a haze of disbelief and relief.

"Oh, Phantom," she breathed in joy when she saw the stallion's black nose and white whiskers. In the next stalls, she found Balik, Palermo, and Dancer.

Her heart still dipped a bit in disappointment as each stall she passed didn't hold the one horse she'd been most determined to find.

No Lubor. And no Wojownik.

Still, she couldn't believe how much more alive and familiar the stables felt. Bret followed behind her, his expression tinged with suspicion and unease.

Adia didn't care what he thought. All was not lost.

"Bret? Adia?" Filip's voice floated down the aisle.

They whirled to see him approach, still bruised and limping from his beating at the Soviets' hands.

Adia rushed to him and took his shoulders. "Is Ewan back? Lubor?"

"Filip," Bret cut in. His somber expression held a gravity that demanded answers. "When did the Germans arrive?"

"Two days ago."

"Who is in charge?"

"A colonel . . ." Filip pressed a finger to his forehead. "Vogel is his name."

The color drained from Bret's face as he glanced around. "Werner Vogel?"

"Yes."

"Are you absolutely certain?"

Filip nodded. "He is quite polite. Said he's been tasked with rebuilding Janów and the breeding program. I never thought I'd say this, but the Germans being here might be a good thing."

"Don't count on it." Bret glowered.

The director ignored Bret's comment, and his eyes shone as he turned to Adia. "They know the location of dozens more horses that were left behind or escaped from the Russians' caravans. They're offering rewards to anyone who brings back a horse with the Janów brand."

Hope turned her blood hot, and her fingers itched to work, ached to check over every horse that had come home.

Why, in the midst of war, did the Germans care about horses? They'd been connoisseurs of fine horse breeding but hadn't put any particular focus on Arabian bloodlines in the past.

Filip took her hand. "And," he said, pausing dramatically until both she and Bret met his gaze, "there are rumors that Lubor has been spotted. As famous as he is, these soldiers are desperate to find him."

Adia's heart raced. "Truly?"

"And . . ." Filip beamed with excitement. "There is supposedly a small Polish boy traveling with him."

Ewan. Lubor. Vogel.

The new information sank in as Bret studied Adia's face when the realization struck her. Ewan was with Lubor.

At the same moment her dark eyes widened and a joyful smile spread across her pink, wind-chapped lips, Bret knew her mind had changed. There was no way she was leaving Poland come dawn.

His stomach dropped as if he were free-falling. Was he disappointed or relieved? Too many thoughts and emotions clamored for his attention.

Focus on the greatest threat first.

Oberst Werner Vogel. If it were true. If the German colonel was really here.

"Filip, may I speak with you?"

"More secrets, Conway?" Adia asked flatly, and he realized it was a losing battle to exclude her.

"Fine," Bret whispered hurriedly, keeping one eye on the aisles in case the colonel decided to stroll by. "Vogel is not to be trusted."

Filip's eyes glimmered in understanding. "You competed against him in the Olympics in '36, didn't you? That's why his name is so familiar."

"Olympics?" Adia blinked. "That's what Filip meant by 'accomplished'?"

Bret sighed. He didn't have time for this. "Vogel is only loyal to the Fatherland. Don't let any of his talk of his love for horses sway you." He shot a look at Adia. "Either of you."

She crossed her arms. "You're leaving."

Was that a tinge of disappointment in her voice? Probably wishful thinking. Her walls were back in place, higher and thicker than ever before.

"I can't stay here without drawing the wrong kind of attention. He'd recognize me, and he knows who I work for."

Filip nodded somberly. "How should I get ahold of you?"

"I'll work something out." Bret shifted. "I should leave. And you"—he met Adia's gaze—"should stay under Vogel's radar. He has a particular weakness for beautiful women."

The words seemed to startle her, but she shook them off. "About meeting at dawn . . ."

"I know." He held up a hand. "You're not going to leave Poland. Not now. And I'll keep searching for Ewan and Lubor whenever I can. I won't be far away if you need me."

Before he gave in to his desire to pick her up and take her to meet Scottie anyway, he left Janów under the domain of a new flag, a new ruler.

And an uncertain future.

23

Adia looked down, brush in hand as she stroked Kasia's coat, while a pair of Germans strode around the corner and headed straight to her and the horse. One was especially tall with Roman-statuesque features and perfect, rigid posture.

Oberst Werner Vogel.

"Were those all we could find?" the colonel asked. Adia's comprehension of their German was unreliable. "Shame. Put the word out: five hundred zloty for every Janów-branded horse returned. We need more stock. The Führer's mission is near impossible unless we find more purebreds. Curse those greedy Russians."

The pair drew close, and Adia kept her eyes trained on the horse's now spotless coat. She hunched her shoulders and hoped her wide-legged trousers, oversized coat, and ratty old hat would hide any identifying features.

The other soldier spoke. "There are no updates on Lubor or Wojownik."

Vogel cursed under his breath, their steps and voices now closer. "A greater reward will motivate. Two thousand for Lubor."

The pair passed as Adia held her breath, both at the news and the

189

proximity to danger. She dared a glance over her shoulder through the lowered brow of her hat.

The colonel walked with his head held high and his sharp blue eyes looking over every horse—and then his eyes met hers.

Her heart thudded as she turned swiftly. The exchange didn't last more than the flap of a hummingbird's wings, but she noted the insightfulness in that gaze.

Moments inched by as she expected their footsteps to falter, for their voices to turn sharp on her and drag her out of the only place she'd called home.

But the smaller man beside the colonel chirped, "When can we expect another inspection from Herr Rau?"

"Several weeks . . ."

Their voices faded, and she was left alone with the four other mares in the stable. She let out a long breath. That had been far too close.

In the two weeks since she and Bret had returned to find the Nazi flag flying over Janów, she'd fallen into an easy routine of caring for the horses and occasionally riding. She was careful not to draw any attention to herself, and Filip had been left in charge of all staffing and menial operations. The soldiers' presence impacted few things in her day-to-day.

She hadn't heard a word from Bret in that time.

So be it. Things were complicated enough without fretting over feelings or—God help her—a romantic relationship with no hope of a future.

But she missed his presence, strength, and well-timed jokes.

She shook her head and patted Kasia absently.

He was doing whatever he needed to do and looking for Ewan and Lubor. And gathering intelligence.

Former Olympian. She shook her head every time she recalled the fact. But was she surprised? Bret had been anything but predictable, ever since their first encounter in the marketplace.

She gazed down the aisle as the autumn rain fell over the starved

Polish soil. *Oh, Ewan. I hope that somehow you and Lubor are dry, warm, safe.*

She returned to her chores, and the clomp, clomp, clomp of tiny hooves appeared and followed her down the hall. Dorek came up beside her and nipped her elbow. She fed the stallions their small rations of grain. They were barely enough to sustain the high-energy animals and far from the lavish portions of their pre-occupation days. It could be a rough winter ahead, especially as the soldiers settled in and drained what meager resources their small corner of Poland could boast.

Dorek reached over her shoulder and nibbled on the edge of a bucket, and she pulled it free. Since he'd been rejected by his mother and bottle-fed by humans, he had no respect for boundaries and was quite mischievous but loyal to her.

"Back off, pest," she hissed, nevertheless grateful for his presence and companionship.

She made a final sweep through the stalls, now quiet as the sun set and off-duty soldiers took to the remains of Wygoda for drinking.

The colt followed her, his tail swishing happily, oblivious to any other world. They crossed the expanse between the barns and the cabins, and the hair on her arms stood on end as she sensed a set of eyes tracking after her and the colt.

She glanced over to see Vogel talking with several soldiers outside the broodmare stalls. He focused back on the conversation, and she hustled Dorek along, hunching her shoulders again and ducking behind her lifted collar. Dorek drew too much attention, perhaps, in acting more like a lost puppy than a colt.

Her pulse jumped, and she forced her pace to remain unchanged, as if Vogel's look meant nothing, as if she had nothing to hide instead of everything.

After securing Dorek in the paddock by her cabin, she slipped inside her domicile and pressed her back against the door. Thankfully, it was the farthest from the stables, and her specific cabin was obscured from view from the barns because of several other outbuildings. But the simple wooden structure provided little protection—neither to the icy winter nor to the soldiers who routinely searched structures with little warning.

After they pilfered anything of value, they looked for any suspected rebels or partisans. For now, all was quiet. Though if Bret returned, and when Ewan returned, she wasn't sure how long that would last. Those two drew trouble like magnets.

She looked around her small home, and a weight of exhaustion and unrest settled on her shoulders. Too anxious, too tired to bother with eating, moving, or even sleeping. She was living in a state of limbo, unable to move forward, backward, or even sideways.

All she could do was wait. For Ewan to return. For Bret to bring news of any kind.

For the war to end.

Or for her presence to be discovered and whatever consequences that might entail.

Bret ducked into the half-demolished pub on the outskirts of a nearly abandoned city near the port of Danzig, where the Nazis had first cut their path into Poland. The dull light from the clouded evening sky cast eerie shadows across the empty town. So far, there were no signs of German soldiers, but then, the Nazis had grown stealthier in response to the increased partisan activity.

Bret wished Antek had agreed to meet elsewhere. This was needlessly risky and entirely too far from Janów, where he'd been watching the occupation from a distance.

With the Russians, he'd had the freedom to walk around as staff, but this was another matter. He couldn't risk Oberst Werner Vogel spotting him. And surely there was a price on his head among German intelligence, which Vogel was known to be connected to.

But how he missed being around Adia every day.

"Conway." Antek's gruff voice sounded at the end of a long hall-way strewn with broken glass and filled with the stench of stale ale.

Bret glanced in each abandoned room as he passed to ensure they were alone. "What's the latest, Antek?"

"We need you to help the local partisan group."

Bret kept his posture relaxed and his expression neutral. Had his commanding officer sanctioned this? How would this serve his mission to report troop movements? He'd mostly been hands-off—observe and report only—with any Polish affairs.

"There's an apartment down the way you can use."

"I'll stay closer to Janów." Since vacating his cabin at Janów, he'd retreated to an abandoned hunting cabin not too far from the stables but well hidden from the road and passing soldiers. "Who is leading the partisans?"

Antek frowned. "Janów is too far. We need you here."

"There's a high-value officer I'm watching."

"Vogel?"

"I'm guessing he's involved in something more than just running a horse farm." Bret had no proof yet, but he also couldn't bear to leave Adia or Filip alone. He knew Werner well enough to know his ambitions were grand, and no horse farm would satisfy someone so eager to prove himself. He must be using the situation for his own gain.

Antek looked away and sighed. "Fine. You'll meet the leader in Wygoda named Nowak. If you insist on staying near Janów, use Tomasz to get to me and Nowak."

Bret blinked. "Tomasz?"

Antek coughed, stood from his rickety chair, and dusted off his pants as he moved to the back of the room. "This way. He can explain everything."

Antek pressed a loose board on the wall, and a hidden wall caved in and opened into an apartment behind the bar. A small group of men with ragged brown jackets lounged around a table with piled-high ashtrays and empty glasses.

Tomasz stood on the other side of the room, looking out a window covered in brown paper with a few narrow slits for visibility. He turned and smiled at Bret. "Good to see you."

Bret moved toward him and clasped his hand warmly. "I'm so sorry about Lukas."

Tomasz's lips tightened and his Adam's apple bobbed. "What of Adia? Ewan? Filip?"

"Adia is well. Filip too." Bret hesitated. "Ewan hasn't been found yet. Nor has Lubor. But the Germans are looking." So was Bret, in every spare moment between errands for Filip, his commander, and now, it seemed, the partisans.

"Where's Rafał?" Bret asked, glancing around.

Tomasz's gaze dropped. "We're not quite sure."

A sense of dread gripped Bret's stomach and spread throughout his limbs. Not Rafał too.

Tomasz shifted and nodded to another partisan who approached. He wore an eye patch and had a fresh white bandage over his leg. He held out a hand to Bret.

"Name's Nowak. We're anxious for your help and military experience. We, uh, aren't too sure what we're doing other than stealing guns and killing Germans. We want to hit them more where it hurts—try to actually loosen the grip they have on us."

Bret frowned. "How many men do you have?"

"Fifty or so between Wygoda and Janów. A half dozen are pretty seriously wounded, but they can set a trap or sit in a sniper hole when needed."

A weight pressed on Bret's chest. How many more would be wounded by day's end? Week's end? How many would die? How many other fathers would suffer the same as Tomasz?

Bret motioned to an empty table. "Tell me more about your men, resources."

Nowak did so, and Bret fought back the urge to check his pocket watch to see how late it might be before he could reach Janów again.

He hated to be so far away from Adia while Werner and his men hovered so close to her—a minnow in a sea of sharks.

And now he'd have to balance coordinating partisan efforts with watching out for the uncertain future of Janów and the hidden American trainer in their ranks.

No matter the cost, he couldn't fail at either one.

24

OCTOBER 29, 1939

Adia tightened her coat against the wind and tucked her hat over her short hair, scanning the aisles as she constantly looked out for German soldiers. Secretly looking for any sign of Bret. No matter the danger or disagreement between them, she felt safe beside him.

She passed through the stallion barn as she wove her way toward the clock tower barn to check on Starlight, a brilliant white mare that was past due with her first foal. As she left the shelter of the tall wooden structure, a violent gust of wind slammed into her and lifted her hat from her head. She whirled and reached for it, running directly into a tall, muscular frame. As she reeled back, her heart lifted in hope that it was Bret. She gazed up and her smile froze on her face.

Oberst Werner Vogel stood before her, his shoulders square and one hand formally tucked behind his back with the other holding her ratty brown cap out to her.

Her pulse raced and cold air froze her lungs as she inhaled. *Do something. Say something.*

But his gaze captured her, deep pools of blue that looked upon her with interest but not even a hint of surprise.

He smiled and bowed slightly at the waist. "Fräulein."

She drew back a fraction of an inch, but somehow her feet were cemented to the hard ground.

He extended the hat. "Fräulein Kensington, is it not?" He lowered his hand and motioned for her to follow. "Come. We haven't been introduced yet, and we have much to discuss."

She shivered. How did he know her name? Bret's warnings flashed through her mind. *"Vogel is not to be trusted."*

"Please, fräulein," he said softly, his accent thick. "It's quite cold. Let's go to my office."

Filip's office, he meant. On the far side of the clock barn. Alone. Isolated.

The empty stalls around her offered her no ally or escape.

Her heart drummed in her chest. Why was he so casual? Why didn't he seem surprised? Had her disguise failed to fool him?

He stepped to her side and led her to the director's office. She walked alongside him, numb and mute and unaware of anything other than the thrumming of her pulse through her veins.

As they reached the simply furnished office, recently stripped of its treasures but patched together by Werner and his soldiers, Adia shook herself out of her daze. She wasn't without options or resources. She knew every location where a trophy still stood, next to a corresponding portrait of the winning horse. She could use those as weapons.

Werner cleared his throat and closed the door, and she jumped. He set her hat on the edge of his desk, walked around to sit in the chair, and motioned to the wooden seat next to her. "Please, fräulein. I've seen how hard you work, and you probably need a bit of a rest."

She clamped her jaw shut and sat on the edge of the chair.

He removed his own hat, and soft golden hair fell over the side of his brow, giving him a boyish look despite the crisp uniform and gleaming brass buttons. Unlike anytime she'd seen him interacting with his troops, his lips held a faint, humble smile as he took her in.

"You're wondering how I know your name. And perhaps how long I've known about your presence at Janów?"

She swallowed and nodded, fiddling with the frayed edge of her jacket sleeve.

He leaned forward, seeming interested and yet not intimidating. He was handsome.

"Your reputation is quite prolific." He chuckled. "And I've known since I arrived. You are in no danger. My men will not bother you." He pointed to her hat. "You've no reason to hide."

She frowned. If he'd known all along, were his assurances true? Had he been protecting her from being discovered or hassled? But she didn't let her guard down. Not yet.

"My name's Werner Vogel." He tilted his head. "And I would like to ask for your help."

She straightened, surprised. "What?"

"I've been tasked with rebuilding the Arabian bloodline in Poland."

Adia bit her lip, a flutter of excitement lifting away the fog of worry.

"I realize you have no reason to trust me, but I've dedicated my life to horses." He motioned to his uniform. "Don't let this fool you. It's a means to an end for me. It allowed me to reach the Olympics, even when I'm only a simple farmer's son."

She leaned forward the slightest bit.

"The Führer is building a better race of horses, collecting the finest horses from all of Europe in Hostau, Czechoslovakia. I've convinced him to keep the Polish stock here, but I'm not sure how long I can delay unless I can show significant progress."

Her chest constricted, as if the walls were closing in from all sides. Horses moving to Czechoslovakia? Images of the Russians leading columns of fine-blooded horses out of Janów, out of Poland forever, filled her mind. No more horses would leave while she had any say.

The colonel continued. "We've heard that Lubor has been seen in the southeastern area, and I've learned you were his primary handler."

Her breath caught, and she nodded.

"Would you be willing to join in our search parties? I'll ensure your safety and see that my men operate with the utmost propriety."

Her mind raced. She could look for Ewan at the same time. He and Lubor were rumored to be together.

"It'd be a great help to me, and I would love to learn all that you know of this renowned stallion and his fellow stock."

When she didn't answer, too stunned, he seemed to read the expression on her face.

"You may think on the matter. I will not pressure you if you prefer to remain on Janów grounds." He stood and bowed formally. He picked up her hat and presented it as if it were a royal crown, not a ratty, sodden pile of wool. "You've no reason to hide from me or my men. If you run into any trouble or need anything to better care for the horses, please don't hesitate to come to me."

She stood, anxious to leave and sort through the mess of new emotions. She tipped her head, took the hat with a trembling hand, and turned to leave.

As she strode to the door, an out-of-place photo caught her eye and she paused to look at the small shelf and simple brass frame. In it, three men in riding breeches and military riding jackets stood on a tiered podium with medals hanging around their necks. The younger visage of Werner Vogel stood on the topmost platform. Adia's eyes locked onto a different face—one that was familiar, his face set in a wry smile that held an air of bitterness.

Her mouth went dry, and she snapped her eyes away, afraid to linger too long and give herself away.

The Olympics.

Bret hadn't simply participated in the Olympics. He'd claimed a bronze medal.

Without stalling, knowing the German colonel's eyes tracked her every movement, she fled the office and raced back to her cabin.

Slamming the door behind her, she leaned against the wood barrier between her and the outside world, unable to catch her breath or fully comprehend all she'd learned. Her room was dark now that the sun had set.

"Have a nice meeting?" a deep voice asked from beside her.

She gasped in terror and whirled, propelling an elbow solidly into the tall intruder's chin.

———

Bret caught Adia's arm, but not fast enough. Pain shot through his face. He groaned, and she gasped as recognition flooded her features.

"Oh! I'm sorry."

He let her go and rubbed his stubble-covered chin. "At least I don't have to worry about you taking care of yourself."

Her furrowed brow deepened as her temper ignited and fire blazed in her deep brown gaze. "What are you doing in here?"

Her anger sliced through him, and his own anger rose in kind. The past weeks had worn out his patience and strength. Aside from assisting the partisans, he'd called in every favor he could of his remaining network and still had found no sign of Ewan or Lubor.

And when he'd finally been able to return to Janów, anxious to check in on Adia, he'd spotted her going into the office with the enemy, Werner Vogel.

"Have you found Ewan?" She took off her coat and hat and tossed them onto the back of a chair.

His own questions came fast, unbridled. "How did Werner discover you? What exactly did you two discuss in his office?"

Her face flushed. "What are you implying?"

"What happened in the time I've been away?"

It was petty to insinuate impropriety. But his mind had wandered through every possibility. He knew Werner was ambitious and unattached. And Adia was devoted to the horses. How far would she go?

Her gaze narrowed as the fire gave way to rage. "You're the spy. You tell me."

He turned to the door. "I shouldn't have come." Anger clouded every sense, and he knew it was best if he were nowhere near Adia.

She slid in between him and the door. Their bodies were close, her face tilted up so she could glare directly into his eyes.

His pulse raced, surprise bubbling up with the too-familiar desire to take her into his arms and kiss each of the worry lines on her face.

Blast it all. He let out a breath and broke away from the intensity of her stare.

"Please," she begged. "Did you see any sign of them?" Her voice trailed off and her eyes filled with tears.

Her pain collided into him, knocking the wind from his chest. How could he be so callous? He'd never answered her most important question. It was clear how it weighed her down.

He shook his head. The anger vanished as he pulled her into his arms, and she melted in silent tears. She was right to worry—the weather was deadly and time was short before snow could impact how far they'd be able to travel to search.

"I'm so sorry, Adia," he said softly. "We'll find Ewan."

She pushed free and wiped at her tears. "It's so cold out there."

"He's resourceful."

"Colonel Vogel." She straightened her shoulders. "He invited me along on their scouting trips to find Lubor. I can look for Ewan at the same time."

His fists tightened instinctively. "You cannot trust him. Give me time. I'll keep looking."

"I need to do something."

She looked up and their eyes held, mere inches apart. At this distance, he could smell the essence of her—soap and hay. He ached to pull her even closer and press his lips to hers, feel her warmth, her passion, her fire.

He closed his eyes. *God, help me get through to her.* "I just don't trust him or his men. Please, stay on the grounds where Filip and the others are close by."

She drew in a deep breath. "You might not trust him, but I feel as if I know more about Vogel after a ten-minute conversation than I do after weeks of being next to you every day."

"You know what he wants you to know."

"Not unlike you, Agent Conway."

He ground his back teeth together, anger spiking his pulse. "Keep your distance from the man."

She swallowed and seemed to inch a fraction closer. "Of the two of us, Bret, you are the expert at keeping your distance."

Her words stung—and her accusation wasn't true. They'd both agreed to keep their distance. To focus on what mattered.

But she was upset, and he knew there was no winning this battle.

Heat radiated off his entire being as he departed her cabin, every moment of training fighting to maintain control. But no one had trained him for this.

25

Most of the soldiers, including Werner, were gone on an overcast day when something new seemed to buzz in the air. Weeks had passed without sign of Bret, and the soldiers occupying Janów had rebuilt both the stock and the structures to nearly their former glory.

But it was hollow without the little Myszko. Without the prince, Lubor.

Adia was lost in it all, unable to find solid footing. Though the daily needs of the horses—feeding, cleaning, exercising—drove her into motion, her soul was unmoored.

The chill of freezing temperatures and the threat of early snow drove Werner and his men to more aggressively seek whatever stock they could find from the countryside. Despite her lingering anger with Bret, Adia had respected his request not to go with the search parties, with Werner.

She had worked with Dorek to train him to use a halter, respond to pressure, and not fight back when she directed his path. The little fireball was stubborn and hadn't taken to it well. Just like his half brother, Lubor, when Adia had been new to Janów.

"Adeeeeeea!" The faint word floated on the wind from across the grounds.

Adia's head snapped up from inside the paddock where she stood with Dorek. Dorek sensed her distraction and slipped out of her grasp, running in pride at outsmarting her.

Her heart thudded against her rib cage. Had she imagined the sound? She looked up into the cloudy sky, where shadows and light intermixed as seasons shifted.

"Adeeeeeea!" High-pitched, childlike.

She dropped Dorek's halter in the dirt, vaulted over the wooden fence, and jogged toward the source of the voice. Her head buzzed with the possibility, though her heart warned against it being true.

Ewan. That was Ewan's voice, no doubt.

She ducked though the foaling barn, racing past Filip, who sputtered and followed at a slower pace.

"Adeeea!"

Oh, God, let it be so. She raced into the clock tower barn and pushed open the large wooden door that led to the entrance and the lot of Nazi vehicles.

Her body froze, boots sliding to a stop.

A hundred yards down the driveway, a small figure walked alongside a lone horse, lead rope in hand. The horse's head was stooped down, but the way he moved was unmistakable.

Filip came around the corner behind her. "What in the world, Adia?" Then he saw them too. "Saints be . . ."

The boy, his clothes ragged and mud-soaked, his hair long and disheveled, smiled brilliantly and waved. "Adeeea!"

Adia laughed. "Ewan."

She raced toward him, the gravel flying beneath her boots. She dropped to her knees, not caring at the rocks that cut the fabric and stabbed her flesh. Scooping Ewan into her arms, she held the small, frail boy tightly as he wrapped his arms around her neck.

Alive.

Filip jogged up behind them and laughed. "Oh, dear boy," he

said. He took the lead rope from Ewan's grasp. "And you found our Lubor."

Adia looked up as if to truly believe it. There he was, watching her and Ewan curiously, his huge black eyes as intelligent as ever. But his fur was matted, dull, and his bones protruded as evidence of the lack of care and food.

Whatever the boy and the stallion had been through, it hadn't been a kind journey.

Adia pulled back and brushed the hair from Ewan's dirty face. His cheeks were sunken and his lips cracked, but he still smiled and beamed proudly.

"I found Lubor!" His proclamation came out as a squeak. "I found him for you."

Her heart constricted. Had he nearly killed himself in order to do this, for her? "How did you find your way home?"

"I found Lubor," Ewan said as if it were a triumphant chant. "And Meester Bret found both of us."

The buzz in her head moved to her ears. He'd done it—just as he'd promised. "Bret?"

Ewan nodded.

She looked around, but the driveway and forest beyond appeared vacant. Emotion swelled from deep inside.

"Where is he, Ewan?"

Bret turned away once he saw Adia run to the little thief. From his position deep in the forest and out of sight of the roadway, he couldn't hear the words exchanged, but he could picture her relief and joy. They probably matched his own emotions when he'd stumbled upon Lubor and Ewan over a hundred kilometers away, nestled in a broken old barn, eating stale hay and grain to survive.

Their trek back had been winding and harrowing, but now they were home. They were both malnourished and a shadow of their former selves, but Adia would nurse them back to health in no time.

Which meant Bret had to return to his mission with the partisans. He had little time to waste.

A twig snapped behind him and he turned, reaching for his pistol, then froze when he saw her behind him.

Adia hesitated for a moment, then sprinted toward him. He hardly had time to respond but caught her as her body slammed into his. She embraced him tightly, trembling.

"Thank you, Bret," she breathed against his neck.

He softened and ran a hand down her back. Words caught in his throat. What could he say after their horrible parting weeks ago? He hadn't returned with Lubor and Ewan just to get into her good graces. The little thief had stolen Bret's heart as equally as he had Adia's, and Bret had been desperate to save him.

"Where were they?" she asked.

"Almost to Warsaw."

She laughed and slowly pulled away, ducking her head as if embarrassed. His hand lingered on her arm for an extra heartbeat, but he'd seen the German soldiers assigned to Janów, including Werner, on their way back, which meant she had only a small window of time to get back to her post or she'd raise suspicion.

There simply wasn't ever enough time with her.

A lifetime might not even be enough. But he pushed that thought aside.

"I-I don't even have the words," she said, meeting his gaze and holding it boldly.

Moments passed as the tension between them sizzled in the air like a lightning storm. The hair on his arms stood on end, gooseflesh appearing under his warm layers of coats. In her deep, vulnerable eyes, he could see some of what she wanted to say. It was more than a thank-you . . . it was surprise and awe that he'd truly lived up to what he'd promised her.

Good. He'd do everything in his power to continue to live up to that expectation. She had put so much on the line in her own life for these horses, and though he couldn't be in the walls of Janów anymore, he'd ensure she felt safe even from afar.

He glanced toward the road. "You'd better get back and see to the boy and horse. The soldiers will be back any minute."

Her shoulders drooped ever so slightly. She smirked. "You're not going to hang around for your two-thousand-zloty reward?"

"Blast! Is that what it's up to?" Bret grinned. "Can you see that Ewan gets the reward?"

"I'll make sure of it." She took a step toward the road. "Where are you off to now?"

He took a step backward, knowing that distance was the best thing for her safety. "It's better if you don't know."

"The life of a spy."

"It's the path I chose." Hadn't he reminded himself of that again and again?

"Thank you," she whispered. Her face had tear streaks down either side.

He put his hands in his pockets to remove the temptation to take her back into his arms. "I won't be far away, Adia. I promise you."

Her gaze twinkled with tears in the dim lighting of the dark winter day. "I believe you."

26

"Oh, meine Güte . . . He is everything I had heard about and more."

Werner's eyes shone as he circled Lubor, his full focus devouring every inch of the stallion. Lubor returned the scrutiny uneasily.

Adia ran her hand over the thickening coat of fur due to the cold weather, absence of muscle and fat evident to her practiced hands. Her mind and body still trembled from the shock of everything. Ewan's return. Bret's role in it all.

"You should have seen him a few months ago," she said, biting back a tone of accusation.

"His fine features are not diminished. A few months of proper feed and your expert care and he'll surely return to form."

A flutter of pride filled her chest at the confidence in his voice. "We could use a bit more grain to ensure the horses don't lose more weight," she said, testing the waters. "It's getting so cold at night."

"Of course. I'll see to it." Werner glanced around. "Where is the boy who returned him? He deserves the reward indeed."

"He's with Filip. He was also tired and in need of food."

"A true marvel, a boy and a horse surviving so much." Werner

208

kept his distance as if awaiting Lubor's permission and acceptance. "The boy was Filip's assistant, you said?"

She nodded, a cough itching at her throat from deep in her chest. She covered her mouth with a gloved hand, and Lubor nudged her elbow.

Werner's gaze darted to her, and he took a step toward her. "Are you ill, fräulein?"

"No," she croaked before clearing another tickle. "It must just be the dry air."

Werner frowned, looking uncertain. "I could call upon the physician to be sure."

"No," she said quickly. "I'm fine."

Though the depth of his concern was reassuring, she couldn't fathom using precious favors from the German officer on herself. There were far greater needs at Janów.

Werner turned back to Lubor and stepped closer carefully.

She expected the horse to nip or flinch when the Nazi reached out to pet him, but Lubor just turned his head and sniffed his arm. Odd. The stallion tended to mistrust men, which was how she'd come to be his primary handler.

"I heard much of Lubor's sire when I was a boy. I was lucky to visit Janów in '29 while on leave. It will be wonderful to fill the fields once more."

She bristled. So many had been lost. Lubor sensed her mood, and he pranced in place, pulling at the lead rope in her hands.

They put Lubor back into his stall and fed him another small ration of grain, and Adia slid the stall latch closed.

In the stall next to Lubor, an equally ragged Wojownik peered back at her.

Her heart fluttered in relief. "I still can't believe you found him too."

Werner chuckled. "A fortunate day for the breeding program, indeed."

Having both fine horses back within the walls of Janów left her feeling more whole than she had in a long time. But then, perhaps it was Ewan's return too.

Wojownik's black eyes were wild, unsettled. She'd have some work to do to rebuild his trust and calm the anxiousness that had always sat under the surface. Whatever had happened to Wojownik while he wandered the Polish lands, whether the gunshots and bombs and rumbling tanks or the lack of food, had left him damaged deep beyond the surface.

She ran her hand along his nose, but he startled and jumped to the back of his stall, pointing his nose into the corner.

"You know, Miss Kensington . . ." Werner's voice went gravelly and thick with emotion. "It really is a wonder that you've overcome so much."

She pressed her lips together. "What do you mean?"

"I don't imagine that as a woman—a young woman—you've had the most supportive of audiences. It was a trial for me to overcome the stigma of my class. A poor farmer's son had no place among the elite competitors."

"And yet you won the gold for Germany in the Olympics," she said.

He flushed. "The military afforded me chances I never otherwise could have had. You did not have such a means, yet here you are."

Here she was, as far from her dream as she'd ever been.

He seemed to pick up on her pensive silence. "The conflict will not last forever. Things will be different from what you've become accustomed to here in Poland, but we can trade and prosper and grow the bloodline as before."

She shook her head in disbelief. "Why do the Nazis even care about these horses?"

"We believe we can create a better breed." He swallowed. "A master race of horses. Though I do not agree with Herr Rau on the mixing of breeds. I believe the purity of each should be maintained, and I intend to see Janów stock remain here and safe."

She nodded and covered another cough, this one feeling rough along her throat.

"I care greatly for these horses, Adia." Werner paused, his deep blue gaze holding hers. "I promise I'll do everything in my power to keep them safe."

She raised her chin and looked to Wojownik, still cowering in the corner of his stall. "So will I."

DECEMBER 20, 1939

"You're absolutely certain of this, Scottie?" Bret asked the youth as they strode through a tense crowd in Wygoda. Civilians glanced at the soldiers patrolling and stationed on each street corner. The once jovial town now felt like a powder keg ready to burst.

"'Course I'm sure. Just remember your side of the bargain."

He did. Scottie's information came at a price. As long as you paid, it was tried-and-true.

"You'd do well for yourself at MI6," Bret said softly as he brushed past a couple huddled together, their eyes darting around nervously.

Scottie huffed. "That might be all well and good for you noble sorts. But there's no money in valor. There's plenty here in the shadows."

Bret couldn't fault the boy his logic. Valor these days came at a cost for all.

But if Scottie's source proved to deliver, at least he could demand justice. Or was it revenge? The lines were hazy in his mind.

Whatever it really was, Charlie was dead, and Scottie had potentially located the man responsible.

A shiver raced down Bret's spine as if gusted by an arctic breeze, though the wind hadn't blown and the mass of bodies around them insulated them from the growing chill of the oncoming winter.

They drew near a towering, narrow apartment building, and Scottie strode through the door without hesitation. "I'll go around back in case he bolts," he said over his shoulder, and slipped away.

Bret froze before the apartment door, the number Scottie had given him. He'd envisioned for months what he'd do if he got his hands on Charlie's murderer. Now his hands shook and his stomach tied in knots.

It was now or never.

He could finally tell Elizabeth that he'd caught the man responsible for her husband's death. Would that mean she'd stop blaming him? Would it mean he would stop blaming himself?

"Quick, Conway! He's going out the window!"

At Scottie's cry, all hesitation fled, and adrenaline took hold. Bret smashed the door in and saw a thin man sliding through a window above the kitchen sink. Scottie came in through a back door in the alley behind the building. Bret raced over, gripped the man's ankle, and pulled hard.

The man cried out, fell, and crashed back into the kitchen. His head slammed into the porcelain sink, which shattered. Bret threw the man up against a wall and held his collar in his fist.

"No, please!" the man cried out, holding his hands up over his face. "Don't hurt me."

"Talk to me," Bret growled. His body went hot, all earlier indecision now funneled into rage. "Let's discuss how you hurt Charlie Knightly. What chance did you give him?"

The man went still. His hands fell slowly, and he looked at Bret, a flicker of recognition dawning. Recognition and . . . terror.

Certainty filled Bret. If the man was terrified, it must mean he was guilty.

"Charlie Knightly?" The man shook his head. "No, no. That wasn't my fault. A German threatened to kill my family."

"Convenient story."

He shook his head again and looked over at a framed photo on the counter. A woman with two young children. "Their death wasn't convenient for me at all."

Something in his voice rang true. The pain. The deep regret.

Bret glanced over at Scottie, who had slackened his shoulders ever so slightly. No. It couldn't be true.

"Who?" Bret tightened his grip. "How did the Germans get involved?"

"I don't know. They knew Knightly and Conway would be meeting with someone in their own network—a Nazi officer gone rogue. They took my family the day before and said they wouldn't be harmed if I delayed the officer from reaching the rendezvous point."

"Why?"

"They wanted to intercept you and Knightly en route and planned to punish the traitor later." The man's muddy brown eyes filled with tears. "They killed my family anyway."

The atmosphere in the apartment went cold. The living room still had scattered toys full of dust, and a woman's apron rested on the counter next to a pile of dusty and rusting pans. It was as if the man hadn't touched anything in the past few months. His ragged clothes, greasy hair, and overwhelming stench echoed the lack of care.

"Whoever you were supposed to meet with was big," he said.

"Why did they leave you alive then?" Scottie piped up.

"Because I didn't know anything. And death would have been a welcome respite." He motioned around the apartment.

"Tell me more about the officer we were supposed to meet." Bret's heart hammered like a thousand cannons firing in succession.

"I never saw his face, but he spoke Polish quite well. Young, I'd guess."

That wasn't much to go on.

A dead end.

"Who else did he know?" Scottie asked, stepping in as Bret fell into a daze.

Bret heard few words but could make sense of what the man said: a whole lot of nothing. Nothing. No hope of justice for Charlie.

No peace for Elizabeth.

No way for Bret to ever face his sister again.

27

As early winter storms shortened the days and snow covered the hillsides, Janów became insulated from most of the outside world. Rumors of Germany's next plans circled the barns, but Adia's days were as they had been months earlier: cleaning stalls, exercising horses, tending wounds, and scrounging up as much food and as many supplies as possible.

The rest of her energy was in minding Ewan, seeing his health rebound, and teaching him to read and write into the night. His presence, and Lubor's, had set many things right within her heart and soul, but the weeks since she'd seen or heard from Bret left her uneasy.

"What is going on here?" Werner's voice boomed out through the aisles of the stallion barn early one morning, and Adia instinctively froze and peeked around the corner as she was dumping grain into a feeder.

The colonel stood in front of Lubor's stall, the door open to reveal Lubor lying in the fresh straw with three blond children leaning against him and Ewan standing at the doorway. Ewan had a book in hand and slammed it shut, tucking it behind his back.

Adia's heart thudded in fear, but Werner only cocked his head and crossed his arms in an exaggerated motion.

Ewan straightened and lifted his chin. "I just showed my friends the greatest stallion, Lubor. That is all."

Adia smelled his lie from all the way across the aisle.

"I heard you singing the Polish anthem." Werner shook his head. "This is forbidden."

"Sing?" Ewan said. "No, not me. I am a bad singer."

Adia bit her lower lip to keep from smiling, though the fear still clawed at her gut.

"And the book you're hiding behind your back?" Werner held out his hand. "Where did you find it?"

Ewan sighed and handed him the small schoolbook written in Polish. Another forbidden item. Adia cursed under her breath. Why didn't he listen to her? She'd forbidden him to take it from the hidden cubby beneath her floorboards. The Germans had shut down all the schools months ago and issued a dozen other decrees to eliminate all Polish history and culture from civilization.

Werner looked over the book and huffed a sigh. "This is quite serious, child. The punishment is imprisonment and hard labor."

Adia gripped the wooden doorway to keep from wavering, but something kept her from rushing to Ewan's defense. Something in Werner's voice.

The colonel tucked the book into his pocket. "You must not convene these school lessons anymore. Do you understand?"

Ewan nodded and motioned to the kids, and they all scurried free from the stall. Lubor huffed as if unperturbed by the commotion, and his ears flicked back and forth.

Werner closed the stall door. When he saw Adia, his face flushed and he straightened uncomfortably, not unlike Ewan did every time she caught him with stolen goods.

She coughed into her fist to cover up a smile that snuck through.

He clasped his hands behind his back and nodded to Lubor's stall. "Did you know about these rogue school sessions?"

She shook her head. "Of course not."

"Rules are rules, fräulein." He shrugged and stepped closer to

215

her, donning his more usual air of authority and confidence. "I am accountable for all that happens on the grounds."

"Then why were you so lenient?"

A smile tugged at the corner of his lips. "Perhaps it is because I see a little of myself in that boy—Ewan, is it?"

She nodded. Briefly, her first meeting with Bret flashed through her mind. How Bret had also feigned scorn while letting the boy off with a much-needed lesson learned.

"This is the only warning he gets," Werner said somberly. "I can't have word getting around that I've flouted the edicts of my Führer."

Her chest constricted in fear for Ewan, the habitual rule breaker. "I understand. I'll make sure he does too."

Ewan's slipup, while small on the surface, only put Adia further into the colonel's debt, and she needed to carefully meter her favors.

But how was she to juggle all that needed to be balanced? Families at Janów were starving, and now Ewan defied German rules every chance he could get.

She tracked the boy down to his favorite escape—a hayloft in the back barn, far from the noise and buzz of the busier barns. There were still only fifty or so horses total, leaving this building empty.

She climbed up the wooden ladder and spotted him tucked in the corner, knees to his chest and face drawn. His tattered coat and undershirts were frayed on the sleeves and elbows, and his pants were getting shorter by the day as he grew taller. The wool socks peeked underneath.

"Myszko?"

He didn't move or respond to her. She ducked to walk under the low ceiling and sat beside him. The wooden loft was swept clean but still smelled of mildew and mouse nests.

"Ewan," she said sternly, "I thought we talked about this. You have to obey the rules—"

"I want to go with Meester Bret and fight the Germans," Ewan said, his face red and tears streaking down his cheeks. "He does not follow these stupid rules. He fights against the bad men."

Her heart fell into the pit of her stomach. She understood the desire. But she knew their limits, and Ewan didn't. "This is the safest place for us, Ewan. And we must look after the horses."

"Horses belong to Poland, not Herr Hitler." Ewan glowered and refused to meet her gaze.

"I know."

"You do not fight."

The words stung. He was still so young, and while insightful and resilient, he'd only known Janów Podlaski as his home and world.

How could she make him understand? She'd never understood children—never felt like she'd been able to be a kid when her parents left her behind with her domineering aunt.

"There's a long winter ahead, Ewan," she whispered. "Bret has his mission and we have ours. Please understand that I've not given up anything. We will make sure these horses are safe and that they remain true to Poland."

Ewan finally met her gaze, his red-rimmed eyes glistening with tears. "I am afraid, Amerykanka. I am afraid Poland is lost."

She pulled him into a hug and squeezed. She didn't have any words to comfort him, not when she had the very same fear.

———

Bret wandered slowly and, in a haze, blindly found his way back to the hollowed-out pub that had become a safe house for the partisans.

He could hardly process all he'd learned from the man, and how Charlie's murderers were still unknown. They'd left the contact shaken but unharmed in his apartment of broken things and dusty memories.

The memory of it all left Bret uneasy, and his thoughts somehow drifted back to Adia. As if the constant nagging doubt that he'd caused his best friend's death hadn't been enough of a reason to keep her and the feelings she stirred up at a distance, this was all the more a reminder.

At the sound of banter from Nowak, Tomasz, and the others, he shed his confusion and frustration. He'd find a new lead, or perhaps Scottie would dig something up in his own right. The kid was relentless.

Their leader, Nowak, sat at the same dusty table in the back corner, playing cards with Tomasz and a few others. He had added a new wound to the collection on his right hand.

Bret nodded to the bandage. "Have you considered trying not to get hit with bullet-shaped projectiles?"

Tomasz sat at the table next to him. "We at least have learned to keep our distance from him when the shooting starts."

Nowak glowered. "Very funny."

"Where did you strike?" Bret's mind latched on to this new topic.

"Supply lines, as you suggested," Nowak said, wincing as he rubbed his arm. "They were more heavily guarded than we'd prepared for. Could use your help next go-round."

"We think Rafał's going to be in the next caravan," Tomasz said.

Bret's stomach clenched, and he nodded. "I'll be there."

Tomasz only slouched farther down as if pressed by the weight of the world. "Just be careful, Bret. You have a role to play beyond this war, and we're counting on you to watch over Adia."

Nowak cleared his throat. "Ah, so there's a girl?"

Bret shot him a glare. "No. It's not like that."

Tomasz chuckled, though it sounded tired. "I sure hope you're better at lying under torture than you are about the fair-faced American lass."

"I'm not lying." Where had this boyish reaction even come from? He hadn't stumbled like this since grade school. "You know the risks of my work. I can't ask that of her no matter what I might feel."

"What is life other than a series of risks?" Tomasz said, suddenly somber and almost challenging with his tone.

"Some risks are more severe than others," Bret fired back. "I'll never ask that of someone I care about."

"Have you given her that choice?"

"She's not too keen on me right now. Perhaps ever."

"We all steal moments from death and must treasure what time we are given with the ones we love. You think I'd go back and wish my Lukas was never born even if I knew the pain I'd endure? Or never marry my Elena knowing a terrible sickness would steal her far too early?" Tomasz's face flushed. "I'd never trade a moment of it. I'd suffer the loss a hundred times over every time."

Bret felt a pang of anguish imagining all that Tomasz had endured. And yet Tomasz so ardently insisted on love. Could he be right? Could it still be worth it?

Tomasz drew in a deep breath. "Forgive me, Bret. I do not presume to know what is best for you." He stood, the wooden chair legs scraping the floor harshly, then stomped out and slammed the door behind him. If they had a lead on Rafał's location, it wasn't surprising for Tomasz to be off-kilter.

A shiver raced down Bret's spine as he watched the closed door. Was Tomasz right? Or was Bret's situation truly different?

Tomasz's choices were his own. Bret didn't have the time or energy to think beyond the more pressing matters. He might not be able to bring Charlie's murderer to justice yet, but he could deliver Tomasz's other son from certain death.

Nowak sighed dramatically. "War." He shook his head and caught Bret's gaze. "It either breaks a man"—he leaned in—"or builds him."

28

DECEMBER 22, 1939

Adia held out her small bundle of rations to Henryk, one of the few grooms who had stayed at Janów and not evacuated Poland. "Please, take this. Zara and the children need it much more than I do." She winced at the cough erupting from her chest, and she covered her mouth with her free hand. Her cough had only grown worse the past few days.

The thin, short, frizzy-haired man shuffled his feet, and tears glistened in his eyes. "Miss Adia, we simply cannot."

"Please, dear friend, I know how ill Andrzej is. There's an entire jar of broth in there." Her throat closed, her eyes watering from the pain in her throat and deep in her soul. She swallowed back the cough that threatened again. "Please," she rasped. "Take it."

Henryk went still, the pain in his eyes stabbing her to the core. If only she'd worked harder, if she'd been able to get more food before . . .

"I'll get more from Werner when he and Filip return from Hostau."

He took the package, mumbled his thanks, and slipped out of the barns to return to his home on the outskirts of the farm.

Ewan stepped up to her side and tugged at her hand. "Amerykanka, can we go home? Will you rest now?"

Adia stumbled, caught herself on the stall door, and let out another cough that clawed at her insides. Its raw force doubled her over. Her throat burned, her head screamed, and her stomach burned from the violent motion.

She'd failed to get Zara and Henryk more food earlier. If she had, their youngest one might not have . . .

"Amerykanka?" Ewan's hand came to her shoulder.

Her skin burned hot under her winter hat and coat, but she brushed off the thought that she might have a fever. It was simply all the exertion today. Half the soldiers were with Filip and Werner in Czechoslovakia, so she was working far more than normal to keep up on the duties.

"I'm okay," she whispered through cracked lips. She drew herself up slowly, her head swimming.

"Home?" Ewan repeated.

She shook her head. "We need to top off the water for the stallions first."

"But—"

She stumbled toward the spigot despite Ewan's protests. The water sputtered out and into the empty metal pail that shook in her hands. Why were her hands trembling? The bucket felt far heavier than normal, so she only filled it halfway, but her balance shifted, and her feet came out from under her. The water spilled onto the frozen earth, and she landed on her side in the mud.

Her chest ached and her brain pounded against her skull. Somehow, even her fingernails seemed tender in their nail beds.

Her vision blurred, and Ewan's cries to her sounded a mile away.

Get up, Adia. Get home, rest a while, and everything will be fine.

"Amerykanka!" Ewan shouted. "I will find Meester Bret."

"No!" she croaked. "Don't fetch him."

Of anyone on the planet, she couldn't face Bret right now. Though they'd parted on neutral terms, she feared the flutter in her stomach and the way Bret saw through everything she said.

He'd figure out in no time that she'd defied his request to keep away from Werner. She'd been steadily paying more and more attention to Werner with the aim of solidifying his attachment to her. It was just now starting to pay off, and she needed to hold on to every bit of progress. Ewan counted on her, especially if he slipped up and was caught pickpocketing.

No, she couldn't face Bret. She didn't need him. A solid night's rest and she'd be fine.

Her eyelids slid shut as her limbs grew heavy, and her body fell completely to the ground. She needed to try to get back to her cabin, but somehow her hands and feet weren't responding to the will of her brain.

Move, Adia. But she couldn't. The cold of the ground seeped through her coat but then faded from her awareness. She'd stay right here a while longer then.

Too tired to fight it, she embraced the darkness around her.

Bret leaned over Adia and pressed a cool cloth to her feverish forehead. Her brow was creased, and she groaned in pain through the fog of unconsciousness.

She had yet to wake from her fall. Ewan had run the entire two kilometers in the cold evening air to find Tomasz to learn of Bret's location. The little thief had slunk into the partisans' hideaway without being seen, giving Bret the scare of his life.

"Adeeea is sick. She will not wake up."

Could any other cluster of words be as terrifying?

Adia had burned with fever since he'd carried her back to her cabin. Her hair stuck to the damp skin of her neck and brow, and her body shivered uncontrollably, no matter the number of blankets he piled on top of her.

"Please wake up," he whispered, his voice husky and his throat tight in fear. Frustration boiled up at the edges of that fear. How had she come this far without anyone seeing how ill she was? Every piece of him wanted to blame Werner or Filip. He wanted—needed— someone to blame other than himself. If he'd checked in with Ewan face-to-face, if he'd been closer to her, if he'd paid better attention . . .

I'm so sorry, Adia.

She moaned and turned to him, her eyes fluttering open.

His pulse raced and his heart collided against his rib cage. He cupped the sides of her face with his hands, the skin hot under his touch.

She covered his hands with her own, her movements slow and groggy. Her gaze searched him and then finally met his. "That little traitor." Her voice was soft and hoarse. "I told Ewan not to bother you."

"He should have bothered me much sooner." He pulled away and reached for a pitcher of water. He needed something else for his hands to do. Surely she could hear the cry of his heart when he sat so close. "How long have you been ill? When was the last time you ate anything?"

Though her baggy clothing disguised it, he had felt just how much weight she'd lost when he carried her to her cabin, and now he could see it in the hollows of her face and the sharpness of her cheekbones.

She gave him a lazy, almost coy smile and took the glass he'd poured. "It's nice to see you too."

"This is no joke. You passed out hours ago."

"I'm not sick, just tired."

"And the fever?"

"I've been working too hard." She took a sip and wouldn't meet his gaze, her hands and limbs still trembling with chills.

"Ewan said you're giving all your rations away."

She lowered the glassful of barely touched water to her lap. The trace of good humor fled from her lips and her eyebrows tensed in sorrow. He'd struck a nerve.

"To the Byzkos?" he probed.

She looked across the room to Ewan, who was curled up in the corner near his open hatch, reading a book by soft candlelight. "They have so many children to feed. They're all starving."

"And if you starve?"

"Halina died last week," she said. The water sloshed onto the blanket in her lap, but she paid it no mind. Her gaze locked onto his, tears brimming on her lashes. "She was two years old, Bret." She lifted the glass and set it on the small table beside her, her hand unsteady.

He mourned with her and for all the children and adults who teetered on the edge of such a fate in Wygoda. Too many to count.

"I'm sorry," he whispered. "I hadn't heard about Halina."

Adia looked away and then burst into a cough that racked her entire being. As it finally subsided, she leaned against her pillow and swallowed with a sharp wince.

He stood and fetched the smoldering stew from the pot that he'd asked Ewan to secure a few hours earlier. When the boy had returned with the small potatoes and a lamb bone, Bret ensured that the thief had, in fact, purchased the goods.

"Yes, with coins you gave me, Meester Bret," Ewan had assured him.

He took a small bowl to Adia, but she shook her head. "I'm not hungry."

"This isn't up for discussion. You can do it yourself, or I'll feed you."

She glowered but slowly adjusted herself and took the bowl. Each spoonful was slow and painful to watch, with coughing fits interrupting her periodically, but after an hour, she'd consumed at least most of the broth.

Her hair fell over one side of her face, the short ends now reaching her chin and curling in an enticing way.

He cleared his throat. "How are things?"

She cast him a side glance though she kept focused on her bowl. "Werner is doing all he can to protect the horses."

And was he keeping a respectful distance? He silently cursed Nowak and Antek for their endless missions that kept him distracted from digging more into Vogel and his intentions.

"Don't look so worried." She set the bowl aside and coughed into one hand. "You look as if I announced my engagement to him."

His jaw clenched at the thought. "Don't even suggest that."

"I don't care for Werner in that way." She coughed again. "You know me better than that."

"War can change people." His mind drifted back to Tomasz and the distance still between them after their argument about love, war, and risk.

"And I thought I was the jaded one." She coughed, more deeply and violently than any time before.

He leaned over and helped her settle back against the pillow when her coughing subsided. Her forehead remained etched in pain. This was serious. She'd need more than broth—more than what he or Scottie could procure. Weeks ago, medicine had simply run out throughout much of the partisan supplies and even in German shipments.

As much as it hurt to admit, he'd need to call upon other options to save her.

"Ewan," Bret said, "fetch Werner when he returns. He can get Adia the medicine she needs."

"Or I steal medicine?" Ewan perked up.

"No!" Adia and Bret said in unison.

She rose partially to meet Ewan's gaze with disapproval. "We talked about this, Ewan."

"Yes, Amerykanka," he muttered, turning back to his book.

Adia leaned back against the pillow, and Bret helped her pull the blankets tighter around her neck. Her pained expression seemed to ease as she closed her eyes and welcomed sleep.

"I'll see about smuggling more food for the Byzkos, Adia. Promise me you'll stop giving away your rations."

She nodded without opening her eyes. "Thank you, Bret." Her

voice drifted, and he prayed she'd truly heard him and understood the gravity of his concern.

As her breathing steadied and all the lines in her face disappeared, he leaned forward and brushed his lips lightly on her warm forehead.

Such a fool, he chided himself. This could never be, no matter how much he wished it were otherwise. What a fool he was to even think he had the ability to protect her in the face of German oppression.

He'd failed everyone he'd ever loved. Why did he think this would turn out differently?

29

Several weeks and doses of sulfa antibiotics later, Adia emerged from the haze of her illness, but she had yet to fully recover from the deep emotions Bret's nearness had stirred.

The New Year had come and gone with no fanfare. A new decade, a new era of life at Janów.

Adia brushed her fingers over her temple as if she could wipe away the recollections that burned her mind and her skin. The fever-induced delirium had done little to lessen the memories. His lips pressed to her forehead. His closeness. His tenderness.

"Fräulein?"

She jumped and looked up at Werner, who stood next to her in the clear, cool light of the January day. What had they been talking about? He'd asked her to examine an abscess in Starlight's hoof.

"Oh yes, let's see." She bent over, grateful to find the action didn't mean instant dizziness. She ran her hand down the horse's silvery-white leg, and Starlight obediently picked up her foot and let Adia hold it gently in her hands as she looked over the crescent-shaped appendage.

But for perhaps the first time she could recall, a horse and its injury couldn't hold her attention.

After Bret had left her cabin, Ewan had dutifully and begrudgingly fetched the acting director of Janów to let him know of her illness. Werner had swooped in with not only one but two doctors and an ensemble of medication, enough to ease an entire small town and perhaps save a dozen lives. It had racked her with guilt to take even the slightest amount. And yet, she was relieved to feel nearly normal.

Physically, at least.

Her heart was another matter. It had been so much easier to hate Bret for his lies while they were out looking for Ewan and Lubor. She had even been able to steel her heart against him and the gentle way he'd cared for her while she was ill. But then she heard Ewan say only that morning, "Food appeared for Henryk and Zara and their family, like from angels!"

Angels, indeed. Bret had assured her he would help, and he had. Suddenly she hadn't felt wholly responsible for the world and for the lives around her. And the Byzkos weren't the only starving family to be visited by the food angel.

Gratitude, admiration, and awe had filled her at Bret's uncanny ability to do all and be everywhere.

Starlight shifted, and Werner cleared his throat behind her.

She set the hoof down, blinking away the sea of errant thoughts. "Yes, it's healing quite well."

Werner patted the mare's fluffy, winter-thick coat and studied Adia in his silent, brooding manner. She should not have let her thoughts wander so far in his presence. It was as if he could sense it.

"You should be resting, Adia. We can get along fine without you for a few more days."

"Thank you, but the fresh air is helpful." She patted Starlight's neck and untied her lead rope to take her back to her stall.

"I don't want to risk your health." Werner followed them. "You are a valuable asset to the operations here at Janów."

She smiled. His concern was genuine, even if she knew it was entirely centered on the horses. Or could it be deeper? She compared

228

Werner to Bret and found similarities in their doting and careful attention. Since Werner had returned, he'd never left her side, which came with its own downside.

Bret didn't show up for any surprise visits, and it also meant Ewan kept his distance, as ordered by Filip, Bret, and Adia separately. They feared the boy's unpredictable ability to keep secrets and his distaste for the man who had seized Lubor in the name of Germany's Führer.

Thus, even with Werner's proximity and respectful attention, Adia was lonely.

She slipped away from him later that evening, claiming to return to her cabin for a rest. She wandered into the stallion barn, now quiet, as all the stalls had been cleaned and the grain distributed. There was at least someone at Janów she could now turn to.

Lubor's dark eyes locked on her, and his sleek black muzzle poked through the metal rails. He blew hot air against her cheek in greeting.

"Hey there, handsome," she whispered.

A deep voice rumbled behind her, "Ah, you're too kind."

For a moment, her heart lifted before her mind fully processed who that warm voice belonged to. It was not the one she'd hoped for, but a wonderful surprise all the same.

Adia whirled and encircled the man in her arms, joy and sorrow whirling inside her. "Tomasz! Where have you been?" She hadn't seen him since the river crossing, though she knew from Bret that he'd been staying and working with the partisans in Wygoda.

"Oh, here and there." He pulled back and looked her over. "I heard you were desperately ill."

"That is a bit overstated." She waved him off. "I'm fine, really."

"Word reached us about Lubor's return." His eyes clouded. "Can you ever forgive me for not getting Ewan and Lubor safely home? I failed them and you."

Tears stung her eyes. "If I hadn't left you all as I did at the river, leaving Ewan behind like that"—she choked on her words—"perhaps Lukas would never have . . ." The ache in her chest and the tiredness in her bones intensified. "I am the one who should beg your forgiveness."

Lukas and Rafał were his only children, though she knew he and Elena had yearned for so many more. And sweet Elena's death a few years ago still felt so fresh.

Adia reached into her nearly worn-out boot lining and pulled out the small, paper-wrapped bundle she'd carried for months. She handed it to him, and he unwrapped the locket carefully, tears slipping down his cheeks for a moment before he wrapped it back up and tucked it safely into his pocket.

Tomasz took her hands and squeezed them, kind and reassuring. Was this the mark of a good father? She believed so. After all, Tomasz had been more of a father to her in a few years than her own had been in his lifetime.

"There is no blame to be cast, Adia. Lukas was itching to go and fight for his country. Nothing would have stopped him." Tomasz leaned in. "I must keep my head low, but I could use your help. It's best if you know little as to why."

She pressed her lips together. "This sounds familiar."

Tomasz lifted a bushy brow. "Oh, give Bret a break. He's doing the best he can."

"So he claims."

"He cares for you." His voice softened. "You know that."

She did. And perhaps that made all the past lies so much harder.

"Does he know about this . . . request?" she asked.

Tomasz adopted a guilty grimace. "Not exactly. We don't quite see eye to eye on this point."

"How so?"

He glanced around. "We need as much information as we can get about the prisoner transfer routes—several of our men are captured." He hesitated. "We think Rafał is a prisoner too."

"Rafał!" Her heart seized.

Tomasz nodded. "I suspect Werner has access to all the information."

"Really?"

"We think he has military command for much of this region," Tomasz whispered.

"But Bret doesn't want me involved."

"Not in the slightest bit."

Indignation rose in her chest, pressing against her already fragile lungs on the cusp of recovery. Of course he wouldn't want her to do this. And after all he'd done to protect her and Ewan, was it fair to defy his wishes? But . . . for Rafał? Was it worth the risk? For Tomasz and all her beloved Poland?

"I won't ask anything other than the next caravan—I just want to find my son."

Adia's heart twisted. Forget about Bret and his reservations. He couldn't protect her all the time, and he wasn't the only one who was willing to risk it all to do what was right.

"I'll help," she whispered back. "What do you need me to do?"

JANUARY 13, 1940

Blast it all. Bret ground his teeth to keep from cursing aloud as he looked at their enemy over the hillside.

Not only were they outnumbered three to one, but they were hopelessly outgunned. Their rifles and handguns with a handful of spare ammunition paled compared to the German convoy's three .50 caliber machine guns mounted into trucks and the shiny new rifles carried by the soldiers.

Tomasz had delivered them information about the location of the motorcade but refused to tell Bret the source or provide further details. It had been a gamble, and now they faced harrowing odds.

Nowak shifted in the brush next to him, his most recently injured foot probably flaring in pain. "Don't worry, mate," he said as if reading Bret's thoughts. "It's a good plan. We'll get 'em all out."

At what cost?

Bret scanned the dozen trucks covered in dark canvas, each loaded with two guards, and the four escort vehicles in the front and rear of the parade. Twenty-five or thirty Germans.

But inside the trucks were one hundred prisoners, some familiar faces among them. Some who knew too much about partisan secrets and operations and would be tortured until they gave it all up. After all, every man and woman had their breaking point.

Most importantly, Rafał was in there.

This was safest—and yet a dozen lives could be lost in this pursuit. Men who'd put their lives, their trust, in Bret's hands.

"They're nearing the fork in the road," Nowak said. "Shall I give the signal?"

Bret's fingers gripped the cold metal of his Luger. If he said nothing, the caravan would pass unhindered, and no lives would be lost today. At least no one under his command.

Confound it all. This was the reason he'd pursued espionage. He'd argued this again and again with the General, but his father would never understand Bret's choice. The General had been hardened to war, to death. But no matter how many men Bret had seen fall, it stung the same each time, and every time he wished it could have been him instead. This was why he'd hoped a life in intelligence could save those around him, no matter the personal cost. Then it was only his neck on the line.

"Conway!" Nowak hissed. "We may never get a shot again."

"Give the signal." Bret flattened against the ground as Nowak made a distinct trilling birdcall.

A heartbeat later, six shots rang out nearly in unison, and six Germans, each of the individuals at the .50 caliber guns, cried out and fell.

In the span of one breath, rifles were racked once more, another chorus echoed, another six soldiers fell.

The vehicles screeched to a stop and all weapons turned on the forests surrounding the convoy.

Nowak had spoken highly of his snipers, and they did not disappoint.

Several more partisans fired in multiple directions, which sent the Germans into a panic.

"Now!" Bret shouted, and the partisans closed in, German soldiers falling in pairs as the closer range led to more accurate hits for the snipers.

Bret rose, held his gun level with his target, pulled the trigger. The soldier fell with a shoulder, and hopefully not fatal, wound. Bret pivoted to the next, mirrored the aim and pull, and moved forward.

Moments later, the gunfire faded to silence as the band of partisans swarmed the trucks and methodically leaned over each downed soldier, stripping weapons, money, and spare ammunition.

Bret focused in on the trucks, his heart hammering in his chest as unease filled him. Too easy.

He jogged up to the first truck and looked in the back. A dozen men with dirt-covered faces and tattered clothing stared back.

"Run—you're free," he said in Polish. The tightly packed truck thinned as the men, eager and quick-stepped, filed out onto the road.

At the end of the group, a tall, lean frame caught Bret's eye. Relief filled him, though his nerves were still taut with adrenaline.

He clapped Rafał's hand hard and slapped his shoulder. "It's good to see you, my friend."

Rafał's deep brown eyes were wide, unfocused, as he scanned the scene around them. A deep bruise lined his chin, and several gashes tore his brow and hands. "You have no idea how glad I am to see you."

Gunfire sliced through the air and both Rafał and Bret jumped, hunching down and looking for the threat. A fallen soldier on the ground, firing wildly with his Luger toward the partisans around him, thankfully missing.

Nowak limped up to the wounded soldier, knocked the gun from the German's hands. "Take this one for interrogating," he sneered.

"Let's get out of here." Bret led Rafał away. "Your father is anxious to see you."

"I imagine. Especially after . . ." His voice faded.

Bret's chest ached at the memory. He knew very well the pain of losing a loved one. Not a twin, though still someone he'd walked through life with every single day since childhood.

"What about Adia?" Rafał perked up a tiny bit. "Is she all right?" There was an all too recognizable gleam in his eye at the mention of her name. It was the same admiration that Lukas had had for her too.

"She's safe, at Janów with Lubor, Ewan, Filip." And a few dozen Nazis.

Rafał smiled as they walked quickly and quietly through the woods. "Oh, good."

"Do I sense a little infatuation? I thought Lukas was her greatest admirer," Bret growled, intending the words to be lighter.

Rafał chuckled. "He was just the loudest about it. And I thought from how much time you and Adia spend together that you two were, well, um . . ."

"We're not." Bret stomped on a frostbitten tuft of grass as he said it, which effectively ended the discussion.

They reached a half-demolished truck that Bret had stashed to make the long kilometers between Janów and his many assignments a little more tolerable. Though the roads were a gamble and he had to hide it in the brush from time to time, it did the trick.

He scanned the road, then they jumped in and bumped down an old forest road that wouldn't show up on any maps.

"So, you think there's a chance Adia and I might, well, um . . ." Rafał said in a teasing tone.

Bret tried to keep his humor equally light. "I'd say your chances are as good as the chance this war ends tomorrow."

30

JANUARY 14, 1940

Adia strode through the barn. Tomasz's quiet words echoed through her mind as loud as a trumpet, and she feared every German soldier she passed could hear them.

Perhaps she wasn't as cut out for this favor as Tomasz seemed to think. She'd managed to overhear bits from the soldiers two days ago about the latest prisoner transports and relay word back to him about a transfer from some camp to the northeast of Wygoda to a camp farther west called Dachau. Tomasz had taken the information and passed it along.

Though he'd said this was all the espionage he wanted her to do, Adia felt compelled to do more. There were other lives at stake—other sons, fathers—and she could save them.

Sweat beaded on her brow despite the cool air, and she swiped back her hair, which frizzed into wild curls. She wove through the stalls until she found Werner speaking with a soldier outside his office. When he saw her, he looked up and smiled. He dismissed the other man and then approached Adia.

"Guten tag, fräulein," he said.

"Lubor seems to be doing well on his grain," she said, careful to keep her voice casual. "But he could use another fifty pounds or so. Perhaps we increase his rations if you can spare more?"

The twinkle in his eyes dimmed. Was that a trace of disappointment? Had he been hoping for her to broach a different subject? A more personal one, perhaps?

"Oh yes, of course. I'll put in a call to Hostau and see if they have further reserves. Grain is becoming harder to procure." He shifted his weight and glanced at his boots, his hands clasped behind his back where they always defaulted to.

She saw the opening in his words and went for it. "I'd love to hear more about Hostau. It sounds like a rather fascinating operation."

He straightened a tiny bit at her rare opening to continue conversation. It wasn't perhaps the most personal of questions, but it was the only thing that came to mind.

"Certainly." He nodded to his office. "I have a few reports I can share if you're interested. They have begun to breed several Lipizzaner lines for more selective traits. I imagine you'd have insight you can lend."

"I'd love to."

She followed him into the office and let her mind shift to her surroundings, taking in the small personal touches he'd added with framed photos. The one with both him and Bret on the Olympic podium pulled at her, but she refused to look.

His desk was a series of neat piles, and her hopes crashed down. There was no chance of observing a map with troop movements or locations when he kept such a tidy display. Today might not be as fruitful.

A safe in the corner of the room caught her eye. Filip had never had a safe. It was new.

Instead of rounding the large desk, Werner pulled a file from the stack, flipped it open, and sat in one of the two chairs in front of the desk. She slowly sat next to him.

"Horses have been shipped to Hostau for some years now, and Herr Rau has taken over the operation to craft the next line of superior horses for work, travel, and agriculture."

"Rau?"

He nodded. "Gustav Rau has been in charge of the breeding program from the start."

"Why bother with horses? It seems your trucks and tanks are more advantageous." The memories of the tanks rolling through the countryside and the truckful of soldiers who had killed the Polish soldiers on the banks of the Bug River burned within her.

"Yes, but the Führer sees the place of horses in supportive applications, and we know with our technology and study, we can improve upon the horse as it is now. There are other programs to breed a better dog as well."

He handed her a few pages and photos of stark-white horses—the infamous stallions of Lipizza, the dancing horses of Spain, Austria, and beyond. Their bloodlines were even more strictly monitored and maintained than that of the Arabian lines.

She pressed her lips together, fighting to keep the hate from her voice. The audacity of the Germans to steal and muck about with farms across the continent. She tipped her head. "But you said you will keep the Arabians here at Janów."

He leaned back in the chair, and his eyebrow twitched. "Rau and I differ in our opinions of this matter. I do believe the Arabian lines should remain pure, same as the Lipizzaners."

That provided some measure of relief.

She looked over the pages with interest, reading through bloodlines and accolades of individual horses, drawings of the horses' features. For several long moments, she was lost in the information and the comfort of this topic she knew so well. She had nearly forgotten her true purpose.

Werner handed her more pages, and as he sifted through the stack, she caught a few pages spilling from another folder. As she pieced the German language together, excitement raced down her spine.

She turned from it and focused only on Werner as he spoke about the different horses and criteria they used to bring horses from all over Europe to their breeding farm at Hostau. All the while, she flushed with the news she'd picked up from that stray report.

She needed to report to Tomasz right away. Another idea popped into her mind as her eye caught the safe once more.

And yet she maintained the act as Werner spoke on and on.

Could she repeat this over and over in the name of saving Rafał and partisans? To gain more information? To protect the helpless like Zara and Henryk and their hungry children? What if her learnings could even save Bret one day? She'd learn to cope and to shift her perception of the work she'd once reviled.

Desperate times called for desperate changes of heart.

Especially when it meant saving those she loved.

———

Bret should have sent Rafał to Janów alone. What had he been thinking?

His body hummed with nervous energy at the thought of running into her.

He was anxious to get back to scouting local troop movements, and an interesting tip had filtered through Tomasz about a potential mass offensive, one that could turn the tide of the war. The old man had been rather vague about how he'd come by such crucial information, the same as before with how he'd learned about Rafał's transport route.

After a day of light conversation and subtle interrogation on how much Rafał might have known, observed, or inadvertently divulged to his captors, Bret and Rafał reached Janów well after sunset.

Bret checked the signal tree and saw the shovel that indicated Werner wasn't on the grounds, then moved silently through the sleepy stables. He'd observed that most of the soldiers didn't dally around after chores were done and horses were fed. They crowded Babka's restaurant for wine and a chance to ogle the young ladies in town.

Both Filip's and Tomasz's cabins were empty, and he made all effort to avoid Adia's, though he knew it wasn't likely she'd be resting no matter how close to death she'd been recently.

A soft glow came from the broodmare barn. A winter foal—rare indeed as most cropped up in springtime. Filip's and Tomasz's voices drifted down the aisle, and as Bret and Rafał drew near, the two men were hunched over the railing of a birthing stall.

"Rafał!" a tiny voice squeaked.

Ewan burst through the shadows and raced to Rafał, who caught the boy and hugged him tightly.

Filip and Tomasz whirled around, and Tomasz's eyes filled with tears, sparkling in the faint lantern light. He stepped closer hesitantly as if in a daze. "My boy."

They collided into an embrace, each whispering to the other, their shoulders trembling.

Filip followed, handed Bret the lantern, and joined in the stream of hugging. At the burning sensation of another's presence, Bret glanced back to the stall and saw Adia step out of it, wiping her hands and smiling softly with her attention locked on Tomasz and Rafał.

She met Bret's gaze and tipped her head in a subtle, thankful nod.

His heart seized. He longed for more of her approval.

He longed for more of her.

But he knew what was best, and what it meant to keep her safe.

Despite his helping her when she'd fallen ill and collapsed in the barn, he knew the tension from his deceit about his true occupation was still there. And he'd see to keeping that wall in place between them.

He nodded back in acknowledgment and then tore his gaze away. He clapped Filip on the arm and returned the lamp. "I must go."

"Bret, no! Stay!" Filip said quickly. "Let us celebrate Rafał's return. I'm sure there are some reserve rations we can dig up."

"No. I need to get back."

Tomasz approached, his eyes liquid and his hands trembling. "Thank you. Bret, just—thank you."

He clapped his friend on the shoulder. "Thankful enough to reveal your all-knowledgeable source?" Bret fought the urge to glance at the one person he suspected to be Tomasz's source. Though he desperately hoped he was incorrect. He and Tomasz had fought at length about whether to ask Adia for anything she observed at Janów, from Werner. Bret knew she'd never refuse such a request. But it was far too risky.

Tomasz smiled and shook his head. "My lips are sealed to protect our lines of information. But my gratitude is eternal, Bret."

Bret nodded, not wanting to press the matter when a father should be able to celebrate the return of his son.

Out of the corner of his eye, he saw Rafał approach Adia, and they hugged for a long moment. Bret's body tensed, despite every synapse in his brain ordering him not to react or care about it. He knew her well enough—Rafał was far too young and not what she needed in a beau.

Bret glanced over to catch Filip watching his reaction. The man's piercing eyes didn't miss a detail.

"I'll be in touch," Bret said in farewell to both Tomasz and Filip. He whirled and strode away, his skin prickling when footsteps followed after him. Soft, light footsteps. Adia?

Hope filled him as he turned and paused.

Ewan stood behind him, wringing his hands nervously. "Can you stay?"

Bret covered his disappointment with a genuine smile for the child. He knelt in front of him, rubbing the boy's arms as he shivered in his threadbare coat. "I'm sorry, I can't."

The boy's eyes dropped to his feet. "Then, can I go with you?"

A sharp knife twisted in Bret's gut. "I need you here, looking after Adia for me. I'm counting on you."

"I do not like Herr Vogel. Lubor belongs to Poland, not Herr Hitler."

Bret looked up as Adia approached. She stopped a few meters away, her features mostly hidden in the shadows.

Her lips parted as if to speak, but she deflated slightly, as if words failed her.

He felt the same way.

Every inch of him yearned to say something, anything. But what good were words to them now? Everything had been said.

Words didn't matter when the world kept them apart.

He gave Ewan a hug. "Be strong, little thief. It will not always be like this."

Was he trying to reassure himself or the boy?

Ewan nodded and raced back to Adia, who took his hand tenderly and tucked him against her side as they returned to Filip, Tomasz, and Rafał outside the mare's stall.

She cast Bret one final, pained glance over her shoulder, and he silently sent the same message.

Be strong, Amerykanka. It will not always be like this.

He had to hold to the belief that this pain, this dissonance in his soul of being so close and yet so far from her, would fade.

He simply couldn't comprehend a future where that was not the case.

31

You do not listen, Amerykanka. Hold the pick like this," Ewan said as they both leaned over a padlock in the corner of her cabin in the early dawn hours.

Adia rubbed her face in frustration. More than a year into gathering information for Tomasz and nearly a dozen lessons with Ewan on how to pick locks, and she still felt inept.

Winter had come and gone since Rafał's rescue, then come and gone once more. After two years under the Nazi flag, life had fallen into a predictable rhythm while the world around them was collapsing into ruin.

At least Ewan had grown into a more mature young man, now eight years old, and had almost eliminated his habit of picking pockets. Perhaps it was the energy Adia demanded of him to help her break into Werner's safe in the office. The timing hadn't been quite right yet, but she needed to know she could do it when the opportunity presented itself.

Ewan had also become quite the little errand boy for the partisans and spies carefully embedded in Janów.

"I saw Meester Bret yesterday," Ewan said thoughtfully. "He misses you."

242

She fumbled and dropped one of the picks. "He told you that?"

Ewan grinned. "No, I just know it."

She drew in a long breath and shook her head. "You shouldn't muddle in people's lives." Though his words spread warmth throughout her body. It had been months since she and Bret had caught glimpses of each other across the fields, usually when checking up on Ewan, who was the sole link between them now.

The truth was, she missed Bret too.

"Try again," Ewan commanded, crossing his legs and angling his head expectantly. His big brown eyes were covered by his unkempt, long mouse-brown hair.

She took the two pieces of slim metal and hunched back over the lock, twisting, pressing where Ewan had shown, and praying for the satisfaction of the lock opening.

The sharp squeal of truck brakes from across the stables startled them both. Ewan quickly gathered the lock and picks and slid them into the hidden compartment below the floorboards. A chorus of truck engines, men shouting, and doors slamming followed as they both rose.

Adia looked out her window but couldn't see much from her cabin on the other side of the grounds. "Stay here, Myszko, no matter what." She tossed her breeches and boots on, tied back her long hair—fully regrown after the Russian occupation—and jogged to the barn.

At the sight of trucks pulling away from the tall clock tower's shadows, her chest tightened in fear and her blood went cold. Flashes of the Russians' catastrophic exit from Janów burned through her mind.

Were they taking the horses? She couldn't tell who—or what—was in the back of the cargo trucks.

She swung her head around in search of Werner. He stood with his arms crossed, the dawn's faint light playing across his unreadable face.

She ran to him and skidded to a stop, breathless. "They're taking the horses? Lubor?"

He held up his hands, his expression quickly changing to horror at his oversight. "Oh, no, no, no. I am so sorry, fräulein, for the fright. Lubor and all others will remain here."

Her pulse slowed to a steadier speed. She turned to the parade of vehicles. "So, what is all this?"

"Our soldiers are needed . . . elsewhere."

Elsewhere. The front—wherever it was now. Yugoslavia? Greece? She'd heard whispers of both. She swallowed back the flurry of emotions. "Are you leaving with the troops?"

He smiled as if he mistook her confusion for personal concern. "No."

She didn't allow for a single movement of her face or body to betray her true feelings. No sliver of relief or disappointment could eke through. Though she truly had no idea what she felt over the news.

"Thankfully, Herr Rau believes me best suited for this post, though he is sending his aide, Herr Christophe Schultze, as further assistance." The colonel's brow lifted in annoyance and his lips pursed in disgust.

The last of the vehicles cleared the driveway just as a new stream of trucks approached. A truck stopped before them and Adia felt the sudden urge to flee, but Werner brushed her elbow with his hand and motioned to the short man who stepped out of the car.

"Adia, this is Herr Schultze." Werner had turned on his charming tone, carrying none of the sneer that had been in his voice a moment ago. "He arranged to bring in more civilians to help with the work now that the eastern front is occupying our soldiers' attention."

More civilians? Of course. With the soldiers all going to the front, that left few workers at Janów. They'd already had several other civilians transferred in.

The short man with gray hair and an arched, narrow nose scanned her from head to toe and back again, and his boldness left her skin crawling.

Werner stepped forward, saluted, and called out, "Heil Hitler!"

The aide smiled, his teeth stained and a few blackened with rot.

"Heil Hitler! I'm very much looking forward to examining your operation here, Oberst Vogel. Is this the trainer you boast of?"

Werner nodded. "May I present Fräulein Kensington."

"British?" Schultze's lip twitched.

Werner shook his head firmly. "American."

"Wunderbar."

"And are you a fellow horse lover, Herr Schultze?" Adia asked, as conversationally as she could manage in broken German.

"Not exactly." The man snickered. "But I do as ordered by my Führer."

She pressed her lips together and held back a retort. This couldn't bode well for Werner and all the progress he'd made. Would Schultze undermine the colonel's power in some way? She couldn't stop the shiver that raced down her spine as she stood next to the dislikable man.

"Miss Kensington will oversee the training of our new workers," Werner said, with a smile at the thin individuals who had just unloaded from the back of the truck. "Herr Schultze, I shall give you a tour. Miss Kensington, I'll leave you to your charges."

The officers departed, and twelve sets of eyes bored into her. The workers' clothes were old, filthy, but their faces were washed, and passive.

Her stomach dropped a bit as the realization came over her. These were not civilian volunteers—they were prisoners.

More helpless lives, all in her hands.

Bret leaned against a tree and stretched his tired legs straight out, scratching at the wrapping of the day-old wound from a bullet that had grazed his forearm. He sat atop the rolling hill half a kilometer from Janów, which had a clear view of the greenery now in the prime of spring growth. Through the blossoming trees and bushes, German tanks, trucks, and troops spanned every inch of the roadways as they plodded eastward.

A twig snapped behind him, and he reached for his gun, but his injury threw off his routine motion. He gave up on his draw when the approaching figure came into view.

"Good thing I'm not a threat." Adia's soft voice floated on the wind.

His skin prickled. Wasn't she?

Adia sat beside him and scanned the valley. Within moments, her soft, clean scent washed over him, and a thousand other details registered: how long her hair had grown in the past year, the soft golden tan of her skin, the faded clothes, the worn-out leather boots.

Did she still stash her cash and documents in the lining of her right boot?

He shook his head slightly to divert his gaze and attention. "How'd you know where to find me?"

"Ewan."

"Powerful ally."

"He's now a hundred times sneakier thanks to your tutelage."

He chuckled and looked back at the military migration, settling into comfortable silence.

She pulled her knees to her chest and let out a long breath. "It's nice up here. I should have thought to pack a picnic."

She smiled distantly, though it didn't reach the corners of her eyes. It had been over a year since he'd seen her truly smile—since Rafał had returned to Janów and the silent truce had been struck between Bret and Adia.

In that time, France had fallen to Hitler, North Africa had been entrenched in combat, and Yugoslavia had been under attack.

And in that time, Bret had checked in on Adia from afar but allowed Tomasz and Ewan to be the main conduits of information between the two of them. This close to her now, he felt like a teenage boy next to his old flame. His heart raced and he smiled at the thought of a picnic on this bluff with her.

Old flame. Who was he kidding? His fire for her had never dimmed, not for even a moment.

She looked over at him, her gaze brushing his forearm before locking onto his face. "Nearly all the soldiers have left Janów," she said, her voice hushed. "They've brought in Polish civilians—well, captives—to help with the workload."

"Interesting."

"Gustav Rau sent an aide to work with Vogel, who doesn't seem happy about it. Christophe Schultze." She shuddered as if equally unhappy.

His nerves rose at her visible reaction. While Vogel had proven reputable and respectful, this new player was an unknown factor. And if Rau sent him personally, he might have as much power or more than the colonel.

"I'll see what I can learn about him," Bret said.

Tomasz and Rafał had remained close to Adia in the past year, but they couldn't be everywhere, and they had to remain in the shadows enough to avoid attention. They'd perhaps be unable to see who or what this Schultze really was.

Bret had heard scattered reports from them about Werner's growing interest in Adia and how she responded in a manner that didn't turn him away but kept him at arm's length. Rafał didn't like it, nor did Bret.

"I can get you the location of the remaining troops," she whispered.

He straightened. "How?"

"Werner keeps it in his office."

He'd gone through this a year ago with Tomasz. Though as always, he could hear the voice of his superiors argue that she'd be the ideal source. She had no idea just how valuable her closeness to Vogel could be. She could set partisan and Allied efforts ahead by months.

He shook his head. "It's too dangerous. If he suspects you—"

"I'm careful. I've been giving Tomasz information for more than a year."

"What?" His voice rose. Curse Tomasz and his deceit. Bret had asked him several times if he'd coerced Adia into gleaning information from the colonel, and he had denied it every time. Yet the information from her was good. It had saved Rafał's life and so many others.

A bitter taste filled his mouth. For someone who'd claimed she couldn't trust him for his career as a spy, she'd hidden this fact for months.

"Tomasz never should have gotten you involved," he said.

"How is you taking risks any different than me?"

He clamped his jaw closed. All the reasons—because he was trained, because he had everything to prove and nothing to lose—felt meager in the face of war. "You have enough to worry about with tending to the horses and minding Ewan," he said, careful to keep his voice even.

"I won't take unnecessary risks."

He said nothing more, listening to the breeze rustle the leaves above them. How he wished she were out of Poland, out of imminent danger.

She leaned back and resumed her own study of the troops on the horizon.

The silence and comfort of being beside her brought him back to their days of searching the fields and ruins of Poland for Lubor and Ewan. Surprisingly, he missed those days.

He missed her.

Desperately.

After several long moments, she looked over and nodded to his bandaged arm. "Are you all right?" Her voice broke at the end.

He clenched his fist to keep from reaching out and taking her into his arms. His chest ached in yearning.

He nodded in answer.

"I wish you weren't so involved in the partisans," she said and looked away. "We lost Lukas and nearly lost Rafał. I could gather information from Werner to help them and keep you or others from harm's way."

How could he argue when he had framed his entire life's work around the very same perspective? But hadn't she held such lies and deceit against him?

"No more feeding information to Tomasz. Please. I need to know that in all of this, you're not going to end up arrested or shot as a spy."

"I'm sorry, Bret." She rose and slipped away, the last of her words drifting on the breeze. "I can't promise that."

32

APRIL 20, 1941

Not again.

Adia fled the ashes of another family's empty cabin and stormed through the aisles, looking side to side for a glimpse of Ewan. She had to get word to Bret, and the boy had some way of communicating with Bret that he'd refused to tell her.

Another family had disappeared, the Kaminskis, with no word of warning and with their domicile in a state of disarray. Weeks ago, the Byzkos had also disappeared without a word or a trace.

Two days had passed since she'd met Bret on the hillside, and a new tension had settled over Janów and Wygoda with the shift of routines and Schultze's presence like a circling vulture. Unlike mild-mannered Werner, the new aide allowed no deviation from the rules. And now, people had disappeared from the village. Some for conscripted work assignments across Poland, others for breaking curfew, others for being suspected partisans.

But entire families?

She reached the long, wide main hallway of the clock barn, the direct path to Werner's office, and heard Ewan's screech of protest.

"No! I'm sorry! I'm sorry!"

A burly Nazi guard pulled Ewan toward Werner's office.

She raced over and took Ewan's arm. "What are you doing?" she asked the guard in German.

The soldier slammed his elbow into her chest, knocking the wind from her lungs, before flinging her to the ground. Her head smashed against the wooden stall, and pain shot down to her toes.

The office door clicked open, shiny boots appeared beside her on the ground, and a smattering of loud German commands echoed through her head. Strong hands lifted her to her feet.

"Ludendorff. Explain!" Werner brushed her chin gently to examine the damage. He shot a glare at the private.

She leaned on Werner as her balance returned, though her stomach churned with bile.

Ludendorff didn't cower. He shook Ewan by the collar. "This boy stole from me," he growled. "I caught him."

Tears streaked down the boy's dirty cheeks as he sobbed, "Amerykanka, I'm sorry."

"It's not on purpose." Adia looked to Werner. "It's a compulsion, and he always returns what he steals. Please, Werner."

A new, booming voice cut in, and the sharp-faced Schultze appeared from the office, tossing Ewan a look of disgust. "Is this your child?" he asked Adia.

Werner stiffened slightly, as if he'd never considered the possibility.

She considered lying, perhaps claiming Ewan was her little brother. But she had no proof. "He's a ward of the director—former director Maier. He's my apprentice."

"An orphan then?" Schultze sniffed.

"Yes, but—"

"He must go to a proper work camp. They have the means to look after him." Schultze clapped his heel down as if it were a gavel. "Vogel, we have more work to do if you're quite done here."

Panic rose in Adia at the finality of his words. Sent to a camp?

She turned to Werner, clutching his uniform and not caring about the tears that spilled over her lashes. "No, please. He's a helpful worker. He won't cause any more trouble. I swear it."

Werner's blue eyes filled with regret—more emotion than she'd ever seen from him in all the months they'd worked together. Hadn't he said when he caught Ewan teaching the children in Lubor's stall that the boy reminded Werner of himself as a kid?

"I'm sorry, Adia. It's a directive I must follow. He'll be with other children, and he'll be safe, I assure you."

"Please, Werner. I beg you." Her voice caught in her throat. "I'll do anything."

"Quit your blubbering." Schultze sneered. "Colonel, you can negotiate with your tramp another time. We must finish our report by day's end."

Adia flinched but didn't release her hold. Schultze strode back into the office, and the guard dragged Ewan into the tack room that had become a prison cell.

"Please, Werner. He's just one boy."

Werner grabbed her arms and squeezed gently. "I'm so sorry," he said in a gravelly voice. "If I push Schultze, I risk all the work we've done here."

"There has to be a way."

He brushed the back of her hand with his lips, the most intimate he'd dared to be, in a gesture of apology and stepped past her.

She fell back to the ground in desperation as he closed the office door behind him.

Her heart splintered into a thousand pieces.

The Germans had captured Belgrade. Sarajevo and Yugoslavia had surrendered. There seemed to be no stopping Hitler's rampage across Europe.

Bret paced the small, abandoned bar, the crowd of shadow soldiers dwindling further every day. He passed the latest report from distant partisans over to Nowak.

"Unbelievable," Nowak muttered as he read. They'd gotten such little information in the past few weeks. His right arm hung in a sling, a magnet for stray bullets.

Bret clenched his jaw in frustration at the latest news. Was he making any difference here? Every country around them had fallen to Hitler: Yugoslavia, France, Poland, Belgium, the Netherlands, Czechoslovakia, Austria. Word was that the bombing in London had intensified. Was Britain next?

He thought of Elizabeth, his mother and father.

"Hey! Lady! How in the—?" A scuffle at the front door had every man at attention.

Bret whirled with his Luger drawn.

"I need to see Bret Conway, now." The firm female voice echoed as Adia pushed past the two men posted at the door.

Bret holstered his gun and strode across the room toward her.

"Lower your weapons," Nowak shouted, and everyone obeyed.

Adia's face was cut along her cheekbone, the skin turning dark blue and swollen. The terror in her eyes and the dried streaks of tears through the arena dust set his heart racing.

Nowak stood. "Who's the beautiful lady?"

"Not now, Nowak," Bret growled as he closed the distance between them.

When she saw him, her forehead smoothed a tiny bit.

"It's Ewan." Her voice hitched. "They caught him pickpocketing. They're shipping him to a camp first thing in the morning." She pressed both hands over her mouth to stifle a sob. He'd never seen her so worked up.

And how had she been injured?

Fear filled his stomach. Rescuing Ewan could jeopardize all he and the partisans had worked for. But it wasn't a question that he'd help the boy.

"We'll get him, Adia. I promise."

She slumped against him, her forehead falling to his chest. He put his arms around her, stirring up all the longing he had spent the past few days trying to rebury as successfully as shoveling sand with a fork.

"How did you find us?" he asked against her hair.

She lifted her head. "Tomasz."

Nowak slid closer, breaking the illusion that they were alone. "What are we talking about?" He turned to Adia. "Name's Nowak. And you are?"

Bret ignored his interest. "I'll need a few men to cause a distraction at Janów tonight." He stepped back from Adia.

She met his gaze. "I begged Werner to let Ewan go. I thought he'd listen." She looked ill at the memory. It didn't come naturally for her to plead for anything. "Won't he suspect me if Ewan is rescued after that?"

"We'll make it appear as if Ewan slipped away. We'll raid the food and supplies, or make it look as though we did."

She nodded, wrapping her arms around her abdomen and hunching her shoulders forward. Never had she looked so defeated, so frightened.

"Perhaps you should stay here," he said, stepping up to her and touching her elbow. "We can get you and Ewan out of Poland together."

She shuddered. "No, then Werner will know I had something to do with it. And Schultze is a dark influence. They'd do horrible things to Filip or Tomasz. Get Ewan out and I'll follow, soon. When the time is right."

Would the time ever be right?

He brushed the bruise along her face. "Did Werner do this?"

She shook her head, her gaze still distant, unfocused. "No. I'm not the one in danger."

He doubted that.

"I can't lose him again, Bret." She trembled. "So many are disappearing without a trace. The Kaminskis are missing. The Byzkos too."

Sorrow filled him at the pain all over her taut features. He pulled her back into his arms, and she clung to him.

"Everything is unraveling, and I can't even find the ends of the string to stitch it back together."

"Take a deep breath." Bret led her to the table where Nowak and Scottie sat. "Let's talk through how we can cause enough trouble at Janów to break that little Myszko from his cage."

33

That night, Adia stood next to Bret, Nowak, Scottie, and a half dozen other men as they loaded up their pockets and belts with spare magazines and covered their faces with scarves.

She studied the confident and mechanical way Bret moved, checked his rifle, strapped on several spare pistols. As natural as the way he handled a horse. Gratitude washed over her. There was no one she trusted more to lead these men to save Ewan.

And yet the lingering warmth of his arms around her left her conflicted.

What if something happened to him in their quest to save the boy?

The final click of a rifle bolt echoed through the darkness of the forest and drew her from her dark thoughts.

Bret looked over each man. "You know the plan. Let's go."

Nowak walked up to her, a goofy grin spreading across his face as his eyes sparkled. "A kiss for luck, darling?"

She caught Bret's intense study as if he awaited her response. She smiled at Nowak and rose to her tiptoes to kiss his stubble-ridden cheek. "Good luck." The rebel had already become a fast ally, though his superficial words and charm didn't work on her nearly as much as seeing the trust Bret held in his companion.

Nowak followed the rest of the band into the forest, disappearing into the black curtain of night.

Bret stepped up to her. "Better get to your cabin soon. Practice your story until it rolls off your tongue in case you are questioned."

"I will."

Silence fell and her insides twisted. So much unsaid. Or was it just that there was so much that was impossible between them?

"Be careful," she whispered.

"Keep your head low. I'll meet where we agreed in a few days with Ewan."

A small smile spread across her lips. "Don't you want a kiss for luck too?"

His gaze darted to her lips for a fraction of a second. "Better not." He shook his head. "I'm not sure I'd be able to focus on the mission afterward."

Though he punctuated his words with a wink, he walked away so fast she felt a stab of rejection deep inside her gut.

Why must it all be so complicated? She shook her head to push it all aside.

Foolish thoughts. Irritating emotions.

Ewan was all that mattered right now.

Bret's shadow disappeared into the trees. Adia had her part to play in all this before she could return to her cabin. She crept back to the stables and rolled her shoulders back, strolling through the barns and checking on the horses as she did every night.

As she neared the main barn, where she would confirm whether Ewan was being guarded and leave a signal for Bret, a figure stepped into her path.

"Ah, there you are." The German-accented voice was like ice.

She swallowed her revulsion. "Herr Schultze. Might I assist you with something?"

He scanned every inch of her, letting the silence stretch. "Your absence was noted today. Where were you?"

She glanced around, desperate to see Werner but knowing it was past the hour he turned in to his own quarters. He was religious about his schedule. Why was this snake here?

"I didn't feel well. Now, I need to check the horses one final time and get back to my cabin."

He didn't move. "I checked your cabin. You were not there."

"I was upset and went for a long walk. I'll catch up on my work tomorrow, I assure you."

She moved to step around him, but his hand clamped on her forearm, hard.

"You'll not leave until I've dismissed you."

Her anger eclipsed her fear and she pulled free, her bones screaming from his clawlike hold. "You do not give me orders. Oberst Vogel is the director here."

She stomped off before his shock gave way at her defiance. She'd made a grave mistake. She'd kicked a snake that was now angry, coiled to strike.

To top it off, if Schultze didn't return to his own cabin soon, she'd need to find a way to get a message to Bret. This was no average guard or civilian staff watching over Ewan. Schultze's presence could destroy the whole plan.

He could get someone killed.

Something was wrong.

Bret felt it in his gut. It had taken too long for Adia to signal whether Ewan was guarded or not and extinguish the candlelight in that barn.

"Where is she?" Nowak whispered, the timbre of his voice echoing Bret's concern.

"I don't like this, Conway," Scottie said. "Smells fishy."

"Nah, that's just yer breath, kid." Nowak chuckled.

Scottie jabbed Nowak's injured arm.

"Ouch!"

"Quiet," Bret mumbled. A hundred different scenarios played through his mind in an instant, many only increasing his worry for Adia's safety. He tried to push them from the forefront of his mind.

With Werner's liking for her, Janów was perhaps the safest place in all of Poland for her. Ewan was the priority right now.

"Let's just go in, assume it's guarded, and get this done," Nowak said.

"That's why ye are always short a limb," Scottie fired back. "Let's nab the boy in transit."

"No. We're sticking with the plan." Nerves humming tightly, Bret stood from his crouched position and nodded. "Let's go. Assume he's guarded and all seven soldiers are on patrol."

The men rose and followed him.

They spread across the driveway, guided by the dim glow of the moon. A few men darted into the storage outhouses and started taking boxes and relocating them to confuse the soldiers as much as possible. Hopefully it would camouflage the true intent of the break-in without depleting the much-needed supplies.

Bret walked down the aisle toward the small tack room he'd hidden Adia in when the Russians had invaded the grounds. How did that already feel like a lifetime ago?

There wasn't a guard at the door or anywhere in sight.

It was too quiet. They needed more of a ruckus to pull this off and keep suspicion from Adia.

He trilled a whistle that set off a series of loud thumps, crashes, and horse whinnies.

A host of German shouts rang out in the distance. They raced to the southern barns, far away from where Ewan was held.

Nowak and Scottie at work.

Bret heaved his shoulder into the tack room door, bursting it open. Ewan lay curled in the back corner on a saddle blanket. He jumped and rose to his feet, blinking rapidly to focus his eyes.

"Come quick," Bret whispered, removing his mask. "And keep silent."

Ewan nodded as the sounds and Bret's presence seemed to register. He took Bret's outstretched hand.

They turned and halted. The man Adia had described as Christophe Schultze stood in the doorway, a gun leveled at Bret's face.

"Not so fast." The German's composure faltered. "Wait. I know who you are—"

A loud thump to the side of Schultze's head cut off his words and sent him to a crumpled heap on the ground.

Adia tossed the shovel aside and then fished for something in her pockets.

"What are you doing?" Bret hissed. "This isn't the plan."

She glared down at Schultze. "I improvised and took a detour to the office for these." She placed four sets of vehicle keys into his palm. "I busted the door open with the shovel so it looks like it was one of you ruffians. I'll give you thirty seconds before I scream."

Four trucks. The entirety of the Nazi motor pool here in Janów. This hadn't been part of the plan but changed the odds significantly. No one from Janów would be able to pursue them, not with any speed at least.

"No." Bret hesitated. "This might be too much. They might suspect you."

"We don't have any choice. Werner will believe me, I know it." She crouched down and brushed Ewan's hair fondly. "I'll see you in a few days. Do as Bret says."

Everything in him wanted to gather Adia in his arms and bring her along. He was still uneasy with taking the trucks, but this would be a huge boon to the partisans. "You sure you won't come with us?" *Come with me.*

She smiled, stood back upright. "You know my answer, Bret."

It had been worth a shot.

"Then . . ." he whispered and leaned in closer to her. "About that kiss?"

Schultze stirred groggily at their feet, and she jumped back.

He bolted away with Ewan in tow. They darted to the driveway, though his heart remained behind in her palms.

34

Within moments of the four trucks tearing out of the gravel driveway in front of Janów, Schultze had fully woken, and Werner came running down the aisle.

"Adia? What has happened?"

Adia feigned alarm and helped Schultze to his feet. "I heard the horses neighing from my cabin, then I heard a scuffle down this hall," she said. "I saw a stranger in a mask and came across Schultze as someone hit him from behind with the shovel. I screamed, and the attackers ran off."

Schultze blinked and looked around, then narrowed in on her and growled. "I don't trust her. Lock her up in the tack room while we investigate."

Werner took her elbow. "I'll put her in my office, Schultze. Not some vile storage room. Mind your accusations." He led her from the tack room. When they were a few steps away from Schultze, Werner leaned in. "I don't know what is going on, and I'm sorry to treat you as a prisoner, but I must get to the bottom of this."

Adia nodded. "I understand."

Werner tipped a gentle smile. "Please wait here," he said and motioned to his office. "We'll be back shortly."

She stepped inside, and he locked the door.

Alone. She looked sharply at the safe in the corner, and her heart slammed against her rib cage.

Now was the time. She had no doubt that Nowak, Scottie, and the rest had left a mess of the grounds, which would keep Schultze and Werner on the hunt for some time. She also knew this opportunity might never come again. And the locked door meant she'd get at least the warning of a soft click before the door opened.

She pulled the two slender bits of metal from her boot lining, raced to the corner of the room, and knelt before the small metal box, latched with a padlock. She angled the lock upward as best she could to slip the picks inside. The office was dark, the only light from a dim bulb hanging above the desk. But Ewan had thought of such conditions and taught her how to pick the lock mostly by feel.

In the shadows, she wiggled and pressed against the mechanisms inside the lock, wishing Ewan were here over her shoulder and giving instruction. But no, he was safe with Bret and far from the reach of Schultze. Thank goodness.

She glanced over her shoulder at the door, hearing footsteps thumping outside but at a fast pace through the aisles. No one was yet drawing near.

Sweat pricked her forehead, and her fingers trembled, faltering in her mission.

Focus, Adia. You have mere moments.

What was more, she knew she couldn't steal the documents. She'd have to make notes and copies onto other pages or risk setting off further alarms.

Suddenly the lock in her hands released. The sound of it was as loud as a rocket in her ears, but the office was still, unmoving around her. She looked again at the door, holding her breath to hear what commotion lay beyond the tiny barrier of wood held in place by a metal bolt.

She set the lock aside and opened the heavy safe door on smooth hinges. Inside, dozens of files were neatly stacked. Werner, ever meticulous, had his handprints all over the system. Each file was labeled in German, but her written understanding of the language was quite poor.

She flipped through the pages for maps. One file, labeled "Barbarossa," showed a Russian map and arrows with troop movements. The soldiers who had just left Janów. They'd been mobilized for this, certainly. The Germans were opening a second front line on the war. A war to the east. A war with the USSR.

She reached for paper and a pen on Werner's desk. Her chest was tight and her stomach knotted as she copied over as much information as she possibly could. Did the Allies know of this yet? It could be the single act that doomed all of Europe, or the single greatest opportunity to strike Hitler while his forces were split.

Five minutes. She'd allow herself five minutes before putting it all back as pristinely as possible. She could only fit a few pages into her boot lining without drawing suspicion anyway.

If Werner or Schultze searched her and found them . . . she'd be dead. No amount of affection on Werner's part would be able to save her.

Her mouth was dry, her writing unsteady beneath the pen.

But this was the right decision. This was what her mother and father had done when danger was at their door, when lives were in their hands. If this could save others . . . if this information could save Bret and Ewan . . .

She scribbled furiously, the scratches of the pen on paper as loud as a screeching barn owl in the night.

The shouts of soldiers beyond the door echoed around her, calling out that they'd found nothing, no one. Time was short.

But each page seemed more and more rife with vital information for British Intelligence, for the partisans who put their necks on the line.

Her hand cramped, but she pushed on. She couldn't stop. Couldn't waste this time.

Minutes ticked by as every creak in the wooden walls around

her, the pitter-patter of mice under the floor, echoed through her head as loud as cannons.

And then the door handle to the office wiggled.

———

"These trucks will come in mighty handy," Nowak said to Bret as they closed the barn doors behind them in the safe house twenty kilometers away from the stables.

Ewan bounded out of the cab behind Bret and followed him closely. Bret's adrenaline still buzzed, but his mind was fixed only on Adia back at Janów. Would she go unnoticed and unsuspected as a collaborator? Would taking the trucks backfire on her directly?

Schultze had clearly recognized Bret. What did that mean? According to his sources, Schultze was an ambitious man, but unliked and not respected among his peers, which left him unpredictable and prone to lash out at subordinates. He had a violent reputation.

Werner still held rank over Schultze. He would protect Adia. Bret was certain of that, at least.

Still, this night had not gone according to plan.

Bret knelt down to Ewan. "You all right, lad?"

Ewan nodded, bruises around his neck that looked about a day old. "Why didn't we bring her with us? It's dangerous at Janów."

"I know. But if she disappeared now, Filip or Tomasz might be blamed."

Ewan's face flushed with anger. "I hate the Germans. Both Vogel and Schultze."

Bret stood and hugged the boy. "I'm just glad we got you out of there."

What they'd do next with the boy, Bret wasn't certain. He and Adia hadn't planned quite that far ahead. But he'd see her in just a few days once the dust settled after the partisan raid and she was able to slip away back to that hidden hillside.

God, let her be there. Keep her safe.

35

Adia fought to keep her back straight and her shoulders square as Schultze and Werner circled like vultures. *Lord, help me say what needs to be said to protect those I love.*

"Let's go over this one more time." Werner leaned against the desk.

"We'll go through this until I'm satisfied that we have the truth!" Schultze said. His face was black-and-blue already from the impact of the shovel. Adia wondered if she should be ashamed of herself for feeling such pride in that swing, that satisfying thump it made against the snake's head.

And the fact that she'd copied the documents and put the safe back in order, all without arousing suspicion. It had been a breath's difference in time, but she'd made it to the chair just as the door opened and Werner stepped in.

Schultze grunted in disbelief. "That rabble in the woods has always been a nuisance, but they've never been so bold."

She kept silent. *"Don't speak unless they ask a direct question,"* Bret had advised.

Werner added softly, "The timing is suspect, Adia. Your little assistant escaped amidst it all."

She met his gaze and tilted her head coyly. "And I won't pretend I'm not happy about that. But as you pointed out, he's an orphan, and he knows how to survive. I'm sure he saw his chance to run."

Werner nodded ever so slightly, and the moonlight cast shadows through the warped windows that caught the deep creases in his forehead. He looked as tired as they all surely were. He wore casual trousers and a tan collared shirt, having been interrogating staff since her scream set the whole premises on alert. Without the Nazi uniform, he struck a particularly dapper figure.

"Schultze, perhaps we give Miss Kensington a respite?"

"Nein!" Schultze fumed. "This is an embarrassment to the entire Reich, Oberst, and a reflection of the Führer himself!"

Adia schooled her expression but inwardly glowed. How embarrassed would he be to learn he'd been felled by a woman?

"Herr Schultze. We've searched the cabins and stalls and found nothing. Those partisans have been plaguing supply lines for months. We have nothing to indicate otherwise."

"And finding our motor pool keys so easily?" Schultze asked.

"They tore through nearly every room and barn," Werner said somberly. "They were faster than we ever could have anticipated."

Schultze cursed and grabbed Adia's chin, jerking her face to meet his gaze. "Or she helped them."

"Let her go." Werner stepped forward, but Schultze pulled a pistol and leveled it at her brow. Werner froze in his tracks.

Her blood ran cold and sweat beaded her skin. The man was on a rampage, the rage in his eyes bordering on delirium.

"There was a British spy among those bandits," he hissed. "Bret Conway."

She blinked, holding back any other outward reaction.

"What?" Werner asked. "You're certain, Schultze?"

"I know who I saw."

The mood in the room shifted, and she shivered. Schultze lowered the pistol. Werner resumed pacing, and a meaningful look passed between the two men.

"If Conway is here . . ." Werner said. He looked back and studied her.

What did all this mean? How could one spy cause so much angst? What had Bret left out of his history with Werner Vogel?

Werner crossed the room to the shelf and took the framed photo of him on the Olympic podium. "You've looked at this before. You recognize someone else perhaps?"

Her breathing became difficult, her stomach turning to stone. "I'm a horse show competitor, Werner. Of course the Olympics catch my interest."

"Not because the man on the bronze dais seemed familiar?" He looked at her with a tiny flare of hostility. Schultze watched her every movement.

"Should I know him?" She didn't lie. Lies could be picked up by trained ears. She deflected.

Werner leaned back, handed his associate the frame.

Schultze chuckled. "I'd forgotten your history with Conway at the Olympics." He circled Adia and brushed a finger along her collar-bone, which brought back the protective, jealous glint in Werner's gaze. "Didn't this Conway make a fool of you in Berlin? Nearly stole your rightful gold and glory?"

Werner looked away. "That was a long time ago."

"Well, it seems he's returned to continue to taint your reputation." Schultze sneered. "I suspect the woman is involved. Kill her now and be done with the matter."

Werner crossed his arms and fell silent. Her fate now rested in his hands.

"Leave us, Schultze," Werner said, his voice sterner than she'd ever heard. Not even Schultze argued with the command, leaving the office. Werner followed him, flipped the lock, and put the image of him and Bret holding Olympic medals back on the shelf. He walked slowly back to her. "This is most troubling."

She clamped her back teeth to keep from speaking. Sweat pricked across her whole body, and her heart rattled in her chest like the wings of a hummingbird.

"I'd been worried about this for some time," Werner continued, his voice low and heavy. "This evening's events have only solidified a decision long coming."

Adia's heart dropped into the pit of her stomach.

"I can't protect the horses here at Janów, especially with so many partisans and so few soldiers. If this man, this Bret Conway, is also in the area, he's no doubt helping the local partisans wreak havoc." He met her gaze and sat on the desk across from her. "I'm going to move our five best stallions to Hostau. Lubor, Wojownik, Palermo, Balik, and little Dorek."

Ice filled the room, froze the breath in her lungs.

"I want you to come with me."

She blinked. "To Hostau?"

Werner leaned forward. "You are the best custodian of the stallions, and even in Hostau, we'll face dangers and challenges. I'd like you to be there with me to ensure their safety and prosperity."

Silence filled the room, and with it despair spread throughout her body. Because she was a civilian, she could refuse and stay with Filip here in Janów. But Lubor would be far, far away.

"I need your answer by week's end, Adia. We'll leave the following day."

APRIL 22, 1941

In the hours just before dawn, Bret paced the designated rendezvous on a hillside a kilometer from Janów, jumping at every rustle of a leaf or distant drone of a vehicle. Two nights had passed since their raid, and he was anxious to know the fallout—and he needed to know Adia was okay.

Ewan was restless in the cab of the truck, where Bret had forced him to remain until she arrived.

"Bret." Adia appeared from the tree line behind him, her approach utterly silent.

The tension fled his body as he searched each inch of her for injury. He couldn't hold back, not anymore. He reached for her waist and pulled her into his embrace. She didn't resist, wrapping her own arms around his torso and clinging to him.

It was as if a wall had blessedly broken between them. A barrier shattered after that night he broke Ewan free of German captivity.

She pressed her cheek against his chest. "Did everyone make it out unharmed?"

He hummed affirmation, finding it difficult to speak with her smell, her presence overwhelming every sense. "Are you all right? What happened with Schultze?"

"Amerykanka!" Ewan squeaked, bouncing out from the truck and running over to hug her side.

Adia beamed down at the boy, slipping out of Bret's grasp to kneel down. "Are you all right? Did Ludendorff hurt you?"

Ewan smiled proudly. "No, I'm not hurt."

She kissed the top of his head and ruffled his dirty hair. "Good. Why don't you go back to the truck for a few minutes so I can speak to Bret?"

Ewan's countenance drooped slightly, but he did as instructed.

"What's wrong, Adia?" Bret asked, sensing a brewing storm beneath the surface.

She reached into the lining of her boot and pulled out folded pages. "I don't have much time before they get suspicious." She handed the stack over. "I copied the original pages and then slipped them back."

He took the pages, scanned them quickly. His breath caught at her scribbles in German. Troop rosters, details about a military plan called Barbarossa. Russia? Hitler was insane enough to invade Russia? The implications . . .

The air fled his lungs as his adrenaline surged. This was good. More information than he'd pulled together in months.

Pure gold.

"Oh, you brilliant, incredible woman." He grabbed her face and kissed her solidly on the lips for the span of a heartbeat.

"I wasn't sure what you needed, so I copied everything I could," she said, her gaze distant and her expression a little dazed.

He noted more of the details as he read deeper. This looked like recent information and was highly valuable.

Could he trust his network to deliver this to headquarters? His gut twisted. No. He couldn't trust anyone with this aside from his commander at MI6. He'd need to take this to England personally.

"How did you find all of this?" He pushed down the rising bile at the realization of the trip before him—the time away from her.

She smiled, eyes dancing with her old sparkle. "They left me alone in the office, and I just couldn't resist."

"This wouldn't just be on his desk," Bret prompted.

"It was in his safe." She flushed. "Ewan taught me to pick locks."

Pride swelled inside him, but then he sobered. "They didn't suspect anything?"

Her smile faded and her eyes grew dark. "No. But there's—" Her voice caught. "There's more I need to tell you."

His body stilled, the noises of the forest fading into a dull buzzing in his mind. He tucked the pages away in his pocket to free up his hands. He'd never heard her voice so tense, so foreboding. Suddenly the air around him squeezed, pressed down on his chest.

She licked her lips, looked away, and drew in a deep breath. She'd never struggled to tell him exactly what was on her mind.

"Adia? What is it?"

She turned, walked over to a fallen tree, and sat on it, shoulders hunched and elbows resting on her knees. He sat beside her and took her hands in his. She gripped them tightly, as if pulling strength from his hold.

"The raid prompted Werner to realize that Lubor and Wojownik are vulnerable here in Poland," she whispered. "And Schultze recognized you, which spooked Werner further."

The blood went cold in his veins.

"They're sending five stallions to Czechoslovakia, including Lubor."

He knew the next words, knew the impact they would have when spoken and given life and urgency. But he wasn't truly ready for that impact.

"Werner asked me to go to Hostau with him and the horses."

The words hung in the air as if they were a feather that seemed so light, so buoyant, it might never succumb to the forces of gravity. It wasn't real, almost. This couldn't be real.

But then she sniffed. "I won't go without your blessing. I could stay here with Filip if I choose. But . . . Lubor . . . I need you to tell me that it's okay."

The world all but collapsed around him. Watching her at Janów from afar had been hard enough. At Hostau, she'd be completely out of his sight. Out of his reach.

Still, she needed his blessing. It sank in slowly, just what that meant. The headstrong, independent, world-traveling horse trainer. When he first met her, she'd needed no one and nothing aside from a stallion and a chance to build her own legacy. Now she'd risked her position at Janów to save Ewan, and she put her next decision in Bret's hands.

What if he insisted that she stay at Janów with Filip? Or better, begged her to go with him to London?

The thought fled as quickly as it came. He knew her too well—he knew now what he hadn't understood back when he'd pushed her to leave Poland.

She would never leave the horses. She wouldn't leave Lubor.

But could he truly say the words to set her on this path?

He could trust her fate to Werner Vogel. He was certain of it. He thought back to Adia's illness and how he'd had to let go of his own limited control and rely on the German colonel to secure the medicine that only he could provide.

The truth was, with bombing intensifying on all fronts and now

271

with this latest intelligence he must take to London, he had no more cards to play. He must face the truth that he had never controlled her or the circumstances around her.

He had to let her go. She'd be better protected at Werner's side.

"You should go with the horses to Hostau." He brushed her cheek, pulled her closer on the log. "There's no one better qualified to look after those horses. And the stables in Czechoslovakia must be better protected from a military skirmish if Werner feels compelled enough to move the stallions away."

Her eyes filled with tears, and she leaned her head on his shoulder. "Thank you," she breathed. "I'll admit, I almost didn't want you to say that."

He chuckled. "If I'd asked you to come to London with me, would you?"

"No. I would have wanted to say yes." Her brows lifted. "But I couldn't leave the horses."

"I wouldn't want that for you." Nor could he have asked it of her. He loved her, every bit of her. And that included her devotion to the horses.

She sighed. "We just never seem to have the right timing, do we?"

"Not yet, at least," he said. *One day, though . . .*

"So, you're going back to London?" Her voice wobbled.

"I must deliver this information personally. It's too valuable to trust to anyone else."

She picked her head up off his shoulder and glanced toward the truck. "Would you take Ewan with you?"

Staying at Janów certainly wasn't an option now that the thief was a fugitive. And Hostau would be the same scenario. There was no other place for the mouse here in the war zone. Elizabeth's face flashed in his mind. His spunky, fiery sister might just be the only other soul in Europe who could keep Ewan from the work camps.

"I will. I know just the person to look after him."

She shuddered as if holding back a sob. "Oh, I hate this. Leaving Poland, losing you and Ewan both. It's happening so fast."

He cupped the side of her face, his body electrified as she leaned into his touch and closed her eyes. "You aren't losing us. You just have important work to do still."

"You as well," she countered. "I've heard all about the ruckus you and the partisans raise. It affects the Germans' morale deeply."

He shook his head. "Finally get a compliment out of you, right before you skip town."

She chuckled, the melodic sounds etching into his soul, reminding him of the days and weeks they'd spent together in the twilight of the war. So many scars ago.

He pulled her close and searched her intoxicating gaze. "Just promise me this—if Werner is reassigned or leaves the stables long-term, you'll find a way to get out of there by whatever means necessary."

"I promise."

"This isn't goodbye, Adia," he whispered. "We'll have our time." He brushed his lips against hers. Her breath caught. He pulled back just far enough to breathe, "I love you, Adia. I've loved you ever since you stood between me and that little pickpocket."

"I love you too." Tears streamed down her cheeks as she laughed. "I think I knew it for a while, but when you brought back Ewan and Lubor in November of '39 . . . I was a goner."

She met his kiss once more, lacing her fingers around his neck and holding him closely. She was warm, her passion a fire that raged between them. His own mind turned primal, taking in every second and committing to memory the indisputable truth: she was made to fit into his arms. They were matched in every way.

And yet she'd be an entire world away. The front lines of the war—tanks, artillery, and thousands of men—would stand between them.

But not forever. They'd both seen how quickly the situation could shift in this war.

"I promise," he said, breaking their kiss reluctantly. "One day we'll go to Babka's for a quiet meal. One day the stars will align for us."

She smiled, leaning her forehead on his and closing her eyes. "I'll hold you to that promise, Casanova."

36

The flurry of preparations for the stallions' departure—for Adia's farewell to Janów—had left her days long and her emotions scattered.

"Oh, and don't forget the lower pasture floods at the start of each fall, so make sure the horses are moved off or they'll get hoof rot," she was saying to Filip as he led her to the trucks awaiting her in the driveway.

Lubor, Wojownik, Palermo, Balik, and the young, unruly Dorek were all loaded into the horse trailers and attached to the military lorries. The trucks had been replaced after Bret and his rebels stole the originals the week prior.

Adia's heart fluttered and her cheeks warmed in thinking of him. His kisses still burned on her lips, and his earnest promises still echoed through her ears.

One day, the stars would align. And then it would be their time.

Days, weeks, months, or years. Whatever it be.

Filip reached over and clapped a hand on her shoulder. "Relax, Adia—we'll manage without you. Begrudgingly, but I'll take good care of everyone until you return."

She looked over and her eyes flooded with tears. He held out hope that this relocation was temporary. Adia wasn't so sure. As they neared the entrance to the clock tower, she paused and hugged her friend and mentor.

He trembled ever so slightly—the smallest bit of wavering that she'd ever seen of this pillar of Poland's legacy. "Be careful out there," he whispered, low so the soldiers couldn't overhear. "Trust no one, and promise me you'll abandon Lubor if it means saving your life." He leaned back, his own eyes glistening with tears.

Unable to say the words, she just nodded.

"Travel safe, Adia." Filip squeezed her hand and turned away, as if he was unable to bear the thought of watching the best stallions, the last vestiges of the breeding program he'd spent his life rebuilding, leave the country of their birth.

She stood beneath the white column of the clock tower arching up into the sparkling spring sky. Any other Sunday, she might have taken a trip into the market for anything that might be available.

But today, she must say farewell.

Hadn't she already endured the hardest goodbye? To the little thief who'd stolen her heart and the man who'd professed his love and devotion. The man she loved in return. Even through the haze of war and uncertainty, she pictured a life growing old beside him. With at least a hundred horses and half a dozen children.

"Fräulein?" Werner's polite voice floated over to her. He stepped from one of the trucks and cautiously approached, his head angled and his gaze studying her as if she might flee or change her mind. "It is time to go."

They had a train to catch. They'd cover the horses' legs in fluffy cotton and flannel wraps to protect them on the bumpy road ahead, then lead them into the train cars. Once they were on board, it was only a day's journey to the small town in Czechoslovakia that would be their new home.

This was the point of no return. She could still refuse, set her backpack of clothing down, and hold fast to her home and her place of refuge. Where she might be with Bret when he returned from London. Where she knew the town, the people, the language.

Babka, Ludwik, Tomasz, Rafał . . .

Instead, the unknown stood before her.

"Shall we?" Werner held out his elbow respectfully.

With a final glance over her shoulder, drinking in the views of the clean aisles, the arched metal stalls, and the light streaming in through the tall glass windows, she whispered, "Żegnam i dziękuję."

Farewell, and thank you.

———

From the back of a farm truck full of crates of rhubarb, Bret watched the border of Poland fade into the horizon as he jostled side to side with each rut in the road.

Would he regret this decision for the rest of his life? What if he never saw her again?

Ewan bumped against him as they sat wedged together, the eight-year-old's gaze as steady and wise as that of an old man. Ewan was no stranger to the trials of the world.

And he was probably missing Adia as much as Bret did in that moment.

The boy was also losing his home, his friends, and the comfort of all he'd ever been surrounded by. He had been stoic and silent for the past few days after Bret and Adia had told him he'd be going to England.

But Bret felt the resistance in him, the same stubbornness he'd felt when trying to get Ewan to cross the Bug River when the child said he couldn't swim.

Ewan held his small canvas bag of clothing and belongings to his chest and rested his chin on top of it.

Bret smiled, remembering what Adia had told him on the hillside. "So, you taught the Amerykanka to pick locks?"

Ewan's gaze snapped over to Bret's. He looked terrified for an instant as if he were in trouble, but when he saw Bret's smile, his body relaxed. "Yes. How did you know?"

Bret wouldn't share enough to put the boy in danger, but he knew distraction was helpful in times of sorrow. "She broke into a very important safe and discovered some very important information." The papers burned from within the hidden compartment in his boot.

"Really?" Ewan's face broke into a smile. "I don't believe it! She was very, very bad at picking locks."

Bret chuckled. "Well, it seems you were a good teacher. She managed it."

Ewan shook his head. "What is the English word? Miracle?"

"Miracle, indeed."

The boy's face fell somber again. "You sure she'll be okay with Herr Schultze and Oberst Vogel? What if the miracles run out?"

Bret wondered and feared the exact same thing. "We just have to have faith and do our best, Myszko."

"But you won't leave me in England, right?" Ewan pressed.

Bret hesitated. That, he didn't know. Once he delivered the intelligence Adia had found on the German plans to invade the Soviet Union, he had no idea what his superiors would command of him. Return to Poland to help the resistance? Remain in London as an analyst?

Bret knew his field experience and undercover missions meant he was too valuable to not have behind enemy lines. There was a strong chance he'd be reassigned to whatever front was most dire. France? Greece? North Africa?

All of it was so hopelessly far away from Adia.

His chest felt split in two at the thought. Was there a way to stay closer to the German occupation in eastern Europe? He'd have to beg for a way to stay within the hemisphere, at least.

But until then, he had to get Ewan and himself through the German checkpoints and smuggled onto a ship bound for London. Scottie had given him careful directions, strapped him with enough cash for bribes, and dropped a few names for him to use if things were dire.

And then, once he and Ewan arrived in London, the truly monumental task of apologizing and appealing to Elizabeth would commence. Would she take in the pickpocketing little mouse? Would she even speak to Bret long enough for him to ask?

He had to keep to his own advice. Have faith.

He reached into his breast pocket, pulled out his grandfather's watch, and lowered it to Ewan. "Why don't you hold on to this for me?"

"No." Ewan shook his head. "It's lucky—and yours."

"Exactly. I think you'll need that bit of luck when it comes to settling into your new life in England. But I know you can do it." *With or without me there.*

Ewan took it hesitantly. "It's smaller than I remembered it being." He chuckled and rubbed his thumb over the engravings.

Bret laughed softly. "That's because you were a good eight inches shorter two years ago when you first nicked it from me."

Ewan winked. "Aren't you glad I did, though?"

Bret's stomach tightened and his arms ached for Adia at the thought. At the priceless memory of approaching her and negotiating a dinner date, which he'd missed entirely. It hadn't just led him to Adia but also to Ewan, Tomasz, Rafał, and so many others who had shaped his life these past two years.

"Don't take this as an incentive to take back up the habit, but yes, I sure am glad you did." He wrapped his arm around Ewan's shoulders and held him close. He chided gently, "You keep that safe from other pickpockets while you're in jolly ol' England. And for now, try to get some rest. We've got some long days ahead of us."

37

The grounds of Hostau, in stark contrast to the castle-like feel of Janów, were utilitarian and simple. The long, rectangular rows of stalls were tucked along the sweeping green hills of the small town. Hostau was quaint enough, with white churches and stone-roofed houses on winding streets.

Even after a month in their new home, Adia was as unsettled as her five stallions seemed to be, pacing in their stalls, nostrils flared to draw in each new scent.

When it came to understanding the Czech language, she felt equally as lost. While slightly more similar to Polish than Russian was, and vastly different from how she'd learned to communicate in German with Werner, the pronunciation of words was so different from Polish. And a similar word might mean something totally different.

One of the locals who worked as a groom in the stables had put forth a small effort to help her fully understand, but the slow development of her understanding frustrated her. In attempting to give instructions, she'd managed to mess up the horse feeding schedule and pasture assignments.

Werner told her to rely on their translators and not bother so much with the nuances of the language, but Adia was planning ahead in case she needed to escape Hostau, with or without the horses. She'd need to navigate the country, and speaking the language would be essential.

At the end of a long week, a small caravan of cargo trucks pulled into the pavilion of the stables, and Adia approached slowly behind Werner.

German soldiers stepped out, saluted the colonel, and motioned to the back of the truck, clattering about excitedly. "Horses from Hungary," they said.

Adia approached cautiously, as she always did with new soldiers she didn't know or trust. One of the men led a shining black stallion down the ramp. His mane was thick and his legs long. A Lipizzaner or warmblood by the looks of him, but black adult Lipizzaners were rare.

"Magnificent," Werner breathed. He smiled over at Adia. "What do you think?"

She couldn't hold back her own smile of appreciation. Her heart was always with the Arabian breed, but she would treasure a straggly old nag the same as a world champion. This horse was certainly a showstopper.

The soldier handed his lead rope off to her, and the horse snorted, pushing her arm gently as he sized her up.

The engraved words on his halter were foreign to her. Hungarian, she guessed. "Do you know his name?" she asked no one in particular.

"Indigo," a man offered. The rest of the sterling white horses were unloaded, examined, and processed as Adia brought Indigo to an unoccupied stall. Lubor nickered at her as she passed by.

Indigo stomped and bobbed his head as if eager to run, eager for action.

Adia smiled and promised herself she'd ride him at the next opportunity. He was powerfully built.

A mountain of chores and work lay ahead for the rest of the day, so she closed the stall door and gave Lubor a gentle pat as she walked by. Beside him, Wojownik looked at her with curious eyes too. They'd all come a long way in bonding with each other and in learning to trust Adia through the strange travel and new location.

What a collection they had here at Hostau—nearly two hundred head, and more filtered in each day. Dozens of white Lipizzaners, Thoroughbreds from all corners of Europe, and Arabians from Poland.

What each fresh dawn would bring, she wasn't quite sure.

Each day ended quite the same, though. Dreaming of Bret, Ewan, and her life once before at Janów. She wondered if they'd reached England yet. If they'd had smooth travels through the occupied countries they'd had to brave. Were they hurt? Were they safe?

Adia slipped into Lubor's stall and ran her hands over his silky coat as she pressed her face to his neck. The stallion nickered and flicked his tail as if acknowledging her unease.

One day, the stars would align. And then it would be their time.

CAMBRIDGE, ENGLAND

The small manor house on a dozen acres outside the city sat as Bret remembered it. Their summer destination whenever he and Elizabeth were home from boarding schools, it was their escape, and the place she'd met Charlie when they were children.

She and Bret had both preferred the house to the larger estate in stuffy ol' London. Charlie and his family had been groundskeepers of this cottage for generations.

Now, to be back without his best friend and brother-in-law, the sight of the stone exterior cut into his soul, and he wasn't sure Elizabeth would even hear him out.

Still, he knocked on the door with Ewan at his side.

Though they'd cleaned up in a safe flat dedicated to MI6 agents' use, the past month of travel across occupied Europe had left them both ragged and exhausted.

Ewan looked up at him questioningly.

"Don't worry," he reassured the boy. "It will all be fine."

Though he had no idea. After speaking briefly to his mother on the telephone in London and learning Lizzy had taken up full-time residence here in Cambridge, Bret wondered if she was still lost in her grief, even two years later.

But then, it was also much quieter and far from the nightly bombing raids of London.

The door swung open, and Bret stared at the mirror of his own features: light brown hair, dark green eyes, and a square jaw. But on Elizabeth, they cast an air of royalty and confidence.

She studied him for a heartbeat and then looked down at the boy.

He realized she might assume that Ewan was his child—Bret had been away from England for nearly eight years, so it was possible, but his sister was not one to jump to conclusions. Except the one where Bret was responsible for Charlie's death. But that could have been true.

"Are you done saving the world then? What else might bring you back home, oh valiant warrior?" Her tone bit as it always had. Always bickering.

"Lizzy, can we talk?"

She looked at Ewan again. "Who's this?"

Ewan glowered back and crossed his arms. In crisp English, he said, "I don't like this woman. Take me back to Janów, Meester Bret."

Elizabeth's eyes sparkled and her face broke into a smile. "Oh, now I'm intrigued. Right then, you both can come in." She swung the door open.

"Golly, thank you," Bret quipped.

Inside the dimly lit house, he noticed the lack of furniture and photos that their mother had prized. Dust adorned the shelves, and the curtains were drawn. The house looked—and felt—more like a mausoleum.

"What's your name?" Elizabeth asked Ewan. "And why don't you like me?"

Ewan frowned. "You're rude to Meester Bret."

Her brow furrowed. "Where are you from? I can't place your accent."

"Lizzy," Bret said, planning to explain everything. But his sister held up her hand to let Ewan answer.

"Your accent is funny to me," Ewan fired back, his ears getting a bit pink as he seemed to flush with irritation.

"How old are you? Six?"

"Eight."

"Why did you steal the small set of keys by the front door when you walked in?" Elizabeth said, her observant gaze apparently not missing anything.

"Ewan!" Bret scolded.

Ewan just smiled. "I changed my mind. This woman isn't as stupid as I thought."

Elizabeth beamed but still held her hand out for the keys. "Stealing is a nasty habit, my friend."

"So is being rude," Ewan said, setting the keys in her hand.

Bret grinned and nodded. Yes. This would all work out quite well. Elizabeth Knightly, infamous for her spunk and keeping up with her older brother and his friend, would be a well-matched guardian for Ewan, the lost Polish orphan.

Bret flicked Ewan's ear to catch his attention. "You go pick out one of the empty bedrooms. You'll be staying here for a while."

Ewan looked up at him. "I will?"

"He will?" Elizabeth echoed.

Bret nodded and turned Ewan toward the staircase to the left of the dining area. "Go on."

After the boy left the room, Elizabeth crossed her arms and angled her head to study Bret. "You look like rubbish."

"I feel like rubbish."

"So, the boy isn't yours?" she asked.

"No, but he's special to me nonetheless. And to the woman I love."

Her jaw fell and her lips parted. "Can it be so?"

Rather than going down that lane of memories, he nodded in the direction Ewan had gone. "Will you look after the boy? I must report back to command. I'm not sure where I'll be assigned next."

Elizabeth turned away, her jaw flexing indecisively.

Bret knew innately that she needed this, needed something beyond her own self and her own mourning. "Please, Lizzy. There's no one better suited within the United Kingdom to tame that boy and set him on the right path."

She stepped closer and nodded. "Sure. But you'll owe me a full recounting of this love story and the boy's rescue over dinner."

"Thank you," Bret said, relief lifting the weight from his shoulders.

"Did—" Her voice broke. "Did you find out who killed him?"

His heart twisted. "I only know it was German agents. I still don't know where the break in our network happened."

She nodded. She'd needed—demanded—answers of him after Charlie's death. But his line of work usually left more questions unanswered. It was part of the risk that someone could disappear without explanation or a trail.

"I haven't given up on looking for the source, Lizzy." He reached out to squeeze her hand. "You know I don't give up easily."

She nodded. "I'm fully aware of your flaws, brother."

He pulled her into a hug, and they clung to each other for the first time in years, perhaps the first step in restitching a bond that had been shattered by death, betrayal, and years apart.

PART THREE

THE GHOSTS

38

JANUARY 10, 1944

Sunshine burst through the towering trees as Adia leaned forward against Indigo's neck. She treasured these moments, as rare as they were lately. Winter had wrapped Hostau in a coat of snow, but the past few days of above-freezing temperatures had left paths of green in the forests surrounding the stud farm.

She drew the stallion to a walk as the forest path narrowed and branches brushed her face. The smell of smoke, which was out of place in this remote forest, suddenly washed over her.

The past three years in Hostau had taught her to be on edge and aware of danger around every corner. No part of Europe was stable as Americans had joined the war and claimed victories in North Africa; the Russians had pushed the Germans back in the Soviet Union; the Italians were in turmoil. Adia heard only rumors and questioned each new prisoner of war brought to the farm as a laborer.

Now she pulled Indigo to a stop and whirled her head around, ready for any possible threat.

And then the click of rifles and stomping on the forest floor.

"Ruce vzhůru!" voices screamed. *Hands up.*

She hesitated only for a moment, considering kicking Indigo

ahead. But if they fired at her—and hit the horse—she'd never be able to bear it.

"I mean you no harm," she called out in Czech, which she'd worked hard to perfect in the past three years. "I'm American! I'm a prisoner of Hostau."

Whispers circled around her, and figures emerged from the bushes, each clad in layers of gray or white woolen clothing and holding guns painted white to blend in with the snow.

The leader, presumably, stepped forward and lowered the firearm. "American?" a crackling old woman's voice repeated. "What is an American woman doing as a prisoner at the horse farm?"

Adia smiled. "That's a long story, actually."

"Are you armed?" The old woman lowered the scarf from her mouth and looked her up and down.

Adia shook her head.

"Get back to your posts," the woman called over her shoulder before walking up to Adia.

Adia dismounted. "My name's—"

"Ach," the woman cut her off. "We don't share names around here, you fool. You can call me Shepherd."

"Oh, okay."

"I'll figure out a name for you if I need it." The lines on the woman's wrinkled forehead deepened as she raised her eyebrows. "What are you doing out here?"

"Just going for a ride," Adia said.

"Prisoners are allowed to saunter through the forest?" Shepherd tensed, her gun lifting ever so slightly.

"I'm the head trainer. I have the trust of the German in command."

Something sparked in Shepherd's eyes. "Do you, now?"

Adia sensed something shifting in the winds and knew whatever this partisan leader had in mind, it would be dangerous.

But these were dangerous times.

"I have no love for the Nazis," Adia whispered, adrenaline surging anew. "How can I help?"

JANUARY 12, 1944
LONDON

Bret walked through the doors of the building on Broadway that had a brass sign reading MINIMAX FIRE EXTINGUISHER COMPANY. It was really the headquarters of the Secret Intelligence Service, and not many in all the world knew the truth of it.

He walked past the plain wooden walls and frosted glass of what felt like a dull, dated office building and knocked on the door of the retired colonel they all called the Commander.

Sir James Whitley was portly, humorless, and cunning. He'd taken a chance on Bret and Charlie when they were only twenty-one years old. Though Charlie had been lost, when Bret had brought back word of Operation Barbarossa in 1941, the Commander had praised him and given him the official military rank of captain and his pick of assignments. While Czechoslovakia hadn't been one of the assignments to choose from, Bret had eagerly returned to France to help with the underground resistance in the hopes that France would be the largest step that the Allies needed in liberating all of Europe.

The past three years of setting improvised bombs, sneaking around occupied cities, and yearning for the days of peace left him with streaks of gray in his stubble and the hair at his temples. But when word had reached him about the Commander calling him back to headquarters for a new assignment, Bret jumped at the chance. He'd been very clear with the Commander back in 1941—whenever an assignment in Czechoslovakia opened up, he wanted it.

Anything to be closer to her.

The Commander motioned to the leather seat across from his mahogany desk. Bret sat on the edge, his back rigid.

"We're planning something big to infiltrate Northern France," the Commander said. "You know the area better than most, and this group is going to be a reconnaissance group behind enemy lines.

They'll need to be fast, silent, and effective. It's a lot more combat than you've seen. But it comes with a promotion."

Bret didn't give a fig about the promotion. His pulse raced. "Sir, would this group eventually venture into Czechoslovakia?"

The Commander's gaze glistened. "General Patton would have them go straight through to Russia and back again if he had his way. But yes. And I know you've got a hankering for that country."

Bret didn't hesitate. "I'm in."

"I should warn you. The plans we're discussing right now are quite risky. Northern France is heavily fortified against any type of Allied assault."

"I don't care. I want the assignment."

"So be it." The Commander nodded and handed him a slip of paper. "You're now officially Major Conway, intelligence officer with the 42nd Squadron of Patton's Second Cavalry. Hope you practiced your American drawl. These are a rowdy bunch of Yankee cowboys."

Bret took the slip and nodded his thanks.

He'd endure whatever it took to reach Hostau.

39

Adia dismounted the tall black stallion at the edge of the Bohemian forest—a forest filled with partisans and the only lifeline between her life at Hostau and the man she loved.

She dragged Indigo's reins over his neck and patted his shoulders. The Lipizzaner had proven an invaluable partner, especially since Lubor was too closely guarded and watched by the Nazis at Hostau. Her freedom to come and go was a tenuous thing. Without Werner's protection, she most certainly would have been sent to a work camp for her insubordination by now.

A woman's gravelly voice drifted from the tree line. "Morning, Angel."

"Morning, Shepherd," Adia called back, as she had hundreds of times since stumbling across this forest last year and offering to help in whatever way she could.

The spring air was crisp in the dawn, though traces of smoke and gunpowder from the nearing front always enveloped the valley. Emerald waves of fields and whitewashed houses rose from the sloping hills, yet untouched by artillery or tanks. It felt a lot like Janów had, before.

"You look tired," Shepherd said, her wrinkled face appearing from the shade of the trees as Adia and Indigo walked up.

Adia chuckled. "You've been keeping me busy. And I wouldn't have it any other way."

Shepherd grinned and the wrinkles of her face all piled together. The fire of youth and strength gleamed through her blue eyes, always reminding Adia of Babka and her undefeatable attitude in the face of occupation.

"I have three packages for you in five days."

"Three?" Adia blinked. Indigo nudged her, sensing her shift in mood. "I'm not sure I can manage that many."

"You'll have to figure it out. We have no other choice."

No other choice. How many times in the past six years of war had she heard the same phrase, felt the same pressure? If the past four years at Hostau had taught her anything, though, it was that sometimes the only path forward was still the right path. She'd step out in blind faith, as she often had.

She nodded. "I'll rendezvous at ten o'clock as normal."

"I've got letters here for you," Shepherd said, pulling out two small envelopes.

Adia's breath caught, and she reached for them like a starving child in hopes of scraps. "Thank you," she whispered, her voice strained.

The woman chuckled. "I'm guessing they're from your man, the way you light up over these letters. Others think it's just your family."

Adia looked at his handwriting, her code name, Angel, printed neatly on the envelope. Her vision swam with tears in anticipation. She couldn't speak, couldn't find her voice.

"Well, have faith, Angel. From what I hear, the Americans are a few kilometers from the Czech border. If the Germans know better, they'll all be running home with their tails between their legs."

Adia swallowed. "Sometimes the cornered dog is the most dangerous."

Shepherd stilled, the rustling leaves the only sound between them. "See you in five days, my dear."

Adia tucked the letters into her boot lining, mounted Indigo, and raced back to Hostau, her thoughts focused on the words waiting on those pieces of paper.

After putting away the stallion, she jogged past Lubor's paddock to check on him. The deep brown horse looked at her and snorted his welcome, his black eyes wide and observant. He'd grown jealous of her time with Indigo, but he was far too recognizable and far too valuable to take on long ventures beyond the stable walls. After feeding him a small handful of the sparse grain, she raced back to her cabin and locked the door behind her.

With her back pressed to the wood, she pulled out the envelopes and opened the first. Emotion choked her, this added gift of working with the partisans almost more than she could bear. After so long, she'd gotten word out of Hostau once she started helping Shepherd. And he'd been able to send her word.

Bret.

The first letter was dated eight months earlier and mostly filled with an update on Ewan and Elizabeth. It was the only topic that wouldn't be censored or dangerous for anyone carrying the letter.

She had no idea where Bret was, other than somewhere on the European continent. He'd left London after taking her little Myszko to his sister's. She liked to imagine he was still causing trouble for the Germans in Wygoda, with Nowak, Tomasz, and Rafał at his side.

> You'll be glad to hear Lizzy has outsmarted E. at his own game. He kept sneaking out after blackout curfew each night, so she started hiding trinkets within the house to challenge his skills in the confines of safe walls. If he doesn't collect all twelve each night, he doesn't win fresh cookies.

Adia brushed away a tear, wondering how tall Ewan had grown in their years apart. He'd had a rough transition to life outside of

Poland, but Bret's widowed sister had found a mission in him and won him over. She was a godsend.

Apparently, the care of the little boy had helped Bret and Elizabeth heal their strained relationship too. But Bret hadn't been able to share the full story in his letters.

> *He's adopted a proper English accent and is excelling at mathematics. He asks about you often.*

And then, the words she lived for, ached for.

> *I miss you, so very fiercely. We'll have our time, one day soon. I love you.*
>
> ### Casanova

The second letter was six months old and filled with more Ewan stories. A short school suspension after stealing all the erasers from each classroom, which drew most lessons to a halt. Bret had found that one particularly clever.

Then, a story about attempting to adopt a stray dog. Ewan had brought the mutt into his schoolhouse schemes, and after the third time the dog was lost in the halls, it had to be sent away to the Conways' other countryside manor.

> *Don't feel sorry for Lizzy. She's rising to the challenge and E. is the one who must face her wrath. E. has been made to atone for his sins, including several hours of cleaning each chalkboard in every classroom at the school.*

Bret shared more of his shenanigans, including how the hard-hearted General and Mrs. Conway had begun to come around to Ewan and now tolerated their missing silverware.

> *Once this war is over, the three of us will retire to the countryside, and we'll find ways to keep the little scamp occupied. I*

dream of this life every day—it soothes me and heals my soul to know you are my future. I love you.

Casanova

Adia read the letters twice more to commit them to memory, trembling as she fought back tears. She had too much work to do to sit here and read them all day. And the upcoming assignment would be her hardest mission yet. She'd need to make provisions and ensure Indigo was ready.

She walked over to her fireplace and set the letters in the still-warm coals from her fire last night. They caught fire and soon were reduced to ash. The safest fate for her, Bret, and Shepherd.

Now, back to the rounds of feeding, exercising, and tending ails of all kinds, in the hope that the Germans would one day soon abandon the farm and the Allies would descend upon them.

This war couldn't last forever.

Could it?

Either way, she'd continue with her own war—the horses and the little special packages she guided to safety under the moonlight.

ASCH, GERMANY

"RPGs!"

"Take cover!"

Soldiers cried out from the back of a half-track lumbering alongside Bret, who operated the gun at the top of a Chaffee tank.

The rocket-propelled grenade upturned another Chaffee only a few hundred yards ahead and sent shock waves over the whole squad. Their intelligence—his own network of spies—had been wrong about the type and strength of ordnances the German soldiers had in Asch.

But these men were the Ghosts of Patton's Army, and they'd never backed down from a fight. At least, not in the past year that Bret had been embedded with the unit.

All the American machine guns targeted the corner of a square where it seemed the grenades—tank killers—had fired from. The meat chopper, their four-barrel machine gun typically used for antiaircraft, made for nothing but utter devastation when used on ground targets.

The guns soon reduced the stone-faced storefront that had housed a handful of SS soldiers to rubble. The narrow cobble streets of this seemingly sleepy town had now become a funnel of firepower. And while the German presence was more than anyone had expected, even their rocket-powered grenades were no match for the herd of metal horses.

The Second Cavalry spread through the medieval-looking town, the windows shut and torn Nazi propaganda posters fluttering from walls or singed at the edges from explosions.

Bret never took an easy advance for granted. The enemy resistance in this part of Germany had surprised him beyond even their long winter in the Ardennes. It seemed Asch was no exception.

As the assigned intelligence officer, Bret could have stayed behind at camp instead of leading in the primary tanks, but his heart wouldn't allow it. It was an honor and marvel to fight alongside these men, and his time with the partisans had shifted his view of what it meant to truly fight for the disadvantaged.

"SS! Contact right!"

Bret turned, instantly barking commands as the wave of new enemies closed in on the right flank of the Second.

A half-track jolted and the cab burst into flames. Bret cranked his Browning machine gun and zeroed in on the man carrying the grenade tube and the three soldiers flanking him for cover. He pressed his thumbs to the trigger, and the M2 Browning spat 50-millimeter lead bullets that rained upon the soldiers and halted their assault with a decisive end.

Just as he sat back to evaluate the surroundings once more, a scream echoed across the column. "Grenade!"

The Chaffee tank beneath Bret bucked like a wild colt, catapulting him through the air in a heat wave that tore across his skin and face.

He landed on his hip and shoulder and skidded to a painful stop along the stone streets, where a nearby private raced toward him.

The boy leaned over and spoke, but Bret's ears rang and pulsed from the explosion. How in the world had he even survived that?

His heart sank. Zane and Kip, who were driving and navigating that tank, certainly could not have been as lucky.

The private hooked his arm under Bret's elbow and helped him to his feet. His head swam with the buzzing and screeching in his ears.

He blinked away the haze and checked his sidearm, then raised it and aimed at each alleyway and window, prepared for anything.

Where had that grenade even come from? The Germans were deeply entrenched in the stone buildings.

"Sir?" The private's voice cut through the ringing in his ears. Bret looked over just as a bullet whizzed past, and the private collapsed.

Bret swung around, saw two SS officers with long rifles aimed his way, and fired his Luger. He dropped both with two shots, paused to ensure the coast was clear, and then knelt down beside the kid.

He spotted his tags. Tyler Erickson. "Tyler?" He searched for the wound. He ripped open the fatigues at his shoulder, seeing a deep red stain growing from just above his heart. "Medic!" He looked around, relieved to see Howards and McCollough racing up with their Red Cross armbands and satchels.

They pushed Bret aside, Howards giving their commander a quick once-over and saying something Bret couldn't hear yet through the ringing tones.

Bret shook his head. "I'm fine. Tend to him."

Howards nodded and turned back to Private Erickson.

Bret stood, swayed slightly, and glanced around to find Colonel Roland, Sergeant O'Connor, or someone who could give him a status update.

The report of M1's had slowed, providing a small measure of relief that they were taking control of the city. The stream of vehicles had thinned as the troopers disarmed German soldiers.

"Major Conway?" A hand gripped his arm. "Major!"

He turned. Colonel Kenneth Roland was speaking quickly and motioning around.

"Speak up," Bret said, pointing to his ears and shaking his head.

"We've secured the main resistance and are working to arrest the pockets who fled."

Bret nodded. "Casualties?"

"At least twenty." Roland frowned and tilted his head. "Dozens of injuries, including you, it seems."

"Zane and Kip? In my tank?"

Roland shook his head.

Bret glanced down at his uniform. Though it was dirty, he couldn't spot a bit of blood or any sign of a broken bone. Then he saw a few drips on his collar and reached up to touch his forehead. It was slick and warm and gritty with dust.

No wonder Howards had looked at him so strangely.

Bret shook it off, fell into stride next to Roland, and began to mentally log each fallen soldier and the ragged state of their Jeeps, trucks, and remaining tanks. Curse those rocket-propelled grenades.

The other lieutenants and sergeants barked commands and motioned to direct the injured and reassign the unharmed. The squadron was a well-oiled machine, and now that the immediate danger had passed, Bret's adrenaline waned, and he felt the rush of exhaustion and the sting along his hairline from whatever cut had left him covered in blood. The buzzing and ringing in his ears had finally cleared, leaving him lightheaded and constantly nauseous.

He relented after all the other injured had been tended to and asked Howards for a row of stitches. As always, he wished it was Adia doing the needlework instead. Just to have her close.

A few hours later, after the last of the town was cleared and the Second Cavalry had settled into their new forward position, Bret approached Jimmy O'Connor by a small fire blazing in an old fuel barrel. The burly man was wrapping a cut on his hand, grimacing while holding a cigar between his lips.

"Conway." He nodded a greeting.

"O'Connor." Bret lowered himself beside the Boston-born sergeant and let out a long breath.

O'Connor tore the white bandage gauze and tucked it in on itself to secure the wrapping. "Three hundred and twenty-two days in this drudge. How many more, you reckon?"

"Too many." It had been two thousand and fifty-eight days of war for him, for Poland. For Adia. But he tried not to make a point of it. The men of the Second Cavalry had fought valiantly and bled much since they'd landed in Normandy in June 1944.

It had been nearly four years since he'd last seen her face, felt her presence. The world was so gray and dark without her beside him. But each village they cleared of German forces was one step closer to Hostau.

Germany couldn't hold out much longer.

But he prayed for Adia's and the horses' sake that Hostau would.

Later that evening, he returned from the forward position at Asch to their headquarters in Eslarn, in the Bavarian forest near the Czech border. Most of the men had filtered back as well, as new groups pushed forward into Asch, eliminating the enemy one building and street at a time.

At camp, he grabbed a plate of chow and sat beside O'Connor in the mess tent.

"Ye hear from yer sister lately?" O'Connor asked. "Those Ewan stories are a hoot. Reminds me of myself when I was a lad."

Bret appreciated how similar O'Connor's brogue was to Charlie's. Both men were Irish in ancestry, but O'Connor's Boston upbringing had left his manner a bit more opinionated and demanding. Still, he reminded Bret in all the best ways of his long-gone best friend.

"Nothing lately." Bret chuckled. "I'm sure Ewan hid her stationery or something."

"Wish I was as skilled as he sounds. I always got caught and walloped good."

Bret nodded, somber at the recollection of how close Ewan had come to life—and potential death—at a work camp due to his pick-pocketing compulsion.

That led him to remember the look on Adia's face when he'd brought the scamp and Lubor back to Janów. It was the first time Bret had seen her unreserved love for the child, and just how complex that woman truly was beneath her tough facade.

Did his letters reach her?

He had no way of knowing, only the luxury of knowing she was safe behind the walls of Hostau. And that he was mere kilometers away. He held to their position here in Eslarn, only five kilometers from the border. Hostau was only twenty-four more kilometers into the country that the Second Cavalry had not yet infiltrated.

But soon enough. The Ghosts were fast, second to none.

I'm coming for you, Adia.

40

Your must listen very closely and obey every word, or we'll all be shot," Adia said in a quiet, firm voice. Three sets of eyes stared at her through the inky darkness of the midnight hour. "You mustn't cry out or scream or even sneeze. We will move very fast, and it will take several hours to get free of the Germans' reach." Her voice shook. "If we are captured, you are to get away and run as fast as you can. Bite, kick, do whatever you must. Do not wait for me or even look back. Understood?"

She'd repeated the words so often, they were seared into her mind. Yet they always drew her back to the days hiding from Germans and Russians with Bret, searching for the lost colts in Poland. And how she'd refused to follow the plans he'd encouraged. She realized now that it was because she'd fallen for him even by then.

The three black-haired children nodded. She didn't know their names, their stories, or where they'd end up. She only knew if she didn't succeed in getting them to the border of the German-held territory, where they'd be smuggled to the Red Cross in Allied territory, they'd be dead.

She wrapped a black wool blanket around their frail bodies and pulled her deep black velvet cloak around her own shoulders and head. The children were so small they appeared to be six, four, and two years old, but they were so undernourished they could be far older.

As they did every time, the children reminded her of Ewan, so distant but at least free from such threats.

She slipped them onto the saddle and led Indigo through the back pasture, where his hooves made only the slightest clomp-clomp-clomp against the hard dirt. Her movements and pathways were deliberate, practiced.

Once she reached a small, forested area, she mounted the horse, tucking the two smallest children in front of her and holding them tightly. The oldest was seated behind her on the horse's rump, holding fast to her waist.

She leaned forward and nudged the stallion's sides with her heels. He responded instantly, bolting into a long, smooth canter. The children gasped, but true to their promise, they made no other sound.

The wind stung her eyes and rustled her cloak around them, Indigo's long mane brushing against the children's faces with each stride. She pressed against the children, exactly the height to avoid the low branches.

Indigo followed the route they'd both memorized—the pathway through Bavaria and to the next safe house within the network that would smuggle the children to the Allied Red Cross. They broke out of the forest, and she glanced around the dark clearing, grateful to see no sign of any military patrols.

She kicked Indigo gently again, allowing him to run faster in the open field. The faster they could cover the twenty-nine kilometers to the border, the better.

The youngest children trembled beneath her, from the cool evening air or fear of the horse's speed, she wasn't sure.

Faster, Indigo. We can't fail these children.

After the moon had crept further into the sky, Adia slowed the panting Indigo to a walk, though he still snorted nervously and energetically. There was a reason she relied on this stallion for such life-and-death matters. He was the best of his breed, unmatched in his stamina and speed. Lubor would probably best him on a race-track, but Indigo wasn't nearly as infamous.

Just as her pulse settled with the knowledge that the border was only steps away, a twig snapped, and Indigo jumped sideways, star-tling all four of his riders.

She pulled the reins back, swerving to flee the noise and praying whoever made the noise wasn't armed—or wasn't a decent shot. Cursed Germans. Must they cover every corner of these beautiful lands?

They were so close to freedom. They couldn't be caught now.

"Hold on," she whispered to the children. She kicked Indigo and he bolted ahead, his hooves digging into the ground and propelling them onward like a locomotive.

The smallest child squeaked a frightened cry. Through the dark shadows, Adia aimed for the shelter of another patch of trees. So far, no shots had rung out, but she somehow felt the approach of bodies closing in around them. She and Indigo had slipped free of close calls before, but that strange, foreboding feeling deep in her bones told her this time was different.

No. She wouldn't allow these children to be taken back to a ter-rible camp, awaiting certain death. The rumors she heard of the detainment centers were too terrible to fathom.

"Come on, Indigo," she muttered, willing him to use every last ounce of his speed to reach safety.

They reached the trees just as a dozen dark shadows appeared, long rifles in their hands and helmets covering their faces from the starlight above.

Indigo jerked to a stop, stood on his hind legs, and pawed at the attackers as they surrounded them.

A hand reached up, clasped her by the cloak, and pulled.

Falling. She flailed her hands, reaching for the children but losing all bearing. And then she landed on her back, air fleeing her lungs and slow to return.

Several faces appeared before her amid a murmuring of voices, commands, and noises. Another pair of hands grasped hold of Indigo's reins, though the horse whinnied and pulled against his captors. The children whimpered somewhere distant, but Adia's mind could hardly make sense of anything over the pain shooting through every nerve.

"Wait," she gasped in German, slowly gaining her voice. "Stop. Don't take the children. They are innocent. Do what you want with me but leave them be!"

"Translator!" a deep voice called out in English.

Her chest constricted, hope blazing like a bonfire on a moonless night. The air returned to her lungs and the haze of her mind instantly cleared.

They spoke in English.

The Allies had reached Czechoslovakia.

"Wait!" she sputtered in English. "Who are you? Where are you from?"

"Blimey!" a voice exclaimed. "It's a broad! She's English."

"American," Adia said. "I was taking these children to the border."

"Well, you found it," someone said.

The group settled around her, the three children each held by several soldiers and Indigo gripped carefully by another.

Under the brims of their metal helmets, they looked curiously upon her and the horse. Others around the edges of the group stared out into the dark forest, which told Adia that they knew the danger that lurked in these woods.

In the dim lighting, she could see the American flag on their uniforms.

Never had a symbol meant so very much. Tears welled at the corners of her eyes. "Can you take the children to the Red Cross? I can't go beyond the border. I haven't the time."

The leader, it seemed, held up a hand. "Whoa, hold on. We'll get to this, but you need to come back to camp for us to verify your story."

Panic seized her chest. Indigo pranced nervously, pulling against the soldier's grip on his reins. "I can't. It is life-and-death if I don't return by dawn."

"Then save your protest and follow us. It's only one klick west. We'll feed and water your horse and see if we can't confirm everything you've said."

She relaxed, but only slightly. Indigo did need the rest and water. An hour. She had less than an hour to spare.

ESLARN, GERMANY

"Get up, Conway." O'Connor's voice came with a boot nudge to the leg.

Bret sat up on his cot and groaned. A quick glance around showed that none of the other boys had been rousted from sleep, so it wasn't an attack. "What is it?"

O'Connor grinned mischievously. "Need your interrogation services. Found something unique on patrol. You'll just have to come see for yourself."

He rubbed his forehead and stiff neck, his head groggy. "It couldn't wait until morning?"

"Not by her account."

Bret slipped on his boots and stood. "Her?"

O'Connor put an unlit cigar in his teeth and jerked his head for Bret to follow.

They wove through the cots of sleeping soldiers, dim moonlight illuminating the ground outside the tent. Starlight shone through the spots of trees along this forest outside Asch. Not enough smoke tonight to choke them out. Bret tried to appreciate these rare moments.

He expected to go toward the command's tent, but they veered toward the stacks of supplies and parked trucks and tanks. Just as

Bret started to wonder if O'Connor was pulling some kind of midnight prank, the unmistakable sound of hooves on gravel brought him out of the residual sleepiness. Behind one of the tanks stood a black, thick-muscled horse with an arched neck and flowing mane and tail.

Lipizzaner. Purebred.

Something caught in his throat. His pulse jumped, a distant string of hope tied to the larger tapestry of the past six years.

Then a voice came from a dimly lit supply tent on the other side of another tank. "How many times must I say it? I haven't the time or breath to waste."

He knew that tone. That spunk.

Adia.

He entered the tent without permission, reason and decorum lost to the impossible.

She stood at the end of the tent with her back turned to him, standing over three young children. She wore a large black cloak, her long, dark hair falling freely over her shoulders.

Surely it was a mirage. A dream. A hallucination. His feet were frozen to the ground. O'Connor stepped up beside him, which drew Colonel Roland's attention to their entrance.

"Ah, thank you for coming, Major," Roland said, stepping past Adia.

"Colonel, I must insist—" Adia turned to follow his path, then drew up short when she saw him.

It wasn't a dream. She was real. She was here.

Her furrowed forehead went smooth, her mouth falling open in surprise.

The air around them went as thick as half-frozen, winter mud. He couldn't breathe. Couldn't speak. Couldn't move.

But Adia could.

She bolted past Roland, dodging two soldiers nearby who tried to reach out and grab the fleeing captive. She ran straight into Bret's arms. Magnetic opposites pulled together with an inescapable force.

He wrapped his arms around her, gripping her, breathing in her presence. She was terribly thin beneath the heavy fabric of her cloak.

She buried her face in his neck, mumbling in breathless waves, "It's you. It's really you."

The soldiers backed away when it was clear she wasn't a threat.

O'Connor cleared his throat. "So, you two know each other?" When neither Bret nor Adia responded, he elbowed Roland. "Should we, uh, give them a few minutes?"

Bret looked over Adia's shoulder at Roland, who scanned them with a suspicious expression. "Two minutes, Conway. Then I need answers."

They all left, the children following O'Connor, who offered them some chocolate bars.

Once alone, Bret kissed her. He cupped the back of her head, finally finding his voice. "What are you doing here?"

She lifted her head just enough to meet his gaze with her own watery eyes. She seemed to take in each inch of his face the way he did hers. While she was as striking and familiar as she'd ever been, the past four years had left her thin, her cheeks pale.

"Me?" she said with a gasp. "Why aren't you in Poland with the resistance?"

"I requested a transfer—hoping to get as close to you as I could."

Tears raced down her cheeks. She looked over at the piles of munitions beside them. "But the front lines, Bret? I thought we agreed not to jump in front of guns." She scanned the stitches along his hairline.

He kissed her forehead. "Your presence here erases your argument. Why aren't you behind the walls of Hostau?"

She flushed and pressed next to him, perhaps as afraid as he was that one of them would somehow disappear.

"I've been helping the Czech partisans get children out of occupied territory."

His heart skipped several beats. "By riding across active hot zones at night? This forest is teeming with SS squads."

She bit her lip, then smiled and offered a meager shrug. "Good thing I'm a fast rider."

Love, admiration, and longing washed over him in the same instant. "How could I have expected otherwise?"

He'd pulled her face closer, bringing her lips to meet his, when O'Connor popped his head into the tent and cleared his throat loudly. "Time's up, Romeo."

"I prefer Casanova," Adia whispered. Her smile didn't waver, but she took a half step back as Roland and O'Connor walked back into the tent. She broke their stare to search the tent. "Where are the children?"

O'Connor motioned over his shoulder. "At the mess, getting some chow other than chocolate."

Roland crossed his arms, and his direct stare cut the side conversations. "Please explain, Major."

"It's a bit of a long story," Bret said, keeping close to Adia to make it clear where his loyalty lay.

O'Connor beamed. "I got all night."

Adia shifted, looking up at Bret. "I don't." Anguish swept over her expression as if she had just realized something urgent. "If I don't get myself and Indigo back to the farm by daybreak . . ."

Bret could assume the rest.

"What farm?" Roland demanded, his voice rising. He had clearly reached the end of his patience.

"Hostau," Adia said. "Two dozen kilometers to the east. The Germans have stolen hundreds of horses from across Europe for the past six years to build up a super race of horses." She motioned to Bret. "We've worked nearly six years to save the Polish Arabian stock from Janów Podlaski."

Roland's eyebrows rose. Bret knew he was a cavalryman of old. He'd led the last mounted war games in the States, before horses were retired from American forces. The men of the Second spoke often about the tales and laurels of their leader.

Roland pointed outside. "The horse outside doesn't appear to be an Arabian."

"Indigo—he's a rare black Lipizzaner from Hungary." Adia smirked. "And one of the fastest horses in Europe."

"How many horses are at the farm now?" Bret asked, as starving for intel as he was for the woman who bore it.

"Nearly six hundred. Dozens of breeds."

Roland reached for a rolled-up map and unfurled it on a wooden crate. "Where?"

She leaned over and pointed out the town of Hostau. "If you keep heading east, you'll bump right into us. Once you secure the town, we can set up defenses around the farm and avoid more air raids—"

"We can't, lass," O'Connor said somberly.

"What?" Bret asked sharply.

Roland's brow furrowed. "After Germany falls, the territory of Czechoslovakia will belong to Russia. Our advance stops at the Austrian and German border."

Adia's face went pale, her jaw slackening. Bret's own stomach roiled in disgust with far too recent memories. Not the Russians—not again. The toll they'd taken six years ago when they'd ransacked Janów and left nothing but the window frames—it had nearly broken Adia.

Adia pressed two fingers to her lips as if she'd be ill. "Is there any way you can reach us? It's just twenty-four kilometers over the border. Twenty-four measly kilometers." She straightened. "We have prisoners at the camp, hundreds of them. Australians, British, Americans."

Roland rubbed his face. "We're under strict orders not to anger the Russians or risk the alliance, though General Patton disagrees and would prefer to keep marching east."

They'd all heard the reports on how ragged and underfed the Russian armies were. How desperate.

"We can't just leave those horses and men to the Russians," Bret said, voice low and resolute.

Roland nodded, but his distant stare indicated he hadn't figured out a way around the chain of command and the realities of defying treaties.

Silence filled the tent, and Bret's mind wandered back to the startling truth that Adia stood before him. And that it wouldn't last. Like so many other moments before, it wasn't their time.

They still had work to do.

Adia drew in a breath and looked at Bret with eyes afire. "What if it wasn't about saving the horses or POWs, but saving German intelligence from falling into Russian hands?"

Roland straightened, head angling in interest. "I'm listening."

Adia beamed. "Near Hostau is a lodge that the German officers and intelligence agents have been using to store documents as they flee Austria."

"Dianahof," Bret supplied, the location clicking in his mind. Yes. It was not too far from the farm. Rumored to be the sanctuary of dozens of former Luftwaffe officers and intelligence stores. His chest filled with pride. That was the Adia he knew and loved. The Adia who seemed to be still peeking at the classified documents in Werner's office.

Adia nodded, and Roland smiled.

"Now that," the officer said with a gleam in his eyes, "I can work with."

41

The hour she'd allowed herself in the Americans' camp passed by far too quickly, but Adia knew sunrise would come equally as fast.

How it ached to leave Bret's side.

Roland, O'Connor, and Bret walked with her to Indigo, who was tied to the bumper of a Jeep with fresh hay and water at his feet. The children followed along, and she knelt beside them.

"You are safe now," she said softly in Czech, catching the oldest sibling's mistrusting stare. "These men will see you get far, far away from the Germans. You'll have food, warm beds, and a new start."

The young girl nodded somberly, a deep despair leaving her empty of emotion or connection. It would take far more than food and a fresh start to bring true healing, and Adia could only pray the next caretaker would do all they could to help the children. She'd taken them as far as she could, and there were other lives relying on her.

She stood upright, and O'Connor inched closer. "Don't worry, Miss Adia—I'll take them personally to the Red Cross station a few klicks back. There's a nurse there I'm hoping to ask to dinner when this is all over." He winked.

Adia smirked and glanced at Bret, who also seemed amused at the parallel to their own first meeting.

"I wish you all the luck with that, O'Connor." Adia slapped his shoulder. "She'd be a fool to say no."

Roland and O'Connor nodded their goodbyes and herded the children back to the encampment, leaving Adia and Bret a moment to say their own farewell.

Once alone, she leaned against him, pressing her forehead into his shoulder.

"Do you want to go over the plan one more time?" Bret said. "What you'll need to convince Werner—"

She put her fingers over his lips and smiled. "I won't soon forget a moment of this night. Not when I've dreamed of such a thing for four years."

He kissed her, long and confident. Her body seemed to melt into his, and she feared she wouldn't have the strength to pull free. She certainly didn't have the desire.

Indigo nudged her elbow and broke their kiss. Adia laughed lightly. "Sorry, he's the jealous type."

"And Lubor is okay with this arrangement?" Bret asked, nodding to the stallion.

"Not quite, but I slip him extra grain rations, so I think he forgives me."

"I can't wait to see him, to have you both back beside me." He brushed her hairline with his fingers gently, his gaze full of worry and angst.

She took his hand and pressed her lips to the back of it. "I feel it—this will all be over soon."

"This will all be over soon."

That was exactly what Bret was afraid of. Not in a blaze of glory but rather in a terrible, horrible end. Was it the two years of endless bloodshed and death that caused such dreary thoughts?

He leaned in, kissed her again, rememorizing the taste of her, the feel of her body pressed to his, and the distinct smell of hay and

314

floral soap. How on earth did she manage to find floral soap these days? Next to her, he felt half the man he once was, and nothing near what she deserved.

She pulled back hesitantly. Neither was ready for her to leave, but they both knew what was at stake.

"I love you," she whispered. "I'll see you very soon."

After four years, almost any span of time felt soon.

He helped her into the saddle, stroked the stallion's neck, and prayed for swift travels. "I love you too, Adia."

She gathered the reins, lifted the cloak hood to her head, and kicked Indigo into a run through the dense, dark forest. The fading hoofbeats turned to faint echoes, and then only the occasional hoot of an owl filled the void.

Roland walked up beside him and crossed his arms. "You second-guessing the plan?" he asked. The colonel was about Bret's age and had run several regiments even before the United States had entered the war. The man was sharp and could see into people's minds.

"I should have gone with her to Hostau."

"It's too great a risk. If she's as clever as she seems and as you say—"

"She is," Bret cut in quickly.

"Then she can handle getting Werner Vogel here tomorrow. We'll see where we go from there."

"Think we can get Patton convinced to rescue the horses?" Bret asked, his gaze still locked on the forest as if he could see her.

Roland drew in a long breath. "Not sure. We're old polo buddies from back in the day, and I know George has no love of Russians. So, if it means keeping the horses out of the Russians' hands . . ."

But the command structure of the Allied forces would complicate everything. Treaties were treaties. Unlike Hitler, they all were bound to those restrictions. If Czechoslovakia was off-limits, there'd be no way to safely send in any number of soldiers to save a herd of animals.

Roland elbowed Bret. "Come on, you'd better get back to your bunk and rest as much as you can. The next few days will be un-predictable."

It hurt to tear his gaze away from the forest. The magical Bohemian forest that had produced the most precious of spoils. If all went according to plan, Adia would emerge again from the same path, the same trees, with Werner in tow so they could negotiate a surrender.

Her life, his future, depended on it.

God, be her shield and wings out there—please, bring her back to me.

42

April 26, 1945
Hostau, Czechoslovakia

Werner? Might I have a word?" Adia's pulse raced at her luck—she'd only just come back with Indigo and returned him to his stall when Werner started his morning rounds of the stables. There was no sign of the leech, Schultze, who'd campaigned for her being sent to camps for the past four years.

Werner turned, smiling kindly as he took her in. "Morning, Adia. This is early, even for you."

It had taken years to convince him to use her given name rather than *fräulein*. Schultze called her manipulative, but Adia had found a true friend in the German colonel who loved the horses as much as she. A lesser man might have demanded more of her than friendship, but Werner Vogel proved to be a rare lily in a field of thorns.

There'd only been one conversation, two years ago, when Werner had asked if he might escort her to dinner. She'd gently shaken her head and said, "My heart belongs to another." He'd graciously accepted this fact, and they'd never spoken of it again.

She glanced around as she approached him, but no person or horse stirred in the predawn hours. "Can we speak privately?"

Her body shook in nervousness, her stomach clenching and her

317

mind still whirring after everything that had occurred in the past twelve hours.

Running into Americans on the border of Germany.

Seeing *him*.

Holding him, kissing him. Like rain after a forty-year drought, it had awakened and brought life back to her weary soul. And if they were to find a way to be together, they had to follow the plan.

She had to get Werner on board. They had to negotiate a surrender for Hostau. If not, Russia would overtake the horses, and they'd be lost to history.

Putting all their faith in Werner was their only hope and their greatest risk. If she'd misjudged him, this conversation could lead to her death by firing squad in the town square.

Bret hadn't been fond of this part of the plan and argued adamantly to sneak into the farm personally to have this conversation with Werner. But Adia knew they had a deep, mistrustful history, and her friendship and trust with Werner was the best shot they had.

He led her to his office and closed the door behind them. "Is everything all right?" he asked, his gaze dark as he scanned her. "Are you well?" He sat on the edge of his desk, but she didn't take her familiar seat in the wicker chair across from him.

She shook her head in response. "I'm sure you know that the Russians and Americans are both closing in on Czechoslovakia."

His body went still, his expression shifting to neutral, no longer warm and caring.

"I ran into an American patrol while I was . . . exercising Indigo."

He blinked and straightened. "Are you all right? Did they harm you?"

"No, but they did tell me something frightening. Should Germany surrender . . ." she said slowly, watching him closely. The ever-practical colonel seemed unaffected by the potential of Germany's defeat. He'd only ever cared about the horses. Not Hitler's quest. "The British and Americans have ceded this land, all of Czechoslovakia, to the Russians."

At that, Werner's forehead furrowed, and his lips parted in horror.

"I was there at Janów when the Russians came," she said, voice thick with emotion. "No horse will survive, no prisoner or German soldier will either."

Silence settled between them, heavy and dangerous.

"How close were the Americans?" Werner asked softly. His gaze was distant, his expression unreadable.

It felt like a test. If she disclosed their location and Werner called it in to local SS troops, they could ambush the Second Cavalry. But if she didn't trust Werner, would he agree to commit treason and negotiate with the Americans outside of his command structure?

"Asch. They're east of Asch."

He nodded slowly.

"The Americans will breach the border and help evacuate the horses," she whispered, uneasy saying such things even behind a locked office door. "If we surrender and offer valuable intelligence."

His gaze narrowed for a heartbeat in confusion. "Intelligence?"

She didn't allow herself to cower. "Dianahof."

"How do you know of Dianahof?"

"Does it matter?" She stepped forward, sensing the uncertainty within him. "This is our only chance."

Werner ran a hand over his face and shook his head. "I've appealed for evacuation for months. Command will not allow it. They say it will reflect poorly on the German army and seem as if we are fleeing in defeat."

She bit back her own retort. Germany was defeated. But they hadn't conceded.

"Will you ride with me tonight to discuss a surrender with the American colonel?" She kept her tone low, humble, and pleading.

He studied her in silence, revealing nothing of his thoughts or conclusions.

Her life—and that of every horse in Hostau's walls—was now completely in his hands.

Eslarn, Germany

"Calm down, Conway," O'Connor said with a wink as they waited outside the camp, where they'd run into Adia the night before. "She'll be here. I saw how she looked at ye. She can't stay away for long."

Bret huffed a short laugh. If only O'Connor knew how long it had taken to get such attention from Adia Kensington.

"So yer really telling me that in the past six years, you never popped the question?" O'Connor pressed for the third time in the last hour.

The dark forest around them rustled quietly, moonlight streaming between the canopy of trees and the haze of distant artillery smoke. The scent of evergreens and rich underbrush battled against the grit and dust that reminded them all of death.

Bret sighed. "I haven't seen her since '41. I knew she was safe in Hostau, but we couldn't risk traveling beyond the borders." Or so he'd thought. Her midnight excursions proved otherwise.

"No wonder you were so ice-cold when you first transferred into the Second," Roland said with a slight smile from a few paces away. His gaze remained fixed on the forest, attuned to any threat.

"Sorry about that." Bret winced. "I was keen on any way to get closer to Czechoslovakia, though I wasn't thrilled about joining the ranks of you Yanks."

O'Connor elbowed his ribs. "Yeah, but we won you over."

"Indeed, you did."

Hoofbeats echoed faintly in the distance, drawing everyone's attention to the east. A shrill whistle sounded from a soldier a hundred yards away. O'Connor whistled back to confirm they'd received the message.

Bret's heart pounded against his rib cage. He ached to hold her again, knowing their time would yet again be limited.

But now they had to focus on whatever terms Werner Vogel would agree to. Adia had been confident: he would do what was best for the horses, not what was best for the Nazis or Germany.

Adia came into view first, hooded in the black cloak astride the black stallion like a medieval princess. The sight of her sent an electric buzz through all his limbs. Her gaze sought him out, and she smiled when their eyes connected. She drew Indigo to a halt in front of him, and he took the reins and patted the horse's sweaty neck.

"You made it," he said softly.

"The hard part's over." She slid off Indigo and nodded to O'Connor. "Evening, Sergeant."

"Aw, just call me O'Connor," the man said with a furious blush in his cheeks. "Did ye have any trouble?" he said, nodding to the tall officer on the horse behind her.

Werner looked down upon the three of them, his gaze locking onto Bret's.

"Translator?" Roland asked Adia.

"You don't need a translator," Werner said in clear English, his voice heavy and slightly defeated.

"Let me see your hands, Colonel Vogel," Roland said, walking up with three other men with handguns drawn.

Werner hesitated only for a second, his gaze flicking between Adia and Bret, and a dawning realization seemed to pass over his expression.

Adia looked up and smiled encouragingly. "You can trust them," she said.

Werner lifted his hands, releasing the reins as the soldiers took the horse and allowed him to dismount. They checked him for weapons, and Werner nodded formally to the colonel. The soldiers around them all lowered their firearms.

Roland motioned to Bret. "Conway, come with me and the colonel to the supply tent. O'Connor, see to Miss Kensington and the horses."

Bret nodded. As he passed by, he discreetly caught Adia's hand and squeezed it softly. She opened her mouth to speak, then just offered a smile. They both had so much to say, so much to share, but nothing needed to be said right here, right now.

O'Connor spoke with Adia and their voices faded into the background as Bret, Werner, and Roland strode the few hundred yards back to the camp.

Once under the cover of canvas, Roland studied Werner with the dull glow of lanterns around the sparse tent. A table of wooden crates stood in the center, adorned by a map of the region with scattered markings.

"Whiskey? Rum?" Roland asked, offering a glass to the German.

"No, thank you." Werner looked at Bret. "Was this all your plan, then, Conway?"

Roland poured himself a glass and cleared his throat. "You two know each other?"

Bret leaned against a crate to give the illusion of relaxation, but he still wasn't sure he could trust Werner. "From a life before the war."

Werner remained upright and tense. "And that little raid at Janów Podlaski? Schultze said he saw you and guessed Adia had to be involved to save that little orphan boy."

And still Werner had protected her. Bret's jaw clamped together so tightly his molars hurt. "Leave her out of this."

"You brought her into this," Werner hissed back.

Roland stepped in between their line of sight. "I see where this is going." He pointed to Bret. "Keep your trap shut unless I ask." Then, to Werner, "You'll be dealing with me, not Major Conway. We clear? Miss Kensington indicated there's a hunting cabin near the farm at Hostau that serves as a storehouse for German intelligence. Is this true?"

Werner looked almost ill for a moment. "I'll need assurances for myself and my men."

"You'll have it, if the intel is good and you surrender peacefully when we come into Hostau. You'll be treated as prisoners of war and protected from whatever Russia would intend."

Werner grimaced. "If I don't put up resistance, I'll be shot as a traitor. Same for those at Dianahof."

Roland nodded. "Then we'll stage a battle, but you'll be responsible to ensure that your men's aim is far from any meaningful damage. To my men or the locals. We clear?"

"Ja, agreed."

"How many prisoners are at the stables?"

"Three hundred."

Roland wrote the number down. "Are they well enough to walk?"

"Yes, though food is scarce for everyone in and around Hostau." Werner scowled. "I've rejected the requests of locals to slaughter the horses for rations."

Roland and Bret both nodded somberly.

"Your men and the prisoners will be well treated by my soldiers," Roland reassured him. "How many are in your ranks?"

"Less than three dozen." Werner softened the slightest bit.

"And what do we expect at Dianahof?"

Werner and Roland hunched over the map, detailing the best forest route to get to the cabin and pointing out the checkpoints and limited artillery along the way. Ten minutes later, Werner shook Roland's hand and the deal was struck.

Roland led them from the tent, but before Bret and Werner exited, Bret caught Werner's arm and leaned in.

"I'm sure it doesn't need to be said," he growled into the colonel's ear, "but if any harm should befall her before we reach Hostau . . ." He let the rest hang in the air.

Werner straightened. "Still so arrogant. Who do you think has kept her illicit rescue of Jewish children from discovery? I've kept her safe for four years at Hostau, two years at Janów."

Bret let go of the man's arm, surprised.

Werner's expression softened. "She doesn't know this." His voice lowered. "I'd prefer to keep it that way."

The realization struck Bret. "You're in love with her."

Werner glanced away, a flash of pain in his gaze. "A condition we both share, I'm guessing."

Bret nodded.

"Well, you needn't fear," he said, rolling his shoulders back to the quintessential German soldier stance. "Her loyalty is to you—and has never wavered."

Werner exited the tent, leaving Bret to his thoughts. Had he been wrong about Werner all along? Perhaps despite their rough start in the Olympics nearly ten years prior, the German really was a man of integrity and valor.

Still, the next two days would be the most dangerous of all. The Russians loomed close and SS fighters dotted the forests around Hostau.

They'd come this far, and they could still lose it all.

43

O'Connor handed Adia a canteen, and she nodded gratefully before taking a long swig. She stared at the canvas tent where the three military men—all from different countries—met to reach the same goal.

"They'll work it all out," O'Connor said, petting Indigo's rump as the horse drank from a bucket of clean water.

She sighed, the weight that had been resting on her shoulders finally shifting ever so slightly. "What good fortune to have run into you all."

"My sweet mother would call it divine intervention." O'Connor winked.

Her chest stirred at the thought. Had God finally heard their prayers? It had seemed so long, the toils so great, that she'd all but given up on prayer. Perhaps this had been His plan all along.

"Ye've sure put up with a lot," O'Connor continued. He shook his head and nodded at the tent. "I can't believe you've endured being around that Nazi filth."

Her stomach filled with bile. "That's rather unfair."

He scoffed. "You haven't seen what I've seen them do."

Anger flamed to life in her. But another voice cut in.

"Careful, O'Connor," Roland said, walking from the direction of the tent. "Miss Kensington has faced four years of war on top of the past two years we've been on European soil. She's seen quite a lot of what the Germans can do."

Adia still fumed but spoke calmly. "Werner has always done what is best to preserve life. Not all Germans are the same."

O'Connor sighed, relenting a bit. "They're all the same to me."

"That's the sort of logic that got us into this war. It's never that simple."

O'Connor held her gaze as Werner and Bret stepped from the tent. He looked over, studied Bret and Werner, and then inched closer. "You have a point. I'm sorry, Miss Adia."

She patted his shoulder. "You're a good man, O'Connor. Don't give in to hate."

As Werner and Bret came close, O'Connor nodded farewell and Roland also returned to the camp, leaving Bret, Adia, and Werner alone with the two horses.

Adia looked between the two men, noting the tension in Bret's jaw and a similar line of stubbornness in Werner.

Bret motioned to O'Connor's retreating figure. "Everything okay?"

She nodded, then smirked slightly at the palpable tension between him and Werner. "And you?"

Werner coughed and reached for his horse's reins. "We should get back to Hostau, Adia." He mounted the horse, his gaze impatient.

Bret shifted next to her, a host of emotions flashing across his worn and tired expression. It killed him to let her go, just as it had the night before.

She put a hand on his forearm, drawing his focus to her. "I'll see you soon?"

He relaxed slightly, closing the gap between them even further. "A day or two, if Patton agrees after we raid the cabin. I'll come to Hostau to notify you and Werner and solidify the arrangements for the surrender."

Her heart seized with hope and terror. "Be careful," she whispered. "I'll count the moments until we meet again."

"As will I." He brushed her cheek with his thumb, holding back anything further in the presence of Werner and the shadow of Roland and O'Connor beyond.

A matter of days. Then it would be their time.

Bret helped Adia mount Indigo, then she followed Werner into the darkness of the forest. She fought back a rush of panic and tears—of joy, of longing, of trepidation.

Kilometers of silent trekking later, Werner drew his horse to a halt outside of Hostau, and she fell into step beside him. The morning sun had started to warm the air but still hadn't peeked over the horizon.

"We must not give any sign of anything being amiss," he said quietly. "Schultze will need to be properly handled when the troops arrive."

She let out a breath. "Thank you, Werner."

He grew still, his eyes roaming her face. "So, all along it was Conway?"

She swallowed, unsure how to read his flat tone.

Werner took that as an affirmation. "At least I can say I took the gold medal from him." His expression went somber and pained. "But I daresay he won something far greater."

She felt torn in two, reading the silent farewell beneath his words. Had he been holding out for a different future once the war was over, perhaps? "I'm sorry, Werner. I truly am. You've been so kind to me, and you'll always have a special place in my heart."

He gave her a weak smile.

"When we evacuate the horses . . ." She faltered. "Will you come with us?"

He shrugged and looked down at the reins in his hands. "That's a question for another day."

If Adia had learned anything from six years of war, it was that another day was never guaranteed.

———

327

April 27, 1945
Poběžovice, Czechoslovakia

"You know the plan, boys," Roland said over his radio next to Bret from the cab of a half-track. They gazed upon Dianahof. "Just a light bombardment. Avoid hitting the lodge itself."

The Germans were already poised to surrender, but they couldn't do so without a fight. So the Second Cavalry would give them a theatrical performance, accept their surrender, collect the prisoners and documents, and hightail it out of this area, as the Americans would say.

They were called Ghosts for a reason—they were quick, and they'd managed to evade countless traps as they blazed across Europe into enemy territory. Some of the magic came from the Second's "always ready" insignia and motto, but some of it came from Bret's years behind German lines and experience with the partisans.

They moved forward, expecting a trap behind every bush or tree, and trusted no one.

Most of all, Bret still didn't fully trust Werner or his word. Especially knowing how deeply he cared for Adia. Would he lead Bret into an ambush to have her all to himself?

Bret shook his head. He could assume as much and do whatever it took to see the Second Cavalry prevail.

The guns boomed across the forest, the shells sending dirt and trees rocketing up into the sky and falling like rain.

After a few moments, Roland held up his hand to signal a ceasefire and looked over at Bret. He nodded, and they jumped down from the truck.

"Let's get out of here as quick as we can," Bret said, scanning the surrounding forest with a wary eye. "There's a lot of SS activity in the area and they'll surely have heard all that."

"Agreed," Roland said, his hand over his revolver in his holster.

His men spread out and held their rifles at the ready, looking for any sign of activity from the tall opening of the building.

The lodge was tucked against a hill with a marbled statue of Diana, goddess of the hunt, at the center of the round driveway. The walls of the building were white stucco and, with the gray slate roof tiles, felt otherworldly among the dense green forest.

A dozen men appeared in the front door, all with their arms raised and holsters empty of firearms. The tall, oval windows looked on like vacant eyes.

The men of the Second swarmed and thoroughly checked all the Germans for weapons.

The Luftwaffe colonel in front of the prisoners nodded to Roland. "Americans, we offer our surrender."

To the Germans who staffed this operation, anything was better than capture by the Russians or being shot for treason by their own people.

"Sir, we located the boxes of intel," a private said, trotting up with a stack of files.

Bret reached for a file, flipped it open, and scanned the documents. His brow furrowed and he nodded. "This is what Werner promised." Lists of names, records of military assignments, secret designs for Luftwaffe planes and weapons. All useful in what would be the post-war tribunals to see that justice was done. "This is good stuff."

Roland whistled to the last of the men in the trucks and Jeeps and waved them toward the house. They tucked their rifles over their shoulders and raced into the lodge at a clipped pace.

"Load it all up," Roland ordered. "Every last sheet of paper."

Bret sifted through boxes as fast as the men could load them. He trusted the boys of the Second to see the lodge thoroughly cleaned out, and fast.

Less than an hour later, Roland poked his head over the back of the truck where Bret sat with a box of paper. "The lodge is cleaned out. Prisoners are loaded."

Bret nodded. "Clear out. We've got to get this to London." And this time, he could entrust the Americans with such valuable cargo.

The rest of his future, his mission, lay twenty-nine kilometers over the border with hundreds of horses and one beautiful American.

But it was up to Roland to convince General Patton to green-light the risky mission. There was no lowering one's guard in the field, where snipers would take out a soldier drinking morning coffee or a disabled vehicle could act as a trap for German artillery.

The Second fled the mountains and left Dianahof and its pristine glory—the legacy of some rich baron hundreds of years ago—to an unknown future. The documents and inhabitants would be relocated, processed, and handled.

When they reached the communications tent outside of Asch, O'Connor and Bret followed Roland in and sat back uneasily as the operator connected them to Patton.

"Cross into Russian territory, herd six hundred horses across SS-filled forests. What could go wrong?" O'Connor puffed on a cigar. "If we do this, can we call it Operation Cowboy?"

Bret smothered a smile, and Roland glowered at his subordinate. He took the receiver and held it to his ear. "Yes, sir. Confirming we have all the intelligence in hand and en route back to Allied command."

Roland fell silent, listening to whatever Patton had to say.

"Yes, sir. About the horses. The trade for the Dianahof surrender was to make our best effort to save the horses from being seized by Russians—"

Roland's words were cut off, and the silence in the tent stretched like a cable holding two tanks rumbling in opposite directions.

Bret crossed his arms and itched for his grandfather's pocket watch. If ever he needed the lucky totem, it was now. But it was safe with Ewan in England.

General Patton hadn't been shy about his disdain for Russia, but the risk of breaking a treaty, especially for what could be seen as stealing a valuable bounty from under their noses . . .

The radio crackled. Roland nodded and handed the earpiece back to his radioman.

Bret held his breath. O'Connor lifted his eyebrows. "Well?"

A grin broke out on Roland's face. "He said, 'Get them out. Make it fast.'"

44

HOSTAU, CZECHOSLOVAKIA

Adia leaned over Matthew's injured foot, carefully placed a splint, and wrapped it with a torn-up uniform. The prisoner, an airman from Britain who had been captured when his plane crashed in Germany in early 1941, winced and thanked her.

"It seems to just be a sprain. We can have the veterinarian review it when he comes to check on the mares later today," she said. When doctors and nurses weren't available within a hundred kilometers, the vet was the next best option.

"You're an angel, miss." He pulled his foot back and tested his weight on the wrapping and splint. "Much better."

"Adia," Werner's voice cut in. The prisoners around her scattered. Though Werner had always treated them well, there was no love lost between the POWs and anyone in a German uniform.

She stood, set her extra cloth aside. Her heart hammered at the urgency in his tone. He took her elbow and pulled her out of the barn, striding toward the seldom-used western gate.

He leaned over. "Dianahof was seized by Americans this morning." His eyes conveyed the rest of the message. Bret would be here any moment.

Her strides lengthened to keep up with his. "Where is Schultze?" she whispered, glancing around for any of his loyal posse.

The lines between his brows deepened, his look uncharacteristically concerned. "I don't know. I'll leave you here to escort Conway. Bring him to my office and I'll see that Schultze and his men are sent on an errand for as long as I can manage."

Her stomach dipped. "If he catches Bret here—"

"I know." Werner muttered a German curse. "Colonel Roland also assured me that if their emissary didn't return to Asch within twenty-four hours, they'd drop the whole of the Second Cavalry upon Hostau, regardless of the horses and prisoners inside."

"What?" Panic rose in her chest.

"There was little room for negotiation. We mustn't delay."

They reached the gate and Werner handed her a small key. "Give me at least an hour before you bring Conway to my office."

And with that, he disappeared.

What if he couldn't get Schultze off the premises? She closed her eyes against the image of the Second invading Hostau with guns blazing. There'd be nothing left. And she knew Roland well enough to know he'd stand by his word. His soldiers would take paramount importance over the horses any day. So, if they assumed Bret had been captured or killed here . . .

She covered her face with her hands. It all got so complicated so fast.

Hurry, Bret.

Bret parked his Jeep off into the forest and covered it with as much foliage as he could, then walked toward the western gate as Werner had described the night before. He'd dressed in civilian attire but knew there were no guarantees.

His heart raced, both in anticipation of seeing Adia again and from the knowledge that he was deep into SS country and Schultze would be looking for his head on a pike if he could only get the chance.

Still, he had insisted on being the one to finalize the surrender and report back to the Second. No one else had more experience in these sorts of things.

Adia was leaning against the gate as the tall fences of Hostau came into view, the green, lush expanse reminiscent of Janów Podlaski and taking him back to those seemingly carefree days.

He broke through the forest, and she raced to him.

The feel of her embrace—it would never get old. He breathed her in, buried his face in her neck as they clung to one another.

She pulled back, breathless. "You got everything you needed from Dianahof? Was anyone injured?"

"Everyone is fine." He looked around for Werner. "How are things here? Where's Vogel?"

She stepped back and shook her head. "He's trying to get Schultze clear of the farm. I'm to bring you to the office and hope that Werner was able to send him off the grounds."

"You think he can do it?"

She nodded. "I trust him, Bret."

He followed her through the farm that burst with horses in every field, all breeds and colors that he could tell. It was beautiful, but a potential land mine if Russia learned of the Americans' plans to sneak out this treasure from right under their noses.

Adia looked over her shoulder. "We'll pass by Lubor's stall on the way."

A few steps later and there he was—the prince of Janów. A little taller, more muscular, and shining in a brilliant coat of dark brown with black accents, the white diamond on his forehead. Lubor huffed and snorted through the rails at Bret.

"Good to see you too," Bret said, holding his hand up for inspection. "Sorry, no sugar, I'm afraid."

Lubor nickered softly, as if recognizing Bret. The horse pawed the ground. Was he sensing the danger in the air too?

"Sounds like he's anxious to get out of here," Bret said.

"Me too." Adia chuckled. "Come on."

They turned the corner, and a manor came into view on the other side of the U-shaped pavilion. A small building on the side seemed to be the office.

Werner appeared on the steps of the manor and met them in stride, motioning for silence until they were inside the small room of photos, trophies, and stacks of files. He locked the door and removed his cap.

Adia seemed to be holding her breath. "Schultze?"

Werner looked uncertain. "Inspecting the satellite barns, but we don't have much time."

The tension in the room slackened only slightly.

Werner handed Bret a piece of paper. "These are the most direct routes to the farm from Asch, and I believe most of the SS groups have pulled back into Berlin."

Bret looked over the information. "What about partisan groups? Should we expect resistance or support?"

Adia remained still as Werner pointed to several positions. "I don't know whether they will impede or aid your efforts." She probably knew more about the partisans than Werner did but hadn't disclosed that to the colonel.

"What about Schultze and his men when we arrive?" Bret looked up from the map.

"I'll do my best to make sure he understands that surrender is our only option." Werner looked over at Adia. "You must stay far away from him and not raise any trouble until he's fully subdued."

Adia's lips formed a line, and she seemed to be wrestling with how exactly to make that happen.

"I'm not sure you know how much you're asking," Bret said with a chuckle.

Adia glared back. "I think I can handle it. How soon will the Second be here?"

Bret looked back at the map, calculating the distances and the speeds at which they could advance through occupied territory. "Twelve, sixteen hours max."

She lifted her chin. "I can handle that. No problem."

Bret and Werner exchanged a knowing look. Neither was quite as confident.

45

APRIL 28, 1945

Avoid Schultze. That was Adia's only mission until the American flag flew over Hostau.

Everything she'd worked for came down to the next day and whether the men of the Second reached the gates before the Russians.

After Bret and Werner solidified their plans, Bret snuck out through the gate and headed back to Asch with hardly an hour to spare on the twenty-four-hour deadline of Roland's.

At dawn the very next morning, Adia rode out to meet Shepherd—to give them all the update on the Allies' plans. Shepherd could help ensure the local partisans didn't hinder the liberation of the farm. She was the leader and well respected by all.

But the forest was empty and quiet of the partisans Adia had worked with for months. The morning was damp after a fresh rain, and the air held the faint odor of distant battle.

Something wasn't right.

She dismounted and stood at the empty clearing, no sign of human occupation aside from the well-trodden paths and faint outlines of campfires. Her breath caught at a rustling behind a small bush. Indigo spooked beside her, but she held tightly to the reins.

"Who's there?" she called in Czech.

"A-Angel?" a small voice squeaked. A slender boy emerged from behind the bush. One of the camp's many children she'd seen around for months. He was only five or six.

A little mirror of Ewan so many years ago.

She stepped forward and knelt beside the boy with disheveled hair and a dirt-smudged face. "What happened? Where is everyone?"

The boy looked around, his wide brown eyes nearly vacant. Adia's own gaze drifted down to the boy's tattered shirt. It was spattered with blood.

Her head spun, and her stomach roiled.

"They killed them," the boy rasped. "The Germans killed them all."

Her chest constricted in horror and pain. Not now. Not when armistice was so close, freedom so near.

"Do you have somewhere you can go?" she asked softly.

The boy shook his head.

She reached out a hand. "Come with me."

It was a risk when they were but a day from the release of Schultze's terror, but Adia couldn't leave the boy behind. She owed it to Shepherd and all the partisans who had given their lives. Where she'd hide the boy was something she'd have to figure out in the moment.

She lifted him into the saddle and mounted Indigo, racing back toward the barn.

Bret, please hurry.

The boy trembled as they rode through an open fence in the back pasture, the eagle of the Nazi flag towering over the stables and looming as death to all who opposed.

"It's okay," Adia whispered. "You're safe now."

"Those are the Germans who killed them," the boy whimpered, pointing to Schultze and his handful of loyal soldiers who stood outside one of the barns.

"Duck down," she said, praying none of them would notice the lump in front of her as she steered Indigo toward a distant barn. She'd have to stash the boy until she knew the coast was clear.

Once they reached the overhang of the stalls, she dismounted, pulled the boy down, and shoved him into the corner of an empty stall, then piled straw on top of him so he was out of sight. "Make no noise," she ordered. "I'll come back for you soon."

The pile of straw only shuddered in response.

Had this been a mistake? Would saving the boy jeopardize the plan they'd put in place?

Her orders from both Werner and Bret were to avoid angering Schultze. But was she to leave the boy alone in the woods to die?

Sweat dripped down her brow as she led Indigo down the aisle of the barn and toward the stallion paddocks. But she was hardly a few steps away from the child's hiding place when a hand reached out and tore Indigo's reins from her and another set of hands grabbed the collar of her shirt.

She cried out and kicked against her captor, but Schultze's voice rumbled in her ear. "What are you up to, you vile woman?"

"Let me go, or Werner—"

"Yes, bring Werner over and let's explain to him why you're returning from the woods where partisans had teemed like an ant infestation."

"What woods? I was exercising—"

He tightened his grip, her shirt twisting and making it difficult to breathe. "You lie. You've lied to Werner for far too many years."

She looked around, seeing three of the soldiers beside Indigo but not seeing any sign of them searching for the child. So be it if she must suffer and it meant his escape.

Schultze caught her look and lowered his face to hers. "What are you looking for? What did you have with you coming back from the forest?"

Panic rose in her, and she struggled to come up with a plausible story. The ferocity in Schultze's eyes was on a new level.

Did he sense his reign was coming to an end? The thought lifted her lips, which caused Schultze to sneer and push her against the ground roughly.

"Spread out and search—she's hiding something."

"No!" She struggled to get to her feet, but Schultze kicked her down again. "Stop!"

An explosion on the horizon drew them all to a stop. They'd been no strangers to gunfire and bombardment in Hostau, but that was the closest and loudest one they'd ever felt. The ground trembled beneath their feet and a roar of tanks echoed in the valley.

"What is that?" one of Schultze's men asked, looking to their leader.

"That'd be the American army," Werner said, walking down the aisle with his hands casually behind his back. His eyes checked over Adia briefly but then trained back on the aide. "I've negotiated a surrender of the stables and soldiers and insist you release Fräulein Kensington or risk quite severe consequences."

A few of the prisoners of war working in the barns emerged from their tasks nearby, their eyes wide and questioning at the words. Matthew limped out from a stall and studied Adia with concern, but he knew not to push Schultze.

Hope blossomed in her chest, but her gaze darted to the Luger holstered at Schultze's side. *What are you doing, Werner?*

The two officers stared each other down as the rumble of artillery and mechanized warhorses closed in around Hostau.

Schultze's eyes were frenzied. "How dare you. I'll see you shot as a traitor."

Werner shrugged. "So be it. But there's no stopping the might of the American forces that will arrive in minutes. If you surrender peacefully, I'll ensure you receive fair treatment."

Adia slid back slowly in the dirt to escape the brewing storm between them, moving silently. Matthew inched closer and leaned down to help pull her to her feet to move her out of Schultze's reach. He took a step toward Schultze, but Adia held up a hand.

"No, don't," she said. They'd all seen Schultze rage and beat prisoners, and she couldn't bear the thought of it happening to Matthew.

The airman shook his head. "Things have changed, Miss Adia." He nodded to the dozens of prisoners around him, and they all sprang into action.

Their target was the short, red-faced German who had abused and berated them for four long years.

Eslarn, Germany

"Tallyho!" a voice shouted as the caravan left the rest of the Second Cavalry behind at first light.

"Get them out. Make it fast."

From Patton's mouth to God's ears. Or so Bret hoped.

The young man driving Bret and Roland in a Jeep looked uneasy. "I don't know, boss. I smell a trap."

Roland hummed a noncommittal response. "Then why did you volunteer for this, Private?"

The kid drew in a long breath, his face bearing the scars of three hundred days of battle against an enemy on a continent three thousand miles from his home. "Well, my sister has horses, see. And I figured if I came home and told her all these war stories but then tell her that I didn't volunteer for this mission, she'd tan my hide."

Bret chuckled, understanding the sentiment. Elizabeth was no different.

"We're Patton's Ghosts, kid," Roland responded confidently. "We'll get the job done."

Bret held his hand to his sidearm as the Jeep bounced down the roads that drew nearer to the border. He and Troop F were taking the most direct route into Hostau, while seventy other soldiers in Troops A and C surrounded the farm from the north and south to clear as many SS strongholds as possible and seek out any additional POWs in the area.

Everything felt familiar from this drive the day before, but moving a mechanized column of troops carried different risks.

They'd gone well beyond the front lines before, the very best reconnaissance group in Europe, to be sure. But if they made a wrong step with this mission, it'd be more than just their own lives at stake. They could jeopardize every diplomatic step to ally with Russia and eliminate the Nazi threat. They could lose horses, prisoners, and every cavalryman who had stepped forward willingly for this mission.

"Eyes sharp," Roland called out as they neared the border crossing and the first known position of enemy fighters.

O'Connor rode ahead in the lead Chaffee tank, one of two they'd brought along with a handful of Jeeps and half-tracks.

"Contact right!" the sergeant called out, leveling his assault gun at a small building and leaving it as firewood.

The threat was nullified.

Roland beamed. "This is what we live for, boys!" He slapped the private on the chest as they cleared the town and blazed the trail toward Hostau.

Within hours of passing uninhibited through small towns and fields of green, Bret heard the words he'd been dying to hear.

"Gates ahead!" O'Connor called back to Bret and Roland.

Adia.

He couldn't rest until she was in his arms, until the Stars and Stripes flew over the Hostau stud farm.

"Gates opening!" O'Connor called out as the vehicles slowed to a stop outside the tall, black metal gates of Hostau.

A dozen ghostlike prisoners filtered into the oval driveway with a few soldiers walking hesitatingly to open the gates, one holding a white bedsheet at the end of a bayonet.

Bret's eyes swept each face, searching for Werner or Adia but finding neither. Where was she?

Rage and terror filled his chest, and he clenched his fists against his desire to race through the grounds and find answers.

The soldiers approached O'Connor, Roland, and Bret with arms raised, holsters empty of weapons.

"Where is your commander?" Roland barked. "Where is Oberst Vogel?"

"I apologize for my delay," Werner's voice cut in. He strode from a barn in the far corner of the U-shaped pavilion. He stood tall, his uniform immaculate and his jaw set. "We had a bit of a complication, but all is resolved."

Bret held back from taking him by the neck. A complication? Where was Adia? Where was Schultze?

Werner glanced at Bret for a heartbeat and then looked away, pulling a long ceremonial sword from his side and offering it to Roland. "Hostau surrenders to the Allied forces."

46

Americans are at the gate!" a prisoner shouted in the crowd around Adia, who was still deep in the barns.

Adia's heart soared at the words, and she put a hand on Matthew's shoulder. He and a dozen others had wrestled Schultze to the ground. Werner, once he was confident the prisoners had complete control over Schultze and his followers, had gone to meet the Americans and urged her to do the same.

"Our liberation is here, friend," Adia said.

Matthew smiled. "Salvation is only found in God, Miss Adia." He pushed his foot a little harder against Schultze's back as the man squirmed, his face against the rocks and his hands tied behind his back. "Though I won't deny this worldly justice does feel quite good."

Adia thanked him, ducked to the stall, and unburied her little partisan soldier from the straw. "You don't need to fear anymore. Come," she said, pulling him to his feet behind her.

The boy gaped at the Germans—now captive to their own former prisoners—but wordlessly followed her through the barns and into the pavilion.

Adia's body felt light and was driven forward by an invisible force. A dozen Jeeps with a bold star on the door circled the flagpole at the center of the stables, and nearly fifty men in olive drab watched as the American flag was hoisted up the pole, replacing the Nazi dominion for the world to see.

This farm was no longer Germany's. She was no longer chained to the fate of her foes.

Tears streamed down her cheeks and her body seemed to float outside her mind. For so long, she'd dreamed of this day.

The boy at her side tapped her arm. "Angel, what does this mean?"

"We're free, little one."

She blinked away her tears, scanning each of the distant faces for Bret's. Werner stood across from Colonel Roland and they spoke intently. O'Connor kicked back in one of the Jeeps, his feet up as he took a long pull on a cigar.

Where was he?

Lubor. He'd expect her to be with Lubor, surely. She motioned to a prisoner she trusted and asked him to watch over the boy. She knelt down and promised she'd return soon to look after him. The kid nodded, his gaze locked on all the new vehicles and people milling about.

Adia took off down the aisle toward the stallion barn. "Bret!" she cried out.

And as she rounded the corner, he was there, walking toward her voice and then racing to meet her.

They melded together, and space and time disappeared around them. She wrapped her arms and legs around his body, and he held her in his strong arms, as steady as the rock he'd always been. She breathed in the richness of his scent, edged with gunpowder and smoke and years of precious time they'd lost together.

All for this moment.

"You saved us," she mumbled against his collarbone. *You saved me.* So many times over so many years. If they'd arrived an hour later, Schultze might have stolen this moment from her, and so much more.

"I'm never letting go of you again," he growled with conviction.

"I won't ask that of you." She leaned back, looking into his battle-weary face with scars and lines and bloodshot eyes. Nothing could camouflage the depth of his love for her or the desire that radiated from his pores.

She pressed her lips to his, tasting the salt and dirt and only sinking into him further. He returned the kiss with passion and confidence.

Though the world around them faded for a moment, the reality came crashing back when voices and the crack of gunshots echoed from the pavilion.

"Contact!"

Bret covered Adia with his body and looked for the source of the gunfire. They wove through the stables toward the pavilion, where all the soldiers were crouched down, facing a distant building in the town beyond.

Sparks pinged off the metal gate and peppered the vehicles lined in front of the farm. Soldiers of the Second scattered into defensive positions in their well-practiced dance.

"It's coming from town," O'Connor called out.

"Russians? Or Germans?" A private walked up beside them, his eyes wide.

Bret and Adia crouched alongside several soldiers behind the small wooden building, splinters of wood flying through the air as the manor and ground took fire.

Bret motioned to a soldier for a spare rifle and handed his pistol to Adia. She took it, checked the magazine to see how many rounds remained, and then nodded to Bret.

They had no idea how many were in the town of Hostau or what the coming onslaught could be. But they were ready for it.

"Look at that!" a private said beside Bret, turning toward the manor behind them.

Werner and a stream of his soldiers and POWs exited. Roland

346

waved them over and offered firearms from the back of a truck, and soon there were hundreds of rifles pointed toward the threat coming from the town.

Bret smiled. Now the odds were most certainly in their favor.

Bullets volleyed back and forth, and several of the Second's snipers took up positions on the second floor of the manor. Dust filled the air, and the taste of metal and grit filled Bret's mouth.

Werner walked around the side of the manor toward Bret and Adia, knelt beside them, and called over the ongoing din of gunfire, "It's the SS. They're holed up in town, and I'm not sure we can dislodge them even with the firepower we have."

"So what do you suggest?" Bret leaned closer.

"Send small groups into town to root them out. I have a handful of volunteers among my men."

"Count me in." Bret stood.

Adia shook her head and lifted her hands. "Is that the only option?"

Werner's gaze softened when he addressed her. "The longer this goes on, the greater the risk of a horse or American being injured."

Werner seemed to understand the implication of escalation if there were Allied casualties in this territory. Adia didn't appear convinced. Bret could feel her hesitation and the years of loss all built up in her. Especially now that they were so close to being free of occupation.

"Wait, please . . ."

Just when it seemed they were at a stalemate, the echo of rumbling tanks filled the valley.

Cheers echoed over the grounds of Hostau. A soldier cried out, "It's the rest of the Second!" Troops A and C, who'd circled around Hostau for this very reason.

Moments later, the gunfire had ceased. Hostau was secured.

For now.

47

Adia wandered through the quiet grounds after the battle and the band of SS soldiers had been neutralized by the American forces, who swiftly cleared out the town of Hostau. That had been close. Outwardly, she'd been confident of the numbers and skill she knew were on their side. But inside, she'd been terrified of losing someone in this final hour.

This had been her plan, just as it had been her plan to evacuate from Janów, which had put Lukas in the path of violence and led to his death.

Bret and Werner had jumped into action once Troops A and C reached the gates, greeting their commander and coordinating further efforts to secure the town. Soldiers filled the premises and wrapped the farm in a layer of protection that left Adia momentarily at ease.

Confident that Bret was safe and occupied, she slipped into Lubor's stall for a moment of solace. The striking stallion nickered in greeting and moved toward her. She pressed her cheek to his hot, sleek fur and ran her hand underneath his thick mane. He stomped his foot, eager to stretch his legs.

He'd get his time to move, soon. In a few days, they'd never see these stables again.

In a few days, could it truly be the end of all this? For six years, she'd known nothing but danger. What would it be like to walk back into her empty stables in Oregon, untouched for nearly a decade? What would it be like to pick up the pieces of a life she'd left behind? What role would Bret step into? Ewan?

She couldn't imagine a future without either of them. Beyond that, her vision was cloudy.

Lubor nipped at the back of her shirt, playful, as if the hours of gunfire hadn't bothered him in the least.

She ran her hand down his long, sleek neck and scratched the spot on his withers that always itched. His head tilted, his lips wiggling contentedly. When she stopped for a moment, he swung his head around, nipping her elbow until she chuckled and scratched his skin more.

As always in his presence, she marveled at the expressiveness in his eyes, the beauty of his rich bay coloring, and the regal confidence in his gait. He had all the traits that Janów Podlaski had cultivated in the decades since the Great War. While everything had been snuffed out a generation before, the Polish people had rebuilt and patched together something amazing.

The same would happen again—it simply must.

And Adia would be a part of it. The same way her mother had sacrificed her life to save these horses. How could she do anything but?

Adia pressed her forehead to Lubor's neck, and the warmth of him soothed the uneasiness in her soul. Was it the six years of this tumult, or was she sensing that the worst was still to come?

The danger of this evacuation and border crossing was unlike anything she'd seen before in Poland or here at Hostau. The Russians, the local partisans, the embittered SS soldiers—everything was out to stop the Americans and the ragtag cohort of POWs with their mass of horses.

The farm was seized, the flag replaced.

The more difficult part was to come.

Werner handed Bret the rifle that Roland had provided him during the heat of the battle. "It seems this is no longer needed."

Bret took the gun and nodded to his former nemesis. His view on the German colonel had shifted significantly. "You're handy in a fight, Vogel."

Werner shrugged. "I'm just glad no one was injured."

"I was wrong about you," Bret said, the words slow to come but long overdue. "I hadn't wanted to trust you, but you've proven to be a man of your word."

Werner stilled, his expression guarded. After a moment, he lifted a brow. "Well, I was right about you all along. I even tried to meet with you and your partner in 1939, but my network was compromised."

Shock shot through Bret. "Wait, what?"

"I'd been in contact with one of your spies, and we were supposed to meet the summer before Hitler crossed into Danzig. Word leaked out and I was nearly tried as a traitor, but with no evidence, I was simply demoted to running the horse farm in Poland."

Realization spread through Bret. Colonel Werner Vogel had been the high-level informant all along. Now other pieces started to make more sense.

"That's why you never turned in Adia for the information she shared, the children she saved," Bret said. "And why you allowed her so much time and access to crucial documents in your office in Janów."

"Partially." The other part, they both understood clearly.

The threads wove together into an intricate tapestry, and Bret now saw the broader picture—how protected Adia and Lubor had been, how her placement had led to greater success for the partisans in Poland and Czechoslovakia, and how her role in negotiating this evacuation would redeem them all. His grandmother would call it God's divine plan. And what else could it have been?

At least Charlie's life hadn't been lost for nothing. Werner hadn't become a true source in their network, but he'd been an ally nonetheless.

"Thank you," Bret whispered, his voice weak in spite of his conviction.

"I didn't do it for you," Werner said in a clipped voice. And before Bret could ask Werner exactly what he meant by those words, the German looked to the east. "You'd better get back to the evacuation plans, Conway. We are victorious today, but time is still running out before Russia discovers your presence."

48

The pregnant mares were loaded onto the trucks that had been converted from troop to livestock transports. Any soldier able to ride was astride a reasonably broke horse. Trucks circled the groups of horses.

In the past two weeks of planning and preparing the horses, the war in Europe had ceased—an armistice declared, Hitler dead in a bunker. And yet there was still a looming dread at the danger across the next hundred kilometers of terrain and the diplomatic mess in the making.

They couldn't make a misstep now.

The air was still fresh with morning dew, but the diesel fumes from the tanks and trucks melded with the smell of warming horseflesh.

Adia stood behind the mass of vehicles and gathered horses, Lubor's reins in her hand as she searched for Werner. She hadn't seen him all morning, and he'd evaded her for days.

But she had to know. She had to see him before it was too late.

She found him in a distant barn, looking through the last of the stalls as if to ensure nothing was left behind.

"Werner?"

He started at her voice, his brow furrowing. "What are you doing back here? You need to be with the group of stallions."

She walked up to him and Lubor sidestepped, anxious at the flurry of strange activity this morning. "Are you coming with the caravan?"

His jaw flexed and he shook his head. "I am not."

Her heart dipped in disappointment. She'd feared this ever since he'd evaded the question when they first spawned this plan with the Americans. "Werner, you must come. You'll be treated fairly by the Americans—I know it."

"I have obligations in Germany."

She grabbed his arm, alarmed for the man who had been her friend and protector for so long. "Germany will be a mess for many years to come. If you stay close to Colonel Roland, he can make sure it's known how you collaborated with us and saved the horses."

He smiled. "I have made my decision, Adia."

Sorrow gripped her. She'd prepared to say farewell to Hostau, her former prison and sanctuary, but she wasn't ready to leave Werner behind in the shell of this place.

He took her hand and squeezed it. "It has been an honor to work alongside you. I have the utmost confidence you'll look after the horses in my stead."

"Werner, I—"

"You should go, Adia." Werner's voice was firm. "This is everything you've worked for. And the Americans will need you to see them through the checkpoints." His eyebrows wiggled. "Especially with all the goodwill you've built up among the Czech partisans."

Her muscles tensed. "You—you knew?"

"Of course I did." He motioned toward the gates.

"For how long?" Relief and disbelief battled within her. Here she'd simply believed she was just so subtle.

"Oh, since well before we reached Hostau." He chuckled. "And now I hope those efforts result in a smooth path ahead, dear Adia."

He took Lubor's reins and offered a hand to help her mount. She let him assist her, bounding into the saddle and gathering the reins.

He'd known about her midnight rides. What else had he done to cover for her in the past four years working alongside her? He'd always been so kind, so respectful of the boundaries she'd put between them. Though she'd been called the Angel of Hostau, had Werner been their true guardian angel?

She thought back to O'Connor's comment about how all Nazis were vile and evil. Werner had defied every expectation. Even Bret would have to admit to that.

Werner looked up and smiled. "I'll escort you both to the gates." He put a hand on Lubor's shoulder affectionately, and they walked side by side toward the chaos beyond.

Bret rode up on Indigo, the partisan orphan boy, Markus, in the saddle behind him. Bret glanced at Werner and a cryptic look passed between them, but each nodded respectfully to the other. It seemed as if they'd already said their farewell or had said their piece.

Werner patted Lubor a final time, passed Adia a regretful smile, and then slipped away.

She pulled Lubor alongside Indigo. "He's not coming with us."

"What?" Bret glanced in the direction Werner had departed.

"He's returning to Germany." She huffed. "Stubborn, stupid man."

"I'm sure he has his reasons."

A moment of silence settled between them, broken only by the young child who couldn't know the complexity of the emotions.

"Angel," Markus said softly in Czech, "I'll ride with you."

Bret looked to her to translate, and she just motioned to the boy, offering her hand so he could jump from one horse to the other.

Once Markus was settled, a wave of nostalgia and anxiety washed over Adia. She pictured beautiful, golden Dancer, dappled-gray Captain, and chestnut Samir as they'd voyaged to Kovel and back, and the way all their efforts had been foiled by the tide of war. Those horses had been lost to the countryside and recesses of her memory, and now six hundred of them stood before her. Awaiting a new security in the voyage ahead? Or the same cruel fate?

"It's time to go, Adia," Bret said, his tone full of understanding and comfort.

She blinked away the memories and pulled in a long, filling breath. It was time.

Bret didn't even have a moment to process Werner's decision or the true impact of what they were doing. All around them, horses stomped their feet, snorted their unease, or nipped at the horse next to them impatiently.

The sea of horses, men, and motorized vehicles covered the landscape. From the narrow gates, they poured out into the town of Hostau and then the grassy hills beyond. Townspeople watched the procession, some with contempt, others with glee.

Though Germany had officially surrendered, these occupied zones were left in tumult and mob rule. Czech citizens had been reclaiming the lands and cities stolen by Germans, and the American army was unable to intercede in the street justice wielded.

Bret only prayed they were able to make it to the German border without confronting those partisans with a chip on their shoulder, bent on revenge of any kind. They were already desperately outrunning Russian interference, but danger lay in every direction until they reached the Allied-controlled boundaries of Germany.

Beside him, Adia and little Markus sat atop Lubor, all three with their eyes glued to the horizon ahead. Love and appreciation swirled in his gut at the sight.

Unlike the similar view six years earlier, they had the might of the American army around them.

Adia must have felt his gaze and looked over, a hesitant smile creeping across her face.

Nothing needed to be said—this had been their goal, their mission, for so many years.

The long caravan inched ahead and picked up traction as the minutes dragged into hours. The springtime sun was warm but not oppressive as Operation Cowboy continued without a hitch. They cleared the town of Hostau after an hour of steady plodding, and then the fields opened up before them as a green ocean of possibility.

As the morning spanned into the afternoon, fields narrowed into towns and then back to forests and further fields. Then, with the sun setting behind them, a strange ripple of tension reached Bret and Adia in the middle of the herd. They'd hung back to help with the group of young stallions, leaving the very head of the column out of view.

Then the whole mass of animals, humans, and vehicles came to a halt.

Instantly, Bret's memories flashed back to the Polish summer of '39, and he saw Adia's nervousness rise. Would this again be a disaster and end with death?

49

FURTH IM WALD, CZECHOSLOVAKIAN BORDER

Adia pulled back on Lubor's reins to avoid hitting the horses in front of her. Something was wrong.

"I'm going ahead," she said, holding on to Markus's arms as she kicked Lubor ahead. She weaved out of the dense crowd of horses and into the clearing of the field alongside the column.

"Adia—wait!" Bret called behind her, but Lubor broke into a gallop and left everyone behind at alarming speed.

Markus whimpered behind her, squeezing her stomach with both arms as he braced against the wind tearing into them. Adia leaned forward in the saddle, one hand clutching Markus's arms and the other holding the reins over Lubor's flat neck as he charged ahead.

Her heart thumped as the mix of horses and trucks stacked up as if it were a slow-moving train derailment. Horses circled anxiously, and the untrained soldiers struggled to control the animals.

The front of the caravan came into view over a long, arching bridge that funneled into a town of tall buildings with an old-world feel to it.

She pulled Lubor to a stop, the horse snorting and panting excitedly.

At the front, several Jeeps stood under the town signage, facing off at gunpoint with several guards at the lowered gate. The guards didn't wear the uniforms of Germany or Russia.

Partisans.

Above the standoff, an etched sign read FURTH IM WALD, and a blocky painting showed a white horse head, severed. She shivered. It was the border town with Germany.

Markus pointed to the sign. "Grandma told me the tales," he said softly. "A bandit tried to escape on a white horse. The gatekeepers closed the portcullis on them, killing the horse."

Adia's blood went cold. The very same thing could happen to their horses—if the gates weren't opened and if they weren't able to enter Germany.

And worse, a hundred rifles were now trained on the small guard station in this town, and if the partisans' fingers slipped on those triggers, the fuse would ignite. The town could be demolished by the might and power in the tanks and trucks behind her.

No more death.

She kicked Lubor forward and called in Czech, "Wait! Do not fire."

The men at the gates turned at her approach, and she looked to a gruff, bearded partisan, who seemed surprised to hear her Czech words.

"The war is over," she said to him, holding his gaze. "You must let us pass."

"Why are there Americans here?" He growled and gripped his weapon tighter. "What is all of this? What more can be stolen from us?"

Adia held up her hands. "These horses are not of Czech blood— they are displaced, and we will return them to their homes."

"I don't believe you."

Markus poked his head around to look at the man, and the guard lowered his weapon slightly.

Colonel Roland, holding a rifle from the seat of his Jeep, cleared his throat. "Get back, Adia."

She waved him off. He didn't speak Czech, couldn't understand the pain of these people in the way she'd seen it for four years at Hostau.

"I helped a woman named Shepherd for many months," she said to the guard. "I know what you've endured. But if you do not let these Americans pass, it is all for nothing."

He lowered his rifle and angled his head. "Shepherd is here." He called behind him to another man, told him to fetch Shepherd.

Adia's pulse raced. Shepherd had survived?

Markus perked up and wiggled behind her. Adia turned just as he slipped off Lubor and raced toward the gate. "Markus!"

Moments later, the familiar figure of an old woman entered the roadway behind the lowered gate.

Adia gasped. It was true. The old woman had survived Schultze's massacre of the partisans in the forest.

"Grandma!" Markus cried out and ran to her. The old woman's face came to light, and she swung the child into her arms.

Grandma? Markus hadn't ever mentioned exactly who his family was.

Adia dismounted, walked through the tight formation of trucks and soldiers near the gates, and paused next to the colonel's Jeep in front of the wooden beam that had halted their progress.

Shepherd walked up, holding Markus tightly, and smiled at Adia. Her aged face suddenly seemed twenty years younger, and her eyes glistened with moisture. "Thank you, Angel."

Tears slipped down Adia's cheeks and she nodded, relieved that Markus had found his home, and that there was a thread of hope for those so beaten and defeated. If these two could find one another through the war-torn remnants of their country, there was a chance others might too.

Slowly, the Americans lowered their guns.

Shepherd turned, hit the burly guard's arm with the back of her hand. "Open the gate, you idiot."

MAY 17, 1945
KÖTZTING, GERMANY

After two days and more than a hundred kilometers under their horses' hooves, Bret and Adia rode into the old Luftwaffe air base that would be the new sanctuary for the horses.

Behind Allied lines.

For the first time since 1939, safe.

Tales of Adia's showdown with the partisan soldier had echoed through the men during the last day of their evacuation. Bret had seen all of it from a short distance once he'd caught up to her and Lubor.

Nothing surprised him about her boldness, her bravery, but still, he couldn't keep the scene from replaying in his mind. If she hadn't been there, would that man have pulled the trigger? Would he have killed an American after arms across Europe had been laid down? What would it have meant for Patton, who'd authorized this reckless, dire mission despite the consequences?

O'Connor stood at the gates with his clipboard, checking off names and counting the horses diligently. He winked at them both and motioned them toward long barns for the stallions to be corralled.

They reached the row of stalls, put Lubor, Dorek, Indigo, Wojownik, and the dozens of others into stalls and paddocks, and ensured all the latches were tight and the water buckets full.

The rest of the soldiers around them strode off to their next tasks, leaving Bret and Adia alone in a quiet corner of the barn. It was strange without Markus at her side, but the joyous reunion with his grandmother was the best outcome they could have hoped for.

Adia looked around anxiously. "I should go get them some grain—they haven't eaten since last night."

Bret caught her arm, drawing her to a stop. Her eyebrows were raised, her hair matted and tangled with the dust from the roads, her skin glowing pink from the unrelenting sun.

"You're not alone in this anymore, Adia," he said. "The men of the Second have everything under control."

Lubor nickered in the stall next to them as if affirming Bret's words.

Her shoulders slackened, her hands fell loose at her sides, and she seemed to fully take in her surroundings. Bret smiled and closed the gap between them, then cupped her face and kissed her gently.

A tear slid from the corner of her eye, and she shook her head as if unable to believe it all.

"We made it," he whispered, his forehead pressed to hers.

"It seems impossible."

And it was. Six hundred horses moved across the landscape. Dozens from Poland, hundreds from Austria, Russia, Yugoslavia, and beyond. All ending up on an airfield where thousands of soldiers congregated, prisoners of war and conquerors combined.

"What now?" she asked, brushing his lips with hers once more.

"Well, we should write to Ewan and Elizabeth so they know we're safe."

She chuckled. "I can hardly wait to see them."

"I know. And you will. Finally, it's our time."

"Our time." She kissed him again.

Epilogue

SEPTEMBER 22, 1946
WYGODA, POLAND

The Sunday market of Wygoda sounded much the same—vendors negotiating prices, old men bickering over the best way to fix a broken wagon axle, old women gossiping about those same old men. Distant church bells of mass.

But as Bret walked hand in hand with Adia through it all, there was something missing. Dozens of vendors were gone, their old cart spots left empty as if they one day might return. The cobblestones were uneven, pitted from tank tracks or munitions. The distant fountain was demolished and still sat as a pile of rubble.

The war was over but not yet a memory.

The light feel of a hand slipping into his coat pocket sent off alarm bells in his head, and as he caught Ewan's hand, he looked over and clicked his tongue. "You're getting sloppy."

Ewan just smiled and raised his eyebrows. Now the boy stood nearly to Bret's chin.

"I gave you Grandfather's watch. Why are you nicking mine?"

The thirteen-year-old with crooked teeth and eternally untamed mouse-brown hair shrugged. "Just wanted to see if I could still do it, is all."

"If you put half as much effort into your studies . . ." Bret started, but Adia squeezed his hand, ending the oft-repeated tirade.

She brushed closer to him, and he caught the distraction in her gaze as she looked over the marketplace. He understood the gravity of this trip for her.

It was their farewell to Poland.

Seven grisly years earlier, he'd met her in this very spot. Now they would go on that date they'd missed. He'd told her about that night in full detail—the car crash and knowing Werner had been the high-level contact. He was living up to the promise he'd made on the Janów bluff before she left for Hostau.

Of course, they were now married and Ewan officially adopted. It was more perfect than he'd ever dreamed. They'd even managed a few letters back and forth with Werner, who had retired to a small farm in Germany and avoided tribunals due to his cooperation. Both Bret and Colonel Roland had filed reports attesting to his supporting Allied efforts throughout the war.

As the three of them passed through the marketplace toward Babka's restaurant, it was impossible to miss the bullet holes and charred stones along the pathways. Only fresh stones and new boards would heal and repair the physical wounds. Time would bring back the buzz of joy and anticipation that used to fill this square.

As they entered Babka's, the old woman squealed in delight from the back corner and rushed forward with open arms. She squeezed all three of them into one large embrace, fussing over Ewan and how tall he'd grown in their years absent. She pointed them to a table and then hurried off to serve up some pierogi.

Ewan looked around. "I need to use the loo," he said and then disappeared.

Adia chuckled. "Such a Brit after just a few years with your sister."

"That's because Elizabeth is a tyrant."

"Thankfully. I don't feel like I need to check his pockets when he gets back." Adia's eyes sparkled. "Do you think she and Roland will hit it off?"

Bret slid into the booth and pulled her close to him. "I hope so. He has big shoes to fill."

The casual introduction when Elizabeth brought Ewan to them in Germany had proved fruitful. Elizabeth and Roland began talking about the horses and the rescue in hostile territory and were lost in their own world for hours.

But Bret's parents would be quite cross if Lizzy did up and marry a Yank like he had. Despite multiple letters of protest from his mother and the General, Bret had firmly stuck with his and Adia's plans to move the horses, Ewan, and their life back to Adia's farm in the States. It would be good to start fresh as Europe pulled itself back together from the years of destruction.

Adia fell silent. He wrapped an arm around her shoulders and kissed her forehead. "Are you all right, my love?" he whispered.

"It all feels so different."

Nothing was the same—nor would it ever be, Bret suspected. He'd seen the scars in his father and grandfather after the Great War, and he very much felt the same fractures in his own soul. The world would always be tainted by what he'd seen, what he'd done, what was lost.

She ran her hand over a small bullet hole in the seat beside her.

"Are you having second thoughts about our plans?" He rubbed her arm gently.

"No." She tipped her chin up to meet his gaze. "And I expect Filip will urge us to keep with those plans."

The soft light of the dim room brought out the depth of her brown eyes, and he was distracted for a moment by the beauty of her. By the joy and gratitude that in spite of all they'd endured, she was finally here beside him.

She pursed her lips. "Wipe that look off your face, Casanova," she hissed. "We're in public."

He chuckled and kissed her before she could react, just in time to hear Ewan return to the table and groan dramatically. "Stop that," he said.

Bret and Adia separated as she flushed and ducked her head, laughing and elbowing Bret playfully.

Babka also stepped up with three plates and winked at Bret. "Well, well, I guess Cupid did his work without my help from the start."

Bret took two plates from her hands and set one in front of Adia. "That old cart horse of yours is probably the one we have to thank."

Adia chuckled. "Oh yes, Lyra."

Babka waved a hand. "I'd forgotten all about that. You know, she came right back home that day she took off into the square. She's near twenty-six years old now and still eating all our grain, stomping on Ludwik's toes."

"I'm glad some things remain constant." Adia beamed.

Babka sobered and pointed a finger at Bret. "You take good care of this woman here."

"Till death do us part," Bret said. "Before God, the military chaplain, and now you."

Babka nodded, winked at Adia and Ewan, and then disappeared. Ewan had already started digging into his food.

"Always hungry." Filip appeared, a hat in his hand, and nodded cordially to Babka.

Adia jumped from the booth to hug her mentor. "Filip! We were supposed to meet you at the farm."

"I was in town anyway, saw this scamp," he said, hitting Ewan gently with his hat.

Bret reached over to shake the elder man's hand. The years had aged Filip severely—he now had dark lines and deep wrinkles from worry, weather, and hunger. He was missing several lower teeth, probably from malnourishment or abuse at the hands of Germans during those most dire years before the armistice.

Ewan continued to gobble up his food as the others spoke.

"So, the rumors are true?" Filip asked, his eyes tired. "Lubor, Wojownik, all shipped to the United States?"

Adia shifted her weight beside him. "We've returned hundreds of horses across Europe, but the Polish government is . . ."

"Overcome with corrupt communists," Filip supplied. He held up a hand. "You don't need to defend the Americans' decision. I am relieved, Adia. Poland is not a safe place right now. I just ask you to look after those bloodlines, as I know you will. I will die a happy old man long from now knowing that their legacy endures."

She straightened and nodded. "We will."

Filip clapped her shoulder. "There's no two"—he smiled at Ewan—"well, three people I trust more with the task." He playfully hit Ewan again with his hat. The boy had cleaned off his plate entirely. "Come, let's go to Janów and leave Bret and Adia to a moment of peace. Rafał and Tomasz are eager to see you and bid you all a safe journey."

Bless you, Filip, Bret thought. He'd hardly had a moment alone with his wife since Ewan joined them while they were stationed at Kötzting with the horses. And the ship would depart in less than a month to deliver the remaining horses and the Conway family onto American soil.

Ewan wiped his face with a napkin and zoomed out the door ahead of Filip, who smiled at them and said, "I'll see you two at the farm whenever you're ready."

The words held weight, as if he knew Adia still wasn't ready to say goodbye.

She slid back into the booth next to Bret. "Well, here we are."

At the beginning. Or where their beginning should have been.

He pulled her closer, not for a moment taking for granted that she sat beside him. No more secrets, active war zones, or occupying forces between them. Now they had nothing but an open future ahead and life together, forever entwined.

"What now, Mr. Conway?" She slipped her hand into his, their hands perfectly fitted together as if they were cast from complementary molds.

"Now we practice the art of small talk." He took a bite of pierogi, the distinct, savory meat, onions, and potatoes bringing him back to his meals with Charlie here, long before the war. Good memories.

Good days. "I was never very good at it, so I'm glad we've skipped the dating part and are now married."

She laughed and slapped his chest. "Maybe call up your old pal Hemingway and get some advice."

He groaned. "Nah, I'll just stick with my tried-and-true method."

She angled closer, their faces nearly touching. "What's that?"

He cupped her cheek with his palm. "Following along as you relocate hundreds of horses across borders, rivers, or continents."

She chuckled and shrugged. "That has worked out for you so far."

"So how about it?" He kissed her lips lightly. "How about we sail across the ocean with a hundred horses, haul them three thousand miles to the West Coast, and start our new life together?"

"With you by my side? Sounds like heaven to me."

Historical Note

This novel came to me as a fifteen-year-old horse-obsessed girl who had recently devoured *Arabian Legends* by Marian K. Carpenter. In that book was a tiny mention of the esteemed Witez II and how he'd been disguised with mud to shield him from German captors in the war. His crown-shaped Janów brand had given him away, and after many years under German occupation, he was later rescued by US soldiers. That nugget of information blossomed into a story that I've rewritten dozens of times over the past twenty years.

The core pieces of this story are true: Poland, its people, its culture, and by extension, its Arabian horse–breeding program faced decimation in both World War I and World War II. When it came to Janów Podlaski, one of several state-sponsored stables, a few brave civilians worked to save the priceless horses in 1939. The efforts of local partisans and civilians cannot be overstated. They faced insurmountable odds, endured brutal occupation, and picked up the pieces left behind.

Alas, Janów and its horses fell to Russian and German occupation. I changed a few pieces of the timeline to better suit my plot and characters. Among historical sources, there are also various pieces of conflicting information, so I selected the most consistent option based on my research.

Several Janów stallions seized by the Russians were used at their stud farm and produced exemplary stallions that would influence Arabian bloodlines for decades to come.

The idea of a German "super horse" program was also true, and Germany pilfered hundreds of horses from across its conquered territories. Many of the staff at Hostau would play essential parts in the liberation of these horses, including veterinarians and soldiers who truly appreciated the horses for what they were. These Germans collaborated with the Allies at the end of the war, and the horses were rescued by General George S. Patton's Second Cavalry. Read Elizabeth Letts's *The Perfect Horse* or Mark Felton's *Ghost Riders* for an excellent accounting of these true stories.

The story of Bret, Adia, and Ewan is entirely fictional, but there were dozens to hundreds of individuals behind the scenes who protected these animals—a part of the culture, history, and art—so that they weren't another casualty of war. Read *And Miles to Go* by Linell Smith for another biographical account of Witez II's life story.

Currently, Janów Podlaski is a shining star for tourism and continues to breed breathtaking horses.

While most of the horses of Hostau were returned to their home countries, many from Poland were shipped to the United States as part of the Cavalry Remount Program, and years later they were auctioned off. American breeders, enthusiasts of the Arabian horse breed, purchased many of these Janów Podlaski horses, and the lineages endure to this day. Witez II (whom Lubor is based on) became one of the most successful Arabian stallions of all time, and I'm proud to say I own a distant relative of his.

The ripples of war are vast and wide, as are the actions of the men and women who seek to preserve life and help the helpless.

Acknowledgments

This story originated in my heart and soul more than two decades ago, and in that time, it has been seen, shaped, and sculpted by more people than I can count.

My family fostered and supported my love of horses early in my youth, and without these animals in my life, I'm not sure my writing would be what it is today. Horses and novels have been the constant passions of my life, followed closely by my interest in World War II.

Thank you to each horse that has shaped me—from the Arabian mare who knocked me off with low-hanging branches as we rode through the forest, to the finely bred horse who claimed regional breed show championships. The Arabian breed is known for their stubbornness and sometimes difficult nature. This helped challenge my resolve and taught me more than I ever thought possible.

To Grunnion, my gray Arabian of Polish descent—the one descended from Janów and the horses seized by Germany in the war—we've had twenty-three years together, and I'm praying for twenty-three more. You've been my companion, confidant, and comedic relief. I'll forever feel connected to Janów and its legacy through you and our memories together.

This novel simply wouldn't exist without the persistence and cheering of my writing community, locally and globally. Dearest Caitlin Anderson and Jessica Carter—my diamond girls—I'm so glad we met at Summer Conference in 2009. To my former roomie and longtime supporter, Sarah Frost—your book insights, eye for design, and endless encouragement have always been invaluable. To my writing group of nearly fifteen years—Melanie Dobson, Julie Zander, Tracie Heskett, Dawn Shipman, Leslie Gould, and Kelly Chang—you're all the best. Truly. To my early critique group who read this manuscript in 2009(ish)—Heidi Chiavaroli, Sandra Ardoin, and Edwina Cowgill—I'm grateful for your influence back in those most pivotal years as I learned the craft. To my friends and supporters at Cascade Christian Writers and within the Books & Such Literary Agency client group—thank you all.

A special mention to WWII author and pioneer Sarah Sundin, who graciously answered my Facebook messages back in 2008 and encouraged me in this genre when it was just beginning to blossom. She paved the way for this story and cemented Revell as my dream publishing house for it.

To my ever-patient literary agent, Wendy Lawton, who has worked with me for over a dozen years and pitched equally as many (yet unpublished) manuscripts of mine—I cannot thank you enough.

To my globe-trotting, Poland-loving editor, Rachel McRae—I am so confident and grateful that God held this manuscript back from every other editor so it could land on your desk at the start of 2022. The world may have seemed a little topsy-turvy, but the stars aligned for us to meet and for this little-known story of Poland's history to come to light.

Last but certainly not least, to my husband and two sons, who have stood by through each rejection, each writing conference, each moment of my mind distantly off plotting a new scene—I love you three so much. John, thank you for being my historical vehicle reference guide and for constantly nudging me with "Shouldn't you be working on your book?" What a journey this has been, and all the better beside you.

Nicole M. Miller lives in Southwest Washington State with her husband and two sons, along with two purebred Arabian horses, chickens, ducks, dogs, cats, and guinea pigs. As a longtime horse owner, she's been involved in many horse organizations, including serving as a Clark County Fair Court Princess and Miss Teen Rodeo Washington.

When she's not writing or tending the animals, Nicole works in people operations for remote tech companies. A journalism major, she's received several national and regional awards for her nonfiction writing from American Horse Publications and the Society of Professional Journalists. See more of her horse and animal stories in *The Horse of My Heart*, *The Horse of My Dreams*, *The Dog Who Came to Christmas*, and *Second-Chance Horses*.

Follow her on Instagram @NicoleMillerWriter and at Nicole MillerWriter.com.

Connect with Nicole

NicoleMillerWriter.com

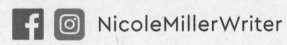 NicoleMillerWriter

Be the First to Hear about New Books from Revell!

Stay up-to-date with our authors and books and discover exciting features like book excerpts and giveaways by signing up for our newsletters at

RevellBooks.com/SignUp

FOLLOW US ON SOCIAL MEDIA

  @RevellFiction

  @RevellBooks

Revell
a division of Baker Publishing Group
RevellBooks.com